Jane Coverdale has worked as a  graphic artist, animation cell artis television drama and commercials has travelled widely in Europe, Asia, America, Russia and India while working on film projects, but it was India and her people that inspired her to write her first historical romance novel, *The Jasmine Wife*. She now lives in the beautiful hill town of Leura in the Blue Mountains, outside of Sydney.

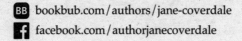

BB bookbub.com/authors/jane-coverdale
f facebook.com/authorjanecoverdale

Also by Jane Coverdale

The Jasmine Wife

UNDER A CERULEAN SKY

JANE COVERDALE

One More Chapter
a division of HarperCollins*Publishers* Ltd
1 London Bridge Street
London SE1 9GF
www.harpercollins.co.uk
HarperCollins*Publishers*
Macken House, 39/40 Mayor Street Upper,
Dublin 1, D01 C9W8

This paperback edition 2022
1
First published in Great Britain in ebook format
by HarperCollins*Publishers* 2022
Copyright © Jane Coverdale 2022

Jane Coverdale asserts the moral right to
be identified as the author of this work
A catalogue record of this book is available from the British Library

ISBN: 978-0-00-854766-0

Printed and bound in the UK using 100% Renewable Electricity
by CPI Group (UK) Ltd

For Adam, Zac, Bridget and Maddy

Chapter One

T he girls hadn't left the house for a week, except when Isobel took Monty to the park across the square where she stood shivering under an umbrella while, with an expression of pained inconvenience, the dog hurried through his business then shot back to the comparative warmth of the house. Then, in a pointless exercise that drove Isobel's frayed nerves to breaking point, he rushed to the window to peer out at the darkening weather and scrape his paws against the glass, as if by doing so he could somehow wipe away the torrent pouring down the windowpanes.

A dull reflection from the feeble sun cast the beautiful old house in a most unbecoming light and showed up every imperfection, especially in the French carpet that had once been their mother's pride and had come as part of her wedding dowry. The pattern of woven pink cabbage roses against a turquoise background, once as fresh as an English

1

garden in May, seemed now to have been battered by the bitterest of storms and left as faded and threadbare as the scene both inside and outside the window.

Violet had a mild cold, and sat slumped, still in her dressing gown, shivering before the meagre fire in a worn armchair, her feet resting on a hot-water bottle while she sipped a cup of thin beef broth.

Her face was a little pale, and her cheeks were tinted with an unhealthy flush. Despite this, she managed to look even lovelier than usual and drew vast amounts of sympathy from everyone in the house because of it. She coughed weakly, as though even that feeble effort exhausted her, though Isobel suspected there was more than a touch of drama accompanying her sister's listless, feverish manner.

The scraping of Monty's nails against the glass roused her now to an irrational fury, and she rushed to the little creature to stand before him and shake her finger in his reproachful face.

'Stop it, you beast! Haven't we got enough to plague us without you making it worse?'

Monty cringed, although Isobel was sure it was for show, then crawled to hide under the blanket covering Violet's lap, glaring at Isobel with accusing eyes.

'Oh Issie … Monty can't help it. This dreadful weather … I feel like smashing at the window myself. Smashing at it till it breaks …if only I could get out of here…'

'Well, you won't need to smash the window to get out of here … we'll be thrown out the back door in less than three months! And God only knows where we'll go when the time comes.'

Violet was the younger and prettier sister, at least as judged by conventional standards, and therefore had not been expected to think about anything as vulgar as money and where it might come from; it had always been assumed she would make a brilliant match – and she might have, if not for the disaster that had befallen them.

'Perhaps it won't happen. Perhaps someone will leave us a lot of money and we won't have to leave after all.'

'Violet, really…' Isobel was astonished her sister could be so naïve. Despite there being only three years between them, she felt far the older in common sense.

'You must face facts. If father had thought to renew the lease on this place instead of throwing away what remained of mother's fortune on his actresses and gambling, then having the temerity to die of alcohol poisoning—'

'Issie! Even to say such things out loud … it's unthinkable! And unladylike! Mother would be shocked! You know it was his heart.'

'For heaven's sake, Violet. Heart, my foot! And Mother is dead. Perhaps it's not the time to be ladylike. I didn't want to bring this up now but there's no choice. We may have to become governesses!'

Violet's eyes opened wide with horror. 'Me? As a governess? You know I can't. What would our friends think? What would John think?'

Almost at once, Isobel was stricken with guilt. Of course it was impossible that the child could ever be a governess. Violet would be sure to fall foul of the first male who found her vulnerable and unprotected.

'I'm sorry, baby. I'll think of something else. Perhaps John will propose at last? And then all this worry will be for nothing. If you say he loves you…'

'Yes, he loves me, but everything is so unfair … his father wants John to marry his cousin with thirty thousand pounds even though he feels nothing for her.'

For the first time a tinge of bitterness had crept into the girl's voice.

'He hinted, though, that because he loves me so much his parents might accept me with a smaller dowry, but I don't even have that. Oh why did father have to be so hopeless?'

'You must stop torturing yourself, Violet. It doesn't help. Really, if John had any spirit at all he'd take you as you are, dowry or not, and let his parents go to the devil!'

'Issie, really, where did you pick up that dreadful language?'

'From our father and his friends. Where else?'

Violet put her hands over her ears and squeezed her eyes shut.

'I don't want to think about it. Oh, why did we have to lose all our money?'

She began to cry now, weak helpless tears. Isobel softened at once and rushed to comfort her.

'Poor thing, you're not well. I'll ask Mary to take you up to bed. You need to rest. Don't worry, I'll think of something.'

Isobel didn't mention that she had already applied for several occupations and had been turned away from all of them.

There had been an opening for a lady journalist in a newspaper office she had thought would suit her very well, but the man who had interviewed her treated her at first with a disdain he didn't bother to hide, then told her in a voice slick with meaning that she was a nice-looking lass and should find a good man to look after her.

Along with a long line of other women she applied for a position as a waitress in a tea shop, but she was driven off by the manageress who told her haughtily that she was trying to take the work away from girls who really needed it. She needed the work as much as the next person, but in her heart she was secretly relieved, knowing how hers was a temperament that preferred to give orders rather than to take them.

It seemed marriage was the only respectable option left for her, but all of the men she had met so far were, to her mind, singularly uninspiring and the marriage state even more so. She was a girl of strong opinions and the very word, 'wife' had become an abomination to her. It might as well be 'cow' or 'dog'. From what she had seen of the marriage state, especially in her own home, it crushed women till their needs were secondary to everything else and left them as helpless victims of their husbands' whims.

Marriage meant her life would be squeezed into a routine of managing household chores, having numerous children and filling in her days with other wives while they waited for their men to come home.

It was a bleak prospect, especially as she usually found the company of other young women in her immediate circle as unstimulating as the men. Their conversation and interests were humble and safe. She saw them as mere dolls, concocted out of pillow stuffing and pieces of fabric, with beads for eyes and a strand of red cotton sewed in a permanently upward smile for a mouth. They embroidered cushions and crocheted doilies, their movements precise and dainty as though controlled by the strings of an unseen puppet master, till such a time they would be controlled by a real master. Isobel struggled against such a fate with an impotent fury that kept her restlessly pacing on the outside of her narrow society while watching on with a fierce, critical gaze that made most men avoid her, sensing she would make a difficult partner in life. Her attitude towards marriage was reinforced too by the newly emerging Female Emancipation Movement and, as she made no secret of her support for their policies, she developed a reputation as a firebrand, setting her apart from her peers even further.

Even so, she was no different from most other girls in that she dreamt of one day falling passionately in love, but only on the condition her prospective husband would respect her ideas of equality in marriage.

This phantom lover took on a vague form; she only knew absolutely he must be strong and capable, and as different in character from her own father as possible. Somehow this fantasy image was tied up too with adventure and foreign travel, thoughts of light and warmth and an endless horizon, of fragrant air and inky starry nights, a dream as far away from suet puddings and butchers' bills as it was possible to be.

But for the moment the responsibilities she had lived with since childhood had blunted romance. She hoped it would come later when she had time for it and she had fulfilled not only her own desires for a more expansive life, but also her promise to her mother to marry Violet to a man who was worthy of her.

While Violet was taking a nap, Isobel went into her father's study to go through his papers once more, thinking that perhaps there was something, anything, of value that might have been overlooked by the lawyers. After a fruitless hour of sifting through legal documents, she moved on to his personal letters. Some of them were from her mother, from the early days of their courting, and were full of love and plans for the future. They had clearly been read many times, as the corners and folds in the paper were almost tattered, the ink was faded now and there were tell-tale signs of blotting where her father must have once cried over them. These tragic traces of his now dead emotions moved her more than she liked to admit, but again she pushed those thoughts aside.

The Blanchards were an old French family who had come over to England to escape the wrath of the Revolution with wealth enough for them to live as gentry for as long as the money held out. But the émigrés hadn't been raised to be men of industry; they were men of culture and indolence and trained their sons to be the same. A true gentleman had no occupation, and so they didn't either. They survived on their French charm and good looks – and by marrying rich women – but by 1911, when their father, the last of the Blanchard men died, it was without dignity and covered with shame.

Thinking of her father brought on the helplessness Isobel was struggling to overcome. His death was still so fresh that sometimes, out of nowhere, she found herself fighting back tears. She told herself to crush those feelings, having seen examples of weakness in both her parents and sister all her life, and she refused to succumb to it.

Chapter Two

A good brisk walk in fresh air was just the thing to bring her out of herself. Isobel rushed down the stairs and pulled on her coat and hat. Monty was dozing before the fire but she stood in front of him waving his lead without saying a word. He at first opened one sleepy eye to look at her, then, in a split second he was up and racing towards the door.

The first rush of cold air revived them both and they flew down the steps together and headed towards the park where Isobel stood under an umbrella in light drizzling rain throwing a stick for Monty to chase while she searched her brain for an answer.

After walking the entire length of the park, she found herself on the other side and in an area of town she didn't often visit. Her mother had believed it to be disreputable and avoided it because she said only people of a certain class lived there – but what that class was she could never be induced to say – but Isobel rather liked it because of the variety of the faces of the people in the street and the profusion of goods it was possible to find in the shops. She stopped at a grocer selling brooms and bananas alongside cheap ladies' hats and bought a pound of chocolate biscuits even though they were expensive because she knew Violet liked them. Then she trailed down the street to stare in the window of a second-hand store.

An icy wind blew a collection of old coats and suits hanging in the doorway into a semblance of life, the arms and legs filling out in a wild dance for a moment before deflating back onto their hangers once more. The wind was followed by a heavy burst of rain, forcing her to sink back further into the recesses of the doorway, dragging Monty behind her.

Her face brushed against a black tailcoat that had clearly once belonged to a man of means. Her father had owned such a suit, though of much better quality, which now hung uselessly in his wardrobe. She looked at the price.

'Two pounds! God damn it!' she couldn't help but cry, using one of her father's common phrases, causing a man who had been watching her through the window of the shop to come out and stand before her, his eyes showing curiosity mixed with a desire he knew he had no hope ever of fulfilling. He was well-dressed himself, but it was obvious his own clothes had once belonged to the unfortunates with whom he dealt, as there was just the faint ghost of another larger body inhabiting his jacket before him.

He had a greasy charm he was employing to the best of his ability, and though once Isobel would have been repulsed by him, now she merely saw the young man as a person who must do what he could to survive.

'Can I help you, Miss?'

'No thank you, I am merely sheltering from the rain.'

He looked at her shrewdly as though sensing her hesitation. After years in the business he could smell poverty, even disguised in the form of a pretty, well-dressed girl.

'It's alright, Miss. Is there anything I can help you with? Have you got anything to sell? Now, that hair of yours, there's money in that. I could give you ten pounds for hair like that, but it would be a pity to take it off such a lovely head.'

She looked at the man aghast.

For a brief moment she considered it and reached up to feel the weight of her hair against her neck, but vanity won and instead she reached into her purse and brought out a card with her address on it. It was the same card her mother had left when making calls to her friends in the long-gone days of wealth and leisure.

'I shall be at home this afternoon at four o'clock if you are interested in buying some gentleman's clothes.'

'No, Miss, got enough already. Can hardly get rid of these.'

'Saville Row,' were the only words she said, and her answer was one lazily raised eyebrow.

'Alright, that is if you—'

He was about to say more but she turned her face away and left. As she rushed home she was thinking of how she could persuade the obviously hardened young man into giving her a good price. She was angry at herself for not having thought of selling her father's clothes before and wondered if it was perhaps pride and shame that had blunted her memory.

———

The camel-hair coat she held up to her cheek felt as soft and fine as a new-born lamb, and in perfect condition. It shocked her to find her father's own particular scent still lingered in the nape of the cloth. A mixture of fine brandy, Cuban cigars, and his own blend of eau de cologne specially made for him in Paris. There was even a hint of something else, something musky and undeniably feminine and forbidden.

The scent was so strong that the image came back to her of the time when he had last worn the coat: a few optimistic moments before a period of dark despair and grief.

He had arrived home from his club at three in the morning, singing an old French ditty and laughing while babbling incoherently. A cabbie had banged loudly on the front door, and she'd rushed downstairs in her dressing gown to open it before the maids discovered the shame of their master drunk and dishevelled, collapsing on the doorstep.

She persuaded the man, who was casting furtive, lewd looks in her direction, to help drag him to the study where she made up a bed for her father on the sofa.

When she tried to remove his coat, even in his almost delirious drunkenness he protested, clutching the lapels and wrapping them around his chest while shouting at her.

'No! No! You can't have it! It's mine! No one can take it off me! Not now!'

Then he opened his blurred eyes for a moment to see her anxious face looking down upon him. He put out his hand to touch her cheek and smiled.

'My Belle, my beautiful Belle. I'm sorry my dear, I'm sorry, I'm sorry for everything.'

She had been stern with him then as she took off his shoes, and almost wept when she saw a large hole in the heel of one sock; she had loosened his cravat then covered him with an old fur wrap.

He had called out to her as she was about to leave the room, 'I have a surprise for you … a great surprise!'

'Yes of course you have, Papa.' Then, impatiently, 'Can't it wait till morning? I'm very tired.'

He had looked at her, half dazed by drink as he lapsed into a semi-coma, only mumbling, 'It can wait. It will be better in the morning…'

Then suddenly his eyes had flickered open and fixed on hers.

'A kiss for your old papa before you go?'

His still fine grey eyes had held an almost urgent appeal, and from the doorway she had hesitated at first, angry enough to walk away and teach him a lesson for being drunk again when she'd begged him not to be, but then, relenting, with an indulgent smile she had returned to his side and bent to kiss him gently on the forehead.

'Goodnight, Papa. Sleep well. I'll see you in the morning.' For a long moment he had clutched at her hand, looking at her with a particular tenderness, then after a moment or two his grip had relaxed, his eyes had closed and he'd let out a long, deep sigh.

Isobel did see him in the morning, but he didn't see her. He had died, the doctor said, around three-thirty, barely minutes after she had let go of his hand and left the room.

The memory was too much after all, and she sobbed into the lapels of the coat.

After a few moments she roused herself, her eyes pink and swollen, and was suddenly alarmed as she thought of the damage she might be doing to the fabric. There was a damp patch right over the pocket. She brushed at it in a little fever of anxiety, feeling as she did so something hard in the inside pocket. It crossed her mind how foolish she was for not checking the coat earlier, but on that awful day the doctor had taken her father's sadly depleted wallet out of his suit jacket, gently removed his coat, and handed it to the maid while Isobel was in a daze of grief.

Now, Isobel reached inside the silk-lined pocket and found a brown leather sachet tightly bound with thin, worn straps. With trembling fingers, she opened it to reveal a sheaf of papers wrapped around a thick pile of banknotes. After a brief count of the money, she found there was four hundred and twenty-five pounds! Not a fortune exactly, but worth a great deal to Isobel and Violet, and it had been hanging in the wardrobe for over three months! It was a great pity there wasn't nearly enough to renew the lease on the house, but the money would buy valuable time and Isobel almost cried at the relief of it.

After putting aside the money, she cautiously opened the small bundle of papers. There were claret stains on the fine parchment, and ink blots where someone had shakily crossed out a name and replaced it with another, followed by an almost indecipherable signature. It was a comfort to see that whatever it was had been witnessed by Baxter, the head waiter at her father's club, a man he revered above most of his more influential and wealthy friends.

It was in places almost illegible, but there in the space marked 'name of owner', she read *Gerald Blanchard*, and his address: 22 *Chester Square, Belgravia*. Further down the page she read:

Silver Mist.

In the state of Goa, India. Ten miles north of Mollum on the Siripi Road.

A solid bungalow of ten rooms including services, sorting sheds, and outbuildings.

50 acres consisting of 5 acres of coffee, 1 acre of pepper, wild vanilla, half an acre of cardamon.

'A plantation! Father won a spice plantation!'

There, standing by her father's bed, was a brandy decanter still a quarter full. After a hasty – and guilty – glance around the room, as though her mother might be hiding there, Isobel took out the crystal stopper and took a long mouthful. It burned going down, but the feeling of being flooded with warmth was very pleasant. Feeling steadier, she sat down on the bed to think.

Her first thought was that the document was a fake. She would have to show it to a lawyer. Her heart sank. It would have to be George Latimer, the family solicitor. At least he could be trusted, but she was reluctant to go to him, knowing he might ask for her hand again, as he seemed to feel it was his duty to try harder now that her father had died. Whenever they met, he would gaze at her in a mournful, half-resentful way that only served to irritate her further. No, she would avoid a meeting with him and send the document through the post instead.

He was a good man – and a kind man – but he was almost forty-five years old, and a contemporary of her father's, and there was something decidedly distasteful in that.

Besides, Isobel was only twenty-two, and though many would consider her more than suitable for a man of his years, she did not. That fact alone irked her. Why should she be considered suitable? She wasn't old, or was a woman's age really worth less than half of a man's? Now though, if the document proved to be legal, none of this would matter. As Isobel stood at the window watching the rain beat against the pane, she was struggling with conflicting thoughts. At that moment she should be rushing in to wake up her sister with the joyous news of the newly discovered deed, but she decided she would wait a day or two and plan a little first. The money was different; she would tell Violet about it at once, and they would celebrate modestly with an outing to the theatre and new underwear, but an unexpected inheritance in India was another thing. This potential fortune so hard won was not going to be easily parted with. Not if she had anything to do with it.

Chapter Three

Arriving home the next afternoon after taking Monty to the park, Isobel spied a familiar walking stick and hat hanging on the hall stand.

Mary came from the back of the house to help her remove her damp coat.

'He's here,' she said in her thick Scots brogue, while making a gesture with her thumb to the drawing room. 'And he's got the appetite of a half-starved dog.'

'John Fitzherbert! Curse him!'

Isobel almost threw her umbrella down, releasing a little of her frustration.

As far as she was concerned, he had no right to visit Violet at all, especially as it was clear he had no intention of ever marrying her sister. She resented too the cost of the large tea he was bound to consume, and she thought bitterly of the ham she had hoped would last a day or two more, wishing he had thought to bring a pound of sausages or a dozen eggs instead of a bunch of flowers.

Even so, he looked romantic as he held Violet's hand in his own and gazed at her lovely face. Long curling tendrils of almost pure blonde hair lit by a thin beam of weak sunlight fell around her neck, giving her the look of a Botticelli angel. Violet seemed entranced by the boy and possibly even genuinely in love, judging by the glow of almost religious fervour in her eyes.

But this vision of loveliness was set against a background of the scattered remains of the tea; he had indeed eaten most of the ham and left the cake a crumbling ruin.

Isobel scowled and straightened. It was all most annoying.

'Mr. Fitzherbert.'

He dropped Violet's hand at once and stepped back looking guilty. His large puppy eyes looked even slightly afraid of the tall, slim figure standing before him dressed in severe black, though the effect was lessened slightly by the damply drooping feather in her pretty hat.

'Miss Blanchard. I was just leaving.'

Isobel smiled, but it was really just a quick grim twist of her lips and he wasn't fooled. She marched past him as she took off her hat and threw it on the couch, giving the impression she wanted him gone as soon as possible. For a moment he just stood there looking, Isobel thought, rather like Monty when he was told to get back into his basket after the failed hope of a walk.

'Well then, I'll come by this evening, if I may?'

'Well, you may if you like but Violet will not be here.'

'Oh.'

'Violet and I must visit our Aunt Bea in Mayfair. I was hoping to persuade her to mind Monty for us. It might be difficult to keep him once we are living in a small, cheap flat.'

She added plenty of emphasis so he could not mistake her meaning.

John looked down at his feet and Isobel took a secret pleasure in his discomfort.

'Aunt Bea also said we may be able to store some of our personal effects,' she said, then added bitterly, 'We can store our possessions in her home but not ourselves. Her charity doesn't quite extend that far.'

'Oh Issie, John doesn't want to hear this.'

Violet tried to change the subject by talking about the weather, but Isobel was not put off, pressing home her grievance.

'Aunt Bea says she'll never have a Blanchard in her home, not even half a Blanchard. Aunt Bea still blames Father for Mama's death. She says Father drove her to an early grave with his gambling and various other misdeeds.'

Violet bit her lip and flushed pink. 'Isobel, really, do you have to tell everyone?'

John swallowed hard and straightened his cravat.

'How very unpleasant for you.' He fumbled with his watch chain while Isobel stood before him and glared. The intense scrutiny was too much and he finally found his tongue.

'Well then, I'll leave you to it.'

John was making for the door in a hurry, and Isobel knew it was because he didn't want to be reminded of her dissolute father.

Violet put her hand through her suitor's arm as though to protect him from her sister's wrath.

'I'll see you out, John.'

Isobel was by his side in an instant.

'No darling, I will. You haven't got over your cold yet. Go and sit by the fire.'

She was determined and Violet knew that tone. It was useless to argue.

Isobel picked up his cane and hat from the hall stand and handed them to him with a finality even he couldn't fail to notice.

'I think it might be a good idea if you didn't come here again.'

He looked at her for a long moment, his mouth hanging agape – again, Isobel thought, remarkably like Monty begging for a treat he wasn't going to get – then he gave her a dry, bitter half-smile and made his way out into the rain.

As he paused on the bottom step and turned to look up at her, it seemed he had the intention of saying something that might soften her look, but she slammed the door as hard as she could, making the house shake.

Violet's voice rang out from the drawing room.

'Issie! Did you slam the door?'

Isobel laughed. 'Of course not, silly, as if I'd do a thing like that. The wind tore it out of my hands.'

The girls had been sitting in their aunt's musty drawing room for some time, almost in complete silence except for the sounds of cups meeting saucers and the occasional piercing squawk from a bedraggled blue and yellow Indian macaw named Billy that the old lady kept on a tall perch by her side. He was an incongruous figure in such a setting, but he had been with his mistress for so long and was so much a part of her personality that it was almost impossible to imagine her without him.

Aunt Bea's tale of woe was infamous in the family folklore. She was the older sister of Isobel and Violet's mother and had once become engaged to a young man with whom she had been deeply in love, but she had been persuaded by her family not to marry him until he had made his fortune. India had been the obvious place to do so, but he had been gone for only two years when a letter arrived telling of her fiancé's death by cholera.

A few months later, Billy had arrived courtesy of a gentleman carrying out the young man's dying wish that his pet bird should be taken to his beloved Beatrice as the only thing of value he had left to offer her. This bird and her overwhelming grief were all the dignity she had been left with, and she clung to both despite the pleas of her family.

The bird was a clever mimic and had learned several sentences in Hindi. Sometimes it would break out in a very recognizable impersonation of its long-dead owner, usually when he gave some phantom servant an order for tiffin around five o'clock in the afternoon.

Despite Billy's flamboyant feathers, the air was dark with disapproval, and their aunt's appearance only added to the atmosphere of gloom. She had entered the room with great ceremony designed to strike awe in the hearts of her visitors. The sounds of her slow progress down the hall reached their ears first. The slithering of her heavy silk mourning gown on the highly polished floor and the echoing tap of her stick seemed to bode ill with every step. She was accompanied by her companion and maid, Miss Blunt, a tender, long-suffering woman with an air of faded gentility, who hovered around her employer's skirts like a bee at a picnic.

When she was settled at last and listening to Isobel's requests with a not too promising expression on her face, Aunt Bea fixed her shrewd eyes on the two girls who were sitting neatly erect before her, Isobel feigning unconcern and Violet frankly scared.

'And what do you plan to do when your lease runs out? If you were married by now this would not be a question that needed asking. Especially you, my girl,' she said, pointing with her teaspoon at Isobel. 'And don't look at me like that. I happen to know you've refused a perfectly acceptable man for no good reason I can see, and it's unlikely you'll get the chance again with that sulky look on your face.'

Isobel raised her chin high as she glared at her aunt. Her pride was smarting, and she longed to say what she really thought of her, but she bit her tongue for Violet's sake. There had been vague talk that Aunt Bea might leave her substantial fortune to the sisters, though the rumour was shaky at best.

'It's that Blanchard arrogance; I've seen it before. Now, Violet, sweet child, praise be, takes after our side of the family.'

Isobel was hurt; it was disheartening always to be thought at fault, though she wouldn't give her aunt the satisfaction of knowing her barb had reached the spot.

'We are not entirely destitute. There will be some money left after we sell the furniture, but naturally the better pieces we will wish to keep – the family portraits, of course, and Mama's carpet. You know how fond she was of it. For sentimental reasons... That is, if you don't mind?'

The woman drew herself up and made a great show of her indulgence towards them.

'Because of your mother,' she boomed, with a surprisingly loud voice coming from such a supposedly hollow wreck of a body, 'I will take the small dog as he may amuse Billy, and you may store your extra belongings, such as they are, with me.'

At first there was a stunned silence from the girls, then they found words enough to express their gratitude while Aunt Bea received their thanks with an imperious nod of her head.

'Now that is settled, what do you plan to do to find a suitable home?'

Violet looked frightened and turned to Isobel for an answer. Isobel took a deep breath before she spoke.

'We will probably take a small, cheap flat somewhere and then find some work…'

'Work!'

The parrot by her side mimicked his owner's voice with a loud squawk and a flurry of feathers. Violet jumped and let out a small squeal of fright.

Isobel, though, burst out in an unrestrained peal of laughter. 'Well yes. At present, we have no other choice that I can see.'

'Good lord! And what precisely do you mean about taking a small … "flat" somewhere?'

At this she gave an obvious shudder.

'Well, I mean perhaps Chelsea, or—'

'Chelsea! Good God! That is not somewhere, that is nowhere! But what can one expect from the daughter of your father!'

Isobel, deeply offended, was on her feet, ready to throw the only lifeline she had overboard.

'Come, Violet, we are wasting our time here. We have a lot to do.'

The banging of Aunt Bea's walking stick on the floor brought everyone to attention, including Miss Blunt who had been watching proceedings from across the room with wide-eyed delight. It was rare to see her mistress taken to task for anything.

'Just a minute, my girl, before you go flouncing off. Stay where you are.'

There was a long silence while the old lady stared thoughtfully at them, and when she spoke, it seemed to pain her deeply to utter the words.

'Contrary to everything I've said in the past, for your mother's sake, you may stay with me till you find suitable husbands. I cannot possibly allow my nieces to work. If anyone should hear of it, your reputations will be ruined.'

'We can't afford to have reputations, Aunt, and I'm beginning to think it might be a lot more liberating if we don't.'

'Issie, please…'

'Your sister is right. Don't talk nonsense! I'm sure you will be able to make yourselves useful to me in some way. Violet has a charming voice – very like her dear mother's – none of this fast modern talk from her!' she said, with a marked emphasis while glaring at Isobel.

'Violet may read to me, and as for you, miss,' she said, 'I dare say I can find something for you to do. Miss Blunt is getting too old to be of much use. I require someone with stamina, and you've always been much stronger than poor Violet.'

Before Isobel could reply, Violet had rushed to her aunt's side and kissed her impulsively on the cheek, causing the old lady to release the ghost of a smile.

'Oh, thank you, Aunt Bea! I must say I couldn't bear the

thought of working for my living, and a cheap flat! *Quelle horreur!*'

'No, of course not, my dear child. The idea's unthinkable.'

She patted Violet's cheek then glared again at Isobel, clearly blaming her for the whole unpleasant episode. Isobel could only smile; she had heard it all before.

Chapter Four

I t was almost eight o'clock when the girls returned home but they found George Latimer settled in the drawing room waiting for them. For Isobel this was disturbing in itself as an evening call under the guise of discussing a business matter might herald the renewal of an unwanted marriage proposal.

Isobel strained to read the expression on his face, looking for signs of elation or disappointment, but as usual he was impassive and gave nothing of his thoughts away. Violet was encouraged to go to bed at once as Isobel was still anxious to keep the secret of the estate to herself a little longer, for reasons she uncomfortably had to admit were not entirely honourable.

'Well, Mr. Latimer,' Isobel said, once the door had closed. 'Is the deed legal or not?'

'It's legal alright.'

She almost danced with the relief of it. Her next thought was to rush to tell Violet of their good fortune, but again, for reasons she was still unsure of, she hesitated, telling herself there was time enough for that later. Instead, she rang for Mary and asked for a bottle of her father's champagne to be brought up from the cellar.

'Well, what do we do next? Is there a problem with us inheriting? There's no impediment in the way, is there?'

'There is nothing to stop you from taking over the property, from what I can see. But from the information I've received, the place is in bad repair and perhaps not as valuable as first thought. You may have to sell it for what you can get.'

'How can you be so sure of all this without having seen the place?'

'I've spoken to the previous owner, the man who lost it to your father. It wasn't difficult to track him down, and I must say he took it like a gentleman. Not a hint of a complaint. Lost it fair and square, he said. A certain Roger Quimp, youngest son of old Sir Cecil Quimp. Absolutely useless boy! He confessed to me he had come back to England and told a cock-and-bull story about how well he was doing with the estate and all the work he's done to improve the place, and the old boy transferred the property into his name as a reward. Well, Sir Cecil will be regretting that now...'

'I feel sorry for the young man – being unfortunate enough to come across my father.'

'Don't. It serves him right. He was drinking heavily and it's plain that the estate was no great loss to him. In fact, he seemed positively relieved to have rid himself of the burden.'

Mary returned with the champagne and two glasses, giving Isobel a warning look as she did so. She at least didn't expect Isobel to accept if George renewed his offer of marriage.

'Here's to Roger Quimp!' Isobel laughed as she clinked their glasses together. 'For being such a determined fool! Now, tell me more about this place – Silver Mist. It all sounds so romantic.'

'Not according to this Quimp fellow. Troublesome locals for a start, and a failed crop year after year – some blight or other. I can arrange to sell it for you if you like, but I doubt if you'll get much. Just a few acres of jungle, he said. Perhaps a few hundred pounds…'

'A few hundred pounds! Is that all? I think I'd much rather keep it. At least we would have a roof over our heads.'

'You can't be serious, my dear. What on earth would you do with the place?'

'I don't know yet. I haven't had a chance to think about it. I need a little time.'

'Well, it seems there was already one offer. Some chap was thinking of buying it to expand his own plantation, but Quimp wasn't sure about it. If you like, I'll cable him and see what the fellow's offering. Quimp gave me his address.'

'Well, I suppose there's no harm in asking what figure he has in mind. How long do you think it will take?'

'Oh, about a week or two I should think. The cable is pretty efficient now. Marvellous progress over the last few years. That and the Suez Canal – hardly any distance at all now…'

He had begun to waffle on his favourite topic: The British Empire and all her achievements. Isobel put a stop to it at once.

'Well, thank you Mr. Latimer, I would appreciate it. You must let me have a bill for your services so far.'

'There's no need for that. You know I'd do anything for you.'

'Please, Mr. Latimer, I insist.'

'Isobel…'

'Please, not now. Can't we talk business without this?'

'I can't help it. Not when I'm this close to you. I have to ask you again.'

Isobel sighed. She would put an end to his hopes once and for all.

'I'm not right for you, surely you can see that. You deserve a nice girl, and I'm not nice…'

His eyes opened wide. He was genuinely shocked.

'What do you mean? Of course you're nice.'

'I'm not. I'm restless and often cross. I don't like a lot of people and quite often they don't like me. I'm impatient and often sarcastic, and frankly, I would try to crush you just for not being exactly as I want you to be. And you know what Mother always said about me: "You never know if Isobel will kiss you or bite you." I'm afraid you would get more bites than kisses, and that wouldn't be fair on you.'

George's face had collapsed now and showed every bit of his forty-five years. He was defeated at last, and he left the house with no intention of ever renewing his proposal.

It was only after he left that Isobel felt a little twinge of concern at her refusal to ever entertain a clearly advantageous marriage to George Latimer, and she rushed to the mirror to assess what would be her value on the marriage market, if by chance it was the only option left to her.

It was a shock at first to really study her reflection for the first time in months. There had been no time for the usual feminine rituals of primping and brushing and embellishing her form, only preparations for burial, poring over accounts, dismissing unnecessary staff, the dyeing of mourning clothes and supporting her sometimes hysterical sister. All this had taken a toll on her charms; she was tired and looked it, but even so she was still proud of the image standing before her.

Her father had always told her she was beautiful, and for that she was grateful. He had not been unaware of the constant favouritism her sister attracted, especially from men, and she felt in her cynical way that he had been attempting to redress the balance. Violet could hold a man's attention in such a way that he was oblivious to anyone else in the room, simply by fixing him with her liquid-honey gaze till they were anaesthetized and captive, but it was her short, plump top lip with its doll-like upward curve that kept them enthralled.

The dimples which often disappear when a child grows to adulthood were still very much present in Violet's nineteen-year-old face, and sometimes when she smiled Isobel was reminded of her mother who had repeatedly told the girls that the dimples were a gift from a passing fairy who had flown over Violet's crib at birth and placed an elf finger there as a blessing.

'It means you are special, my darling, and destined for a grand marriage...'

For Isobel, a child without dimples, the prophesy had taken on a great deal of importance, and consequently she always felt inadequate, and her mother had done very little to restore her confidence.

Violet took after her mother in both appearance and personality, being light-hearted and at times even light-headed, while Isobel, according to her father, was a true Blanchard.

The Blanchard women, he had always said, were like the queens of ancient myths, with the most transparent, pale skin and abundant honey-blonde hair – 'the colour of the best French champagne,' he would often say as he raised a glass of that same favourite beverage.

Old family portraits showed that in the days of plenty before the dreaded Revolution, the women were painted elaborately bewigged and bejewelled, their faces showing their great pride matched only by their great wealth. Their sly, alluring smiles and painted cheeks adorned with strategically placed beauty patches showed an unusual spirit and style that shone out of the canvas; that perhaps had allowed them to survive even such a catastrophic event as the French Revolution.

Isobel did not know it yet, but she had inherited that spirit in abundance, and now, with George Latimer well and truly dismissed from her life, she experienced a surge of elation. She felt she was at a crossroads, unsure about which direction to take. But now, with the sure knowledge that the inheritance was real, there was an opportunity that might pitch her into something life-changing, and she had no intention of wasting it.

Chapter Five

The house was almost bare, and Isobel wandered around the echoing rooms in which both she and her sister had been born, with feelings close to despair. It was an elegant eighteenth-century confection with a delicately carved central banister and an old-fashioned garden, already a rarity in that part of London, as most of the surrounding houses had been demolished to be replaced with blocks of dreary, red-brick mansion flats. Now her own lovely home was to meet the same fate and every memory of the Blanchard family, pleasant or otherwise, was to be demolished with it.

The rain had stopped at last, but Isobel's walk in the garden was bittersweet. It was one of the last times she would stop to admire the old oak in the centre of the lawn; no more would she breathe the scent of the crimson roses that grew in abundance against the iron railings of the fence and heralded the coming of summer. Here was peace and beauty, and beyond the confines of the garden was an uncertain future. For a moment her courage almost failed her.

The postman's whistle brought her to attention, and she hurried to take the large envelope held out to her, then she rushed back inside to eagerly tear it apart.

The package itself was intriguing. It was battered by travel and the imprint of many hands and covered with a large quantity of colourful stamps bearing the postmarks of Goa and Bombay. She drew out a letter that was curiously impregnated with a fleeting and unfamiliar fragrance and written on extremely good quality paper.

There, embossed at the head, was the imprint of a name. Then, underneath, an ink drawing of a grand but indistinct house surrounded by tall cypress trees, bearing the name 'Casa Margarida'.

Dear Madam,

I have been advised by your lawyer that you and your sister are now the owners of the neighbouring property, Silver Mist, due apparently to the dissolute actions of the previous owner...

Isobel raised a smile at that. The writer was clearly a man who didn't mince his words.

Of course, the estate can have no interest to a pair of women such as yourselves, residing as you do in England, so I'm offering you the sum of four thousand English pounds for the house and land. The estate is in disrepair and the land has been neglected for some time, but against my better judgment I'm prepared to be liberal just to get this matter finalized at once before the need for harvesting is upon us.

If you agree to my terms, I can have my lawyer draw up a deed of sale etc....

The letter was followed by a signature written with a dramatic flourish.

Phillipe Santiago Almeida.

Isobel's first thought was that the sum of money seemed enormous, perhaps just enough if she forfeited some of her own share to produce an acceptable dowry for Violet so she could marry her beloved John. Her second was that she was so overwhelmed by the arrogance of the writer's tone that she felt a desire to thwart him in some way. He clearly expected there would be no opposition to his offer and that annoyed her, but she felt she had no right to refuse. Violet must be consulted now. It wasn't fair to hide their good fortune from her any longer, even though she knew for certain what Violet's response would be.

Violet could never be persuaded to go to India to find out if this man's offer was fair or not, as travelling had never held any interest for her. Even their occasional visits to France had been met with foreboding, and abject horror at the customs so unlike what she was used to.

Violet would insist on selling, and she most probably would be right. It was the only sensible thing to do.

Then, as Isobel picked up the envelope to replace the letter, something fell out. At first, she thought it was a piece of gaily coloured fine paper but then the object revealed itself to be something quite different. It was a butterfly, around eight inches across, obviously long dead, but even in death the most beautiful creature she had ever seen. She held it in the palm of her hand where she gazed at it in wonder. The weak sunlight creeping through the window illuminated the glories of the delicate velvet wings. There was turquoise and cerulean blue and emerald-green flashed with silver and even a faint dusting of gold, like stars across an inky sky. How had it got into the envelope and how had it remained intact after such a journey?

In that damp empty room with its pale-grey walls and bare floors, the butterfly grew in magnificence. It was a rare and exotic jewel flashing in the palm of her hand, hypnotizing her, and at the same time instilling an overwhelming desire to see the land where such a creature could have lived.

After a short, guilt-ridden struggle combined with a wild fluttering sensation in her stomach, she made her decision. Violet would have to stay ignorant of their good fortune for a little while longer.

For some time, Isobel had been longing to travel, and Egypt was one of the destinations that most appealed to her. From Egypt there were ships that sailed directly to Bombay in just under two weeks.

The idea became more and more feasible in her mind if India was never mentioned. At the first sniff of such a destination, Violet would be sure to protest and insist on selling without having seen the inheritance at all.

It was settled.

They would go on a voyage under the guise of a cruise to Egypt for the benefit of Violet's health, and then she would break the news of the estate and the trip to India when it was too late to do anything about it.

Then, if the estate was truly as this Almeida fellow said, she would sell it to him at once.

If, however, the place proved to be better than expected, she would then drive a harder bargain. There was another reason too for keeping their good fortune secret a little longer. In her heart she truly believed it would be a mistake to encourage a marriage between her sister and John Fitzherbert, even if John's father did agree to it and despite Violet claiming to love him madly. As far as Isobel was concerned, Violet didn't know what was good for her, and this cruise would perhaps make her see the sense of waiting till a more suitable candidate turned up. There was something else driving her to escape London too: she would avoid the necessity of decamping to her Aunt Bea's. The thought of spending even one moment as a barely tolerated dependent relation, no matter how temporary, was impossible to contemplate.

After gently placing the butterfly in an old cardboard box, she dug a small grave under the rose bushes and buried it with a prayer that the creature's soul would find its way back to the country of its birth, then she placed her favourite hat on her head and left the house to take a cab to the city.

An hour or two later, she walked out of Thomas Cook & Son with three first-class tickets for Cairo. She also had the name of a ship they could pick up from Port Said direct to Bombay. Again, a brief flutter of guilt crossed her mind when she thought of Violet, but she cast it off almost at once, saying she would cross that bridge when she came to it.

The tickets plus the need to buy clothes suitable for the tropics would certainly eat quite a hole in their limited funds. However, Isobel calculated the risk was worth it. Now, all that needed to be done was to tell Violet about the cruise and to soothe the wounded vanity of her Aunt Bea.

Of course, Violet reacted as expected, but Isobel was determined and stood her ground.

'It was very unfair to do it without consulting me, Issie, even though I know you were only thinking of me and my colds.'

Isobel flinched at that delusion on Violet's part, but now was not the time to be feeling the pressure of guilt.

'I can't return the tickets now but think of the fun we'll have. A proper holiday with just us. We can do what we like without anyone telling us what to do. Imagine! And of course we must give up wearing mourning for Papa and buy new lighter clothes for the trip. I know he wouldn't mind.'

The idea of giving up mourning for new clothes was a tempting thought for Violet, and she was comforted more than she would let on. Even so, her voice was almost a wail now and tears rolled down her cheeks.

'But what about Aunt Bea? She's gone to so much trouble for us already. And to be away for months... What will John think when he hears about it?'

'I don't care what John thinks and you wouldn't either if you had any sense. If he really loves you, he'll wait for you. If he doesn't wait... well, he didn't really love you anyway. And where is he now, if he's so fond of you?' Isobel added, conveniently forgetting that she had banned him from the house.

Violet only cried louder, and Isobel was in despair, as ahead of her was the likely fury of her Aunt Bea. She would have to brave the old lady face to face, and alone. Violet would have nothing to do with it.

'A cruise! To Cairo!' the frail old lady boomed, and Billy leapt off his perch and into the air with a loud shriek, a wild flutter of wings, and a word in Hindi that might well have been a curse. 'What on earth are you thinking of?'

Isobel abandoned her meek manner almost at once.

'There's nothing unusual about it. Lots of people do it—'

'Not my nieces! Alone on a ship with God knows what temptations. I won't allow it.'

'Well, Aunt Bea, we won't be alone. We will take Mary with us, of course, as a chaperone. And anyway, it's too late now. The tickets are bought, and we leave on Wednesday of next week … and there's nothing you can do about it,' Isobel added, with more than a touch of a smug smile.

The walking stick hit the floor with a loud thud.

'I've a good mind not to have you here with me after all. After all the trouble I've gone to. It would serve you right if I went back on my promise.'

'I'm very sorry, Aunt, and of course you must do as you see fit.'

The surprisingly sharp eyes narrowed. 'But then, as you say, there's nothing I can do. And you were only thinking of your dear sister's health, so I forgive you this once.'

'Thank you, Aunt Bea.'

Then, as an afterthought she added, 'Purely as a matter of interest, on what rat-infested craft are you attempting this ridiculous journey? If it sinks, *The Times* will at least inform me of the fact.'

'It won't sink, Aunt. It's a very fine ship, *The Solaris* – highly recommended, of course.'

The sharp eyes narrowed further. 'How long did you say you would be away?'

'Just three months. When we return it will be the middle of spring in London, which is so much better for Violet and her colds, and so much more pleasant for you,' Isobel said, almost with a touch of gaiety. 'Think of it. You won't have us under your feet through winter and there's so much more we can do together in summer. Why, we might even take a trip together to the seaside if you think you can manage it. Perhaps even as far as Scarborough?'

The old lady looked at her with a canny glint in her eye.

'A trip to the seaside, you say? How very thoughtful of you. I'll think about it.'

Isobel stood to leave before her aunt could betray any further signs of irritation.

'Well then, I suppose that's it. I must go. I have so much to do. You will keep Monty then?'

'Yes. He can live in the kitchen.'

'In the kitchen?' Isobel tried to disguise her concern with a weak laugh. 'Oh well, I don't suppose he'll mind that much as he'll be closer to his food bowl. He will have regular walks though. He does so love his walks.'

Now that grim reality had set in, Isobel started to feel guilty and a little sad. She began to think she might even miss the irritating little creature.

'One of the maids will accompany him on a daily walk to do his business.'

'Well then,' Isobel said again as she bent down to kiss the parchment cheek, 'thank you, Aunt Bea. Thank you for everything. We will see you in three months.'

Her progress towards the door was easier than she'd

hoped. At any moment she expected an explosion of wrath, but the old lady even managed a grim smile.

'Have a pleasant voyage,' she called out, in an almost friendly way, just before Isobel hurried off, relieved to have escaped so lightly.

Chapter Six

They were on board *The Solaris* at last and would leave in just a few minutes. Isobel took a long, deep breath, willing herself to relax, feeling sure that nothing could go wrong now that they were almost under way, and she was free at last to look forward with pleasure to the trip before her.

Even so, her conscience bothered her. She still hadn't found the courage to tell Violet about the plantation. Many times, she had been at the point of spilling all, but at the last moment she would falter and turn away with an expression of angry frustration, causing Violet to wonder at her sister's erratic moods.

In the end, however, her secret became too much for her to keep to herself, and she resolved to tell Mary, who accepted the news with her usual comforting common sense.

'Of course you wouldn't be silly enough to sell your property without having seen it first. That's just good judgment, but your little sister now, she's a darling and we all know it, but hasn't the sense of a rabbit when it comes to business. No, it's best we keep it to ourselves for the moment.' Then, after a few minutes, she came back into the room with a wide grin on her fine, strong-boned face. 'India... That's something. I've always wanted to see the place...'

So as far as Violet knew, they were going to Cairo for her health, as the air was supposed to be good for her delicate lungs. Isobel would tell Violet they would be travelling on to Bombay once they were in Cairo, hoping by then that Violet would have begun to enjoy travelling and would take pleasure in the thought of a more adventurous trip.

While Isobel was struggling with her conscience, Violet was sitting resignedly on a deck chair already complaining about the smell of the ship. She felt at that moment that she would never forgive Isobel for taking her away from the man she loved, even if that man had turned out at the last minute to be a slight disappointment. Even so, she didn't blame her darling John. She blamed Isobel for being so ... so ... so heartless and so cruel!

John had somehow come to hear of the proposed trip, and on that very morning had braved a visit to Violet with the vague intention of asking for her hand, despite the objections of his father. He had waited outside of the now almost empty house for hours, trying to screw up the courage to knock on the front door. He had almost given up and was about to walk away when, watching from behind a tree, he saw the front door open and the elegant figure of Isobel step out, look about at the unusually mild morning with a pleased smile, then trip lightly off down the street.

He waited till she had disappeared around the corner then rushed out of his hiding place like a stoat out of its burrow to tear up the front steps and knock at the front door.

Mary tried to hide her annoyance at seeing him there and was about to say that her mistress wasn't home when Violet herself, who had seen him from her upstairs window, called out that she would be down as soon as she had made herself presentable.

John sat in the empty room on one of the trunks that had already been taken downstairs and labelled with its destination. He poked sadly at the label with his walking stick.

'Cairo, Egypt.' Something inside of him disapproved heartily. If it were Italy, well now, that might be a good thing. A continental tour was respectable and perfectly reasonable considering Violet's fragile health, but of course, he thought resentfully, Isobel Blanchard would choose some inconvenient and barbaric location, when something more suitable would do. It was while he was muttering something about bad blood that Violet swept into the room and almost took his breath away.

He had almost forgotten how very lovely she was, as she stood before him in her light-grey travelling dress, a look of dewy-eyed joy on her face.

'John! I had almost given you up!'

For a long moment there was an awkward silence while she stood before him with an expectant smile on her lips, then at last he managed to blurt out a few words.

'I couldn't stand the thought of you going away without seeing you.'

Tears filled Violet's luminous eyes. 'Oh John, I don't want to go, and I've missed you so much.'

First he stared, tongue-tied, then, all of a sudden, he fell to his knee and took her hand in his.

'I can't bear it. I must have you for my wife. Please, Miss Blanchard, Violet, will you marry me?'

Violet at first stood with her mouth wide open, then the words came tumbling out.

'Yes, oh yes. Of course I will. Oh! I'm so happy!' He was about to take her in his arms and at last kiss that captivating mouth, when the door burst open and Isobel stood before them, her smile quickly evaporating.

'What is the meaning of this?'

Violet rushed to her and threw her arms around her neck.

'Isobel, oh Isobel, I have wonderful news. John has just asked me to marry him.'

Isobel turned to face the boy with a deceptively sweet smile on her lips.

'And does your father know of this?'

'Well no, but…'

'But what?'

John found the courage to speak, despite the look in Isobel's eyes that reminded him of an eagle about to attack a rabbit.

'I hope I may convince him. He has hinted that even with a small dowry he may be persuaded.'

The words 'small dowry' shook Isobel a little, though she betrayed no sign of it.

'And what would he consider a small dowry?'

'I don't know, a gentleman doesn't speak of such things. It doesn't sit right.'

Isobel's lips curled into a bitter smile.

'My dear Mr. Fitzherbert, even if Violet had ten thousand pounds, no sister of mine will marry into a family that needs convincing she's good enough for them. It's up to me to decide if your family is good enough for us!'

Violet was almost in tears now.

'Isobel! You have no right! If John wants to marry me then that is good enough for me!'

Isobel ignored her sister and spoke directly to John.

'You can marry my sister when I have a letter from your father clearly saying he would be delighted for you to marry into the Blanchards, dowry or no dowry. Till then I must ask you to leave. We have a ship to catch this afternoon.'

'Issie! Please!'

Isobel was unmoved.

'Well, Mr. Fitzherbert, you have a choice. We sail at six o'clock. If you can return within that time with a letter from your father saying he agrees to your engagement on the promise of no dowry, then I will also agree, and Violet may stay in England with our Aunt Bea in Mayfair. But till then there can be no engagement. Come, Violet, we still have a little packing to do.'

Then Isobel softened at the mournful look on her sister's face.

'Try to understand. You're only nineteen, darling. Not much more than a child really. You have so much time to be in love…'

Isobel put out her hand to her sister who reluctantly took it, while at the same time giving her lover a look of painful longing.

'Try, John. Try for me…'

'I will, darling. I'll beg him if I have to.'

Then he gave her one last despairing look and left.

That was the last Violet had seen of him, but even now, as

the gangplank was about to be drawn up, she held out hope. Then, as though her prayers were being answered by a higher power, she heard a commotion on the wharf. There was a great deal of noise accompanied by a loud squawking. She thought it was very odd but supposed the noise must be coming from a crate of chickens waiting to be taken on board.

Then a voice rang out from the shore asking for the gangplank to be held.

Violet leapt to her feet, her hand on her heart, sure it was him. John had arrived with the letter, and she would be able to leave the cursed ship! For to the depth of her soul she was afraid, afraid of the sea and what she saw as an almost inevitable voyage of disaster.

She looked across to where Isobel was standing near the rail with a look of absolute frozen horror on her face, for there, making her way slowly and ceremoniously up the gangplank with the aid of her walking stick and a great deal of bustling and issuing of orders, was their Aunt Bea, followed closely behind by a flustered Miss Blunt who was struggling with Billy in his cage and Monty on his lead.

———

Violet was the first to speak, as Isobel could find no words.

'Aunt Bea! What are you doing here?' After first giving the old lady an impulsive hug, she bent down to take Monty in her arms to give him a quick kiss on the nose, relieved to find that some of the world she had left behind would be accompanying her on what she saw as a fool's expedition.

The old lady looked up from under her mourning veil.

'I've always wanted to go on a cruise, and what better

opportunity than now, when my nieces would see so much sense in my accompanying them.'

Then, turning to Isobel with a sly smile she said, 'You did mention how we might take a trip to the seaside together. Well, here I am.'

It was too much for Isobel, who couldn't even find it in her to be polite at such a moment. She could only walk away to give herself time to control her temper and to curse aloud at a crate of cabbages on the deck, using one of the cruder expressions borrowed from her father, while lamenting the fact that she had been outfoxed.

It was when they were disembarking for a day in Marseilles that Isobel overheard one of their fellow passengers laugh not too discreetly as she and her party walked by.

'Good God! How standards have fallen on the P&O these days.'

The woman was referring to Aunt Bea, the endlessly ruffled Miss Blunt, Mary, Violet and herself plus Monty and Billy. It was useless to protest that Billy should be excluded from shore excursions, as it was believed he would benefit from a day on foreign soil as much as any other creature. He sat on the old lady's shoulder attached to a long ribbon which she tied around her waist. Isobel was certain Aunt Bea insisted on towing the bird with her everywhere as a kind of perverse and mischievous punishment to her nieces. She seemed to enjoy the sight of their flushed cheeks and embarrassed sidelong glances whenever someone approached them with a comment about the unusual arrangement, but usually strangers just laughed and pointed, making the girls squirm with shame.

There were some attractive men on board and Isobel thought how much fun there might be if any one of them could be persuaded to overlook the eccentricity of the group or be allowed to get close enough. She had also hoped that by meeting other eligible men, Violet might forget about John for a moment and be less resentful.

But getting past Aunt Bea took a very brave man and so far no one had found the courage till a handsome young Scotsman, Charles Cameron, who was on his way to take up his position as manager of a tea plantation in the north of India, broke through the barricade and opened the flow of other eager young men. He was clearly already besotted with Violet even after only one dance, but she showed no signs of returning his interest. Isobel knew it was more than her being faithful to John. It was because Violet was a snob, and not about to throw herself away on a man, no matter how attractive, who had only a yearly wage and the promise of a bonus if the tea yield was successful.

But even so he persisted and paid the steward more than he could afford to have himself seated at Violet's table night after night. She might be immune to his charms, but Isobel wasn't. Apart from his broad shoulders, thick reddish-brown hair and warm hazel eyes, she found him intelligent and funny and strong enough emotionally to be able to weather Violet's changeable moods. Then a letter arrived from John with the Marseille mail, fuelling her sister's love with more promises of being able to convince his father to agree to their marriage. Charlie Cameron was only just tolerated as a useful diversion with which to amuse herself, and Violet passed her days in a cloud of resentment against her sister.

But there was so much about ship life Isobel found to enjoy that she could at times almost forget she was the cause of her sister's unhappiness. She delighted in everything: the fresh ocean breezes that whipped her cheeks into a rosy, healthy glow, the roomy cabin lined with dark teak, the comfortable bed and the crisp white sheets, the cunning little bathroom, the long, luxurious meals in the dining room, and for once not having to come up with ways to make the roast go further.

She was enjoying being a girl again, free from responsibilities, and more than one man on board noticed her beauty and was beguiled by her charm. She danced and flirted in full view of her aunt's cautionary looks, enjoying the carefree girlhood she had been denied in the past, though always in the back of her mind was the fear of the storm that would inevitably break over her head when they arrived in Cairo and she would have to tell the others of her intention to continue on to Bombay, revealing to them at last the truth about the plantation. It wasn't so much her fear of Aunt Bea's reaction, as the old lady had proven herself to be so far a hardy and uncomplaining traveller; it was more her dread of Violet's inevitable rage. For not only had she dragged her sister away against her will, but she would also have to confess to have had all along the means in her hand to give Violet a dowry, small as it was, with which to marry the man she loved.

While contemplating her dilemma, she had the idea that after the scheduled six weeks in Cairo, she would suggest that Violet return to England with Aunt Bea and Miss Blunt while she went on alone with Mary to see the plantation for herself. In a rare fit of unreality, she argued that no one could possibly object and all would be well. This self-delusion allowed her to carry on showing a public face that was outwardly more than usually charming and which drew a marriage proposal, from a man who even in her Aunt Beatrice's eyes would be considered highly eligible.

The proposal came the evening before disembarking at Alexandria. There he would be leaving the ship to return to his posting with the Foreign Office. For a moment, Isobel was tempted by the idea, despite the man being a little stuffy and pompous. From Alexandria he would move on to Baghdad where he had a large house and had enchanted her with tales of his life there: his visits to the camps of the great sheiks and the glorious sight of the camel caravans as they appeared as if by magic out of the shimmering haze of the horizon; the desert tribes and their mysterious customs, the beauty of the oasis pools and the wide rivers – the Tigris and the Euphrates – names she had read on her schoolbook maps, names that filled her with longing.

But it was no use; she knew in her heart if she accepted him, it would be only because she was more attracted to the idea of life in an exotic and mysterious country than the man himself, and she parted with her deeply disappointed suitor in the morning with absolute composure and barely a tinge of regret. Most of all though it was the mysterious lure of Silver Mist that kept her eyes firmly fixed ahead. In her mind this almost mystical Shangri La had become the answer to all her problems and all else shrivelled in significance before it.

Chapter Seven

The exhausted group of travellers arrived at their hotel just as large flocks of noisy ibises were settling for the night in the grassy mounds and banks alongside the Nile, then the sun seemed to drop from the sky, rapidly turning the darkening night into the deepest of lapis lazuli blue. For some minutes, the occupants of the carriage sat silently as they absorbed the magnificence of the scene before them while they stretched their stiff limbs and slapped the dust from their clothes.

On the amber-tiled hotel terrace, as a rather shaky string quartet played Chopin, a smiling Sudanese servant in an immaculate white uniform and wearing a red fez gave long glasses of bright-pink pomegranate juice mixed with champagne to a group of elegantly dressed ladies and gentlemen who had gathered to enjoy the scented evening air and watch the flow of humanity passing before the grand hotel staircase.

On the dusty street before them, a small, thin girl with bare feet and a wide, brilliant smile was performing somersaults for the hotel guests, but every minute or so one of the waiters would wave her away; she would retreat behind a pillar to peek cheekily out until the man's back was turned and then she would reappear to perform even more somersaults, much to the delight of the ladies on the terrace who threw her coins which she instantly snatched up to hide in a little bag tied to a string she wore around her neck and hidden down the front of her ragged red dress.

A team of heavily laden camels led by a group of wild-eyed young Bedouin in long black robes brought the romantic air of the desert with them, and the men paused to stare at Violet who was looking particularly pretty as she straightened her wide-brimmed hat. Then they broke out in an unintelligible but excited babble as they gathered about her, their harsh eagle-like eyes raking her body and blonde hair, till she shrank back, alarmed, into the watchdog presence of Aunt Bea who shooed them off with a few harsh words. It was impossible to guess at their expressions, hidden as they were by their headscarves, but their eyes told everything. It was a mixture of lust, fascination and absolute contempt for Violet's protector.

Intriguing women, covered from head to toe like phantoms and sometimes bearing huge vases on their heads, looked out cautiously from behind their mesh face veils onto the world that separated them. Every now and then, young women, their foreheads decorated with a swathe of silver coins above eyes painted like the figures from the tombs of the Pharaohs, captured the attention of watchful men who tried to perceive a glimpse of an alluring face half-hidden by a veil that only hinted at the beauty beneath. These girls rushed by with quick, confident steps as though on important missions, the fine fabric of their robes billowing about them and allowing a glimpse of dusty sandalled feet decorated with henna markings and trim ankles encircled with gold bangles.

A troop of soldiers from the Foreign Legion lounged about in their sand-coloured uniforms and took up a position near the front steps of the hotel while they laughed and smoked strong-smelling cigarettes; they blocked the path with their heavy, almost threatening presence while their sharp eyes darted about on the lookout for anything, human or otherwise, they might be able to exploit or profit by. They too noticed Violet and Isobel, but they expressed their interest in a subtler though infinitely more dangerous way.

Groups of exhausted tourists covered in dust, just arriving back from touring the sights, dragged themselves up the front steps with hopes of a warm bath and a cool drink before dinner. It was plain some of them were at the stage of wondering why on earth they had bothered to move out of their pleasant homes to risk life and limb in the pursuit of whatever it was that had driven them to such an inhospitable world, to eat food that made them ill, and to sleep in beds not as comfortable as their own.

Every now and then, a soft tinkling laughter rose from the women seated on the terrace, one of whom was particularly striking for her quiet elegance.

She had a head of almost pure black hair parted strictly down the middle like the Madonna and held back with a pair of ornate gold combs. Heavy, intricate gold earrings studded with rubies hung almost down to her bare shoulders. Her skin was sallow and her mouth pale and rather thin, but even so she had a beauty of sorts that was at times compelling. A gold cross surrounded by diamonds hung around her throat and fell to rest above the demure décolletage of an obviously expensive Parisian black silk gown. Her most attentive admirer was a tall, distinctly handsome man who appeared to be aged around thirty years old with the same perfectly cut eyes and pale olive skin, though his eyes glistened with a lustre the young woman lacked, as they flashed from left to right, while taking in every detail of his surroundings. There was a restlessness too in his manner that showed in the way he smoked his cigarette, taking short, sharp puffs then stubbing it out with a frowning edginess.

But there was some other emotion that sometimes took over his face when caught in unguarded moments. As though being reminded of something unpleasant, a hidden melancholy would seem to overwhelm him, giving the impression his mind was elsewhere, in a much darker realm; then he would mentally shake himself, and bring his attention back to the present.

Two other women at the table, one clearly a lady's maid and the other, much older, flanked the girl and fussed over her wants with an attention that bordered on suffocating. Overall, there was an air of entitlement and exclusivity about the little group that made others less fortunate look at them in a type of wonder and envy along with a vague resentment.

It was into this oasis of refined calm that Isobel and her party had arrived, tired, dishevelled and hot, and in Aunt Bea's case, resentful now to the point of not bothering to hide how she felt, as the only carriage left available to hire for the journey from the train to the hotel had been almost comically shabby, though the owner had tried to enliven its façade by painting it with the brightest colours of the rainbow, which had only succeeded in making matters worse.

There had been trouble too about a huge metal trunk belonging to her aunt that Isobel found such a burden, she had wanted to have it shipped back to England. They had several fierce arguments about the necessity of this unwieldy item, but to no avail. The trunk must accompany them wherever they went, taking up valuable space and considerably slowing their journey as it needed four men to lift it onto whatever means of transport they were employing.

This constant bickering finally ended with Isobel losing her temper at last. She ordered the carriage to turn around and suggested in no uncertain terms it might be a good idea if both the trunk and her aunt stayed in Port Said while the others went on to Cairo.

This brought about an immediate thin-lipped and haughty silence from Aunt Bea, along with various reactions from the other inhabitants of the carriage. Billy squawked a shaky response that sounded a rebellious note in the ensuing quiet; Violet was frightened her aunt really would defect and take her money with her; Mary was unmoved, having seen it all before; but Monty saw the sense in lying low and sat close to Violet, not moving except for an occasional nervous glance at Isobel until they pulled up in front of their hotel.

The loaded-down carriage drawn by the aged horses, both wearing straw hats against the sun, had made for a comical entrance before the elegant crowd who stopped what they were doing to frankly stare.

Mary drew the most attention as she was in charge of Billy, who seemed to be the only creature amongst them to have maintained some form of dignity. He sat high on his perch, proud and unflappable, unlike Miss Blunt who was being harassed by her employer for allowing Monty, who had suddenly recovered his spirits, to leap out of the carriage and run up the street, his lead trailing behind, in pursuit of another dog of highly questionable parentage. Isobel was occupied in getting the attention of the servants to deal with the baggage, who all appeared to be looking the other way when they saw the size of the trunk – while she helped her still peevish aunt down the rickety steps of the carriage. Violet alone stood radiant, lovely and composed, as she fanned herself prettily while looking up at the hotel with an approving smile.

The dark, good-looking man on the terrace held his glass halfway to his lips with a scornful smirk, then turned to the woman by his side to say a few words, just loudly enough for Isobel to hear. He spoke in a tongue with which Isobel was unfamiliar, but she thought it might be Portuguese; having had Spanish rammed into her by her old governess, the formidable Madame Joubet, Isobel understood enough to be offended.

He had said something like, 'It seems we are about to have a travelling circus descend upon us…' before his voice was lost in the woman's well-bred laughter.

For almost the first time in her life, Isobel blushed, but she recovered enough to stare back at the man in an impudent way, making it plain that she had heard and understood him.

He held her eyes with his own and showed no sign of shame, only briefly lifting one enquiring eyebrow and giving her a haughty glance before turning away and pouring a great deal of exaggerated attention onto the girl by his side. He did, though, for just a moment, allow his eyes to flicker over Isobel's neat form as she skipped lightly up the steps of the hotel.

Isobel saw this elegant group only one more time a few days later. They had chosen a large table quite close to hers because it was the only one left that had a view of the Nile, even though there was already a neatly written *Reserved* sign placed clearly in the centre of the table.

She watched them as they came into the room. As usual, they were richly dressed – in Isobel's opinion too richly dressed for the daytime – the long gowns of the women sweeping the floor behind them, their heads held high as they rejected one table after another while ignoring the maître d' as he ran ahead as though trying to block their path to the reserved table. The women didn't even see him; their eyes were on the desired spot, and the outside world and the concerns of others were of no consequence to them. Then, with no sign of emotion or even making eye contact, the gentleman lifted one elegant hand and waved the maître d' away with a handful of notes and an air of absolute disdain. He did, however, notice Isobel at the next table; he seemed to come to with a start, then gave her a hasty bow while muttering a thickly accented greeting. She inclined her head coldly but said nothing in return.

Isobel had come down to breakfast early in the hope of avoiding the usual fuss that accompanied her at mealtimes. Violet liked to sleep late and have breakfast in her room, but Aunt Bea was usually annoyingly present at an early hour with a long list of demands about the exact timing of her eggs and tea; so far this morning, Isobel had managed to eat her breakfast in peace and even read an old copy of *The Times* without interruption.

Every now and then she hummed a little tune to herself as she ate. Everything was such a pleasure. Fresh grapes and melon at breakfast! And the flavour of the eggs! Surely they didn't taste like that in London. Even the bread had a wonderful earthiness and texture she had never experienced before. And the coffee was a fragrant dream, tasting faintly of nutmeg and cloves. It was so delicious that she was inspired to ask the waiter why it tasted so special.

'It is Arabica, Mademoiselle. The best there is … from India.'

'From India?' She laughed. 'I would have thought it came from Arabia with such a name.'

'Well, it did, but so long ago, the origins are forgotten.'

It crossed her mind then that perhaps there might be such a variety growing on her own estate. *Estate.* She couldn't even say it to herself without a little thrill of excitement.

The waiter returned with the bill, and she signed it without looking at the amount because she didn't want any thought of money to ruin her day. She was glad she had chosen the most expensive hotel in Cairo, though she knew it was probably a little reckless. The added expense was easily justified by the thought that if she wanted to attract wealthy men as suitors for Violet, the right hotel was a necessary expense; she was, however, uncomfortably reminded of how she might be seen to be following in her father's footsteps of wild extravagance.

A faint titter of laughter from the opposite table drew her attention towards the exclusive little group seated there.

After straining to listen to the conversation for a few minutes, Isobel concluded that the young woman must be either the wife or fiancée of the arrogant man who had been so rude to her when she first arrived. But then when he left the table for a few minutes, the talk became immediately about him.

The two women began to speak in what Isobel again believed to be Portuguese, but then the girl implored her mother to only speak French as she wished to practise it for when they shopped in the bazaar.

The younger woman threw a quick glance in Isobel's direction and said, 'Perhaps she can hear us...'

The older woman replied with particular scorn, 'She is English. They know nothing but their own coarse language.'

It was tempting to answer the woman in her immaculate French, but Isobel was more amused by the idea of overhearing their conversation, even though some of their words were unintelligible.

'When you are married,' said the older woman, 'you will have to insist you live in Lisboa. It is impossible you should be so far from me. To think of living in that terrible place...' This time, though, her daughter replied with a little furious hiss.

'Please, Mama. He hasn't asked me yet...'

'Your uncle Tiago wants the marriage very much, so he will influence the nephew.'

'I do not need the influence of my uncle. He will ask me; I am sure of it.'

'If your uncle desires the marriage then you will have to obey him, now that your dear father is dead, even though I am against it.'

The girl sighed rather pointedly. 'Yes, Mama.'

Then her mother said with particular bitterness, 'He had better ask you soon since you've brought me all this way from Lisboa. He must suspect something. Besides, you're nearly twenty-six.'

'Please don't mention it again. You make me ashamed.'

'Why shouldn't I mention it? And to think, you could have married our dear Benedito and been a princess...'

'I told you I don't love Benedito. You know who I love, and I want only him.'

'You are spoilt. A husband is not a new dress or a piece of jewellery.'

'I don't care.'

'Well, thankfully you are rich enough to marry whom you like, but I still say you are a fool to want him when you could have—'

'I know, Mama. I could have been a princess.'

'And there is the boy. Do you really want to be a mother to another woman's child?'

'He can go to school. I need not have anything much to do with him.'

Then, after seeing their handsome companion approach their table, their voices dropped into furious whispers and Isobel could hear no more, but the moment he sat down the two women resumed for his benefit an outward display of harmony.

The man didn't seem in the mood for chatter, and only watched the scene between the mother and daughter play out before him with a benevolent eye, though just once Isobel thought she saw the faintest sign of irritation pass over his proud face. But mostly their public behaviour was marked by its perfection, and the sense that the group were divided from the rest of common humanity by an invisible wall, like the invisible wall of royalty, and that peculiarity finally drove Isobel to ask the young waiter who they were.

He replied with a faint sneer.

'The countess D'Souza and her daughter. They are very rich.'

'And the gentleman?'

'I do not know, but he is Portuguese too, I think.'

To Isobel he seemed more Italian than Portuguese. There was something about the liquid glance in his eyes and the shape of his red lips that reminded her of the paintings of the beautiful youths of the Italian Renaissance.

Regardless of his origins, he didn't have the appearance of a modern man; he should have been wearing a stiff, white, lace ruff around his neck along with a pointed black beard and a dagger in his jewelled belt. It was the face of a man who might well feel compelled to travel to new worlds in search of gold and rare species to pique the interest of his queen.

He had pushed his chair away from the table and sat leaning back, crossing one elegant leg over the other as he sipped his coffee. Once he stood for a moment to help the countess retrieve her dropped napkin and Isobel could see that he was quite tall, broad shouldered, and straight backed. Too straight backed, she thought; he was clearly as pompous as he was rude. She watched as he sat down, combing his fingers impatiently through a thick wave of dark, shiny hair that had fallen forward over his face before throwing back the remains of his tiny cup of syrupy coffee in one shot.

For a not very heavy man he seemed to take up a lot of space, with a presence that was indefinable, and Isobel noticed hers were not the only eyes in the room observing his languid movements. Overall, though, Isobel thought that despite his very attractive features, he looked sulky and spoilt and clearly used to getting his own way.

Chapter Eight

Peace reigned for only a few moments longer as soon there was a commotion at the door of the dining room which foretold the arrival of her aunt who was making her usual dramatic entrance. Her steps were slow, ponderous and noisy, drawing the attention of everyone in the room as she bent heavily over her walking stick and with her long black veil trailing along behind. She was accompanied by Mary with Billy on his perch even though Isobel had demanded he be left behind in his room, at least for the duration of their stay in the hotel.

Isobel looked hastily around then whispered to her aunt, 'Really, Aunt Bea! You promised you wouldn't bring Billy into the dining room. You promised most faithfully.'

The old lady looked up with an expression of childlike innocence in her eyes but said nothing. Isobel was surer than ever that the parrot was used as a means to taunt her.

The waiter flew to stop her.

'You cannot bring this bird in here, Madame! It is unhygienic! The other guests…!'

'Unhygienic, my foot! He's cleaner than any human I've ever met, and his table manners are better than most! Bring me a bowl of Huntley and Palmer's water biscuits at once. They're his favourites.' The bird looked at the waiter with an expression that seemed to confirm his mistress's request.

'I cannot, Madame…'

'Do so at once.' The old lady didn't even bother to raise her voice, only fixed him with her formidable stare, and the waiter left waving his hands impotently in his despair, knowing for certain he was beaten.

Isobel looked towards the opposite table and was punished by the sight of the dark man trying not to laugh. The girl too had bent her neat head closer to his, but Isobel heard distinctly his words spoken in Portuguese, '*O Inglês ridiculo.*'

She glared in his direction, but he didn't notice her, being too busy trying to stifle his laughter. 'How dare he! Again, he insults us. Now he calls us ridiculous!'

But there was worse to come when Miss Blunt appeared at last. A very different Miss Blunt, somehow looking considerably younger and even mildly pretty, due to her best hat and a wide exultant smile on her face. For a moment or two she almost hopped on one foot before the little assembled group, looking as though she might burst with the news she was so obviously dying to report. Then she took a deep breath and blurted out the words in a rush.

'Madam, I am here to give my notice. I wish to leave your employment, at once,' she added, with obvious joy.

At first there was no response, only an irritated twitch on

the side of the old lady's mouth as she raised her teacup to her lips.

'You wish to leave, Blunt? What are you talking about? Sit down at once and order some fresh tea! This is cold! By the way, where were you this morning? I called and called.'

'I was with a man,' Miss Blunt said proudly, making no attempt to lower her voice.

'With a man, Blunt!' Aunt Bea echoed, and Billy shrieked a response, sounding disturbingly like the voice of his mistress.

The people at the opposite table laughed openly now, not bothering to hide their amusement, and Isobel blushed with shame. Miss Blunt drew herself up proudly.

'I was with my fiancé, Mr. Leigh—'

'Fiancé? You have no fiancé. I believe you have been dreaming. The heat has gone to your head. Well, you can't leave. I haven't finished with you yet,' she added ominously.

Isobel was the first to recover. She remembered then how Miss Blunt had appeared to be unusually happy on the ship, and how she had even spied her several times on the lower deck out of sight of her mistress and deep in conversation with a short, bald man with an ecclesiastical collar.

'Please, Aunt Bea. You haven't been listening. Dear Miss Blunt is engaged to be married.'

Aunt Bea remained unconvinced.

'I must say, Blunt, this is highly inconvenient for me and very inconsiderate of you. Just who is this fellow you say you're engaged to? Are you sure he's not toying with your affections? Why on earth would he want to marry you?'

For a moment, Miss Blunt was about to show signs of her former subservient manner. She trembled visibly; her thin courage shaken. A shadow of doubt passed across her face and tears formed in her eyes.

Isobel rushed to her defence.

'Mr. Leigh is that very sweet curate from Poona, isn't he? I had no idea you had formed an attachment.'

'Neither did I till last night. That is, I thought we had become good friends on the ship, but I never dreamt...' She blushed prettily, then added, 'Harold is very impulsive.'

Isobel tried to compare the picture of the nice but strait-laced vicar with the suddenly imbued actions of an impetuous lover but could not.

'There's a ship leaving Port Said tomorrow for Bombay, so to avoid any hint of a scandal' – here she gave a little half smile as though relishing for the first time in her life the thought of being at the centre of salacious gossip – 'we'll marry here so we can have our honeymoon on the ship ... our honeymoon,' she repeated, almost as if it were a dream. Then she rushed out of the room, without looking back.

At the mention of Bombay, Isobel paled, having been jolted back to the problem almost at hand. Soon there would be no avoiding having to confess the real reason for their trip, but with Miss Blunt leaving, her situation was becoming more complicated by the minute. Now she must feel the inevitable guilt of sending Violet back to England with no one to help her with her aunt.

The next half hour passed in a constant air of irritability while Isobel served the tea and pretended to listen while the old lady poured out her usual long list of grievances in a voice loud enough for the group at the next table to hear.

'Wretched woman! Now you'll have to help me up, Isobel.' Aunt Bea was leaving the table with her usual fuss and ceremony and Isobel realized with a start that the duties of a maid would now inevitably fall on her shoulders, and just for a moment she cursed Miss Blunt for having the temerity to fall in love with the nice Mr. Leigh.

The old lady was heavy, and it took some pulling to raise her to her feet. The chair had to be pushed back from the table, plates and glassware had to be moved and incessant grumbling had to be endured.

Then the man from the next table offered his help. He stood before them with his immaculate black suit and patronizing manner, one graceful hand outstretched towards the old lady. He spoke almost perfect English, though with a faint hint of an accent more Italian than Portuguese.

'May I be of assistance, Madame?'

Aunt Bea looked pleased and fluttered a little before the man's cool charm, but Isobel was irritated, and she narrowed her eyes. She saw his polite intervention as a kind of game he was playing, almost as though he had been dared to enter the circus ring in order to see up close if the exhibits were even more freakish than he first thought them. Isobel looked around to see the women at the next table hiding their smiles behind their coffee cups and she noticed there was just a hint of a sly smirk playing around the man's lips.

'No thank you,' Isobel said with as much of a superior manner as she could muster. 'I am quite capable of managing by myself.'

His dark eyes widened in surprise, and he stepped back a pace.

'Let the gentleman help if he wishes, Isobel.'

Aunt Bea was almost girlish as she held her hand out to him.

'No need, Aunt.' Isobel's tone was firm. 'As I said, I can manage!' She almost snatched at the offered hand and tugged at the old lady who seemed to be doing her vindictive best to make herself heavier than usual as a punishment for having opposed her.

This time he couldn't hide his smile.

'As you wish, Miss…?' He pronounced the word 'Miss' as 'Mees', and there was just a hint of a suggestion of wishing to be introduced, perhaps as a kind of atonement for his behaviour, but Isobel turned away, not caring if she offended him or not.

It took all of Isobel's fragile self-control to calm herself. Her one thought was that he had laughed at her family. Aunt Bea was ridiculous, it was true, but she was her Aunt Bea, and no one was allowed to laugh at her except herself.

He stepped back and gave a brisk half-bow, then returned to his table to watch their awkward retreat from the room.

Isobel was aware of three pairs of eyes boring into her back and the faint sound of girlish laughter, but she straightened her spine and half turned at the doorway to deliver a final contemptuous look in their direction. She noticed that the man wasn't smiling; he simply half rose in his seat and bowed briefly before making a show of turning to the girl by his side, taking her hand and again raining his full attention upon her.

Chapter Nine

E verything felt a little flat after the departure of the happy couple. The sudden change in Miss Blunt's fortunes made everyone aware of how life can take an unexpected turn in an unforeseen direction and it made for a certain uneasiness, but just in time, Violet's ardent admirer from the ship, Charlie Cameron, appeared from his cheap hotel on the other side of Cairo, saying he had decided to postpone his journey to Bombay for a week or two and would be available to squire the little party of ladies to whatever sights they might like to visit.

At all times he was charming, gallant and attentive and a useful guide and protector from the hordes of touts and con men who hounded their every step. Isobel was even a fraction envious of her sister's luck in attracting such a man, as in her eyes he came closest so far to her idea of what a husband should be. Everything about him indicated strength, warmth and honesty. The character traits she admired most in a man. But he could see only Violet, being blind to the charms of all other women.

But Violet didn't seem to notice any of his qualities and saw him only as a pleasant friend and useful companion. Her very lack of interest made her more desirable still as there was never a hint of restraint or any sign of feminine guile when around him; it also meant she didn't notice the almost painful expression of unrequited love in the poor man's eyes when he gazed at her.

Violet laughed when Isobel hinted that Charlie Cameron was in love with her.

'You think everyone is in love with me, Issie, and the only man who truly is, you refuse to have any sympathy for. Mr. Cameron knows I love John and that I intend to marry him, despite you doing everything you can to prevent it.'

It never occurred to Violet that the obstacles in her way could not be overcome. As a spoilt child, somehow everything she had ever wanted magically materialized and she couldn't see that having John as a husband would be any different.

So, they saw the pyramids and the tombs of the ancient kings, and rode on camels at dusk, and bought exotic but useless souvenirs that once home would gather dust in the attics for a later generation to find and wonder over. On the surface they appeared to be a cheerful little set, though the only truly happy members of the group were Aunt Bea, who proved to be an indefatigable tourist despite her outwardly fragile state, and Mary, who found fascination in every new sight and pleasure in the first true holiday she had ever had. Charlie Cameron, despite his eternal good humour, was desperately unhappy and became more so the closer his time of departure came. He felt he had made no headway with Violet, and he loved her more than ever. The prospect of a future without her seemed unendurable and his only comfort was knowing that Isobel was sympathetic to his situation despite him being poor.

Violet, despite her sunny exterior, had moments of severe dejection which increased if no letter had arrived that morning from her beloved John, and nothing could shake her out of it till the next post brought the loving words she was waiting for; if the letter contained what she wanted to hear she went through the days with an expression of radiant joy that made her more attractive still. Isobel watched her sister's moods from afar with increasing guilt and a sinking heart, and every hour that passed while she carried on her deceit became unendurable.

It was Charlie who ultimately forced the situation. He announced after dinner one evening that he intended to catch the next ship to Bombay, which left on the following Friday. There was a general cry of disappointment around the table, as everyone had become reliant on him in some way. Even Aunt Bea, who disapproved of him as a suitor for Violet, found him invaluable as a steady arm on their various expeditions. He also didn't seem to mind when it came to taking his turn holding Billy on his perch, and he seemed impervious to the stares and smiles of strangers as they passed. Now he stood before Violet with his emotions firmly under control, though Isobel could see clearly the pain written there.

'So, I have taken a ticket on *The Indian Rose*, a fine ship with a fine captain. I know it well...'

Isobel was listening intently; it so happened it was the exact same ship she hoped to catch. She had already enquired about tickets and found passage was easily available. All that remained was to tell the others. She too had come to rely on

Charlie, and if she was going to Bombay she wanted to travel with him.

Violet must be told of her plans first, and it was with a dreadful sense of foreboding that Isobel joined her sister in their bedroom. At first, she took the trouble to order tea and cakes in their room – something she knew Violet loved to do – and by way of anaesthetizing her sister against inevitable fury, Isobel handed her a large slice of strawberry cream cake.

Then she sat back to watch her sister eat.

'Is the cake nice, dearest?'

'Yes, Issie, very. Why don't you have some?'

'I'm not very hungry just now. Perhaps later.'

Violet looked up to see her sister pacing the room.

'Why don't you sit down?'

Isobel stopped, took a deep breath, then flopped into a chair with the air of someone who was resigned to her fate.

'Violet, I have something to tell you. It's very good news… You remember when I found the money in Papa's wallet?'

'Yes of course, Issie. What's the matter? You are quite pale.'

'Well, darling, there was something else. I found a deed … a deed to a coffee and spice plantation. Papa had been playing cards and he won an estate in the south of India. It's just a hundred miles or so south of Bombay, in a place called Goa, but there's a steamer, I believe, which is not too uncomfortable and from there we—'

'Isobel, stop! What are you saying? Papa won a plantation and you kept this from me?'

'Yes.'

Violet stared, the cake halfway to her lips. She let the fork fall with a loud clatter.

It was the closest she had ever come to losing her temper.

'You had no right, Issie!'

'Well, I was sure you would want to sell it and I didn't want to. Not at once anyway…'

'You mean it's worth something?'

'Yes, of course. A few thousand. There was an offer but from someone very unpleasant. I didn't like his tone and I thought it might be worth much more, but how can we tell without seeing it?'

'Do you mean to tell me that all this time you had the means to give me at least a small dowry and you kept it from me?'

'Yes, but—'

'And you didn't accept what sounds like a perfectly generous offer because you didn't like the man's tone?'

'Yes, but I'll show you the letter and I'm sure you'll agree with me.' She rushed to a dresser and produced it with a flourish. 'Listen, I'll read it to you—'

Violet raised her hand.

'Stop! I don't want to hear it. The truth is you're jealous!' Her voice had a touch of hysteria now. 'You're jealous of the love John and I have for each other! You couldn't bear it that I had someone worthwhile in love with me and not just a musty old solicitor like George Latimer. Issie, how could you?'

'I'm sorry, darling, I really am. I just wanted the chance to see if we could make more money, that's all, but as soon as we see the place, and see what it's worth, we'll sell it, I promise, and you can have a dowry to marry John…'

'What do you mean, "see it"?'

'Well, we must go to India of course, to see it.'

'You'll never get me to go to that place. India! Ugh! I

couldn't bear it! It's bad enough here in Egypt.' For a second or two there was silence as the truth suddenly dawned upon her.

'Issie, really! How could you?'

Isobel hung her head.

'I'm truly sorry. Would it make you happy if you went back to England with Aunt Bea? It would mean no maid, of course, but perhaps one of the ship's stewards will be of help to you. I'll go on to India with Mr. Cameron and Mary and I'll see the place and sell it at once. First thing tomorrow you must write to John and tell him you have a small dowry and that I agree to your engagement. You can have my share of the money. I'll probably never marry. No decent man will ever want a girl who would lie to get her own way!' Here she laughed weakly, but there were tears in her eyes. 'Will that make you happy, darling? I'm so sorry, really sorry. Please forgive me.'

'I don't want your money, Issie. I just want you to trust me to make the right decisions, to trust my judgment as well as your own.'

'Do you forgive me? You must. I'll be miserable if you don't.'

'Well, I don't forgive you. It was wrong of you, very wrong.'

'I know, but I've paid a hundred times over. I've been so unhappy.'

'You didn't look very unhappy. In fact, you seemed to be having a perfectly marvellous time.'

'Smiling on the outside, but inside...' Here Isobel gave a look of such genuine despair that Violet laughed.

'Well, it's over now, and Cairo has been fun in a way. And I do feel very well; I haven't coughed for weeks. I'll write to John at once and say that as soon as we sell this inheritance of

Papa's I will have at least two thousand pounds. Surely that will be enough to sway his father.'

'You must not get your hopes up darling. John's father may not shift on his demands.'

'But when he realizes how much we love each other…'

'I'm not sure for him love enters into this transaction. He is a banker, remember. And are you sure John is who you want? Really sure? Because I'm not certain yet he's right for you.'

'Quite sure. I will never be happy with anyone else. One day, when it happens to you, you'll understand exactly what I mean.'

'When or if it does happen to me, I hope I won't be such a slave to it. I would find it too exhausting. But will you come to India with me? Don't you want to see your property? Probably the only property you'll ever truly own – that's not your husband's, I mean. Just imagine, one's own house and land… Papa's final gift to us both.'

'No, I want to go home to John. Don't try to stop me, Issie. I can't bear being away from him any longer.'

Here she burst into tears but allowed Isobel to comfort her, thereby paving the way to much improved relations between them, which, for the first time in weeks, allowed Isobel to sleep the sleep of the guiltless.

Chapter Ten

I sobel rose in the morning refreshed and with a new determination to face what was ahead with courage. She would tell Charlie Cameron at once that she would accompany him to Bombay and from there she would catch a ship to Panjim in Goa.

Everyone had gathered for breakfast at their usual table and Violet almost skipped into the dining room, a lighter, more hopeful girl; she even bent to kiss Isobel's cheek, showing that she had truly forgiven her, then she sat down to eat a huge breakfast for the first time in weeks.

'Well then, Aunt Bea,' began Isobel, 'I have something to tell you. Mary and Violet know already, and Mr. Cameron might as well know now...'

Then she began, all the while keeping her eyes on her aunt while she braced herself for the inevitable storm that would break over her head.

'So, therefore, Violet has decided she would like to return to England with you, Aunt Bea, and I am going on to India with

Mary on the same ship as Mr. Cameron. To see our property and to get the best price I can for it.'

There she stopped and smiled in Charlie's direction. He smiled in return, though it was plain he was stricken with the news that Violet would be returning to England where he had no hope of ever seeing her again as a single girl. In his usual way, he raised his chin and hid his despair.

'I would be happy to be of service to you, Miss Blanchard, in any way I can.'

Isobel folded her hands on her lap and waited for what she felt must be the inevitable response.

'Thank you. Well, Aunt Bea?'

The old lady smiled grimly.

'Nothing you do surprises me, young lady. Typical Blanchard. No thought for your poor sister at all.'

'Yes, I know, Aunt Bea, but—'

'No buts about it. Disgraceful behaviour. It's the way you were bought up – not enough discipline and too much freedom.'

'Yes, I know.' Isobel was impatient now and couldn't hide the sulky, defiant expression about to spread over her face. She bit her lip. In another minute her anger would bubble through to the surface.

'No decent girl could maintain such a deception for as long as you have.'

'Yes, yes, but what's done is done now, and if I want to—'

Violet glanced at her sister. The eruption would happen any moment now.

'However, it is as you say. What's done is done and—'

Isobel's eyes opened wide. There seemed to be a distinct

75

softening in the old lady's tone. Not what she expected at all. She took a deep breath.

'Well then, that's settled. I'm glad you see the sense in it.' Isobel stood to leave. 'I must arrange passage for myself and Mary on *The India Rose*. I will of course see about the tickets for you and Violet on the next ship back to England. How pleased I am that the matter is settled at last.'

The old lady's eyes narrowed to thin slits.

'You seem to have planned everything to perfection.'

'I hope so, Aunt. Now, I really must go. There's so little time.'

Isobel began to walk away but was halted by the booming voice of her aunt who seemed to be thinking aloud.

'I have always wanted to go to India, and I would have if my dear Archie had survived. And, of course, it's where Billy is from…' She turned to the bird and spoke in a peculiarly gentle voice she reserved solely for him and sometimes Monty.

'You would like to see India again, wouldn't you, Bill? You would like to see your true home?'

The bird bobbed his head and squawked his response, and curiously it seemed as though his expression brightened a little.

'There's a good chap. Well then, you may yet.'

Violet had been watching the proceedings with varying emotions. Her head darted from her sister and back to her aunt as though watching tennis.

It was Isobel who mumbled out the first hesitant words.

'You can't possibly be suggesting…? But Violet hates ships. She hates travelling. She wants to go home to lovely Mayfair, as you must, and Monty will hate the tropics,' she added uselessly.

Aunt Bea was undaunted; in fact, she seemed quite rejuvenated.

'Violet will enjoy it once she's on board – as will Monty – and we'll be perfectly safe with Mr. Cameron to accompany us. And,' she turned to Isobel with a look that put any idea of protest out of her head, 'no tricks, Madam,' she said, shaking her finger. 'I'm going on that ship with you and that's that.'

Chapter Eleven

Violet didn't enjoy it once she was on board. Mainly because every mile sailed towards India took her further and further away from her beloved John. There had been no final letter on the day of departure from Port Said and there was no chance of one till she reached Bombay. His last letter too she had found slightly disturbing. He declared his love for her as loudly as before, but it was full of reproaches towards Isobel, blaming her for taking Violet away from him. 'When we are married,' he wrote, 'I do hope your sister will not be making her home with us. She has at times a most wilful manner and I believe is lacking in respect towards me...'

For the first time, Violet found herself slightly irritated by his tone, though she told herself her dear John would love Isobel just as much as she, once he knew her better.

She had written back with the news of her impending dowry:

Isobel thinks my share may be as much as two thousand pounds …
but she has offered her half of our inheritance to me as well, even
though I refused it. Does that make you think more fondly of her?

The weather became hotter now and the girls changed into lighter dresses more suitable for the warm tropical days and nights. Even Aunt Bea, who swore she would never take off mourning for her long-lost Archie, changed out of her heavy wool and into a black linen skirt and grey blouse, reducing her crepe veil by several feet so now it floated gaily behind her as she walked the decks with Monty in tow, his little legs pausing and bracing at each rise of the ship. Contrary to Isobel's prediction, Monty seemed to be enjoying himself very well and had made friends with a rather unpleasant bulldog, the constant companion of an elderly colonel who was returning to India after failing to adjust to life in England after spending almost thirty years in the Punjab.

Following the lead of his dog, he had made friends with Aunt Bea who seemed to be getting younger with each passing day, at times becoming almost schoolgirlish with excitement as the little group neared India. Isobel began to have a grudging respect for her aunt's enduring spirit which kept alive her own sometimes flagging optimism. She was more than ever burdened with the thought that she had made her sister unhappy and was constantly reminded of the fact by the sight of Violet's increasingly wan expression. Even Charlie Cameron, who could usually coax a smile from her, failed to lift her mood, and by the time they reached Bombay, the glow that usually shone out of her beautiful eyes had faded and her brow seemed almost constantly puckered into a frown. It was clear to everyone that she was anxious to hear from John and even Charlie was perversely beginning to hope for the longed-for letter if only to see the light return to his beloved's eyes.

Again, he delayed his trip to Assam for a few days to see his friends settled into their hotel and to help arrange for their steamer passage on to Panjim. He had become so attached to the little group that he was finding it increasingly difficult to say goodbye even though he knew he must. Isobel too anticipated their parting with misgivings. She had begun to rely on this fine, strong Scotsman more than she liked to admit, especially now in this foreign world that at times appeared so confusing. His knowledge of Hindi too had paved the way through the madness of the docks to their hotel with very little effort. He had fought off the clamouring mass of touts and beggars with only a few sharp words and a handful of well-placed coins, but it had been the scene they had witnessed moments after setting foot on this foreign soil that had caused so much distress that Violet had had to be half carried along the pier to the long line of waiting carriages, her lovely face ashen with fear.

The ship had berthed at a long pier that protruded out into the ocean on one side and bordered a sandy bay on the other. It was Isobel's fault of course, as it was she who had drawn attention to the scene. It was the curious chanting that drew her first and she wandered to the edge of the pier to look at what seemed to be the beginnings of a bonfire on the sands near the water's edge. Then all in the party were gripped with horror – all except Charlie who had witnessed such an event many times before – but as though in a trance, Isobel could not be persuaded to drag herself away from the ritual in front of her.

A young woman dressed in purest white was sitting on the

sand at the end of a large mound of neatly cut wood that had been piled in a crisscross pattern to a height of around four feet. Then a priest appeared with a group of mourners tottering under the weight of a bier, holding the body of what they supposed to be the woman's late husband, covered thinly with a muslin net and scattered with wilting marigolds.

The body was laid upon the pile of wood, his head half protruding out of the cloth at one end and his bare feet at the other, then a fragrant oil was poured over the body by the chanting priest.

Isobel stepped closer, gripped by a curiosity that was stronger than revulsion. This was her first encounter with a custom so vastly different from her own and she did not want to shy away from it.

Violet's voice rang out with a scream.

'Issie! Please! Come away!'

But Isobel did not hear. She was mesmerized by the sight of the young woman who walked three times around the body of the deceased, touching his forehead each time, then stepped forward with a handful of lighted straw, igniting the pyre into an inferno that swiftly consumed the body.

There were no unseemly displays of emotion from the mourners; just, it seemed to Isobel, a quiet acceptance that the deceased had passed onto a higher plane and would surely soon be leading a happier life elsewhere. The wife was led away by her relations, but something in the way she held her shoulders showed a deep despair – perhaps not as much for her husband as for herself and her uncertain future.

Throughout it all Isobel couldn't help but think that as confronting as the whole process was, there was also an honesty and acceptance of death that seemed to her far healthier than the European way of disposing of their loved ones. For her, there was a greater terror in the thud of the soil on the closed coffin, along with the loneliness of an eternal sleep beneath the cold damp earth.

'Isobel! Come away at once!'

It was Aunt Bea, whose ladylike roar could not be ignored, and Isobel followed the others quietly as they hurried along through the crowds on the wharf. But all the while she was thinking that here was life, even if it was at first sight extremely disturbing.

Monty barked wildly at everything and had to be restrained from leaping out of the carriage to chase an evil-eyed little monkey wearing a tiny, jewelled fez that passed by on the shoulder of a street magician.

Aunt Bea smiled grimly through it all. To Billy she whispered, 'You're back home at last, old chap, where you belong.'

Billy managed a weak squawk in reply.

In a fit of generosity, Aunt Bea had booked them all into the grandest hotel in Bombay, consisting of three floors of pseudo-English luxury where even the waitresses were young English girls imported especially for the task. The hotel had been recommended by Aunt Bea's friend the colonel who said goodbye to the little group over a final afternoon tea before leaving for his home in the hills of Simla. Isobel was amused to see an almost tender scene between the old man and her aunt when they finally parted, her aunt fluttering and giggling and promising to write, much as Violet had done when parting with John. Her mourning veil had now been replaced by a rather smart black hat with a short matching piece of black transparent silk bought in the French Quarter in

Cairo, which lent her a distinct touch of almost flirtatious charm.

Inside the walls of the hotel, it really was possible to believe they were staying in Bournemouth instead of Bombay, even down to the muffins at breakfast. Isobel, despite her impatient desire to experience something of the real India, felt relief at not having to pay the bill for once, and gratitude that Violet had a comfortable place to recoup her energy and spirits as it seemed it may well be quite a few days before they could move on.

Every day delayed brought increased frustration. She longed to be in Goa and to see the inheritance that had offered her so much hope as well as so much conflict. Now though she was certain she would sell the property at the earliest opportunity.

She would approach this man, this Almeida fellow who had offered to buy it, try for a higher price, accept without too much haste to preserve her dignity, and retreat at once back to England.

She could never admit openly just how shaken she was by the India she had seen so far, despite the fragrant beckoning air at night that drew her to her balcony to breathe in the life and atmosphere of the great city she was surrounded by. Her heart fluttered with anticipation at the thought of the adventure before her, but it all seemed so big and unfamiliar, and made her feel powerless and insignificant. She was too at times uncomfortably reminded of the thought that the British had colonized the country she now had a stake in against the will of the inhabitants, and she tried to picture how she would feel if the situation was reversed. It took not much reflection on her part to realize she would deeply resent it, but she pushed that feeling to the back of her brain as she wrestled with her own need for survival.

Panic crept in too at night when she was left alone with her thoughts, knowing absolutely that whatever disasters might befall them all from then on were due to her folly alone, and she must live with it.

Violet was unwell with a stomach complaint and even the mere mention of stepping outside the hotel brought on an explosion of fury at Isobel for dragging her to a place she loathed. Mary too found the heat unbearable, so it was only Aunt Bea who appeared to have the stamina to venture on a tour of the city and its outskirts. Together they visited spectacular shrines, went to the markets and bought numerous cashmere shawls and yards of multi-coloured silks to purchase a little joy for Violet.

Isobel began to enjoy herself despite the drenching heat she was so unused to. The vivid colours and scents of this new world enchanted her, but the incessant crowds and the acute poverty, which was almost always present were often so confronting, it was impossible not to be affected.

Even so, she found the few people she encountered gracious and kind despite their often-desperate circumstances, and she was buoyed up as well by Aunt Bea's fascination for the country.

'I might have had a residence here if only poor Archie had lived,' or 'We would have walked together along this seashore if only he hadn't caught that terrible disease...' were refrains she heard over and over from her aunt.

She mentioned his name often, usually accompanied with a deep, sad sigh of regret. Once, when Isobel asked what he was like, she said, 'He was the dearest, sweetest boy you would ever meet, and we loved each other very much. He wrote to me every day for two years and described in detail all he had experienced in India. I lived every moment of his Indian life with him, except I was stuck in that miserable house in Mayfair with my miserable father!'

Then, with a deep bitterness that shocked Isobel to the core, she added, 'I'll never forgive my father for not allowing me to go with Archie. If I had gone, he wouldn't have died.'

Isobel didn't argue with her. Knowing her aunt as she did, she was sure Archie probably wouldn't have died. He wouldn't have had the nerve.

Chapter Twelve

The long-awaited letter from John didn't arrive before it was time for the little band of travellers to board a steamer to Panjim. Despite her wan expression, Violet had been buoyed up by the news that the English mail had been held up by a storm in the Gulf of Arabia and any post would have to be forwarded to their new address – the most romantically named, Silver Mist.

It would take at least two full days to reach their final destination and Isobel secretly confessed to herself to being anxious about the trip, though she didn't indulge in these fears for long, for if she thought about what failures might lie ahead, she would lose her courage entirely. As was her way, she felt it was best to forge blindly ahead and deal with the consequences later.

Now the burden of the unknown would fall entirely upon Isobel's shoulders as Charlie was leaving them at last to take up his position in Assam. As his final service to the women, he had hired as a guide and protector a rather grand gentleman, a

Sikh with a magnificent moustache by the name of Darshan Singh who spoke perfect English and wore a carved kirpan tucked into his crimson sash. He had been the long-time retainer of a senior government administrator who had returned to England and left his beloved friend and servant with excellent references and a taste for the English ritual of high tea and the game of cricket.

He had been hired by the month and it was Aunt Bea who offered to pay his wages and any other costs incurred on the journey. Isobel didn't let pride stand in her way. She had exactly one hundred and three pounds, ten shillings and a few hundred rupees between herself and poverty – not even quite enough to pay for the return passage to England.

That was something she didn't care to think about and as usual hastily pushed the thought back to a place reserved for all kinds of unpleasantness.

'What's done is done,' she said to herself, but whenever she took a furtive look in Violet's direction it was difficult to hide her guilt, even from herself.

Charlie stood on the pier waiting for the steamer to depart, bravely hiding his despair at having to leave the little group of which he had become so fond, and above all having to leave Violet potentially forever. When she asked him to write and let her know of his safe arrival in Assam, he cheered up at once, and was able to walk away without looking back. Except for the brave squaring of his shoulders and his averted eyes, no one could suspect his true feelings.

The steamer to Panjim was a very different vessel to the one in which the group had sailed from England. It was rather small with a peeling, wide-bottomed stern that had once been painted red but was now a faded rust colour that mingled with the only too obvious rust beneath. The upper deck was open on all sides but protected from the sun by swathes of faded canvas that hung from tarnished metal rods in loose folds and fluttered noisily at the faintest breath of wind, seeming to threaten to blow away the moment they headed out to sea. A handful of tiny, rickety cabins were clustered together at the back of this upper deck for those like Aunt Bea who insisted on maintaining British standards for herself and the girls, even though the interiors were far from luxurious. There was only a narrow bunk covered with a thin mattress, a tiny but immaculately white pillow and sheet, a single blanket neatly folded at the foot of the bed, and a bucket in case of sea sickness.

At the sight of the ship, even Isobel experienced more than a tinge of doubt, but she swallowed it with a forced smile for the sake of Violet. Violet had at first flatly refused to get on at all and had to be coaxed on board to the sound of bitter whispered accusations and recriminations under her breath directed entirely at her sister.

'It will be a miracle if we survive this trip. I'll never forgive you for this. Never! I'll be sick all night, I know it!'

Then she went straight to her bunk and lay down with her face to the wall, refusing even to look at Isobel who by now knew that it was best to keep out of her way till the journey was over.

It was much more cheerful on deck with the other passengers anyway, who seemed to have no fear of the journey ahead and had already opened tidy bundles of food from woven baskets and piles of fresh coconuts from which they drank after cutting off the top with a machete. Everywhere there was an air of gaiety; someone had produced a battered squeeze box and was playing a melody that would be more at home in Europe than India. Some men, who to Isobel appeared to be somewhat piratical, had arranged themselves at a small table set up on the deck and were playing cards while drinking a rose-coloured wine from a flagon and smoking small European cigarettes rather than the bidis the Indians smoked in Bombay. They were speaking a confusing mix of Portuguese and Hindi that was totally alien to Isobel's ears and it became clear to her then that she had already crossed into a vastly different culture from the one she had left behind. She rejoiced in it, for she realized she had moved from being merely a tourist following a well-trodden path, to that of being a traveller, at the beginning of what might be the great adventure she had been searching for all her life.

With a great deal of shouting, general confusion and laughter, the little ship finally slipped away from the turmoil of the Bombay shore. Only an hour into the journey, a new world revealed itself in the form of a coastline of gently waving coconut palms and pristine beaches against the vivid turquoise-blue background of the Arabian Sea.

A fresh breeze had sprung up and every now and then a cry would ring out from the passengers as they spied dolphins swimming alongside the ship or something more ominous, either real or imagined, following along behind.

A handsome young boy wearing only a white loin cloth

wandered the decks balancing a tray on his head that held neatly tied parcels of fish and rice wrapped in banana leaves and a mound of various local fruits. Isobel was hungry and was tempted to taste the delicious-smelling concoction wafting towards her, but she had been warned by Charlie that under no circumstances should she eat anything that might have been lying too long in the fierce sun.

Isobel saw her aunt walking the decks with Billy on her shoulder and Monty in tow. She called the boy over and handed over a coin in exchange for a portion of the food. She clearly had no fears for her health and settled down on a rickety canvas deck chair to eat while she watched the sun go down. Billy sat quietly on her shoulder with his feathers being lightly ruffled by the breeze, and for once the bird seemed suited to his surroundings, scarcely drawing a look from the other passengers.

Mr. Singh joined Aunt Bea then and the two older people sat together in compatible silence to watch the sun go down.

Aunt Bea had taken a great fancy to Mr. Singh and the pair were often discovered deep in conversation or laughing at matters that were usually beyond the understanding of her young nieces. Theirs was a peculiar relationship, coming as they did from vastly different worlds, but Isobel was thankful for it as it deflected attention away from herself and the usual criticism that followed.

It was a bewitching time. All of a sudden, the sky was flooded an unearthly pink; the sea was as calm as a pond and painted a silvery iridescent blue. As the ship cut through the gentle waves, a phosphorous glow bordered the foam from the waves while a school of flying fish raced ahead, their slick bodies fringed in that unearthly radiance.

Everyone on board had stopped their chattering and lapsed into a gentle reverie. A golden light illuminated everyone's faces, making even the most plain and humble person godlike for a moment. In the distance, the silhouettes of the palms trees on the shoreline formed a black lacy embroidery against the burnt-orange sky. Sharp peaks in the shape of volcanoes or small jagged islands punctuated the landscape, creating in Isobel a mysterious powerful desire to see up close such enticing places.

Isobel was intensely moved by the beauty of the scene. The chaos of Bombay was forgotten and even forgiven, as at last the journey to India was living up to her expectations.

Mr. Singh left to join some other men in a game of cards, and Isobel sat beside her aunt, wanting to share these magical moments with another person, even at the risk of being blamed yet again for having lured them all on what may turn out to be a fool's errand.

She took a cautious peek out of the corner of her eye and was almost shocked. Her aunt's face was free of her usual stern mask, and she wore an expression of tranquil bliss. Isobel saw for the first time how her aunt wasn't as old as she liked to make out, and in fact her true age couldn't be much more than fifty. Her skin was very pale from so many years confined to her house in London, but she was quite unlined and there were even signs of a faded dignified beauty revealed by that magical light.

While Isobel was wondering if she should apologize again for her bad behaviour, her aunt spoke as if in a dream.

'I'm so very glad you tricked us all into coming on this trip. It would have been a pity indeed to miss such an experience. Archie wrote often of such journeys.'

Isobel was so relieved that she felt hot pin-pricks of tears fill her eyes. She called the boy to her and asked for a parcel of the food, and the two women sat together saying very little but finding a quiet strength in each other till darkness fell and they retired to their cabins.

———

At dawn they were sailing past the Chapora Fort, the first sighting of the state of Goa, its gloomy grey walls adding a forbidding note despite the beauty of the morning. Then the seductive golden sweep of Anjuna beach, followed by a sighting of the Baga Hills in the distance. They continued around Fort Anguada, a formidable structure projecting out into the sea built by the Portuguese in the seventeenth century as a warning to anyone apart from themselves who might be foolhardy enough to attempt to rob this land of its riches.

Finally, they turned into the wide yellow Mandovi River to disembark, with an ashen-faced Violet clinging to her aunt's arm after a sleepless night spent in fear of the ship's inevitable sinking.

Chapter Thirteen

The sight of Panjim was uplifting, though Violet remained aloof to it all and seemed even more determined to show a wounded face to the world.

It was a pretty place with a fresh sea breeze and the wide, placid Mandovi River keeping the temperatures at bay a little. There too was a curious sense they weren't in India at all, as most of the buildings had a quaint Latin charm, with white-washed walls, high windows, balconies draped with vividly coloured flowers and sloping red-tiled roofs.

Very tall, thin palm trees and great fragrant trees grew everywhere between the often-charming houses and churches, and on the nearby hill and dominating the landscape, an exquisite pure-white cathedral built in layers like an elaborate wedding cake hovered over the town and somehow despite a conflicted history, imparted an air of benevolence and sanctity.

Panjim was inhabited by people of all races and religions, Christians and non-Christians, Goan Hindus, Chinese and

Buddhists. There were black people who not many years before had been enslaved and now with the coming of freedom had been left in the streets to beg. Smuggling was a thriving industry, plying their trade along the Mandovi River and through the passes from Bardez into Bijapur. The warehouses that opened onto the bustling streets were full to bursting with caskets trimmed with tortoiseshell and silver, desks and wardrobes in woven cane and marquetry, and food stalls piled high with mangoes jackfruits, melons and coconuts.

There were stately mansions too, surrounded by beautiful, overgrown gardens, but nearly all of them in a crumbling state of disrepair. Most of them had been built in the eighteenth century at a time of enormous wealth, but when fortunes failed with changing times and regimes, their owners either died or returned to Portugal, or migrated to more affluent parts of India, leaving their lovely, graceful homes behind to collapse into rubble.

The illusion of Europe transplanted continued with most of the street signs, on which Portuguese names were largely displayed. The name *Almeida* appeared on a very grand rice warehouse near the river and Isobel wondered as they drove past if he could be the same Almeida who was interested in buying her estate. Thinking of the estate and being so close to their journey's end brought on a feverish desire to leave Panjim at the earliest opportunity, but it wasn't till a few days later that Violet felt well enough to travel. The trip on the steamer, she said, had almost been the end of her, and her resentment against Isobel grew until she no longer bothered to hide it.

But the train to Mollum was almost the end of them all; that is, all except Aunt Bea who again took a grim, stoic pleasure in every discomfort, even the suffocating heat of the carriage as it rattled its way through the outskirts of Panjim.

She ate everything offered her by the peddlers at the stations or from a little man who pushed a trolley through the carriages, including every sticky pastry or fragrant curry without suffering any ill effects, whereas the others in the party all had stomach upsets, and being unused to the hot spices, had to make frequent trips to the makeshift toilet at the back of the carriage. Coming back from one of these trips, Violet was so outraged that she could contain her anger no longer and could only mutter weakly to Isobel, 'I hate you. I really hate you and I'll never forgive you,' before collapsing back on the hard wooden bench that acted as a seat. Despite an almost overwhelming feeling of guilt, Isobel was too sick and exhausted to care, and by the time they arrived at the little village of Mollum, everyone, except Aunt Bea, was thoroughly disheartened.

As the train pulled out and left them on the immaculate wooden platform surrounded by their piles of luggage, it was plain that Mollum was hardly the hub of commerce and culture Isobel had been hoping for. But the air here was cool and refreshing, and everywhere was thick green jungle that in places had begun to encroach on the little township.

After paying a porter to watch over the luggage, they set out in search of some refreshment and a vehicle to take them the remaining few miles to Silver Mist.

Apart from a pretty white church on a raised bit of ground, there were only a few mudbrick and timber buildings running down both sides of a dusty street, and an open market where groups of women sat on woven grass mats with their produce laid out in front of them. The Portuguese influence was everywhere as there were one or two little shops selling coffee and cakes as in Panjim, so it was decided they would break their journey for tea while Mr. Singh went off to secure a carriage and buy enough provisions from the local market to make a meal when they finally arrived at Silver Mist.

A Goan man with very long pointed fingernails and wearing a thick shawl over his dhoti appeared like a genie before the ladies and gently steered them into a café at the back of his shop.

The coffee was presented on the rustic wooden veranda with as much elegance as if they were dining at the Ritz, with everything being scrupulously neat, only with cracked China plates and limp yellowing napkins. The effect was shattered by the appearance of a monkey with an embarrassingly bare and red backside that came rushing out of the undergrowth to steal a biscuit from Violet's plate then eat it with unusual delicacy just out of reach of the waiter's broom.

Violet's face was frozen now into a grim, tight-lipped resentment that increased further when Mr. Singh returned with some added passengers as well as the fruit and vegetables from the market. A half a dozen scraggy chickens in a woven bamboo cage were dumped unceremoniously next to Billy who resided in his own more splendid enclosure so the birds could spend the rest of the journey to Silver Mist very silently studying each other.

There was further disappointment waiting for them as no horses and cart could be found to take the group from the village to Silver Mist till the following morning and they were forced to spend the night in the local hotel where the owner was unkempt and surly, and the beds were little more than bunks covered with rough blankets. The cook had left for the day, and the little group were in danger of having nothing to eat. But here again Aunt Bea proved to be a valuable travelling companion. The large trunk she had with her, that Isobel had thought so unnecessary and over which so many battles had been fought, was opened with a flourish and shown to contain, amongst various mysterious packages, a pith helmet, a fly swat with a pearl handle, a small spade, a portable kerosene stove, three pairs of fine linen sheets, silver-plated cutlery and stiff cambric napkins, a box of fine China dinner plates, half a dozen heavy crystal glasses wrapped in straw, a wide selection of tinned goods, and six large bottles each of brandy and gin from Fortnum & Mason in Piccadilly.

'I always travel with my own sheets,' the old lady announced with more than a touch of smug self-satisfaction.

'And your own alcohol; there seems to be rather a lot,' added Isobel with a bite of sarcasm.

'Medicinal purposes only,' shot back her aunt with her haughtiest look.

'You must be planning on being ill very often,' Isobel couldn't help but add, but she was careful not to show too much gratitude for the contents of the trunk, seeing as how she had so hotly opposed it. But in truth she was angry for not having thought of bringing such items on the trip herself. This lack of thought showed just how unprepared she was for a venture that might well turn out to be a complete disaster.

Her Aunt Bea had outsmarted her again, and she had to humbly admit her valuable common sense.

After a meal of salted biscuits, tinned ham, tomato relish and plum pudding, a bottle of the gin was opened and enjoyed with tonic water, 'To fight off the malaria,' added Aunt Bea, and despite alcohol being frowned upon for young ladies, the rules were relaxed for once on the grounds of it being, as Aunt Bea had said, 'for medicinal purposes only.'

The next day, after securing two wiry little horses and an ancient cart that showed signs of being a survivor of the previous century, then climbing up winding steep hills for some hours, the travellers reached a kind of plateau where a faded sign announced in Portuguese and English that they had reached the Siripi Road at an elevation of three thousand five hundred feet. It was a comforting sight in the apparent wilderness and brought with it the knowledge that Silver Mist could not be far away.

The cart rattled along what had now become almost a dirt path surrounded on both sides with thick coconut palms and jungle, broken now and then with views of rich green undulating hills. As they climbed, the air had become progressively cooler and everyone gratefully breathed in the fresh mountain air, even reaching for the cashmere shawls they had bought in Bombay. Sometimes a glance behind revealed through gaps in the thick jungle, the pale, steamy turquoise blue of the Arabian Sea and the red roofs of distant Panjim. Far below, curls of smoky white heat floated up from the swampy, humid plains, making everyone feel grateful for having left it behind.

They passed over tumbling rivers and waterfalls that sprayed their faces with a fine rainbow mist as they crossed precarious bridges, but the countryside was so beautiful and lush that even Violet's scowls couldn't dampen Isobel's excitement as they drew close to their journey's end.

During the final miles of their expedition, the travellers had passed several plantations, some of the houses appearing to be well tended and almost grand. This fact gave everyone hope, almost believing now that 'the inheritance' would be equally fine. However, all thoughts of splendour quickly fled as, about five miles from the last estate they passed – a neat-looking place with a freshly painted sign announcing *Propriedede de Santa Maria* – they came to a stop at last in front of a pair of ornate but peeling wooden gates bearing the name in faded script, *Silver Mist*.

Mr. Singh jumped down and untied a tattered piece of rope attaching the gate to the fence post. Then, with a great creaking groan, the gate fell backwards into the dirt with a resounding thud.

'Oh Issie, where on earth are we?' Violet's voice took on a frightened, peevish note. 'This can't be it...'

'Not much of an introduction to the place,' said Aunt Bea from her position in the cart. 'Looks as though you might have inherited a pig in a poke. Typical! You should rename the place "Wit's End" as you must have been out of your wits not to sell it when you had the chance!'

Isobel ignored such unhelpful remarks and leapt down off the cart while Mr. Singh began to drag the fallen gate out of the way. Then she held out a hand to Violet. 'I can't wait. Come with me. Come and see what Papa has left us.'

But Violet silently shook her head and turned away, so Isobel could only sigh before running ahead down the overgrown driveway, eager to see this much dreamed-of property before anyone else.

Chapter Fourteen

It was useless to pretend any longer. The house was a disappointment at first sight, though there were signs of a certain rustic charm. It sat on a slight plateau, solid, long and half-hidden under a high thatched roof in what must have once been neat, wide lawns and gardens, though these were now unkempt and in parts out of control. Wild and lovely plants grew up almost to the veranda rails, some of which she recognized. Frangipani in particular was everywhere, filling the air with scent, as well as a gnarled peach tree and a flourishing plum, obviously planted by a previous owner many years before.

Running down behind the left side of the house and about twenty feet away from the veranda were stables, of sorts. Next to the stables was a series of large sheds that seemed to have once been used for separating the various spices, as enormous flat cane dishes were piled up in abundance or lay scattered about the wooden floors as though abruptly left by the workers at a moment's notice.

Ragged woven grass mats hung in places from the tin roofs, providing dense shade from the sun, and clusters of bamboo grew in wild thickets that made a peculiar moaning sound as they swayed in the breeze.

Everywhere were huge trees, some as high as a hundred feet tall with a pretty, light-green foliage hung with long brown pods. It seemed they were a crop of some kind as there was a certain order in the way they had been planted, but it was difficult to tell as time had almost obliterated the paths that had once kept the trees from growing into each other.

An ancient well stood in a stone courtyard surrounded by a high wall on two sides, and various clay jugs and bowls obviously used for carrying water to the house sat neglected in the sun. Isobel laughed at her own naivety. Water! She had never even thought about it before now. It had just appeared in her bedroom, placed there by a housemaid.

Now there was the question of whether it would even be fit to drink, and again she cursed herself for her own lack of foresight.

Everywhere was an unearthly silence, as though all the animals and birdlife sensed an intruder in their midst and were watching her with unseen eyes.

She began to feel uneasy and wondered why the others were taking so long, then the bushes nearby moved with a sudden violence, causing her to jump in fright. Something brown, furry and unrecognizable fled in alarm, crashing mindlessly through the undergrowth till it came to a silent breathless standstill.

It felt safer on the terrace, and while she waited, she counted eight stone pillars placed at regular intervals gracing the front of the building. The walls of the house seemed to be made of huge mud bricks once painted a saffron yellow that had bleached in patches to a mottled cream, while the wide double doors were painted a faded turquoise blue.

The French windows ran from the stone terrace almost to the height of the roof but were so covered with a strangler vine thick with sticky red flowers that in places it must have been difficult to see out of the rooms.

Four weather-beaten planter chairs sat sturdily on the terrace and as Isobel moved around to the side of the house, she found an empty whisky decanter where a fierce-looking spider had taken up residence, and a glass lying on its side on a bamboo table.

A straw broom made of fine twigs lay against the wall in the corner where it had been placed. Clearly the servants had all left, tired of waiting for their master to return.

Everywhere had an air of sudden abandonment, as if the previous owner had had a final drink before walking away and had not looked back. What happened later apparently was seen by him as a blessing. He had thought so little of the place, he was prepared to gamble it away without a second thought, almost with the intention of freeing himself of the burden of having to return to a life he clearly did not care for.

Isobel tried the front door and found it unlocked. The door swung open into a wide, cool hall with rooms running off both sides. Her footsteps made a pleasant click- clack sound on the dark wooden floors, and though they had not been stepped on for many months, they had a hard, dull shine broken in places by brightly woven rag rugs.

The ceilings were vaulted and lined with dark teak boards that gave a sense of solid endurance to the structure. Most rooms too had an interior fan-shaped window that could be propped open with a long metal rod, allowing a breeze to come into the house on the hotter days.

Hanging overhead like thick woven blankets on an indoor line were punkah fans left over from a time when the servants would pull the ropes back and forth to keep the occupants of the house cool through the warm summer nights. Isobel tugged at the long trailing rope and the fan creaked into life, causing a gentle gust of cool air to dislodge a little grey mouse that had taken up residence in the folds. Fearing itself under attack, it skidded in a panic across the floor near her feet.

Isobel didn't scream as she had always liked mice and marvelled at the beauty of their tiny pink hands and feet, but she was grateful Violet wasn't with her as she always made an enormous fuss about the little creatures and wouldn't enter a room if she knew one was hiding there.

A huge fireplace set in a stone wall graced almost the entire end of the sitting room, with a pile of neatly stacked logs lying waiting to be lit; clearly the nights often grew cold, and Isobel anticipated the cool of the evening with a deep pleasure.

Through the open door she could hear the cart pull up out the front and various voices raised in loud exclamations coming down the hall, clearly not flattering to the house, though she was relieved to hear Mary at least trying to put the best possible slant on their new home, temporary as it was.

Her cheerful brogue echoed through the house exclaiming, 'This will clean up very nicely. I'll get the tea things out – we could all do with a cup.'

Then she heard Aunt Bea's more refined though cantankerous tones. 'Billy could do with a Huntley and Palmer's also, Mary; the potted shrimp and some of Billy's biscuits will do very nicely for our own tea. That is, if you can spare a few, old thing,' she said to the bird in a gentler voice. She returned to addressing Mary. 'And the tin of Scotch shortbreads I bought at Harrods before I left. Then perhaps Mr. Singh would be so good as to light a small fire. I believe it will be a chilly night,' she said, with added relish.

Monty came barking up the hall and skidded on one of the rugs. Then he ran around in circles chasing his own tail. There was at least one creature happy to be in this new home.

———

There were six bedrooms furnished with huge divans – more like platforms than beds – made from carved teak and hung with yellowing mosquito netting suspended from bamboo frames. The cotton mattresses were rolled up at the foot of each bed and, judging by the fine layer of dust coating the striped linen covers, had not been slept in for years.

One of the better rooms, obviously having been inhabited by the previous owner, was still made up with rather dingy white cotton sheets and a faded maroon quilt, perhaps in anticipation of his return. There was even a copy of a book entitled *Great English Cricketers* lying on its face on the bedside table where it had been left.

For a few brief moments, Isobel crept between the folds of the mosquito netting draping the bed to lie down to test the mattress, a practical measure that turned into an unexpected pleasure. Inside this white diaphanous world, she was immediately enveloped with a sense of peace and safety, like the sensation of being in a makeshift cubby house as a child, but there was something highly sensuous too about this veiled space that made her want to linger there and lapse into wild daydreams.

In the wardrobe, some of young Quimp's clothes still hung – mainly serviceable khaki shirts and two pairs of riding jodhpurs from the Army and Navy stores in Bombay, still with the price tag attached, plus, tucked away in the back of a chest of drawers, a hoard of gin and two full packets of cigarettes. Isobel decided the room would do her very nicely and the gin would be appreciated by her Aunt Bea, though she pushed the cigarettes further back in the drawer to retrieve later. She had been used to having an occasional cigarette in the evenings with her father and associated that vice with pleasant times, his abundant warmth and his wicked humour.

Even so, she would keep her secret weakness to herself, as even she couldn't face the furore likely to erupt if she dared to smoke in front of that virtuous lady.

Seeing the somewhat poignant remains of his possessions, for a moment Isobel felt sorry for poor Quimp, thinking it must have been very lonely for a young man with a background fit for nothing but the drawing rooms of London to find himself alone in such a place and with the added pressure of being expected to make a success of it.

The kitchen was a cheerful room with a floor made of wide planks of hardwood that had been bleached almost white with scrubbing over the years, as well as a gigantic, obviously homemade table standing heavily in the centre of the room. A modern sink with a copper tap poured water from an outside tank that seemed if not clean, then at least clear after first spurting out a quantity of brown sludge.

Huge copper pots and pans hung from a wooden rack above the sink and surprisingly there was a substantial set of fine crockery in the wooden cupboard against the wall. Isobel turned over a teacup and saw the mark of a very good French manufacturer and marvelled at how it had come to be in such a remote place. There was something extremely moving about the sight of such delicate beauty painted with charming pastoral scenes of a land so far away, and she imagined the teacup in the hand of some hopeful bride, perhaps come out to marry the original owner of the estate. It was more poignant still to imagine the fate of the woman who had owned the set, as surely if she had left the place alive, she would have taken such a valuable possession with her.

There were three bathrooms, all of them consisting of a stone floor with a drain hole in the middle and a bucket hanging overhead attached to a rope. It was plain one was meant to soap first then pull the rope to release a torrent of water over the body. The main bathroom was lined with blue and white Portuguese tiles and contained a free-standing stone bath big enough to hold three people. It was primitive, true, but in a way more convenient than the arrangements in their old home back in London where servants had to carry heavy buckets of hot water up two flights of stairs whenever a member of the family wanted a bath. The basin was almost elegant, being surrounded by a magnificently carved cabinet grand enough for a palace, though when Isobel opened the door of the cabinet she found a very rustic tin bucket inside, dissolving at once the idea of modern elegance.

Isobel muttered a hasty, 'Thank God!' for she had not thought about what they might do if the house should prove to be uninhabitable and she was not so prissy as to be put off by a little inconvenience.

The back of the house revealed a good-sized room with

French doors draped in blue linen and half drawn against the light. In the semi-darkness, she could see that the furniture was respectable, being mostly of a serviceable woven cane with chintz covers that matched the drapes. It was clearly a summer room as there was no fireplace to be seen. The latch on the doors was stiff and it took some pulling to finally wrench the doors open.

At first the light blinded her, then the view stopped her breath. The ground suddenly sloped away from the terrace and wild, untended lawns ran down about a hundred feet to where there grew plants of a kind she couldn't recognize, higher than a man's head, unkempt and irregular, with narrow trails running in between. There were signs the bushes had once been cut into uniform shapes but had now returned to how nature had intended them.

But it was the mass of white blooms that filled the landscape that took her breath away. It was almost as though there had been a snowstorm, so thickly were the flowers clustered together. Myriad bees and insects flew lazily in and out of the bushes, drunk with the honey amassed from such a bounty. She had never seen anything like it before. It was unearthly in its loveliness.

Then, with a shift of the breeze, an almost overpowering fragrance came towards her, a scent unrecognizable to an English nose used to the delicacy of roses and violets. This was an assault on the senses so intoxicating it bordered on unpleasant, like the perfume worn by certain women she had passed in the London streets whom her mother would have called common or cheap.

Gigantic rhododendrons topped with crimson blooms grew everywhere unheeded, and at first Isobel thought they must have been haphazardly planted there. Then she remembered standing before such a tree in the Kew Gardens bearing the plaque: 'Rhododendron – native to the Himalayas and the slopes of the Indian Ghats.'

A distant silvery river ran through a wild, undulating landscape filled with vast thickets of what seemed to be untamed jungle. Starkly irregular navy-blue hills half enfolded in the evening mist leaped up before her, craggy and magnificent.

The sky was filled with what she thought were birds, but the jagged black shape of their wings silhouetted against that vibrant sky showed them to be something quite different. Bats! Isobel prayed fervently Violet would not notice as she would be sure to demand to leave at once. Huge flocks of them filled the air as they fled, squeaking, towards some unknown destination, leaving behind a strange, pungent though not too unpleasant odour. On one of the trees nearby, more bats hung upside down like tiny plump babies suspended in blankets, while others were slowly unfurling their wings as though waking from a deep night's sleep.

Then a butterfly danced before Isobel's spellbound eyes, of the very same species that had somehow found its way into the envelope bearing the letter from the mysterious Almeida. The very same butterfly that had precipitated the long journey to this almost mystical place.

The creature flashed before her, iridescent blue, green and silver with a dusting of gold, with a wingspan of at least eight inches. Then, as suddenly as it had appeared, it fluttered away on a puff of light breeze.

Tears sprang to her eyes. Here was magic as well as beauty. It was worth it!

It was worth it to have come so far, and to have endured every discomfort and doubt, to see her property at last. Her property! The words had a very comforting sound. A great peace fell upon her as she realized that she may have found at last what she had been searching for. Something to love with a passion and something worth fighting for.

In her heart she knew it was impossible now to sell it. Not now she had seen the view. Familiar footsteps came up behind her and a gentle hand was placed in her own.

'Well, we've seen it, Issie, and I hope you're satisfied now. Anyone can see the place is impossible. As soon as we can, we must see the fellow who wanted to buy it and go back home.'

At first Isobel experienced a stab of disappointment much stronger than she had ever felt she was capable of. Some small part of her had hoped Violet might like the place and want to keep it, but now she could see the idea was hopeless.

'It is lovely though isn't it, Violet? You must admit there is beauty here.'

'Well, yes, I suppose so. It is lovely, but it's so very wild. You will sell it, won't you Issie? I'm frightened, really frightened, and you promised faithfully. You know you did.'

Isobel took a deep breath and crushed her disappointment.

'Yes, I promised, and I won't go back on it.'

They stood together, arms around each other's waists, and looked out towards the darkening sky.

The last rays of the evening sun struck a hill in the distance on which, through the gaps in a steadily increasing mist, they could just make out a magnificent house. It appeared to be in places more than two storeys high, with a number of tall turrets built of a gold-coloured stone topped by a russet-tiled roof and surrounded by what appeared to be acres of well-tended gardens and ancient trees. Rows of tall, thin, dark-green cypress punctuated the distant landscape, giving the house the look of a European palace more at home in Italy or Spain.

'Do you think that grand house belongs to our neighbour? This mysterious Mr. Almeida?'

'I hope so.' Isobel laughed. 'If so, it seems he has money, and I intend to get a high price for this place. Four thousand pounds indeed! It's worth at least twice that; anyone with half a brain can see that.'

Chapter Fifteen

The first night passed almost without incident except for Monty having cornered a banded black and white snake that had been sleeping under the bed in the bedroom Aunt Bea had chosen for herself.

Without flinching, Mr. Singh picked it up on the end of his long, curved knife, flicked it in the air and cut it in half with one stroke. The two pieces writhed for a second on the floor then lay still.

'Such a little thing,' said Isobel, faintly annoyed. 'Surely we could have let it live.'

'It was a krait, Madam. It will kill you in ten seconds if it bites you. It is better for us all it is dead. Anyway, there are probably hundreds more out there ,' he said, indicating the garden with his knife. 'The gods will forgive us this once.'

His words were hardly comforting, and every bed was stripped and shaken before anyone had the courage to get into it, but with another good shot of Aunt Bea's brandy everyone fell into a type of exhausted coma punctuated by moments of wakefulness.

The house appeared more hopeful with the dawn, and thankfully the bright morning sun didn't expose any obvious faults such as cracks or peeling paint in the walls.

It was pleasant to put bare feet onto the dark, shiny wooden floor and open the long windows to step out onto the terrace and look out upon such a glorious sight. The white flowers seemed fresher and even more snowlike in the soft morning light, as though the cool night had given them fresh life, though the fragrance was not as intense as the day before.

The mountains were a light blue in the dawn but as she stood there with her white cotton nightgown billowing in the early breeze, Isobel felt again the deep pang in her heart when she thought about selling Silver Mist. But it must be so, and she berated herself for being a romantic fool to become so attached to a place she as yet knew nothing about.

Her heart should be firmly rooted in the place of her birth; it was natural and right. Though when she tried to conjure up an image of London, she could only picture it in sepia like a photograph; it seemed now to be all just a dim memory. Perhaps it was the still-fresh pain of what she had left behind, the death of her parents that still brought sharp tears to her eyes and the loss of her beloved home, but distance from such events was a balm to her wounded soul and for the moment that was what she needed.

After a very satisfying late breakfast scrambled together from the contents of the trunk and some delicious fresh eggs the enterprising Mr. Singh had obtained from the market in a nearby village and cooked with an expertise that surprised everyone, there was in general a more cheerful attitude amongst the little group, except for Violet, who looked about with a pale, frightened expression and only picked at the food on her plate.

There had been sounds of scurrying alien feet on the roof throughout the night that had kept her awake and it did no good to reassure her it was only the monkeys who had perhaps seen the lights of the house and were being curious. She was sure she had heard a roar of some sort followed by a horrible scream of some poor animal being torn to pieces, even though Isobel had only heard what seemed to be birds. Unlike their English feathered cousins who had the decency to go to bed at night and sleep through till morning and only then waken the humans with their gentle warbling, these foreign creatures had the nerve not to know night from day and kept up a persistent volley of long, loud mournful whoops, wild screeches and trills that lasted throughout the long night and strangely only fell silent with the dawn.

Mr. Singh's appearance in the village had apparently caused quite a stir, for several people who had once worked for Quimp in the house and the garden had much to tell of their previous master. They said he had done nothing but drink and wouldn't pay them their wages. In the end, one by one they had left him to his bottle, but there were several people who needed work and would be happy to come back to Silver Mist if the ladies would have them.

'There are two women who would be a great help to you, Miss Isobel – very respected in the village– and a boy or two for the yard would be very useful. It is not appropriate you have no servants here. I have asked them to come and see you tomorrow.'

'Thank you, Mr. Singh, but we won't be here long enough to employ staff.'

'You will be here longer than you think, and they need the work. The people are very poor here.'

She was a little taken aback by the certainty of Mr. Singh's prediction but could see no real harm in his suggestion.

'Well, as you have asked them to come, I'll see about it. I shall speak to Aunt Bea and if she agrees to pay their wages then it will be alright.'

Mr. Singh came back also with the news that the Casa Margarida was indeed the imposing house on the hill that could be seen from the terrace of Silver Mist. The distance was perhaps four miles and could be reached by following the clearly marked signs towards the plantation.

'They are a most important family, Madam, very, very rich, but not popular with the people I met. There are some problems at that house, but no one would say what. They don't trust me enough to tell me.'

He had also met one of the Casa Margarida house servants when he had purchased the eggs and discovered that the master was presently not at home though he was expected any day now.

The news came as a surprise to Isobel as she had written before she had left Bombay telling Almeida of her intention to visit him and discuss the terms of his offer.

She had received his returning letter at her hotel, written in what she felt was a most self-important manner, informing her that he would be available to receive her between the hours of ten and twelve any weekday. He had also added with a touch of scorn:

I find it most unusual Madame that you would bother to come all this way simply to see if I have been fair with my offer when the matter could have been settled so much more easily if you had stayed in London. But you will soon discover for yourself how very rundown the previous owner had allowed Silver Mist to become, and frankly if you have any intentions to farm it, I cannot imagine two single women could do any better than the young drunkard who came before you…

At the time his words had shaken her, and now she had seen Silver Mist for herself she could see the truth in what he said. It was impossible she could ever imagine raising crops from the devastation around her. He had her in the palm of his hand really, but she certainly wasn't going to let him know it.

In the meantime, however, she set about making her new home as comfortable as possible and she took an enormous amount of pleasure in being the mistress of a place she had already begun to love despite knowing her ownership of it would most likely be temporary.

Mr. Singh established himself as a general household help as well as a cook and as one of his first acts he cut the large patch of grass in the front of the house with a rusty lawnmower he found in one of the sheds, creating a pleasant place under the trees for afternoon tea.

'It is most necessary,' he whispered to Isobel, already divining that Violet must be protected from any unpleasantness, 'in case of snakes, Madam.'

'Of course.' Isobel smiled. 'I would be very grateful if you would continue to keep it to yourself – about the snakes, I mean.'

He nodded. He had also understood early on that Violet must be protected at all costs and it was Isobel who would have to bear the truth of anything unpalatable; he also soon learned that it was Aunt Bea who must be indulged in all her wants as quickly as possible.

The two women who he had recommended were just as he had said, both very pleasant and highly competent. One was an older lady of around forty years of age who had once acted as housekeeper to the young Quimp.

Like the rest of the household, she had waited dutifully for him to return, despite having not been paid, but eventually she had gone back to her little house in the village nearby, only sometimes returning to sweep the rooms and dust the furniture in case he should suddenly appear.

The tale she told of her former employer was a not a pretty one. He had arrived full of enthusiasm and seemed to enjoy the life for the first few months, then he began to drink, usually alone, and found it difficult to get out of bed in the morning. Then one day he was gone, and she hadn't seen him since.

Her name was Constanza, and she spoke excellent English and wore a mixture of western and Goan dress, usually consisting of a bright muslin sari topped by an old grey oversized man's cardigan that Isobel suspected had once belonged to her former employer. Under her sari she wore long, thick fawn-coloured socks, indicating how much she felt the cold – again, perhaps these too were remnants of Quimp's belongings. Over the socks she wore open brown leather sandals that made a loud flip-flop sound as she moved through the house, usually accompanied by her off-key singing of the religious songs she had been taught long ago by the nuns.

Her hair was always combed back neatly into a heavy bun at the base of her neck. Her face was round and shiny and usually appeared to be cheerful because of the wide gap in her front teeth that gave her an almost cheeky smile.

She was a Catholic whose family had been converted by the Portuguese a few centuries earlier, though Isobel soon noticed she still clung to a few Hindu traditions, such as setting up a little shrine in her bedroom and praying to the various gods when she thought no one was looking. It soon became apparent she was a most necessary addition to the household as she had an ear open to all the goings-on in the neighbourhood and knew all there was to know about the families on the nearby estates – including the Almeidas. Unfortunately, though, she could not be induced to speak about them except to say that they were very proud and grand and perhaps not very popular with the local people.

The other house servant was a much younger girl, Aashi, who was the daughter of the leader of the local tribe, who were highly regarded for their knowledge of Ayurvedic medicines usually gleaned from the herbs and plants growing in the surrounding forests.

Aashi put everyone's minds at rest by saying the water from the well at Silver Mist was unusually pure as it came from an underground spring deep beneath the ground. All the local people knew of it and in the past had used the water for cleansing rituals, though no one was yet convinced enough to stop boiling the water before they drank it.

Apart from her usual duties in the house, she soon found her niche in the preparing of various potions for headaches and upset stomachs and in the cooking of vegetable curries, which became much more delicious when thickened with the cream of cashew nuts and flavoured with the fresh limes from trees that grew in the abandoned vegetable garden at the back of the house. Without being told, she dug up the old dead plants and began to talk about the planting of fresh ones, despite Isobel telling her it was probably a waste of time as they would be sure to be gone long before the vegetables grew.

Some days, Aashi would dress herself in her best sari, comb and oil her black hair into a neat plait, then follow a trail through the overgrown coffee plants and disappear into the thick jungle in the gentle valley below Silver Mist. At first Isobel was anxious for the girl's safety but Aashi showed no sign of fear and always returned an hour or so later with an expression of almost beatific joy on her pretty face and usually with a basket of strange plants and herbs. When Isobel asked where she had been, she would say mysteriously, 'To visit the trees of the ancients, Madam, to pray for us all and to speak with the forest spirits,' but she would say no more, assuming that was explanation enough. Isobel didn't question her further, thinking that perhaps Aashi was a little melodramatic and that surely one tree was no different from another.

She was also a skilled masseuse and earned extra money by offering her services to Aunt Bea in order to alleviate some of the pain she obviously suffered from, but the massages proved to be invaluable also in smoothing out built-up tension that otherwise might have developed into full-blown arguments between Isobel and her aunt.

Sometimes when Isobel paused at her aunt's bedroom door and heard the grunts of pain emanating from the room, she couldn't help but smile with a grim pleasure at the sounds of that lady's suffering, as she saw it as a small reward for having endured her sharp tongue and generally overbearing manner for so many months.

But these treatments resulted in more than an improved appearance; soon Aunt Bea was moving with a much greater speed around the house, and this, most annoyingly, allowed her to make surprise attacks on anyone who might be slacking at their duties.

The two boys Zoze and Nikel, employed to look after the horses and chickens and to keep the grounds under control, were both aged around fourteen, with uncombed wild black hair, beautiful teeth and flashing eyes. They were very good friends and spent a lot of their time laughing uncontrollably at each other's jokes that were incomprehensible to the rest of the household. But their presence was a happy addition to Silver Mist, and everyone soon grew used to the pranks they continuously played on each other and the often hilarious consequences. They were both keen to learn English and Aunt Bea took it upon herself to spend an hour each day to teach them. It was an amusing sight to see them sitting side by side on the front lawn, their hair slicked down with coconut oil as though in school and listening attentively to their teacher, of whom they were so terrified that they learned very quickly and were soon reading halting sentences from a copy of *Tom Brown's School Days*, which young Quimp had left behind.

With the addition of four more people, the house began to

hum like a well-oiled machine. Mr. Singh ruled over the domestic arrangements with a gentle but firm hand, leaving Mary to act as lady's maid mostly to Violet and Aunt Bea. Again, Isobel mentally blessed Charlie Cameron for his genius in finding such a man.

Chapter Sixteen

During those first weeks, the entire household was kept busy with getting the house to a standard fit to be lived in. Every floor was swept and mopped; every surface polished till it gleamed.

Sheets were washed and laid out on the lawn to be bleached by the sun, and as a final touch, vases were unearthed from the kitchen pantry and filled with large bunches of sweet-smelling flowers from the prolific garden, making it, if not a grand residence, certainly a very pleasant one.

Monty padded up and down the hall now with a distinct air of ownership and he slept in front of the fire at night in a basket put there for that purpose, though sometimes he slept with any member of the household he chose to grace with his presence. The huge garden and abandoned sheds provided an abundance of sniffing places and strange scents, enough to keep any dog happy, though sometimes he came rushing back to the house after one of these tours of the garden with an air of alarm and his hackles raised, skidding down the hall back to the safety of his cushion while keeping his eyes firmly fixed on the front door.

He had given up his occasional ill-tempered growling which all in all made for a much more pleasant dog and if there was such a thing as a smile on a dog's face, then it was on Monty's.

Billy too had undergone a change for the better. He seemed to have lost his downcast air and even his feathers looked brighter and less droopy in the clear, new light. He spent most of his time on his favourite perch in the garden looking up at the sky or watching other birds as they settled in the trees nearby. Sometimes one of his own species would fly past and make a derisive remark in the form of a catcall, but Billy would always look away as though puzzled or offended by this flying rabble and return to nibbling his biscuit with an air of wounded pride.

Isobel secretly loved this new world and often went about the house with a hidden sense of satisfaction saying to herself, 'This is my house, these shining dark floorboards are mine, these rooms are mine, this comfortable bed is mine,' and when she walked in the garden and breathed in the many scents and admired the view towards the distant hills, she found it hard to imagine selling it, though all the while knowing she must.

Amongst the former owner's possessions were a series of handbooks on the running of a spice estate and in the evenings, she took to poring over these books while she gnawed at the end of a pencil. There were also old accounts from a long-ago, much more successful owner showing the price per hundredweight that the planter could expect from a good coffee yield. In the most successful year, Isobel saw that the estate had grossed one hundred rupia per hundredweight. She knew one Portuguese rupia was equal to one British shilling.

'One hundred shillings!' She was so stunned that she called out, causing her Aunt Bea to look up from her sewing and stare at her with suspicious eyes. Isobel's brain began to tick over. She was sure the place could produce at least five hundred times that. Pepper was the most valuable crop – that is, if she could manage to unearth what remained of it from the all-consuming jungle and somehow learn how to process it.

She estimated that barring unforeseen circumstances, in a good season the estate must be capable of making more than a thousand pounds profit a year, 'And that thief Almeida wanted to pay only four thousand.' She mused to herself, 'Why, in four years he would have gained his investment back and with more to come! Over my dead body!'

Violet continued to be unsettled, though at times she showed signs of her former infectious gaiety, causing everyone in the house to smile upon her with a pleased indulgence. At others, she would be overwhelmed by a dark despair, especially as she had not yet received the long-awaited letter from John, despite the post arriving with a miraculous regularity for such a far-flung colonial outpost.

Twice a week, a skinny little old man on a battered bicycle, wearing an equally battered uniform matched with a faded blue turban, came to the front door with the mail.

He performed his duties with the aplomb of an army sergeant, usually saluting Mr. Singh as he handed over the letters and parcels taken from his worn knapsack.

He was then offered a cup of tea, some food and a rest, which he would always gratefully accept, and after twenty minutes or so, during which time he would have a chat with Mr. Singh, he would get back on his rickety bicycle and career off down the hill. It was a ritual the household looked forward to, as not only did it give hope to Violet, it also brought some order to their day while they waited for the great Almeida to return from Panjim.

Aunt Bea in particular seemed to have a healthy stream of correspondence, much of which she kept to herself, only giving a complacent smile as she looked at the name of the sender on the back. Isobel often wondered who it might be from, as the contents usually put an extra zest in the lady's step and she would go about the house humming to herself, and for a time was unusually indulgent to everyone – even Isobel. But still no letter arrived for Violet, and she was becoming increasingly miserable.

But a welcome distraction from her preoccupation with John came when three men on gleaming, well-fed horses came up to the house with rifles carried over their shoulders and the limp bodies of some small furry animals slung across their saddles.

At first there was a little frisson of terror at the sight of the strangers and Isobel had great difficulty preventing Mr. Singh from herding the women into the drawing room under lock and key while he confronted the men on the terrace with his knife drawn.

The reality was much more benign. One of the strangers was an Englishman by the name of Harry Saunders who lived a few miles away across the border in British Karnataka, and the other two men were his Indian servants. They had been on a hunting expedition, had seen the gate to Silver Mist was open, and had thought to visit the young man who was the previous owner, thinking he had returned from his trip to England. It came as a great surprise to find two lovely girls, their maid and an older lady, all of whom were overjoyed to meet a fellow Englishman in the jungles of India.

He was almost handsome with his neatly oiled light-brown hair, a well-clipped thin moustache and pleasant manners, and the girls felt a measure of comfort in knowing he was not far away if needed.

He too declared himself thrilled to find such beautiful ladies in the neighbourhood and offered to help in any way he could. He owned a thriving estate of over five hundred acres of prime coffee which kept him occupied most of the time, and some very profitable interests in the mining of iron ore, but his chief obsession was hunting, and he said with a self-deprecating laugh that he was devoted to the sport.

After tea he invited the women to his estate to view his trophies; he claimed to have hundreds of various species, both rare and otherwise. He had been out that morning at the news there had been a sighting of a rare black leopard in the area, a creature he was keen to add to his collection.

Despite Isobel's disapproving glares, Aunt Bea accepted his invitation for them all to visit his estate, having in mind that Saunders might be a good match for Isobel.

'There are leopards! Here!' Violet's dreamy eyes opened wide in alarm as she ran to the window and looked out, then turning to Saunders she frowned prettily as she gnawed at her bottom lip.

'Oh surely not. Please say that's not true.'

'Most definitely it is true,' Saunders's chest swelled, 'but you'll be safe if I'm around. Still, you must never go outside after dark, as that's when they like to hunt, and keep the dog inside after sundown. They can pick up the smell of a dog on the wind very easily.'

Violet rushed to Monty to pick him up and hug him. 'Did you hear, Monty darling? You must listen to this kind gentleman and never ever go outside at night.'

Then she gazed up at Saunders with what could be thought of as worship, though in fact Violet was quite short-sighted and it gave her at times the dreamy, wide-eyed look of a kitten.

Saunders was entranced, and Violet had another man on the verge of falling in love with her. Isobel was forgotten, especially as her original charm had evaporated and she was looking at him now with her eyes flashing and her mouth pursed in a way that could only be called scornful. She began with a few terse remarks.

'Why do you have to shoot the leopards? Surely, they cannot cause too much trouble?'

'Isobel! Don't ask such foolish questions. I'm sure Mr. Saunders has a very good reason for shooting them.'

Aunt Bea had learned to recognize the warning signs that showed that Isobel was displeased in some way, and her plans for a marriage began to look decidedly less likely.

'My dear young lady,' Saunders addressed Isobel with a tone she instantly despised, 'surely it's obvious.'

'Not really. It is, after all, their home and always had been before we came here. And you can't eat them. That is, I don't think I've ever heard of leopard soup.'

'I can see you have radical views. You won't find many people around here agreeing with you.'

'You know everyone around here, I suppose.'

'I think so.' He looked very smug. 'That is, everyone around here knows me.'

'Is Mr. Almeida a friend? We are all very curious about him.'

'Phillipe Almeida? An acquaintance only. I don't think he has many friends around here.'

'Why ever not?'

'Far too grand. The Almeidas think they're better than anyone else. The family has been here for over three hundred years, since the first Portuguese set foot in the place, and they don't let anyone forget it.'

'I have already some sense of what he may be like. He says what he thinks.'

'Oh, Almeida's alright in his way, but it's the old man, his uncle, Count Tiago.'

Isobel laughed.

'A count? Here in this place? It seems almost ridiculous.'

'Not to him. He's very proud of the title, and he never lets anyone forget it, even though legally it means nothing. It's his nephew who's the real count by descent, but it's Tiago who runs the show and he's a wicked old devil. A bit harsh on the natives, by all accounts, but he's away in Bombay now, I hear. He spends most of the year there running the main warehouse. They deal mostly in rice and copra – the coffee is more of a side-line.'

'And Phillipe Almeida's parents?'

'The father died many years ago, and Tiago took over running the place. But his brother's wife, Phillipe Almeida's mother, lived at Casa Margarida for a while after her husband died. I've never met her, before my time – and I believe she went to Europe a long time ago, where Almeida grew up.'

'And does Phillipe Almeida have a wife? Or is he so unpleasant that no woman will have him?'

'He did have one. I only saw her once, a lady not quite as grand as himself but very beautiful, but she died in childbirth, poor creature, and if he should ever marry again, I doubt if there's a woman in this country he would think good enough for him, though he hasn't as yet seen you two ladies.'

With that parting gallant remark, and a glimmer of romantic intent in his eye, he rose to leave, but not before extracting a promise from the girls to visit him as soon as possible to see his estate. It was plain, however, to everyone in the house that for good or bad, they had not seen the last of him.

———————

That night Isobel lay awake long after the rest of the household were asleep, as usual planning what she might do with Silver Mist if it was in her power to do so.

The evening was particularly beautiful and with the linen curtains drawn apart, Isobel's room was flooded with moonlight. In the past, moonlight would always stir feelings in her that kept her awake and restless, and now in such a wild and lonely place, the feelings were intensified to a degree that left her more disturbed than usual.

It was while she was telling herself not to be foolish that she heard the sound that sent a shudder of pure fear down her back and instantly made her sit upright. It was just the faintest of movements in the undergrowth outside the window but judging by the sudden sway of the bushes and the way they snapped back; it was obviously a large animal. For a long moment she lay frozen as she tracked the sound to the window outside Violet's room, next door to her own. With great stealth and speed, she crept out of bed and down the hall before feeling her way to the open door of Violet's room. Her curtains too were wide open, and a beam of bright moonlight fell directly onto the scene before Isobel's eyes.

There was almost complete silence, except for the faint sound of Monty's snoring as he slept at the foot of Violet's bed. There was nothing of the watchdog about him as he lay prone, his little body sunk deep into the coverlet with his legs straight out in total abandonment.

Violet too was in deep sleep with one arm flung out behind her on the pillow, and Isobel couldn't help but envy her sister's ability to sleep soundly throughout the night no matter what the situation, while she often suffered from fits of insomnia.

Then she saw the leopard. It was sitting only a few feet away, high on the stone wall of the courtyard, giving it an unobstructed view through the long windows into the room. It sat lazily licking its paws, the long, spotted tail waving slowly back and forth, and its green glinting eyes fixed on the sleeping forms in the room. But it was the majesty of the beast that kept her enthralled as Isobel stood motionless at the open door. The creature moved lazily, stretching itself luxuriously before settling back to watch its prey, and Isobel could see the gleaming muscular beauty of the spotted black and gold coat, patterned as though woven by the skilled fingers of a maker of Turkish rugs.

The animal turned its head to the light and Isobel saw it had a curious pattern on its forehead. Two perfect circles of black streaks were formed into the shape of a crown, giving the animal an even more regal appearance, and the eyes were bordered by thick black almond-shaped markings like the kohl worn by the Indian women.

She had always loved cats but as a child was never allowed to have one because of the cavalcade of her mother's various dogs who took precedence over every other animal. Now she was revisited with the same desire and admiration but amplified a thousand times over.

The leopard must have known it was impossible to catch its intended prey at that moment as the window was firmly closed, but it was almost as if it were indulging itself with a little light fantasy before settling down to the serious business of hunting for the night, and yet Isobel felt with a deep horror and an absolute certainty that because of the unhurried nature of the beast and the total confidence of its manner, if she were not careful to prevent it, in the end the creature would triumph and it was only a matter of time before Monty would be no more.

A sudden painful bite from a whining mosquito caused her to jump, and with that movement the creature became aware of her presence, leaping to its feet and stiffening, the magnificent yellow-green eyes capturing her gaze with its own and fixing her to a terrified standstill.

Her heart skipped a beat while the animal stood rigid, its head lowered, as if deciding what to do next. Would it throw itself at the window and tear everyone in the room apart? It certainly had that capacity if such a thought ever entered its head. Beads of sweat stood out on her forehead as she waited, too frozen with awe and fear to cry out. The animal gave her a final, almost benign stare, a proud flick of its tail, then sprang off the wall with an unhurried grace and disappeared.

The next morning Isobel asked Mr. Singh that all the windows in the bedrooms be fitted with bamboo shutters as an added precaution. When Violet asked why, as the shutters ruined the view from the windows, Isobel replied as casually as she could that it was only sensible to take precautions after their conversation with Saunders, even though she felt he was likely exaggerating the dangers in order to impress the women.

Knowing how Violet would react by demanding a mass exodus from the house, she reluctantly decided to carry the secret of the leopard alone, though she did suggest everyone should stay within the confines of the house and garden during the day and no wandering into the surrounding shrubbery.

'You don't have to tell me, Issie. I have no intention of going beyond the veranda while we're forced to stay here. Not after seeing that hideous snake. God only knows what's out there.'

'And I don't think Monty should sleep on your bed anymore. He made a mess the other day in the house because he couldn't go outside. From now on he should sleep in the bathroom, as the floor is stone there and if there's an accident...'

At this Monty looked up from his bowl and gave Isobel a look that said he had never made a mess in the house in his life, then shook himself, stuck his nose and his tail in the air and marched off.

Aunt Bea was faintly suspicious at Isobel's tone of voice but didn't contradict her. She had her own exercise regime which didn't include wandering into the jungle paths.

If she felt the need to stretch her limbs, she did fifty rotations of the house and gardens with Monty, to whom she had taken a great fancy, trotting along beside her, then, with the routine never varying and not till the last circuit was complete, they would return to the drawing room and collapse back into their favourite chairs. Isobel thought of this daily exercise routine with a great deal of concern as now she couldn't dismiss the thought of the innocently unaware Monty on the end of the lead as a tantalizing morsel of bait for the lurking leopard.

It was only Mr. Singh who wasn't fooled by Isobel. He recognized the quiet urgency in her voice and set out at once to do as she asked, and by nightfall, with the aid of the two boys, the house was almost a fortress.

Chapter Seventeen

The day finally came when Almeida was home at last and ready to greet his neighbours.

In line with the importance of the event, Isobel chose to wear a neat, grey, linen suit that showed off her trim waist, matched with a rakish black velvet hat and veil, an outfit probably much more suitable for a day's shopping in Paris than a morning jaunt in Indian hill country.

As she put on the hat and pulled the veil over her eyes, she felt she looked rather good. 'Pretty but not too feminine,' she declared, but in fact the mannishness of her suit made her appear even more feminine and certainly more alluring.

A knock on the bedroom door announced her aunt, who with every passing day appeared to gain fresh vigour. No more could her hesitant approach be detected by the slithering sound of silk on the floorboards and the tap of her stick; now her approach was more likely to be heralded by a loud, determined step and a waft of the perfume she had bought on a shopping excursion in the French Quarter in Cairo.

Her dress was reduced now to a simple black linen skirt and a mauve or grey blouse – the only colours deemed suitable for semi-mourning. Even the ugly brooch she habitually wore, woven from her dead fiancé's hair, had been replaced with a large Victorian cameo worn at the throat. Her hair too was arranged into loose curls that fell over her forehead and somehow made her look ten years younger. The source of the curls was a mystery till Isobel found them snuggled into a box like a little furry animal on the dressing table in her aunt's bedroom. The once grey cheeks were rosier now and the explanation had revealed itself to be a jar of rouge that a shocked Mary had found hidden amongst the old lady's hairbrushes, again obviously brought in Cairo. The walking stick now leaned almost permanently against the wall and was used only occasionally to hoist herself out of a chair or to wave at a passing servant to get attention.

It was an unspoken agreement between everyone in the house that these changes would not be mentioned, given how prickly the subject might be.

But as though sensing the curiosity of the household, Aunt Bea declared one morning how wonderful the daily massages and the climate were for her health, even crediting the warm days with almost curing her rheumatism and the mountain air with having revitalized her complexion.

Even so, Isobel couldn't help but wonder what had brought about this sudden transformation, especially in a woman who had declared loudly and often that she would never come out of mourning for her late fiancé.

Her aunt stood behind her now with her hands placed youthfully on her newly slimmer hips as Isobel adjusted her hat before the mirror.

'Are you going alone to see this man?'

Isobel had hoped to avoid her aunt but as usual the sharp eyes were on the lookout for any of what she called 'unladylike behaviour'. That was something that hadn't changed.

'Violet says she is not well enough, but I know it's because she was hoping for a letter from John today. It's useless to tell her it will come whether she is here or not, and Mary has far too much to do.'

'Then it must be me.'

'Not this time. This is not a social call. I have business to discuss.'

'All the more reason why I should accompany you.'

Isobel turned to look at her aunt. It was on the tip of her tongue to tell her to mind her own business and hint again that it was perhaps time for her to return to England.

But there again was the familiar stubborn look in her aunt's eyes and Isobel was reminded of the bulldog belonging to her aunt's friend the colonel, with whom she used to walk around the decks on the trip out to Bombay. After living with her now for almost three months, Isobel had developed a strategy to get her own way; she wanted no spy to accompany her on this most crucial visit. A small, wicked smile broke out on her face.

'Well then, I shall wait until you are ready.'

There was a returning thin streak of a victorious smile from her aunt.

'I'll change my clothes and get my hat.'

Isobel waited till her aunt disappeared into her bedroom then raced out the front door where Mr. Singh was waiting with the cart.

'Go, Mr. Singh! Go!' she whispered, and Mr. Singh, liking any opportunity to test the horses, raced off down the drive with Isobel looking anxiously behind her. It was a ruthless strategy for which she would pay on her return but on no account did she want anyone with her to curb her dealings in this most important business transaction, especially as her Aunt Bea had humiliated her enough on previous occasions. She might insist on taking Billy, which would automatically place them both in the category of eccentrics and easy targets for contempt. For Isobel this long-awaited meeting was a serious matter and required her to always have the upper hand, and cool, resolute dignity was a part of that plan.

They drove briskly along a narrow road that ran through at least three miles of semi-tamed jungle. Small huts stood in cleared patches where chickens flapped wildly between packs of bare-footed children who ran around calling out in high, excited voices. Lovely women in bright saris with kohl-rimmed eyes and black lustrous hair tied neatly in long glistening plaits stood at the front doors of their simple homes and smiled at Isobel's wave as they drove past. Mr. Singh stopped the carriage and bought vegetables and fruit for Silver Mist's larder, so it was later than expected when they came at last to an elaborate set of gates announcing the Casa Margarida.

A rather magnificent but severe guard carrying a rifle came out of his sentry box and gave a sweeping bow as they drove past, but did not smile, a curious omission in a land of smiles and blessings.

Inside the gates was a world of strict order. In the near distance, thick jungle still lined the perimeters of the property but everywhere within the confines of the bordering wilderness were countless rows of immaculately trimmed bushes with the remains of the same overpoweringly sweet-smelling flower that had grown in such profusion at Silver Mist. They drove along a hard dirt road where on both sides the foliage grew in perfect lines towards the house, though it was broken at regular intervals by hundreds of tall, thin shade trees that had been heavily pruned, allowing the plants beneath to benefit just enough from the warmth of the sun. Groups of workers wearing shabby loincloths and mud-coloured turbans moved slowly in and out of the fields, snipping at the occasional unruly leaf and overhanging branch, sometimes pausing in their work to glance up as Isobel drove past. Again, there were no smiles and hardly any acknowledgment of her presence; instead, there was an air of listlessness and suspicion about the men, and even a deep sense of hopelessness.

The cart stopped, Mr. Singh helped her down, and Isobel stood awestruck by the sight before her. It was really more of a palace than a house. Even though the sign had said *Casa*, the name was far too humble for such a structure. The façade was unique in appearance, being a mixture of cultures from both the east and the west, with high-arched double windows of the type seen in a Gothic church but crisscrossed with small panes of glass that flashed with a multi-faceted light when hit by intermittent beams of golden radiance from the sun. Behind the house, a newer wing boasting several turrets gave the place the look of an ancient monastery, while around the turrets several black crows flew in lazy circles, filling the air with their mournful cries.

The lower two storeys were divided by a long, low veranda hung with an ancient vine that grew up in regular intervals from the ground and twisted its serpentine way around the stone columns, creating an arbour of deep, almost gloomy, shade. It should have been a pretty spot to rest away from the heat of the day, but there could be no relaxing in such a place. There was a chill emanating from those hard stone walls and the narrow mahogany benches set against them acted much like the pews found in the strictest of convents and monasteries where the need to guard the body against laziness was a constant daily reminder.

However, behind the house, in a curious lapse of the almost regimented condition of the rest of the estate, the gardens ran almost wild. The rhododendron bushes were as tall as trees and hung with the richest blood-coloured flowers, while masses of hydrangeas of the most intense deep blue ran in rivers around the great cypresses and into the nearby woods themselves.

Isobel had visited France several times with her parents and had seen the magnificence of the chateaux sitting solidly against their backdrop of gentle countryside and appearing very much as though they belonged there. This mansion though, despite having been built over three hundred years before by the Portuguese forefathers, had an air of discomfort about it still as it sat bizarrely in the semi-tropical landscape, looking much as she would if she had unintentionally worn a ballgown to a picnic. The uncomfortable clash of cultures had produced such an astonishing house but gave the whole place a sense of disquiet.

There were no sounds coming from inside the house; all was in absolute silence except for the crows and the sigh of a cold wind coming down from the nearby hills. Isobel shivered and wished she had brought her cashmere shawl with her.

She let out a sigh of relief at the sight of a child's toy train painted a joyous red and blue lying discarded on the flagstone terrace. That simple, commonplace object cast off some of the gloom she was feeling and shook her back to the present time.

'These people are very important, Madam,' said Mr. Singh as they stood before a worn row of marble steps. 'I wish I had thought to put on my new turban and puttees. This place shows up all the signs of my carelessness; there is a stain on my shirt I didn't know was there.'

'Well, you know what they say, Mr. Singh,' said Isobel, trying to appear unimpressed by her surroundings, 'distrust any venture that requires new clothes. They will have to take us as they find us.'

Nonetheless, she straightened her hat and quickly examined her clothes for similar stains, before walking smartly up the staircase where several house servants were hurrying down to meet her.

They were ushered through a series of grand, echoing rooms hung with fine crystal chandeliers and huge paintings, the subjects of which were almost lost amongst the dark patina of age, and elaborate gilded mirrors disfigured by the murky fog of time.

When she stopped for a moment to straighten her hat again, her usually vivid reflection showed only an indistinct blur, almost as if the house had swallowed her up and reduced her presence to that of a visiting ghost.

The walls had been papered long ago with scenes from a

different world – quaint villages and ornate bridges over picturesque streams and tame views of a country now only a romantic dream – but over everything hung a greyish tinge, almost as though the finest of invisible webs had been spun to cover the furnishings and walls, sealing them forever in the long-dead past.

Isobel caught a glimpse of a dining room that housed a mahogany dining table long enough to seat sixty people, before being led into a somewhat smaller drawing room with windows that opened onto a terrace and looked out on the scene she had so recently driven through. From above, the view showed just how extensive the property was. On the right it ran in cultivated rows for what seemed like at least a mile or two down to a wide shining river, but on the left, in the valley below, lay Silver Mist half-hidden on the rise of land in its little hollow encircled by a few overgrown fields and the wide, wild patch of jungle that dropped back into the valley and down to the river below. Isobel could see now how Silver Mist might appear to be a blot on the agricultural landscape to someone who wished to see every foot of earth productive and profitable. But she was a romantic at heart and something within her sighed at the thought of this last patch of jungle being sacrificed to economy. She stepped back into the drawing room and began to look about her.

The walls were heavy with the portraits of Almeida ancestors who resembled each other to an alarming degree. There were sickly white-faced ladies with unnaturally pink cheeks, hollow eyes and thin lips, dressed in tight embroidered bodices which flattened their breasts and held them captive in stiff brocaded dresses held out by bizarre trapeze-like petticoats.

A painting of a sallow, thin-faced man with cruel black eyes, wearing a single gold earring and a huge white ruff, glared down at Isobel as she took a seat in one of the hard, elaborately carved chairs placed around the room, set amongst rather ugly highly polished tables with barley-sugar legs.

One table held a pair of silver cutlasses in a glass case beside a single jewelled glove with three missing fingers, covered with what looked suspiciously like long-dried blood. Another held a huge book bound in leather and held together with iron bands, attached to the table leg by a long iron chain. The gold script on the battered spine read in large, proud lettering, *A casa de Almeida. Uma Familia Nobre*; clearly a volume of great importance to the present Almeida family.

Mr. Singh was moved enough by his surroundings to speak. 'I do not like it here. It is all this death about me. All these ghosts.'

'I know what you mean, Mr. Singh,' Isobel began, then in the acute silence of the background there could be heard the clatter of fast-running feet on marble floors, followed by a small figure who rushed into the room and skidded to a stop before them.

It was a little boy around six years old with dark, tousled hair and huge blue eyes in a pale face, out of breath and holding a wooden toy in his plump little fingers – the same toy train Isobel had seen only minutes before on the terrace. He was dressed in a lace-collared white silk shirt and black velvet trousers – a quaint form of clothing that hadn't been seen in England for fifty years at least.

He rushed up to Isobel, softly touching her hand before putting a chubby finger to his lips and appealing to her with his huge eyes before fleeing to a thick brocade curtain against the wall and hiding, just moments before a woman, with thin grey hair scraped back in a tight bun and dressed in strict black, tore into the room.

She bobbed a curtsy when she saw Isobel then spoke a few words so fast that Isobel couldn't understand.

'I'm afraid I don't know what you are saying. I am English.'

The woman seemed surprised but answered in a thickly accented voice: 'Forgive me, Madam, but 'av you seen a boy come in here?'

Something about the woman sparked in Isobel an instant sympathy with the child and she spoke without hesitation: 'I think I saw a small boy going towards the garden.'

She pointed at the open doors and in an instant the woman had flown through them and down the stairs.

After a moment or two the child emerged from behind the curtain to stand shyly before Isobel once more. Children usually held no interest for her but inexplicably she was entranced by this child's sweet, flushed face. She bent down on one knee and couldn't help but smooth the hair away from his forehead.

'Do you understand English?'

He nodded, still uncertain.

'Is she your nurse?'

'No! I am too big for a nurse! She is Senhora Clara, my teacher. My papa wants me to know three languages before I turn six, but today I don't want to learn. I want to play.'

Isobel could identify with the child at once, as the same strict regime had been applied to her by her own governess, the formidable Madame Joubet.

'And what is your name?

'I am Marco.'

'And who is your papa?'

There was a hush for a moment while the boy studied his toy train, then a voice interrupted the silence, making her jump.

'I am his papa.'

Chapter Eighteen

I sobel looked up. She rose to her feet, her face clearly showing her shock.

It was the man from the hotel in Cairo who had laughed at her.

There he was with the same cool, elegant stance and superior manner. Even at leisure he was dressed formally, in a black suit and loose bowtie with a white shirt that had a ruffle running down the front in the style of a Portuguese grandee. If he was shocked too, he showed little sign of it, but Isobel could detect just a faint twitch in his cheek and a quick flash of recognition in the proud, dark eyes. Even so, he seemed intent on pretending he had never seen her before, and Isobel was too proud to be the first to admit to having recognized him.

'It's Miss Blanchard, is it not? We meet at last. Phillipe Santiago Almeida at your service.' He gave her a snappy, almost military bow.

'But 'aven't we met before?' He rubbed his forehead with his graceful gold-brown fingers as if to prompt a thought. 'No, but I 'ave seen you somewhere, I think.' His voice was deep and pleasant to the ear, though thickly accented.

Isobel frowned and pursed her lips as if struggling to remember. 'I cannot imagine where. No, I cannot recall seeing you at all.'

Giving up the game, he let out a hesitant little laugh. 'Oh yes, yes of course. Now I remember. In Cairo. You were with the old lady and the parrot, and the little dog. How strange…' It was plain he could barely keep from smirking.

Before she could stop herself, Isobel responded and gave herself away. 'Oh yes, of course. I was in Cairo.' Then, with a snap in her voice, 'With a travelling circus.' She smiled, though her voice was cool.

His eyes flashed as he processed her barb. 'I'm very sorry. The comment was not meant for your ears, and I was not to know you understood Portuguese.'

'I don't, but I understand enough Spanish and some of the words are similar. Even so, in whatever language it was spoken, it was not a nice thing to say.'

'But you must admit, the old lady and that absurd parrot…'

'You must mean my Aunt Beatrice. A most respectable lady and,' she said, raising her chin with great dignity, 'Billy is not absurd at all. He is a member of the family.'

Her response was so silly, she wished she hadn't said anything. He looked as though he was desperately trying not to laugh.

'A most distinguished family, I'm sure.'

'There was a circus?' asked the child, who was following the conversation with great interest. 'A dog? Did it do tricks? And a parrot?'

'No … yes. A dog, yes, but not a circus…' Almeida could

think of nothing more to say. He snapped himself back into a more business-like manner.

'Forgive me, I'm sorry to 'ave kept you waiting. It was unavoidable, and I see you 'ave already met my son.'

Isobel smiled first at the boy, then turned to Almeida. She was still astonished at the coincidence of their meeting.

'It is most strange that you should turn out to be the same Mr. Almeida I have been corresponding with, and then to be at the same hotel in Cairo…'

'Not so strange really. The 'otel …' He seemed to remember how to use the letter 'h' and with a great deal of effort corrected his pronunciation, 'the *hotel* caters to the London–Bombay route. Everyone stays there, and everyone meets there. I was there myself to meet a cousin who had come from Lisboa. My cousin's father died, and the ladies were alone, so they have come to Goa to seek refuge with my family for a while—'

He stopped suddenly, as though aware of having said too much. He became business-like again.

'But why did your sister not accompany you today? You are both owners of Silver Mist, are you not? I remember her – a pretty girl with very fair hair.'

It was on the tip of her tongue to ask him why he remembered Violet so clearly but not herself. She was beginning to hate him.

Again, she calmed herself, though she was finding it increasingly difficult now to be even civil.

'Violet was not well, but as you can see, Mr. Singh has accompanied me.'

'Oh, I am sorry. Nothing serious, I hope?'

'No, a matter of the heart only.' As soon as she had said the words she regretted them, as he responded with a rather cynical smile.

'The most painful of all afflictions.'

He turned to Mr. Singh.

'I would like a moment alone with Miss Blanchard, if you don't mind.'

Mr. Singh looked reluctant to leave her alone with a strange man but after a moment of indecision he bowed stiffly and left.

'And you may go too,' Almeida said to the child, with just a hint of a cold smile. 'You should be at your lessons.'

The boy moved closer to Isobel. 'I want to stay with … *cette jolie dame.*'

'Well, you can't, you little charmer. Be off with you. We have business to discuss.'

The child left reluctantly, but at the doorway he stopped and turned. 'Will I see you again, Mademoiselle? You hear, Papa? I remember my lessons.'

Isobel laughed at both the compliment and at Marco's use of the French terms.

'I would like to, if your papa will allow it.'

The child smiled but looked at his father with his rather sad eyes.

Phillipe Almeida decided not to respond to her remark but merely waved the child away, and that annoyed her too. The boy was clearly neglected, and his father was impossible.

He went to an embroidered bell pull hanging down from the wall and jerked at it with unnecessary impatience. In a moment a servant arrived wearing an immaculate white kurta and blue turban.

'Ah Jose, please put down an extra setting in the dining room and see that her servant has some food and drink.'

The man nodded and hurried away.

'Thank you. I'm sorry, I have arrived at an inconvenient time. Our trip took longer than expected.'

'No one is turned away from here without refreshment. Hospitality at Casa Margarida is a serious matter and has been so for over three hundred years. But let us get down to business. You have seen Silver Mist, and do you still consider my offer unreasonable?'

His dark eyes showed no sign of warmth as he fixed her gaze. Even so she found the courage to stare back with an equal lack of warmth.

'Your offer was reasonable enough but surely the estate is worth much more? I have been reading over past accounts and—'

'Silver Mist is worth nothing unless it is worked, and as far as I can see you have no means of working it.'

'If I intended to work the place, I am sure I would find the means.'

'Do you have any idea of what is involved in running a place like this?'

He crossed to the open window and indicated the rows of plants. 'Do you even know what is happening here? Do you know what those flowers represent, for example? They are not there only for their beauty and their scent.'

'No, but—'

'Each one of those little flowers will be a coffee bud – that is, if they come to fruition at all. There is sometimes blight, there is disease, no rain or too much rain, a myriad of things that can go wrong. And then there is the fact that this district is already not entirely suitable for the growing of coffee; it is still an experiment that often fails.'

Isobel crossed to the window to stand beside him and look out upon the scene. Even though most of the blooms had fallen to the ground and begun to wither, the sight was still enough to inspire joy.

'I had no idea growing coffee could be so beautiful.'

'There is no romance in this business.' His voice was harsh now. 'It will rain heavily tonight by all accounts and the last of this will be gone tomorrow. We could be left with nothing but mud.' He gave a despairing wave of his hand. 'And as I said, if the rain continues, that might mean half the crop lost.'

She turned to face him, as if struck by a sudden thought.

'And what do you intend to do with Silver Mist when I sell it to you?'

He raised his eyebrows at this. 'My uncle owns the estate on the other side of you.'

'The estate Santa Maria?'

'Yes. Silver Mist is in between, and he feels it is…'

'An eyesore?'

'No, of course not, but he has a desire to own it all.'

There was a peculiar bitterness to his voice that Isobel picked up on at once, but he recovered his balance and continued.

'In answer to your question, my uncle would extend, of course; remove the jungle and plant more coffee.'

'Remove the jungle? What do you mean?'

'Burn it, of course.'

'All of it?'

'To make the place pay he would have to.'

'But the people and the animals, where do they go?'

'They move on, I suppose…'

'But where?'

'I can see you are not rational. We are talking business here.'

'But surely this place is enough for you. It's so very grand. It must make you—'

'If you mean, is my uncle rich? I suppose so, but if I increase the offer to you, he will be less rich and he would not like that. Now we will dine.'

He offered his arm and she placed hers in his with a wry smile. The whole ceremony seemed so formal, especially for the middle of the day. It was a curious sensation to walk with him down the wide, silent hall, her hand hooked into his rather rigid arm.

She stole a glance up at him, looking for signs of warmth or humour, but he kept his eyes straight ahead, almost as though she didn't exist. She did notice that his hand was trembling, but it was so slight that it was almost imperceptible.

They moved into the dining room where two places had been set opposite each other at the end of the long mahogany table. The plates were of the very finest duck-egg-blue porcelain bordered by a wide gold band that seemed to Isobel's eye to be real gold.

They were so exquisitely fragile that it seemed a shame to use them for anything as mundane as mere food, but Almeida seemed not to notice as the servant filled his plate with a delicious fish and a vegetable dish smelling of garlic and herbs.

The silverware was heavily carved with a pattern of briar roses and lay on cambric napkins bordered by thick yellowing lace and initialled like scar tissue with the Almeida crest.

'So very beautiful…' Isobel said, as she placed one on her lap and hoped fervently, she wouldn't drop any food on it.

'My great grandmother made them, I believe.'

They ate in near silence, only conversing briefly about Cairo and her voyage to Bombay. Again, she noticed, as before in Cairo, that he ate little and waved his food away half-eaten.

At the end of the meal a servant entered bearing a silver platter with a plate of delicious-looking little pastries. Each one was wrapped individually in the finest pink or blue tissue paper with cut-outs representing different flowers and birds.

Isobel held one of the tissue papers up to the light. It was delicately cut into the shape of a peacock.

'I have never seen this before. It is so charming.'

'It is an old tradition. The nuns in Portuguese convents make the little paper cut-outs. In the past they were offered as gifts to invading armies in the hope they would be left unmolested by the soldiers. Will you have one?'

It was an alarming tale and like everything in this strange house, there was a hint of savagery.

'No, thank you. I don't really like sweet things, though my sister loves them.'

It wasn't strictly true, but somehow even the act of eating something so flaky in front of him was impossible. His eyes were too penetrating and under such scrutiny she was sure to drop the crumbs all over herself.

'Will you have coffee or tea? The coffee is Arabica, grown here of course.'

'I think it had better be coffee. Is there Arabica at Silver Mist?'

He gave her an almost pitying look.

'We would not be offering to buy the estate if there wasn't.'

'Oh,' she smiled to herself, 'I see.' It was the Arabica that sold for one hundred shillings a hundredweight.

'And now I must ask you, if all goes well with the crop, how long does it take till the coffee is ready for picking?'

'By late October usually, but then there is only a small window of opportunity to pick it. This place will require every worker available. Even if you had plans to see a crop through to the end, you might find it difficult...'

'Why difficult?'

'Because ... as I said before, there are many reasons why the crop could fail. Then there is finding workers enough...' There he paused and it seemed for a moment he might say more, but he only gave a grim smile and tossed back a short black coffee with, it seemed to Isobel, a touch of anger.

He rang for the servant then, and spoke rather quickly, as though he was annoyed in some way.

'We will finish our coffee on the terrace, Jose.' Then he added, almost under his breath, 'This room closes in on me...'

Once settled outside on the terrace, he brought out a gold cigarette case and lit a cigarette. It was the Turkish kind her father liked to smoke.

'Will you offer me one?'

He was too shocked to reply but without a word handed her the open case.

She took one and leaned forward to have him light it.

Then she looked up at him from under the draping of the veil on her hat and fixed him with a long, slow look from her lovely grey eyes before relaxing back into the chair while crossing one long elegant leg over the other, showing her trim ankles.

'Well, will you increase the offer?'

He seemed momentarily stunned.

'Will I what?'

'Will you increase the offer?' she repeated.

'I might…' He seemed to shake himself back to consciousness. 'What will you do if I raise the amount?'

'Leave at once and go back to England. You see, my sister is engaged to be married and naturally she wants to be with her fiancé.'

'And you?'

'I must go where my sister goes. That is, until she marries. After that…'

'So there is no fiancé in England waiting for you to return?'

She almost said it was none of his business but decided to be polite instead.

'Perhaps.' She smiled. 'If I decide it to be so.'

'Oh, then the man has no say in the matter?'

'Yes and no. It depends on the man.'

'You seem to have very firm ideas on matters of the heart.'

'Not really. I have other much more important subjects to think about – like providing an income for myself and my sister until her fiancé takes her off my hands. Anything else, I don't really give a—' She almost said 'damn' but caught herself just in time.

Even so, he gave her a long, curious look, then stood up and walked away from her to stare out at the scene before him, deep in his own thoughts.

'You'll have to give me time to think about it. I must discuss it with my uncle, of course.'

'How much time do you need?'

'It may take a week or two. I shall have to investigate our finances … and, as I said, I must talk to my uncle.'

'A week or two? Oh.' Isobel thought uncomfortably about Violet and how she expected the sale to be finalized at once.

'But then, the original offer still stands. I can write you a cheque at once if you like.'

She thought for a moment. How easy it would be to just accept, especially as she hadn't even enough funds to pay for their return journey to England, but after having come so far, she felt a need to at least profit by it, even if only by a few hundred pounds to cover the cost of the trip.

'No thank you. I prefer to wait for better things.'

'Then we are at a stalemate.'

She stood to leave. 'Well then, I must be going. Will you come to see how we have improved the house? It's amazing what a couple of women can do in only a few short weeks.'

He flinched at that, but let it pass.

'Please bring your son. I think he would enjoy visiting a circus. He looks as though he could do with a bit of fun.'

He said nothing, only looked at her as though humouring a child.

His manners seemed to Isobel to be almost over-formal as he gestured with a wave of his hand that she should go ahead of him through the echoing rooms, and it was with a sense of discomfort that she did so, as all the while she was aware of the peculiar prickly sensation on the back of her neck, knowing full well that his eyes were upon her.

To come out into the bright sunlight again was a relief after the oppressive gloom of the house and she almost skipped down the marble steps to the cart where Mr. Singh was waiting.

As Almeida helped her up into the cart, a servant came hurrying from the house with a basket, which she put on the seat beside Mr. Singh.

Almeida gave one of his rare smiles.

'They are for your sister in the hope that she may feel better soon.'

'Oh, the little tarts. So many... How wonderful. Violet will enjoy them so much, as will we all. Thank you.'

'It would be a pleasure to see your sister again – and yourself, of course,' he added with an almost sly smile, though Isobel felt again that surge of anger as he made it clear she was merely an afterthought.

Chapter Nineteen

It was late afternoon when Isobel finally arrived back at Silver Mist and was just taking off her hat and gloves when Violet hurried to meet her in the hall, anxious to hear about the outcome of the trip to Casa Margarida.

'Well, what was the great Almeida like? Will he buy Silver Mist?'

'It was most odd, and a strange coincidence. Almeida was in Cairo, at the same hotel as us, with some ladies.'

'I don't know who you mean.'

'You saw him in the dining room once and commented that you thought he was very good-looking, and he remembered seeing you. He called you a pretty girl. He has sent you some cakes.' She handed Violet the basket, half empty now, as she and Mr. Singh had eaten half of them on the return trip home.

'Oh, how lovely. I wish I had gone now, and the mail hasn't come after all. But what did he say, Issie? When can we have the money?'

'Soon, darling, soon. These things take a little time, of

course, but yes, I had him eating out of my hand.' She added, with a slight quaver of uncertainty in her voice, 'He will buy Silver Mist, and I believe for a lot more than the original offer.'

'I hope so, after us all coming so far, but when? He must have given you some idea.'

'He said a—'

Then, to Isobel's great relief, Mary came hurrying into the room with the mail.

'It's late but it's a miracle it arrives at all. Here's one for you, Miss Isobel. It looks like Mr. Latimer's writing. That man simply won't give up, and two for you Miss McGregor,' she said, handing a letter to Aunt Bea. 'Here's one from Miss Blunt – or I should say, Mrs. Leigh, and another from…'

Mary turned over the envelope to read the name on the back, but the letter was almost snatched from Mary's hand and hastily tucked into the little embroidered drawstring bag Aunt Bea always wore at her waist. She gave it a complacent pat as she smiled mysteriously to herself, and Isobel wondered again who it could be from.

'One for me,' said Mary, 'from my sister in Aberdeen, and who is this one for? Oh, of course … Miss Violet Blanchard, Silver Mist.'

'Oh, give it to me Mary, don't tease me any longer.' Violet blushed. 'It's from John of course. At last! I was beginning to think…'

Her eyes scanned the envelope as they filled with tears of relief, her pretty mouth curved into a dazed smile. 'But if you will all excuse me…'

Everyone smiled in return, almost as grateful for the letter as Violet – all except Isobel who looked down at her hands with an expression of profound guilt.

Oh please, please, she prayed, *let him not ask about the dowry. Not yet...*

'And here is a letter from Mr. Cameron,' said Mary. 'Addressed to you as well as Miss Violet, but I suppose you will read it to us.'

'Later, Mary dear, later. It can wait.'

Violet fled from the room, her face radiant with joy, clutching the long-awaited letter from John to her chest.

Aunt Bea nodded approvingly.

'This separation might have been a good thing after all. The young man clearly misses her, but I suppose this will hasten our return to England.'

Isobel looked up at her aunt; there were clear signs of reluctance in that speech.

'Not quite. There is still the matter of selling this place.'

'I thought that was assured?'

'Well yes, it is, but it might take a little longer than I thought.'

Her aunt was alert now and scrutinizing Isobel's face.

'What have you been up to, my girl? And I have a bone to pick with you! Running off like that and leaving me behind. Absolute cheek! But I've grown to expect that kind of behaviour from you.'

There was no time to answer her. Violet stood in the doorway, the open letter clutched in her hand, her previous radiance replaced by a look of absolute horror. Her complexion had turned a ghastly white as she stood shakily, staring at Isobel.

'For God's sake, darling, what's the matter?' Isobel stood and rushed to her side. 'Darling, what is it? Tell me...'

Violet recovered herself enough to speak, though in a voice very unlike her own.

'I hate you! I hate you! And I'll always hate you! I didn't want to come here … to this … this living hell! Don't ever, ever speak to me again!'

Then she turned and hurried out of the room, wiping the tears from her eyes, the letter torn in half and thrown to the floor.

Isobel snatched it up and read the words she had both hoped for and dreaded.

'He has given her up, and he intends to marry his cousin. Listen…'

I'm sorry my dear girl, but I hope you will understand and not take it too badly.

If you had stayed in town this may well not have happened, but I've been lonely and having turned to my cousin Adelaide for comfort, I discovered, as my father has always said, that I have a great deal in common with her. But it's more than that. I can't believe your sister kept the truth of your joint inheritance from you then tricked you away from me. It shows a sly nature and one to which I could never adapt myself. Your sister would always stand between us as I know she has never shown any respect towards me and probably never will…

A harsh voice in Isobel's head told her Violet may well be right. If only she had kept out of it, things might have been different. If she hadn't tricked Violet into leaving England, then perhaps John would not have been left to find solace elsewhere. But a more rational voice consoled her with the truth. Despite John keeping Violet's hopes alive with the promise that he could eventually bring his father around to accepting her with a small dowry, he was essentially too weak to go against his family and the promise of a fortune. Isobel's unwanted interference was a convenient excuse to take the attention away from his own failings as a man. In the end he didn't love Violet enough to fight for her, but that was a truth too bitter to swallow. It was so much easier to blame Isobel.

Aunt Bea mercifully, for whatever reason, held her tongue. Instead, she came to sit by Isobel for a moment then gave her a clumsy pat of comfort on her shoulder, before rising to go to Violet who could be heard sobbing in her bedroom.

Chapter Twenty

There followed a period where all within the house were uneasy and tiptoed about for fear of causing Violet any further pain. She stayed in her room for two days and refused to eat or drink until finally a determined Aunt Bea managed to coax her way into the room with a pot of tea, the beautifully wrapped tarts from Casa Margarida and Monty, who immediately threw himself on Violet with enthusiastic barks of joy and a comforting lick.

The novelty of the gift and a few stern words on the topic of self-indulgence were enough to spark an interest in eating again, and gradually Violet began to involve herself in the day-to-day activities of Silver Mist, though at times it was almost as though she was sleepwalking her way through life.

Eventually her vanity was revived through being the centre of much interest from Harry Saunders who had returned to Silver Mist with the evident intention of making her his wife.

Being a cautious man, he began slowly and treated his wooing in much the same way as he employed methods of hunting a wild beast. He worked by stealth, not showing his hand till he felt, in a vulgar manner of speaking, he 'had the creature in the bag'.

He let slip, drop by drop, information about his income and his prospects. His estate and interests in iron ore were worth four thousand pounds a year and even though he was only the second son of a prosperous merchant from Liverpool, he was bound to inherit the tidy sum of fifty thousand pounds at his parent's death. At this information, Aunt Bea sat up and took notice, overlooked what she saw as a background firmly rooted in the dreaded 'trade classes', and encouraged his visits, even initiating a trip to Cardamon Hills where she could assess the value of the estate with her own eyes.

Violet desperately needed a break from Isobel, and Aunt Bea could see the sense in it, despite having some misgivings. It was difficult to ignore the frigid silences and even the occasional waspish remark from Violet when she was reminded of what she saw as the treachery of her sister, so it was with a deep sigh of relief that Isobel waved them off with Mr. Singh who would return the following day, leaving her with Mary, Monty and the servants. Billy, too, was to be left behind as even Aunt Bea, with her usual lack of concern for the opinion of others, had a vague sense that Saunders, being a highly conservative man, might find a visit from a parrot a little eccentric.

In the great silence that followed their departure, Isobel felt momentarily bereft, and even a little afraid as she stood on the terrace and looked out at the silence of the mysterious, dark undergrowth surrounding the house.

She thought of the leopard and the possibility that the creature might sense there were only women and boys alone in the house and take the opportunity to crash through the doors and devour them all. But she knew after reading a well-thumbed book stained with the rims of wet gin tumblers, left behind by poor young Quimp, that leopards were shy, solitary creatures who usually only hunted at night. They were rarely seen in daylight hours, except for occasionally the fleeting glimpse of an indolent tail hanging like a lure from a high tree where they sometimes took their dead prey to eat, unchallenged by other animals.

However, despite her faint feelings of trepidation, she was imbued with a wonderful sense of unbounded freedom.

She could do as she liked – have breakfast late or not at all, wear her hair uncombed down her back, read till all hours without her aunt, who refused to knock first, barging through her bedroom door and ordering her to put out her lantern if it was past eleven o'clock.

A whole range of otherwise forbidden activities were now open to her – and most especially the opportunity to indulge a secret desire she had been waiting to satisfy for some time. So, almost as soon as the carriage had passed through the front gates of Silver Mist, she dashed to the wardrobe in her bedroom and flung the doors wide open.

A pair of khaki jodhpurs and a shirt belonging to the previous owner were taken off their hangers and laid on the bed. She slipped out of her long dress and petticoats till she stood only in her chemise and tried on the pants. It was an odd sensation to be wearing an article of clothing meant exclusively for men, and a little disturbing as well when she struggled with the row of buttons in the front meant for a member of the human anatomy she didn't possess.

Quimp must have been short for a man and very slim as

the jodhpurs fitted almost perfectly, despite being a little firm against the roundness of her bottom. Quimp's long, soft leather boots were a couple of sizes too big but with the aid of a thick pair of his socks, she could walk about quite comfortably. The shirt was easy, and even though too big in the shoulders, she undid the top buttons, freeing her neck, and tucked the rest into the pants before pulling on the wide brown leather belt. Then she stood before the long mirror to assess the finished result. There was no doubt the look suited her, with her long, slim legs and neat waist. She turned around to view the curve of her bottom. There was nothing to be ashamed of there, and in fact she thought she looked rather dashing.

But it was the sense of boundless freedom that gave her a strange sense of joy, combined with a tinge of bitterness that such clothing should be forbidden to women. She raised her arms over her head and swung one leg as high as she could to test the range of movement.

Here was proof that men had the advantage in playing all forms of games and sports. It was difficult to hit a tennis ball when dragging a few extra pounds of petticoats around, even though she often won when playing against men. It was only in archery there seemed to be any equality, and in that sport Isobel had excelled.

In her jewel box was a collection of little gold arrows she had won over the years, the only jewellery she'd had difficulty in parting with; she had excused them from sale on the basis that they were really trophies and could be kept as a tiny insurance against future needs.

She strode about for a few minutes with her hands on her hips and mimicked the movements of men while she laughed at herself.

Mary chose that moment to walk into the room. At first, she stood stock still with her mouth agape.

'My goodness, Miss Isobel! What are you up to now?' Then she laughed. 'It's a blessing your Aunt Bea can't see you! She'd have a heart attack without a doubt, poor lady, and if she has any plans to leave you anything you'd get your inheritance early for sure...'

The new outfit, despite being oddly picturesque, was meant to serve a practical purpose. Since the episode with the snake, Isobel was reluctant to walk through the long grass around the property without being properly shod and wearing something impenetrable around her legs. There were spiders too, huge and hairy, that crept into the house from the trees and appeared on the walls without warning to stare down at the occupants of the rooms with what seemed like malevolent intent.

Often it was Monty who spotted them first. He would look up with a vague expression as though catching a scent on the breeze, rouse himself to focus, and then simply stare at the wall with a grim dog smile, before letting out a sound more like a strangled squeak than a bark. Mr. Singh would then be called upon to dispatch the beast without mercy while the women huddled together in the corner of the room. Mr. Singh was clearly as terrified as everyone else, and his fear made him incompetent so there was usually a nerve-wracking game of dodge around the floor before the final kill.

At times like these, when all eyes were turned towards her for an answer to the problem, Isobel too was almost made insensible with an irrational fear and proved to be as helpless as the others when it came to dealing with the creatures. In fact, she had developed a horror of them and would cautiously enter her bedroom at night, holding the lamp up to scan the walls and floor before she felt safe enough to leap into bed.

One memorable night, when Mr. Singh was otherwise engaged, it was Aunt Bea who, on looking up from her sewing, saw a particularly hideous representative of its clan hanging from the wall. With admirable calm and a quiet stealth, she picked up a heavy copy of the Bible she kept at her side and flung it with all her strength, scoring a direct hit. The book bounced off the wall and left a thick brownish mess and a few crushed legs for the girls to make horrified squeals over.

Then Aunt Bea calmly went back to her sewing, only muttering to herself, 'I'm sure the good Lord was having a bad day when he designed such a creature…'

Now, Isobel strode about the grounds with a thick stick in case of snakes or any animal small enough to be discouraged by it, while clutching a notebook and pencil in the other hand. Instinctively, she avoided the left side of the house where she had last seen the leopard and explored the grounds that led down to the front gate. As she walked, she thought about what she might do if the house wasn't sold. The gardens were so overgrown with huge rhododendrons mingled with other unknown shrubs that it was at times difficult to find a path through, but her plan was to calculate how many viable coffee plants were on the plantation so she would have an accurate knowledge as to their quantity and value.

In front of the property, she counted two hundred and seventy coffee plants almost entirely hidden under the foliage, and then, gathering her courage, made her way to what she saw as the safe side of the house to stand before the long, wide sloping field that led down to the distant stream and the forbidding jungle.

As she stood there breathing in the fresh mountain air and gazing upon the beauty and grandeur before her, she again experienced the peculiar and unexplained hush that came from all the creatures about her when she ventured into their territory. It seemed even the insects who usually gave out such a cacophony of sound seemed to collude to be silent in her presence, apparently watching her suspiciously; then, almost as though in agreement that the intruder amongst them was no threat, the forest noises began again in unison, only louder than before.

It was a strange and even unnerving sensation, but the awakened animal instinct in her sensed that at that moment of the day it was a benign response to her presence. When darkness fell it was a different matter, and any person or creature foolhardy enough to venture into this forbidden territory must expect to be fair game.

With her eyes screwed up against the sun she calculated at least a thousand more plants half-hidden under the trees that could be coaxed into productivity before the next harvest.

The nights spent chewing on her pencil and going over past yields had not been for nothing. She had learned that the profusion of tiny fragrant flowers was a sign of a good yield, and that wild, uncultivated coffee was often of the best quality. With the right conditions and enough labourers to pick the buds, the crop might really be worth at least a thousand pounds!

Walking back to the front of the house, her mind was racing ahead. If only Violet could be convinced to stay a little longer and at least see one season of the coffee yield come to fruition. Aunt Bea would have to be called upon to make a loan of course, but something told Isobel she might be persuaded. The old lady—

There she corrected herself. She could be called an old lady no longer. She was certain now that her aunt could be no older than fifty or so, and, she noted with derision, seemed to be getting younger every day. Her aunt had proved to be surprising in many ways, and not nearly so fearsome as she liked to make out.

Violet was really the only sticking point and if all went well, Isobel could show that ... that ... Almeida person just what he was dealing with.

Chapter Twenty-One

Her thoughts were interrupted by the sound of Mary's voice calling for her, coming from the front of the house.

Isobel hurried towards the sound. Rounding the corner, she came to an abrupt halt. Almeida himself was there in front of her, helping a young woman down from the carriage – the same young woman she had seen in Cairo.

She was elaborately dressed, but as before, still in mourning in a black velvet gown embellished with Belgian lace and matching ribbons on her hat. She appeared out of place in the bright sunlight, as to Isobel's mind she belonged in the same gloomy seventeenth-century paintings she had seen at Casa Margarida where the women were depicted with an air of being constantly under the threat of disease and impending death.

But there was a sweet smile on the girl's pale mouth and there was something rather touching about her obvious adoration of the handsome Almeida, who seemed to indulge her in a somewhat kindly patronizing way, though certainly not as a lover. Isobel couldn't help but think that if they did marry, he would always be in her debt as her love for him was so transparent.

The girl's mother had already alighted, smoothing her silk gown while gazing about her with a look of disdain. The countess was feeling the heat, waving her black lace fan with an air of impatience which stopped abruptly as her face took on an expression of shocked horror. She had turned and now she saw Isobel standing before her in jodhpurs, men's boots, and a battered, wide-brimmed hat, desperately pretending her clothes were so commonplace that they were beyond comment.

Almeida turned his head to see the cause of the woman's dismay. At first his dark eyes widened, then they lit up as his mouth twisted into a half-smile as though he was trying not to laugh.

Isobel stood before him with a defiant expression on her face, mingled with acute embarrassment. But she had already decided to brave it out, much as she did when caught doing the wrong thing as a child.

'Mr. Almeida, this is an unexpected pleasure.' She looked at the now-empty carriage. 'You promised you would bring your son – I am disappointed.'

Almeida took some time to answer, as he was still struggling with a mixture of dismay and admiration.

'Forgive me, but he's already in the house. He saw the little dog and took after it at once.'

The countess broke into the conversation, her voice a peculiar nasal whine.

'He should not have been allowed to come. He was most

rude to his governess. I would have made him stay behind to finish his lessons. And he made it worse for himself by crying.'

'Oh, poor child. Then Monty and Billy will cheer him up. I will see if Mary has some cake.'

'Not a poor child. He is a most naughty child.'

Almeida stepped forward and gave Isobel a brief bow. 'Forgive me, Miss Blanchard; this is my aunt, the countess D'Souza, and my cousin, Miss Carolina D'Souza.'

Carolina smiled pleasantly but it was clear she didn't know how to react to Isobel's unusual attire and decided in the end to try to ignore it.

'What a strange coincidence it is to find you here. Phillipe has told me you were the same girl we saw in Cairo, at the hotel with the old lady – she is a little eccentric, is she not? But then I have often heard it said that it is not an unusual trait in English people.'

Isobel thought briefly of defending her nation, but when reflecting on Aunt Bea's behaviour and looking down at her jodhpurs, decided she didn't have a case.

'That is most unusual clothing you are wearing, Miss Blanchard,' said the countess. 'Indeed, I have never seen a woman wearing trousers before. Phillipe, I think we must go. Perhaps another time when you are appropriately dressed, Miss Blanchard…'

'Well, forgive me. I thought I was alone, and I didn't expect visitors. Bloomers have become quite commonplace for bicycle riding in London, and the Indian ladies wear trousers, especially when they're working.'

'That is no excuse. The Indian women are almost savages, and I include anyone who wears' – here she almost choked –

'bloomers! But I am not going to argue with you. Phillipe, we are leaving. Come, Carolina.'

Then Marco appeared at the open front door weighed down with Monty in his arms. For once the dog was being compliant and even looked as though he might be enjoying himself. The boy waved when he saw Isobel, almost dropping Monty who hung in an undignified way from the boy's arms. Marco appeared to be the only person totally unconcerned by her appearance.

'Papa, come and see! There is a tame parrot that talks! It is almost a circus after all.'

'And here we have the ring master,' Almeida said quietly, so only Isobel could hear, with a sly look at her jodhpurs.

She decided to ignore him and turned to the ladies, dragging out all the considerable charm she had.

'Oh, please Countess. You've had a hot drive and you must be thirsty. Please do step inside and have tea. The boy will be so disappointed if you don't. I was in the fields working...' With great reluctance she made a hasty gesture at her clothing. 'It's because of the snakes. Mr. Singh says there must be hundreds out there.' She waved vaguely at the landscape and shivered. 'Skirts can be so dangerous.'

The countess sniffed but seemed to soften a little, then Mary appeared and took control.

'This way, Madam, Miss.'

She led the way down the hall and the women followed with reluctance, holding onto their skirts and lifting them higher than they needed, as if in danger of being polluted by the ground beneath them.

Then Almeida bowed and made a gesture with his hand.

'After you, Miss Blanchard.'

Isobel was waiting for him to go first.

'No, after you, Sir.'

'That would be unforgivable. After you.'

There were definite signs of mischief in his eyes that in a way made her like him a little bit more. He had unstiffened just a touch, but it hinted that there was perhaps more to him than the rigid, uncompromising figure he presented to the world.

It was unavoidable that she must go first, so she walked swiftly down the hallway, highly conscious of the way the men's clothes revealed the shape of her body. She was burningly aware of his eyes upon her as he followed.

Mary had made a great effort with the tea, and as Constanza had not yet baked, she had delved into the bottom of Aunt Bea's trunk to produce a tin of Scotch salmon, water biscuits, French Macaroons, and tinned Fuller's cake as a special treat for the boy.

Isobel had almost decided not to change as not only had the damage already been done, but also because she felt a perverse pleasure in setting herself even further apart from her guests, but in the end, she hurriedly slipped into one of her best tea gowns, a white muslin with transparent sleeves that showed her slim arms. She poured the tea as elegantly as a duchess, but the countess had not forgiven her yet and hardly responded to her as Isobel handed them their teacups. Almeida made it worse by saying nothing at all, only staring at her more often than she liked, and making her feel distinctly uncomfortable.

She thought them all frightful snobs and had no interest in

cultivating a relationship with any of them and, except for her business dealings with Almeida, she decided she would avoid them as much as possible. That is, everyone except the child. She felt an unaccountable fondness for him as he sat next to her on the settee, swinging his little legs and humming a childish song as he fed a biscuit to Billy and patted the unusually obliging Monty. Once, when the boy patted him perhaps harder than Monty liked, there was an uncomfortable moment when it looked like he might get even with a sly nip, but when he caught the warning in Isobel's eyes, he thought better of it and returned to giving a passable impersonation of a lap dog.

The silence was becoming uncomfortable and grew worse when Almeida excused himself and left the room for a few minutes. The countess kept her eyes fixed resentfully on Isobel who found it difficult not to fumble over the teacups.

The rare delicacy of the macaroons was soothing and went a long way in improving the relationship, but the countess was suspicious still and had many questions that needed answering.

'And your aunt? Where is she? And where is your younger sister? I remember her. A pretty girl, very ladylike...'

Again, Isobel had to crush a feeling of resentment. The question was clearly a veiled insult directed to herself.

'They are visiting a neighbour of ours in Karnataka, Mr. Saunders. They will be back in a few days. My servant, Mr. Singh, will be here tomorrow.'

'You are alone! Without a man!'

'All of us here are quite capable of looking after ourselves.'

Isobel's certainty was far from doing her credit in the eyes of the old countess who merely sniffed her disapproval.

After an uncomfortable minute, Isobel changed the subject by sticking to topics that she hoped couldn't provoke any violent reaction in the countess.

'And are you enjoying your stay in India? A most fascinating place, I'm sure you agree.'

'It is not fascinating at all. It is a very dirty place, and the people are savages!'

'Then I think differently on this point,' said Isobel coldly. 'I believe in a very short time I have developed a love of this country. And a deep respect for the people. They have had to endure so much, especially from people who wilfully refuse to make any effort to appreciate their culture.'

There was no reply from the countess except a thin-lipped glare.

Carolina seemed a little ashamed of her mother's response and hurried to make amends.

'My uncle, Count Tiago, had written to my mother insisting we come and stay with him as there is no man in our family now, and Phillipe and I have known each other from childhood.' Her face lit up when she mentioned Almeida's name, making her for a moment radiantly pretty. 'He was always very kind to me.'

The countess interjected, 'As our only male relative, Count Tiago is head of our household now and we must follow his advice in all things.'

Isobel was passing the cake to Marco to take a second piece. His hand was poised to do so when the countess called out, 'You have had enough!' and the little boy dropped his hand and shrank back behind Isobel. His fear of the woman made Isobel speak out when she might have remained silent.

'Surely you are capable of making a decision for yourselves without a man?'

'In Portugal the man has absolute power. It is written in our laws and we women are very happy for it to remain so.'

Isobel laughed. 'In my family it was I who made most of the decisions. My father was charming, but hopeless I'm afraid when it came to practical matters.'

'How extraordinary...' The countess raised her eyebrows and stared.

'It is right that Count Almeida should make decisions for us. The Almeidas and D'Souzas have been intermarrying for over three hundred years so we are almost one family, and in that way the bloodline has maintained purity.'

'You mean that marrying anyone not an Almeida or a D'Souza will pollute the blood? What a very strange idea.'

'In a more practical way this rule has preserved our fortunes, but times have changed, and now I see for myself how barbaric this country is, I cannot imagine any civilized girl wanting to attach herself to such a place.'

The remark was clearly aimed at Isobel, and at her daughter, who sat squirming in her chair and blushing profusely.

'But our bloodline can also be maintained by marrying into royalty. This is the only exception.'

'Please, Mama.' Carolina looked up with a pleading expression. It was plain she still harboured the hope that her plans for marrying Phillipe Almeida would come to pass.

Isobel began to feel sorry for the girl and even admired her a little. She hoped she would succeed, if only to thwart her very unpleasant mother.

There followed a period of absolute silence till Almeida

walked back into the room and everyone let out a collective sigh of relief.

He'd been making a tour of the house with Mary and had taken a hasty look at the grounds as well. He leaned elegantly against the fireplace and took out a cigarette while fixing his eyes on Isobel. He made a slight taunting gesture towards her by holding out his cigarette case in her direction when the other women weren't looking, challenging her to take one, but she pretended not to notice him. After a few moments he sat down opposite her, tapping the end of the cigarette on the case before lighting it.

'You have made the house charming, I admit, but the grounds are a different matter. So much to do to get the place viable again, an added expense – and there are the sheds, which are almost rundown...'

He was amused as he watched her eyes darken and her fingers flinch, knowing she longed to contradict him. Then he straightened and smiled, as though all at once reminded by a more pleasant thought.

'But this is not the time to discuss business. We have come on a different matter.' He leaned over to where Carolina was sitting and raised her hand to his lips while holding her gaze with his own.

She smiled up at him, the open adoration showing in her eyes.

'We are hosting a party at Casa Margarida to introduce Miss D'Souza and the countess to our little community...'

Marco looked up with an enquiring gaze, first at Carolina and then at his father, then with a little squirming movement he moved closer to Isobel, almost leaning his head on her lap.

'You will make a mess of Miss Blanchard's dress. Sit up at once!'

It was the countess who spoke, and the child sprang to attention, his eyes wide with alarm. Isobel put her hand out to touch his cheek, causing him to give a wan smile.

'He was not crushing my dress. I like him being here.'

Almeida made a move to leave.

'Well, I think he has been spoilt enough for one day. Come, my boy.' He turned to Isobel. 'We have decided on the Friday of next week. Your sister will be back by then, I hope? And your aunt will accompany you, of course. I will have rooms prepared for you all and your maid.'

In the hall, Isobel let the women pass then paused before Almeida, hoping for a quiet word with him.

'You have thought about the offer? I would like to give my sister some idea of our progress when she returns.'

'Oh, the offer, of course. I haven't given the matter much attention this week. I have been very busy with my visitors, but now I have much food for thought.'

He gave her an intense, dark look that almost unnerved her, but she stared back at him, calling his bluff.

'Well, I suppose that must do, but, if you are having second thoughts about buying, perhaps I should advertise. It might be a good thing to have a comparable offer. Yes, I think I will advertise after all.'

He answered with haste, giving himself away a little.

'No, that won't be necessary. I am interested in buying but you must understand there are many little details to iron out, and as you know there is my uncle as well; he must be consulted. We can discuss the matter further when you come to Casa Margarida on the fifth.'

'You were ready to buy Silver Mist quickly enough before. I can't understand your hesitation now.'

'Things are different now and I am adapting to conditions.'

'Do you always like to toy with your victims, Mr. Almeida? Because that is what it feels like to me.'

'Victim? You? You are the last person I would see as a victim of anything.'

It was said in such a way that it was difficult to tell if it was a compliment or not, but as he raised her hand to kiss it, he gave her a look that left her a little shaken out of her usual poise.

The countess gave Isobel an almost curt nod on parting, but the boy called out to Monty in a final joyous goodbye. At the sound of his name, the dog rushed out onto the front lawn to first run around in frenzied circles trying to bite his own tail, before bolting off through the front garden to chase the carriage down the driveway.

Chapter Twenty-Two

Violet returned from her visit a different girl. A week of continuous praise, and attention to her every desire, had almost restored her to her former self. She was in raptures about 'Cardamon Hills,' which she declared was a lovely house at almost the standard of an English country home with every comfort including at least thirty servants and a room large enough for dancing. And there had been two evening parties while she was there, and she had played and sung for the other guests to much acclaim. Both she and Aunt Bea returned with lengths of rich silks for themselves and for Isobel, which they had bought in a little shop in the township, and they had borrowed a quantity of the latest novels from the lending library. There were also frequent visits to the English club where they had met many of the other planters and had dined on roast beef and Yorkshire pudding. Isobel couldn't help but pull a face at that. It all seemed so unappetising now she had grown so used to Constanza's delicious, mostly vegetarian cooking.

Violet had already heard about the party at Casa Margarida as Harry Saunders had also been invited and it was widely speculated that it was then that Almeida would ask his cousin from Portugal to marry him. Thankfully, Violet didn't push the subject of the sale of Silver Mist, only asking briefly if Almeida had agreed to buy yet, before rushing on with a story about the well-known bravery of Saunders and his collection of leopard pelts, the best of which he promised he would have made into a hat and muff for Violet, as he knew a tailor in Bombay who was almost as good as anyone in Savile Row.

At this Isobel scowled and reminded her sister how inappropriate it was to accept gifts of clothing from a man, especially one who had not yet made his intentions clear.

Violet only gave a sly smile at that, almost implying the time would soon come when he would show his hand, as he had been very attentive to her throughout the visit. One memorable evening he had produced his collection of precious stones he had bought over the years while living in India, including a huge, square-cut blue sapphire he hinted would make a beautiful ring for the right girl – and judging by Violet's devious smirk, it was plain he meant her.

Saunders had also told her he had almost had enough of India and was planning to sell Cardamon Hills and his shares in the iron ore mine for an enormous profit, which would enable him to return to London and set himself up in a comfortable establishment there. There was also mention of a country estate he had his eye on in the Cotswolds where he hoped he would raise a family one day.

At this, Aunt Bea had interjected by nodding her head and saying Saunders was a good match for anyone smart enough to take advantage of his single state. Violet once more looked very coy, though Isobel frowned when she thought of her sister marrying him. There was nothing glaringly wrong with him – he was more than presentable – but there was something hidden, something distasteful about him that had not yet made itself felt. However, because of her previous disastrous intervention in Violet's affairs, she made a pact with herself she would do her best to keep out of her sister's life and let matters run their inevitable course, even though it was sure to be difficult.

To Isobel's relief, the subject of returning to London at once seemed to have been forgotten with Violet's new social schedule ahead of her and it was only sometimes apparent that Isobel had not yet been forgiven. But when Isobel cautiously asked her sister if she longed to return to London quite as much as before, it was then that Violet showed the true depth of her bitterness.

'Why would I want to return to a place where I'm a laughingstock? What would happen if I should accidentally meet John and his—' There she faltered as tears filled her eyes. 'His wife? I can never live it down, never. Everyone knew about our engagement even though it was supposed to be a secret.'

'You didn't tell anyone, did you? Violet, you should have thought. You know how people talk.'

'I was sure we would marry, and we would have if you—'

There she stopped, only turning her face away from Isobel and biting her lip.

'And by now everyone must know how he jilted me. I must stay here, at least till I...'

She left the sentence unfinished, but Isobel knew her sister had no intention of returning to London unless she had a husband by her side – and a rich one at that – who she could flaunt in the face of the man who had rejected her.

———————

The week passed quickly with Violet spending a lot of her time reading her new novels and choosing a suitable gown for the coming party at Casa Margarida. She went about her daily chores, sometimes humming a little tune, but with at times a strange, cold expression on her face as if bent on a distasteful mission that must be accomplished at all costs, causing Isobel to suspect she was seriously thinking now of encouraging Harry Saunders in an offer of marriage.

With great reluctance, Isobel broached the subject one evening when Violet was sitting on her bed, her large amber eyes misty with some pleasant thought while she brushed her hair.

'Let me do it, dear. It's been months since you've let me.'

It was clear that Violet was cautious and clearly reluctant when once it had been the time she had enjoyed most with her sister, but she handed Isobel the brush with a faint smile.

'Well, if you want to.'

Isobel touched the hair as gently as she could and soon Violet began to relax with the rhythmic motion of the brush. Isobel came to the point at last.

'What do you think of Harry Saunders?'

'I like him. I like him a lot. He makes me feel safe.'

'Safe from what?'

'Oh, I don't know, the world, I suppose…'

'Do you still think of John?'

Violet pulled her head away with a sudden jerk.

'Sometimes, but I don't want to talk about him.'

'You don't think perhaps because of what happened with John, you might be a bit hasty in giving your affections to someone else?'

Violet was angry now. She snatched the hairbrush out of Isobel's hand, leapt to her feet and began to pace about the room.

'Is it really any of your business, Isobel? Especially after what happened with John. I'm surprised you haven't learnt a lesson from that.'

'But do you love him? Really love him? Marriage is for life, you know. Didn't you ever notice how unhappy mother was with father? I believe she had nothing but contempt for him in the end. Do you want to take that risk with a man you hardly know?'

'I love him enough if that's what you want to know, and he would take me away from here, which is what I want most in the world, and especially to get away from you. You choke me! Choke me!'

She threw the brush down on the bed where it bounced and landed with a crash on the floor.

In the next room Billy squawked loudly and Aunt Bea's voice could be heard through the wall soothing him. 'What's the matter, old man? Time you were in bed…'

There was at first a profound silence from both the girls, then the night noises from outside the window burst into life, making them feel their own personal tensions more deeply.

'I'm sorry, it's only that I promised Mother I would look after you. I want you to be sure, that's all.'

'I don't think that's the reason at all. You're jealous of me and always have been, and because no man will ever want you because you're too opinionated and wayward, you set every man you meet against you. You know you do. You'll be a bitter old maid, Isobel, just as Mother always said!'

'Did Mother really say that?'

'You know she did.'

There was silence again as Isobel thought what to do next, but for a long time she was too hurt to speak and all she could do was to stare down at her hands and fight back the tears beginning to well in her throat.

Then Violet's voice came, cold and unforgiving.

'I wish you would leave. You know I want to be alone.'

Isobel dragged herself to her feet and left.

Chapter Twenty-Three

Harry Saunders unexpectedly came to stay the day before the planned excursion to Casa Margarida. He had heard there were bandits in the area and in a fit of concern for the unprotected ladies had left immediately for Silver Mist, bringing two of his men and their rifles with him.

He made a very impressive appearance as he stormed heavily up the hall in his thick leather gaiters and boots with his rifle slung over his shoulder, ordering his servants to unsaddle his mount and to be quick about it. Everyone smiled at his powerful masculine presence, especially Aunt Bea who seemed to lose all common sense when around members of the opposite sex, but to Isobel he came dressed in the guise of a fox that had crawled his way under the chicken wire to steal one of the hens.

Isobel studied him from afar, rarely speaking and only answering him if spoken to.

It was as though she had trained a microscope on him deliberately to expose his every flaw. This was a serious examination of his character, as she didn't care much about what he looked like, though she felt there was something repellent and brutish about his appearance despite his scrupulously groomed hair and trimmed moustache. His eyes she found the most unsettling feature, being of a cold ice blue, giving them the lifeless look of the dead creatures he liked to collect and hang on his walls.

He seemed to find it his right to order others about and once when he snapped at Mr. Singh to take away his boots to clean, he didn't notice that man's humiliation at being asked to do something so obviously beneath him. It was only when Isobel intervened and sent for one of the young boys to do the task that he muttered a sort of half apology. He was insensitive to anyone else's pain, and that was what Isobel most objected to, as it did not bode well as a trait in a future husband.

Isobel went to bed weighed down at the prospect of Harry Saunders being a permanent fixture in her life, causing her sleep to be broken by a series of nightmares that seemed so alarmingly real that when she was awoken by a terrifying roar followed by rifle fire, at first, she thought she was still dreaming. But then a series of louder shots made her leap out of bed and pull on her dressing gown before running down the hall towards Violet's bedroom.

Violet too had awoken and stood shivering with fear in the arms of Aunt Bea and Mary and even in her agitated state, Isobel couldn't help but wonder why no one had rushed towards her room.

Monty sat cringing in a corner of the hall with his hackles

raised and his eyes bulging. There was even a tell-tale puddle next to him, which told of his terror.

Violet was almost hysterical with fright.

'Oh, why did we ever come to this horrible place? I won't stay here any longer. I won't.' Then, when she saw Isobel, she became more frantic still and for a moment it looked as though she might lose control and attack her, as her eyes were almost crazed with fright.

'Why did you make me come here? Why? If only Mother were alive... It isn't fair...' Then she seemed to lapse into a kind of dream, her voice dropping almost to a whisper, saying mysteriously and with a suddenly cunning smile, 'I don't have to if I don't want to...'

A few minutes later there was the sound of male voices coming down the hall led by Harry Saunders who was exclaiming loudly, 'She's a beauty there's no doubt, the biggest I've ever bagged, but by God did she ever put up a fight. Six shots to finish her!' followed by the laughter and congratulations of his servants as they gathered about him.

Only Mr. Singh's voice had a note of regret as he muttered, 'A female, and a beautiful lady...'

Isobel's mind flew immediately to the leopard and in almost a blind panic she ran down the hall to stand trembling before Saunders. Before she could stop herself, the words came rushing out.

'What have you done? What have you done, you brute!'

Saunders, having clearly prepared himself for the rightful tributes awarded to the conquering hero, was taken aback to say the least.

'She was after the dog. I could smell her. I know the smell

of leopard anywhere, then I saw her from my window sitting on the wall. She would have taken the dog!'

'How? How could she have taken Monty? There are bars on all the windows! He was supposed to be in the bathroom. Who let him out? Everyone knows he's not to sleep on Violet's bed.'

'It seemed a bit cruel to keep him locked up so I let him out. Poor fellow was putting up a bit of a fuss, whining at the door and such.'

'So, you decided against my expressed wishes—'

'Sometimes you ladies make decisions that are not always sensible.'

'I did it for a very sensible reason.'

'Do you mean to say you suspected there was a leopard out there?'

'I wasn't sure,' she lied. 'You said yourself there might be leopards about.'

Violet wasn't convinced.

'I don't believe you. You knew about this … this monster all this time and didn't do anything about it! And you didn't tell me! Isobel! How could you? I might have been killed – any one of us might have been killed!'

'I didn't want you to panic, and you would have. Anyway, there was no danger of you being killed as you never go outside the door, and he had no right to shoot it. He's a beast. He only wants to look like a big man in front of you.'

'Isobel! Stop it at once! How dare you!'

'What do you mean? I'll say what I like! He had no right to shoot an animal on our property without my consent!'

'Well, it's my property too and he has my consent!' She paused for a moment to give more weight to her words. 'As he has in another matter.'

Violet's face showed a range of expressions. First there was a faint shadow of doubt crossing her forehead, then a clearing half-smile as she made her decision.

She moved close to Saunders and slipped her hand into his. In return, his eyes lit up as he took her hand to kiss it. 'You mean you will…?'

Then he put an arm around Violet and squeezed her with the confident ease of ownership.

'My darling, my little girl…'

Aunt Bea was the first to speak.

'What does he mean? What's he talking about? Could you please take your arm from my niece? She is not appropriately dressed.'

Violet laughed then, even though it was a little shaky.

'It's alright, Aunt Bea. Last night Harry asked me to become his wife; I wasn't sure, and I told him so, but now I am sure, so he has every right in everything to do with me…' Then with a barbed meaning impossible to mistake she fixed her eyes on Isobel. 'Harry is the man of the house now.'

Not bothering to dress, Isobel made a cup of tea and waited in the drawing room till light broke through the windows, then made her way outside the house to where the leopard lay underneath her favourite perch, drenched in a pool of blood. Isobel crept towards the creature with great stealth as though any moment she might wake and launch herself at her throat. As Isobel got closer, she realized there was never any chance of that. It was an ugly sight: one of the beautiful paws Isobel had once watched her clean so carefully had been shattered; an eye was blasted away, and her belly was ripped apart by the force of the bullets. But there was beauty in her death as well, the great rippling muscles under the skin had not yet completely collapsed and the fur still held a lustrous gleam.

Isobel put out a hand and began to stroke the still warm fur. 'There, there,' she said gently, 'it's over now.'

Then she began to cry – deep, painful sobs such as she had never experienced before.

But a deep instinct inside her told her she was crying for her sister perhaps even more than the leopard. She was sure Violet would be unhappy with such a man.

She remembered then an episode from childhood where she had been punished soundly for a small misdemeanour and had refused to cry, and then overheard the servants talking about her.

'She's a hard little piece, that's for sure, with a heart like a rock…'

Now as she sobbed, her only consolation was that the beautiful head was too damaged for Saunders to make a trophy of her; she at least would be spared that.

As Isobel sat, oblivious to the damage the dirt and blood was doing to her silk dressing gown, she heard a noise coming from the bushes a few feet away.

She watched, her heart in her mouth, as the bushes parted, and a baby leopard came tumbling out of the undergrowth and waddled towards the body of its mother.

The little creature seemed confused at first and sniffed and nuzzled as if hoping to prod her dead mother back to life.

Then it stumbled about trying to suckle at the mother's nipples and at the same time covering its fur in the mother's blood. It was a bleak sight and at first Isobel was unsure what to do.

Then, after a quick look about, she scooped the cub up in the end of her dressing gown and hurried towards the house. The cub made loud mewing noises and twisted its fat little body in an effort to get away, but she wrapped her dressing gown tighter and held it close till she could get to her bedroom and examine it more closely. It was obviously a female and had the same corona-shaped pattern on her forehead as her mother.

There were stronger, darker markings around the bright yellow eyes, giving her a sweetly fierce look which Isobel was sure would become terrifying as she grew older. The little creature stared up at her with more curiosity than alarm, though all the while keeping up a loud constant mewing.

She was obviously well nourished and perhaps aged, Isobel thought, about six months, so there was every chance the cub would survive if she could be persuaded to take a bottle. Then Isobel thought there may be more babies out there in the wilderness that would surely die without their mother. It would be pure folly for her to venture into the jungle without some protection and she reluctantly concluded she would have to tell Saunders of the cub's existence. She left the baby on the bed then dashed to the kitchen and found a large, deep cane laundry basket which would serve as a nest.

After lining the basket with an old blanket and gently placing her inside, Isobel was at leisure now to truly admire the beauty of the cub as she tumbled about. She knew it was imperative she should be fed as soon as possible, so she washed the leopard mother's blood off her hands and dressed with haste before going to the dining room to face Harry

Saunders, who by now she thoroughly hated, and who was soon to become her brother-in-law.

The entire household was at breakfast, and they all looked up with various levels of reproach written on their faces as she came to sit, pretending not to be intimidated by their expressions.

Mary showed her usual unwavering loyalty by pouring Isobel a cup of tea and patting her on the shoulder as she passed. The simple act gave Isobel courage to face the inevitable storm before her, but she decided to soften the impact by drenching Saunders with the immense charm she knew she had when she decided to use it.

'I'm so sorry I called you a brute, Mr. Saunders. It was fright really that caused me to lose control. You know how women can be – quite unstable without a man to guide them.'

Aunt Bea looked up at that and gave an audible huff of disbelief before returning to her breakfast, though keeping a shrewd eye on proceedings.

'And allow me to say how happy I am you have become engaged to my dear sister.'

'Well thank you, Miss Blanchard. And when we're married, of course you must make your home with us – that is, until some other lucky man comes along.'

'Well thank you, Mr. Saunders, but I have other plans.'

'You are happy for me then, Issie?'

'Yes of course, darling, very happy.'

Violet was moved enough to go to Isobel and kiss her gently on the cheek and Isobel felt almost guilty. Violet would marry Saunders over her dead body.

'And now I have a little surprise for you all...'

Aunt Bea looked over her teacup, saying dryly, 'I thought as much.'

'It would be kinder to drown it at once...'

It was Saunders who spoke first and as if Isobel hadn't already hated him enough, she felt that emotion rise to a new level.

Aunt Bea was scathing. 'It's not a kitten, Isobel, that will grow into a house cat. It's a wild animal. Have you thought about what you'll do with her when she's grown? Typical!'

'But she's so sweet.' Violet put out a hand to pat the cub but when she saw a little of the mother's blood had stained her lovely hand, she stepped back in disgust, only murmuring to herself, 'We must try to save her at least,' then she added vaguely, 'or have her taken away somewhere...'

Mary was unsure but as usual was loyal. 'I'm sure Miss Isobel knows what she's doing. She usually does.'

Both Constanza and Aashi stood back, puzzled at the curious behaviour of the English lady. They agreed the leopard cub was healthy and might well live if able to tolerate a substitute milk.

Mr. Singh too was confident the cub would survive.

'I have raised them before, in Simla. Sometimes the gentlemen brought in a baby or two from their tiger hunts. I know what to do.'

'And did they live, Mr. Singh?'

'Some of them did – that is, until they were let loose when they were old enough for the gentlemen to shoot them...'

Isobel looked at the cub with an expression of horror. That

would never happen to her cub. Never. She would move heaven and earth to prevent it.

Saunders was unconvinced. 'I still say it would be kinder in the end to drown it…'

Isobel now forgot any intention she may have had to be pleasant.

'That's probably what your mother said when she saw you for the first time.' It was said with a laugh, but he took it in the spirit it was meant and looked deeply offended.

Chapter Twenty-Four

L ater on in the morning, Isobel, led by Saunders and his servants carrying rifles, made a search of the surrounding bushes and the ever-encroaching jungle.

Again, the strange silence that fell over every living thing as the group walked through the thick forest was uncanny and a little unsettling. But everywhere there was a profound beauty: in the distant sounds of birdsong, in the dappled light that filtered through the dark green canopy and the brilliance of the wildflowers as they fell in tangled disarray down to the rich black earth.

As Isobel walked through that magical place, she was overcome with a deep reverence for the spiritual nature of her surroundings. This was different to walking through the charming but manicured parks and countryside of her homeland that she had always loved and admired. But there it was tame country, and here was the mystery of the unknown that stirred her blood. She wondered where these unlikely feelings came from, then she remembered from her childhood a glamorous Blanchard cousin with whom, even from the age of sixteen, she had been in love, who had set out to explore the far reaches of the Amazon many times and returned throughout the years to entertain her with stories of the wonders he had seen there and tales of what drove him like an addiction to go back again and again, till finally he was seen no more and all that remained of his life was the beautifully carved case of a blow pipe belonging to a once lost Amazonian tribe.

It had arrived in the mail a few months after he had disappeared and was addressed to Isobel with an accompanying letter. He spoke of returning to England in the summer and the joy at the prospect of seeing her then, but with a peculiar inner instinct Isobel had known at once that she would never see him again.

They crept on, hardly making a sound. The evidence of monkeys was everywhere, but they kept to their outposts high in the trees, swaying back and forth on the branches while peering down at the invaders with unsettling, resentful, little human faces. They became excited and let out loud, piercing cries that sent shivers down Isobel's back when the group came upon a clearing surrounded by tall trees covered in a kind of thick green moss on which clung masses of tiny vivid orchids like coloured spiders. Rays of silver light illuminated the figure of a half-human stone deity placed on a dais in the centre of the grove surrounded by piles of other carved grey stones, some of them lying about haphazardly amongst the roots of beautiful and strange plants.

A champak tree was a peculiar and lovely sight standing alone in this cleared space, radiant and blooming against a background of the jungle. It was almost as if the tree itself emanated a powerful but benevolent force that was both calming and discomforting at the same time.

There were huge butterflies too, some of them striped like the fur of a tiger or painted like the leopard, and others like the one Isobel had found in the envelope another world away, but it seemed that here was the source of the creatures as they floated lazily around in that almost mystical place.

The guides stood back and muttered amongst themselves as though afraid.

Isobel too was overcome with a vague fear. 'What is this place?'

One of the guides answered her in a whisper. 'These trees are sacred to our people. They are the trees of the spirits…'

Saunders made it clearer. 'It's a sacred grove. There are a lot of them around here. The natives believe it's a sin to kill anything from here or to take anything without the permission of the gods. Lot of nonsense, of course…'

'Nonsense to you perhaps, but not to the people who come here to worship,' said Isobel, not caring if he was offended or not. She felt he didn't belong there. In such a place his lack of sensitivity became even more glaringly apparent.

A few metres from the stone deity and at the foot of a shallow cave, one of the men found a deep indentation in a mound of soft grasses.

'Leopard!' said Saunders. 'This is where she kept her cubs. Well, not anymore…'

Saunders poked at the soft grasses with the end of his shooting stick. 'There's nothing here. We might as well go back.'

Then came a faint mewing and there, crouching against the wall of the cave, could be seen a glimmer of yellow-green eyes.

As Isobel moved closer, she could see the cub was coal-black all over which was why he was at first difficult to see.

'Oh, you little beauty!' Isobel was enraptured with the little creature that struggled at first, making brave, lashing motions with its baby paws.

A great rush of love for the animal brought tears to her eyes and at the same time she wondered why she felt such a deep passion for a creature not even of her species when human babies had never roused such sentiments in her – in fact quite the opposite; she found them grub-like as well as terrifying.

Saunders had come to stand behind her and roughly took the cub out of her hands to determine the sex before handing him back to Isobel.

'A black leopard! And a male. That's a rare thing. It means the sire must be black too. So, then the rumours of the sightings must be true…'

The hunter in him was roused, and every inch of his body was on the alert. His eyes were darting from left to right; he was almost salivating with the thought of a kill.

'He must be still out there somewhere.'

The tone of his voice made Isobel instantly alarmed.

'And there he will stay as long as he's on my land!'

He answered her with a smile and with what seemed to be a veiled threat.

'As you say, for as long as it is your land.'

She refused to answer him, even though he had ignited a stray thought that perhaps Saunders might have an acquisitive eye on Silver Mist. He had often remarked it could be 'a nice little property if managed well.'

Instead, she pressed her face into the warmth of the little cub's body. How she hated that man, and how she cursed the stars for allowing such a beast to cross her path and that of her innocent sister.

They walked further, keeping an eye on the trees in case a leopard should be watching from above, and on the ground for signs of fresh prints, but eventually Saunders declared the area safe from any other wild leopards – at least for the moment. They returned to the house, Saunders to the fond smiles and gentle caresses of Violet who of course attributed the find of the new cub to the resourcefulness of her fiancé, and Isobel to her room, where she found enormous consolation in watching the joy of the little cub as he was reunited with his sister, and afterwards the pleasure of watching him fall asleep in her arms after devouring an enormous bottle of warm milk.

The following morning, just before leaving for Casa Margarida, Isobel was walking past the drawing room when she overheard Saunders speaking to Mr. Singh in hushed tones.

'Now there's two of them, there's little chance they'll survive. It would be best if you smother them while we're away. Miss Isobel will be none the wiser, there's a good chap.'

'Miss Isobel would be very unhappy and if she should ever find out she would never forgive me.'

'She'll soon get over it – you know what women are. She'll have forgotten all about it in a week.'

'Not Miss Isobel. She's different to other ladies.'

'Just do as I say, man. I'm almost head of this house anyway and what I say goes. There will be a few extra rupees in it for you.'

'I don't want any money,' Mr. Singh said proudly. 'I am paid very well here.'

Saunders put his hand back in his pocket.

'Well, that's a first, but keep this to yourself, won't you?'

Mr. Singh said nothing, preferring to keep his eyes down in case he should betray his true feelings.

Listening from the door, Isobel wondered if she should burst in and confront Saunders at once, but for Violet's sake she held back, and she had no doubt where Mr. Singh's loyalty really lay. Her faith in Mr. Singh was justified when a few minutes later he knocked on her door to confess the whole thing and how he had been told to do something he never could.

'He is a big man, Miss Isobel. He could make trouble for me.'

'Over my dead body he will. Thank you, Mr. Singh. I'll deal with Mr. Saunders. He won't bother you again.'

A quiet fury settled in Isobel's heart now, but if she openly made a stand against Saunders, Violet would be sure to dig her heels in. She would have to move carefully, but now all her best intentions not to interfere with her sister's life were swept aside, and all she could think of were ways to destroy him, and how to be rid of him forever.

Chapter Twenty-Five

When the party from Silver Mist passed through the gates of Casa Margarida, the guard sent a boy to race ahead on his horse and warn the inhabitants of the estate of their coming, so by the time the carriage swung into the drive before the house, Phillipe Almeida was waiting for them, immaculate, handsome and smiling. Isobel, however, sensed an underlying tension in that smile and suspected his charm was forced.

He stepped forward at once to help the ladies down, exerting all his masculine charisma with Aunt Bea and Violet in particular, who blushed prettily at his rather extravagant flattery while she looked about with a childish joy at the grandeur of Casa Margarida. He was more restrained with Isobel as if he sensed she would accept his compliments with a more cynical eye, but as he took her hand to help her down, he felt such an unexpected and powerful flash of shivering heat from the mere touch of her fingers that he could not meet her eyes; instead, he turned away and barely recovered his composure enough to hand the party of ladies over to his housekeeper.

He seemed anxious to be rid of them, and Isobel watched his hasty retreat with a feeling of vague disappointment as well as a touch of resentment. She had felt Phillipe Almeida had begun to like her a little, which could mean a higher price might be extracted from him when it came to the sale of Silver Mist, but now it was clear he scarcely even noticed her.

Isobel was shown to a room containing a four-poster bed with brocade hangings depicting gentle pastoral scenes from the far-away world from which they had come centuries before. The sheets and pillows were of the finest cream linen edged with almost a foot of Belgian lace that lay spread over a blue silk coverlet embroidered in gold thread with the Almeida crest.

Isobel crossed to the windows to let in some light and air. Up close she could see the hundreds of panes were not of glass at all but of a peculiar, polished shell set into little wooden triangles, laboriously handmade by some worker in the past.

Placed by the bed was a book meant for visitors on the history of the Almeida family marked *Uma Familia Nobre*, obviously a smaller version of the huge, chained volume she had seen before in the drawing room. This edition though was written in both French and English instead of Portuguese and she settled back to learn a little of this ancient family.

It seemed that the earliest settler was a certain Alphonso Almeida, also known as Alphonso the Just, who arrived in 1550 with one hundred slaves left out of the two hundred he had started the journey with, a signed proclamation from King John III, 'The Colonizer', giving him the right to claim for himself and his sovereign anything that might be of use or value, and a wife fifteen years old – and there Isobel couldn't resist a laugh, a certain Margarida D'Souza, showing the tradition of marrying their cousins had indeed been a practice between the two families for hundreds of years.

They settled first on the island of Goa before then setting out to claim for themselves vast tracts of what was supposedly unoccupied land.

There followed descriptions of such vile practices, Isobel couldn't help but wonder how on earth he managed to earn the title of 'The Just', especially after emptying an area of one mile square of the original inhabitants and claiming for himself the land on which he built his home. There was a curious little added detail of continued protests from the local people who had taken exception to the burning of a sacred forest – an area of five acres at least:

The savages risked death and paid for their foolishness in high numbers in order to save this place of devil worship, but it was to no avail as it was on that most favoured position I chose to build my mansion house...

Isobel looked around at the grand room with its trappings of luxury with a strong feeling of dread. The beautiful house had been built on the bodies of the slain who had died defending their most cherished land, and if she were superstitious, she would have thought it was a great risk to build Casa Margarida on the burnt remains of a sacred forest. At the very least it was an unsettling thought; at the worst, the house might be cursed in some way, which might account for the feeling of unease that seemed to permeate the very walls.

Even from the softening distance of time, Isobel felt a pang of regret and injustice. If the sacred forest Alphonso the Just had destroyed was as lovely as the forest near Silver Mist, it was clearly a crime against nature, as well as the people of Goa.

Isobel skimmed over a rather bloody one-sided description of a war with a local Maharaja who had understandably taken exception to his country being pillaged, the accumulation of more land, and an enormous bounty of fabulous jewels taken from the vanquished Maharaja.

She was deeply absorbed in the description of the jewels and wondering if they were still in the hands of the Almeida family when, as she lifted the book to get a more comfortable position, a thin, yellowing envelope fell out almost upon her lap.

It had been addressed to: *Maria Baronti, Piazza san Francesca 21, Lucca Italia*, but had obviously never been sent. Isobel stared at it for some time, put it back into the book and tried to ignore it, but eventually curiosity overcame her, and she quickly opened it to read it.

It was written in Italian in a fast-flowing, elegant script and largely incomprehensible, but some words were easy to decipher:

> *I'm afraid of him … I want to get away but he watches me night and day … he is half crazed with jealousy … last night he came to my room and he tried the door but I made sure it was locked … I know it was him … he is a beast … he has paid the servants to watch me so I can trust no one…*

There was no signature as the letter was clearly unfinished, almost as though the writer had been interrupted before secreting it away in the book. It was obviously a woman, but who? Could it be Phillipe Almeida's wife? Could it be he who was half crazed with jealousy? She was known to have been very beautiful and must have been attractive to other men.

Was Phillipe Almeida's rather cold and distant manner hiding something far worse?

Isobel was so engrossed by the desperate tone of the writer that she sat up with a start when there was the sound of a sharp knock on the door, returning her with a certain amount of relief to a much less tempestuous world. She had only just enough time to push the letter back into the pages of the book before Violet ran into the room, nearly breathless with excitement.

'I had to tell you, Issie, it couldn't wait!'

Isobel sat up, putting the book aside.

'What is it, Violet?'

Violet paused for a moment to look around the room.

'My goodness, what a mausoleum. You should see mine – it's even worse.'

She sat down on the bed and seemed to steel herself before speaking.

'Listen, I've been talking to Harry. He doesn't want to wait. He wants to marry as soon as possible.'

She paused then to wait for a response, but as none was forthcoming, she went on:

'We thought in about a month from now. That will give us time to sell Silver Mist and we can all move to Harry's estate. Well, it will be my estate too then, Issie. You'll like it there, I'm sure – so much safer than Silver Mist and he said everyone can stay – Mary and Aunt Bea… That is, till she returns to England and' – she shuddered prettily – 'no wild beasts to deal with.

Then Harry said he will sell his estate and we'll all go back to England together and you can live with us. Oh Issie, I'm too frightened to stay at Silver Mist any longer, since the leopard—'

'Wait! In only a month? So soon? You can't be serious. Violet, you hardly know him, and I don't want to live with Harry Saunders.'

'I knew you would say that, but it's not fair! You get your way in everything and it's what I want, really want, and you know you owe this to me...' The words swept out in a rush as though she wanted to get them out before she lost courage.

'Because I took you away from a man who took pleasure in keeping you on a string and wouldn't have married you anyway?' Isobel's voice was calm, but there was an underlying tension she struggled to keep control of.

'How dare you! You know John loved me and we would have married if—'

'I know no such thing.'

'Well, whatever you say doesn't matter. It's my right to sell if I want to and if you don't get something for us to sign in the next couple of days, I'll ask Harry to take over as he said he would.'

'Oh, he did, did he? How very thoughtful of him.'

'It is thoughtful. He's a busy man but he said he would take care of the matter for me – for us, I mean, and as he said, ladies don't have much of a head for business. He said he would get us a much better price than you could.'

By now Isobel had leapt off the bed and begun to pace the room.

'Oh, I'm sure he did say that, and I suppose you just smiled sweetly and agreed.'

'Well, I suppose so, but I'm not like you, Issie. All I want is a comfortable home and a man who loves me, but I must have a dowry in order to marry. And this is the best solution, the best for us all.'

There was such an air of finality and confidence in her voice and Isobel's heart filled with a sudden bitterness, for they were not Violet's words but those of Harry Saunders.

She was all at once very tired and for the first time she resented the promise extracted by her selfish mother to always put Violet first. She resented the blatant favouritism that had followed her across the years and haunted her even now, long after her mother had died.

Her resentment spewed out in a torrent of angry words.

'It doesn't matter anymore. You can do as you like. Marry the fool! But I'll be damned if I'll go and live with him! As soon as I sell Silver Mist, I'm taking my money and going my own way. And don't worry, I'll talk to Almeida at once. Tonight! I won't have that murdering pig Saunders speak for me. You'll have your money to marry him. Marry him tomorrow for all I care!'

'Murdering pig! Is that really what you think of him?'

'Yes, it is what I think. Do you know he tried to make Mr. Singh kill our cubs! Why would he want to do that? Not because it makes any sense to do so but only to teach me a lesson for defying him! Can you imagine what your life would be like with a man like that? All will be well as long as you remain beautiful and sweet and do exactly as you're told, but heaven help you if you get old and ugly and don't conform to his ideas of how you should behave. This is for life, Violet. For God's sake!'

'Harry was only thinking of the cubs. He said they would

be sure to die slowly of starvation. He was only thinking of them!'

'He thinks of nothing but himself. I loathe him! And if you had the sense of a rabbit, you would too.'

With her lips contorted with rage, Violet turned and left the room, slamming the door as she did so.

For Isobel everything was over, and all her plans had turned to nothing. Her much-loved sister – much-loved still, despite everything – would sell the only security they had from under her. All the time she lay there, leaving large, wet patches of tears on the silk coverlet, she could only think of two things: the leopard cubs and their future, and the view from the summer room at Silver Mist.

Chapter Twenty-Six

T he greeting of the guests into the drawing room before the party at Casa Margarida was almost as formal as if they were about to be received at the Portuguese court.

The visitors filed past their hosts one by one, made a brief curtsy or a bow then mumbled a few words before moving on and collecting in little groups around the room to drink champagne and gossip. Nearly all the people were from neighbouring areas, most of them Portuguese and some Frenchmen from the coast, though others were important members of the Portuguese government in Panjim. They were not what Isobel had expected in government ministers, as they appeared to be on the whole a shady lot with sharp, suspicious eyes and an air of hiding something unsavoury under their almost too perfect manners. The French were mostly merchants who traded in luxury silks from the great warehouses in Panjim and Bombay. Most of them had lived so long in India they had unconsciously taken on an Eastern character, giving them a unique identity that would forever set them apart from their fellow countrymen and make them unfit for living anywhere else. They had not, though, lost their French manners, and made a great show of admiring the girls with a lot of hand kissing and outrageous compliments.

There was a rather self-conscious, plump and heavily perspiring Maharajah who kept pulling at the unaccustomed tie around his neck, while wearing an old-fashioned tailcoat and pinstriped trousers matched with a magnificent bright-pink turban on which sparkled an enormous yellow diamond. Isobel couldn't help but stare and wonder if it was one of the Maharajah's jewels of state that had survived the ages and the rapacious greed of Alfonso the Just.

He had brought his entourage of handsome servants and several women to accompany his favourite wife, who was tiny and shy and mostly half-hidden under a diaphanous shawl of the finest silk from behind which she took cautious peeps with her huge kohl-rimmed eyes when she thought no one was looking.

Set apart from this incongruous gathering, the countess D'Souza and her daughter held themselves stiffly upright on their throne-like chairs placed on a dais in the corner of the room, their curiously opaque black eyes showing no emotion but barely concealed boredom, their neatly folded hands appearing white against the stark black of their silk gowns. They were displayed on a background of pale-pink brocade, amongst a setting of crystal chandeliers, grey lace-patterned wallpaper and the almost morbidly dark oil paintings of the Almeida ancestors, who bore a striking resemblance to the living descendants beneath them. It was obvious the custom of marrying their cousins had produced some unfortunate results.

Both the women were wearing their finest jewellery, in particular a string of huge pearls attached to a ruby cross worn by the countess and a pair of emerald and diamond earrings worn by her daughter that by comparison threw the Maharajah's diamond into the shade.

Phillipe Almeida stood behind the pair, one hand resting on the back of the couch where his perhaps intended fiancée sat, with the other resting elegantly on his hip. He too was wearing strict black and his customary pure-white shirt, which threw into stark relief his slick black hair, intense dark eyes and pale olive skin. At his throat he wore a thin bowtie, again in the style of a Portuguese grandee.

The little group was a tableau of their own sense of superiority, but Isobel couldn't help but think they looked as though they all needed winding up from the back to encourage them into any appearance of life. Because of that frantic letter she had read in her room, she watched Phillipe Almeida more closely now, looking for signs of a latent cruelty in his eyes. But if it was there, it was very well disguised, as usual, with his faint, complacent smile that gave very little away.

Mostly though, all three wore expressions of utmost self-assurance, though Isobel thought she could perhaps see faint signs of anxiety in the eyes of Phillipe Almeida, who was casting uneasy glances at Carolina and her mother, as well as taking hasty glances towards the open double doors as though he was waiting for someone.

Isobel had held back till the last moment as she was enjoying being a hidden spectator to such a scene and also because she felt it was beneath her to have to stand before Almeida and his D'Souza relations and curtsy like everyone else in the room, but when the crowd thinned at an inconvenient moment, she was exposed to all and had no choice but to step forward and make her appearance known.

There was a just-audible gasp from the old countess, a sudden shifting in her chair from Carolina and an abrupt movement from Phillipe Almeida who rose out of his languid position and stood alert, his eyes flickering into life and showing, along with surprise, signs of definite admiration as she walked towards him from out of the crowd.

Though almost shockingly modern, her gown of deep-yellow silk, embroidered with the tiniest black silk roses on the bodice and hem, was the perfect exercise in restraint, despite the unusual colour.

She had bought it on a last extravagant shopping spree in Paris with her father in the final months before he died and even though it was amongst the most expensive dresses in the store, he had insisted she have it because she had loved it so much. It was cut low and square in the front and even lower in the back, exposing the elegant curves of her shoulder blades, and was tied just above the waist with a wide black velvet band. Her slim arms were bare except for a pair of long black velvet gloves, an almost bohemian oddity in a room where everyone else wore inoffensive white. She wore no jewellery except for a very long, thin strand of jet beads tied once around her throat then falling from her neck to below her waist, emphasizing the black touches on her gown perfectly.

Her abundant champagne-blonde hair was gathered up in a loose twist of waves and held by a silver diadem across her forehead embellished with an enamelled fleur-de-lis hair clasp. She shone in that beautiful but severe room as the very picture of flaming youth, and hardly anyone was going to forgive her for it.

All eyes were upon her, and each told a different story.

The Countess D'Souza's expression was clearly disapproving and unconsciously she reached out to her daughter and placed her hand on hers in a subtle sign of support. Isobel noticed the woman's behaviour and rightly interpreted that she was seen as a threat, and even though she felt it was petty she couldn't help but feel a touch of feline triumph for having unsettled such a smug and self-important woman.

Carolina's face had crumpled at first into a moment of insecurity and jealousy but only for a brief instant. She withdrew her hand from her mother with a sharp, not very subtle tug and smiled at Isobel.

'As usual, Miss Blanchard, you manage to astonish us – first trousers and now you appear in what could be considered almost revolutionary fashion. Mama would never allow me to wear such clothes—'

'Which are most unfeminine. You will be wanting the vote next, like those wild creatures in London who have been causing so much trouble!'

Isobel struggled with the idea that she was supposed to hold her tongue and move on for the sake of good manners, but with Violet's marriage now unavoidable, more than ever she was in no mood to be interrogated by a woman she had no interest in. Her whole heart was feeling her outrage at the countess singling her out when everyone before her was able to pass unmolested. She raised her chin and spoke clearly and precisely so there could be no doubt of her answer.

'I want to have a say in how the world is run. Is that so very terrible?'

'You are a young girl. You must leave these matters to your betters to decide.'

'Oh, and so any man is my better? No matter what his education or position in society, he has more right to express his opinion than I, simply because he is a man?'

At this, Phillipe Almeida gave a faint smile.

The countess was furious now and made no attempt to hide it.

'I think, young woman, you have ideas which can only lead you into an unhappy life. You should be content to be what you are and to accept your limitations.'

For once Isobel held her tongue but Carolina frowned and looked at her mother with an expression that showed she was not pleased. Then she gave Isobel a small, sweet smile showing she was on her side.

'I think, Mama, that Miss Blanchard is right. I have often wondered what is the point of my excellent education if I can do nothing with it? There are not many men who can equal my—'

'That's enough Carolina!' The countess could scarcely hide her rage now. 'And as for you, Miss Blanchard, your attitude is dangerous and can infect others.' By this she clearly meant her own daughter who was now looking down at her hands, her face flushing crimson.

It was impossible to argue with such a woman, so Isobel began her retreat, first giving Carolina a grateful smile of thanks for her small rebellion, knowing how much it cost her to speak out against her mother.

Turning to Almeida, she asked for a few moments alone with him later on in the evening to discuss a business matter that had suddenly become critical.

After a few seconds during which she received no response, Isobel repeated her request. 'I will probably leave earlier tomorrow than I anticipated. I have urgent matters at home I wish to attend to.'

Still there was no response. It was as though he was in a trance and even the countess's loud clearing of her throat did not stir him. All the while, Carolina was also staring anxiously in his direction and even ventured to softly call his name, but he did not hear her.

———————

At his first sight of Isobel, an avalanche of consciousness had overwhelmed Phillipe Almeida, making him almost unaware of where he was and oblivious to all around him. Everything and everyone that had once seemed so important to him was suddenly meaningless.

It was as though every creature and every object in the room had vanished and left only himself and the lovely girl standing before him.

For the past few hours, he had been struggling with the sensations he had experienced when he felt the touch of her fingers on his own. It had thrown him into a daze of wonder and doubt about his feelings for her, but now he saw her with a blinding clarity – her striking elegance, her unusual beauty, and the calm poise gently disguising what was clearly a tempestuous and original personality. Every woman in the room was cast into shadow by her presence, including the very lovely sister. It wasn't just her gown; it was what that gown represented.

She was indeed a 'new woman', and he could see too that she was also the future of womankind.

In a flash of understanding, he saw that he had been attracted to her in an almost compelling way from the very beginning, even though he had refused to admit it. He remembered the first sight of her in Egypt and the way she had paused on the steps of the hotel and glared back at him when he had been so obnoxious as to criticize her family. From the very beginning he had been dishonest with himself. He had called her ill-bred for responding to his remarks – a lady would have ignored him – but her striking face and the defiant expression upon it had fixed him to a standstill. Many times since then, and usually when he was finding it difficult to sleep, her image came back to him, clear and compelling as well as insolent and lovely.

But he had ruthlessly denied his attraction to her, preferring to retreat to the safe, compliant smiles of Carolina and a future that would surely reflect those smiles.

But most of all, he felt that to truly give his heart again was a betrayal of his beloved Silvia who had died because of him. His punishment must be to forever live a kind of half-life as a penance for his crime. He had chosen the black veil of mourning to hide under, and Carolina would have joined him there, allowing him to continue as he was – undisturbed, numb and remote.

But passion, it seemed, was a cloaked imp, and now that she had sprung before him in such an unlikely and inconvenient way, he knew he didn't want to marry Carolina at all.

He had been left with a grief that could allow no brightness in, but there before him now stood the very embodiment of spring after a long, icy winter – not in her manner, as even he, almost blinded as he was by her radiance, could see she would never be an easy, compliant partner. She would always be difficult and even wayward, but he wanted to embrace the chance to learn from her, to bask in her warmth and to love her if she would let him.

But now there was the question of being able to extract himself from a difficult situation. Clearly, he was expected to announce his engagement this very evening, but now he knew he never would, regardless of the consequences.

'Mr. Almeida?' Isobel's rather husky voice roused him from his dream.

He realized then he had been simply staring at her for at least half a minute and not hearing a word she had said.

'Mr. Almeida, I think you have not heard me. I wanted to ask you to spare me a moment alone this evening to talk business. There are things I must settle as soon as possible. You see, some things have changed…'

He saw then that her eyes were a little bruised, as though she had been crying. Though he could not imagine her in such a state, there was something broken about the way she held herself that he had not noticed at first, and she was doing her best to hide it.

The orchestra from Panjim had begun to warm up their instruments, then all at once began to play one of the more seductive Strauss waltzes that brought him abruptly to life.

'Not tonight, Miss Blanchard. Tomorrow. It is not a night for business, it is a night for dancing, and I hope you will do me the honour…'

The words were out before he realized what he was saying, and what's more, he found he had stepped off the dais and was now holding out his hand – which he noticed was trembling slightly – in her direction. A brief glance back showed Carolina's shocked face and the obvious fury of the countess who had half risen in her chair. It was the ultimate insult to a girl who as his intended would rightly expect the first dance of the evening to be for her. But he didn't care; he wanted to feel the warmth of that glorious shining girl in his arms. The blood was rushing through his veins, igniting little fires throughout his body and unsettling his sense of balance. It was almost painful.

She seemed taken aback at first but complied readily enough, even though from across the room her Aunt Bea gave her a look that warned of scandal if she dared to dance with an engaged man when it was plain the first waltz belonged to his fiancée. But Isobel turned away, choosing not to see her. The expression in his eyes was so intense, so burning, she was almost afraid to refuse him.

As he stepped forward to take her in his arms she yielded ever so gracefully to his touch and allowed herself to be led to the centre of the room with every eye upon them.

Chapter Twenty-Seven

A t first, he was almost overcome by the nearness of her. At each turn there was a fresh sensation. The faintest glimpse of the swell of her breast under the thin chiffon and silk, the curve of her chin, the flushed velvet cheek, the half-moon of her eyelashes against the pure skin beneath; a quick warm gasp of breath from her mouth as he spun her around, the fine strands of softly curling hair where it met the back of her neck, the delicate arch of her throat, then a glimpse of her white shoulder as the yellow silk slipped a little.

Her scent was Lily of the Valley, as fresh as the lovely creature in his arms; he often hated scent on women, especially when it soured on contact with the skin. He bent his head slightly to breathe in the fragrance of her hair. His fingers could feel the flesh underneath the thin silk. He experimented a little with pulling her closer and she melted under his grip, and all the time his eyes were fixed on her, enraptured and trapped. He was unable to speak, and now he experienced a hot, sharp pain in his belly as he found himself unable to look away from the soft curve of her pale-pink lips that seemed to tremble slightly, or did he imagine it?

Her lips especially intrigued him; there was a painting he remembered hiding somewhere in Casa Margarida of a playful Greek nymph with similarly carved lips wearing a silver diadem across her brow, and again, with the same touch of wickedness lingering around the smile. He decided he would seek the painting out at the first opportunity and take it to his room so he would have a reminder of his love always at hand. *My love.* He longed for the day when he could tell her his secret and hear the same feelings he was experiencing repeated by that lovely mouth.

He took delight in the feel of her hand in his, the palm warm and smooth. How much he longed to feel that hand on his face, on his chest... At some future time when she was his and it would be natural for her to do so.

He was aware too, though, of a need not to frighten her away with any sign of uncontrolled ardour. He seemed to sense she was perverse enough to reject any form of intrusion on his part in order to gain the upper hand and make him suffer for it, as even he, almost blind with love, could read her faults.

Isobel looked up, evidently puzzled by his expression, and completely unaware of the effect she was having on his self-control, and he admired what he saw as her complete lack of coquetry.

He had always had a secret horror of the false employment of the feminine arts. It embarrassed him to see the simpering smile on a woman's face when she deferred to him, or a demonstration of helplessness around a man, but he had accepted it as normal for women to behave in that way. All these things he had never liked, but it was only on meeting Isobel Blanchard that he was made aware of the artificiality of it all.

From her point of view, Isobel saw a man who was certainly even more strikingly handsome up close, even though at that moment he seemed sculpted out of marble, so pale was his face, and for a moment she wondered if he might be ill and doing his best to cover it up, as his eyes glittered as though he had a fever. He seemed unwilling to speak, and she began to feel uncomfortable with his eyes constantly upon her. She was starting to experience the same sensation she felt while standing alone in the wildest parts of the gardens at Silver Mist, a sense of unknown impending danger, something primal and threatening, and a tremor ran down her back when he held her close to turn in time to the music. Was that hint of danger something that had grown into a frightening jealousy that terrified Phillipe Almeida's poor wife half out of her wits? But looking at him it seemed unlikely. There were even signs of a vulnerability around his very attractive mouth, but now as he looked at her without even a shadow of a smile on his lips, she had to wonder again what secrets lay behind his impassive expression.

His hand firmed behind her back and drew her slightly closer as they swirled across the floor. It was pure pleasure to lose herself and forget for once the problems that had begun to close in on her.

It was rather wonderful, too, to be with a good-looking

man who knew how to dance and how to make her feel as though she were the only person in the room.

None of the men she had danced with in England or on the ship were as accomplished. All she could remember was the feel of a sweaty palm in hers, bad breath or adolescent mumblings and awkward silences – or worse, being held too close by a predatory older man, and the feel of his hand as it moved sneakily lower to push her hips towards his own, as well as the smell of whisky as he leaned forward to whisper something highly inappropriate in her ear.

Phillipe Almeida was none of these things, but when she smiled up at him, to her dismay, he turned away from her with a stern frown.

He was to her a mysterious creature, always holding himself so erect and severe. Though once, when he smiled at a light remark she had made, there had been a sudden flash of brilliance that lit up his face and made him appear much younger.

Up close, she could see his eyes were not black as she had always thought but a very dark blue with the tiniest flecks of darkest brown around the iris. They were fine, proud eyes but there was a strong hint of sadness there too, and she imagined it must be because of his wife who had died so young. After seeing a little into the depths of his soul, she felt it was impossible now to believe he could terrorize any woman. She sensed such behaviour would be beneath him, but then she knew men could become different creatures when in the grip of a consuming passion.

He had been closely shaved, but still there was the faintest shadow of bluish re-growth around his lips and chin. He smelled divinely of soap and there was a small square patch of unshaved skin below his left ear she longed to tell him about; she smiled to herself as she thought how mortified he would be if he knew. She spent some time studying his glossy black eyebrows and how the tiny hairs had shaped themselves into a perfect wing. His eyelashes were long and very black, but she couldn't help but think what a waste they were on a man, especially one who seemed so unaware of the power of his masculine charm.

To break the tension, she attempted conversation, despite him not wanting to talk business. She began with Violet's engagement.

'You know my sister will be married soon?'

He roused himself to speak.

'Saunders informed me of it. She seems very young, a child still…'

'I think so, too, but it is her wish.'

The music ceased and, taking her arm, he led her away to a seat in a quiet corner of the room, even though when momentarily glancing back to where Carolina stood, he could see the silent plea written so clearly there. To his shame he turned away from her. Now he was within the realm of his desire, he could not tear himself away. Every moment with Isobel had become precious to him and he guarded them jealously, like an animal over a stolen feast.

'He wants us all to live with him.' She looked away as she tried to hide her doubt and grief, but he saw her lips tremble. 'That is, till he sells Cardamon Hills and returns to England. He doesn't much care for India and Violet hates it.'

'Will you like living with Saunders?'

'I confess the idea is not very appealing. In fact, as you have asked me … I hate him.'

He smiled just a little, showing again a flash of very white teeth.

'That is most unfortunate, considering the circumstances.'

'He has threatened to interfere if I do not soon come to some agreement with you, even taking over the handling of the sale of our own property. Why do men think they have the right to lord it over women like that?'

'Because some men only feel safe when they've crushed everything and everyone around them. They must bend everyone to their will. It's a type of madness.'

Isobel reflected a moment.

'You seem to have experience of such men.'

'I do,' he answered with a great deal of feeling, but seemed unwilling to say any more.

Her guard was down now and, feeling she may have a sympathetic ear, she let show some of the fury she felt, her eyes burning with the injustice of it.

'Saunders killed a leopard at Silver Mist – in my opinion unnecessarily. A mother, with cubs. I have decided to rear them, much against his advice. I suppose you think I'm foolish, like everyone else…'

'As a child I had a little leopard cub myself, a victim of a hunter like Saunders, but unfortunately it died without warning. It nearly broke my heart. I hope that doesn't happen to you.'

'You have never been a hunter?'

'Fortunately, I grew up in Italy and there was no occasion for it. There is enough death in this world without adding to it.' Then he said with a particular bitterness, 'My uncle is the hunter in the family. He enjoys it.'

'Your uncle is not here tonight?'

'He's been in Panjim for a few months. We have a warehouse there and business must have delayed him. It was his idea to have this party tonight. He was most particular about the date. He is very fond of Carolina, and her mother.'

'I like Carolina. She shows great promise, if she can ever escape from her mother.'

He smiled.

'I like her too. Very much. We were great friends as children.'

Then he frowned, and again a dark cloud swept over his features.

Isobel thought she must have offended him for making the remark about Carolina's mother, and at the same time, unaccountably, she experienced a faint tinge of jealousy.

But it was a wasted emotion. It was plain Phillipe Almeida would marry his cousin, and soon.

Meanwhile she felt like shaking him up a little.

She began with a sly smile, 'Why, when we met here at Casa Margarida, did you pretend you hadn't seen me before?'

He was taken aback by this, and it took him some time to answer.

'I'm not sure. It was unforgivable. Perhaps it was because...'

Then he paused and gave her another of his intense looks.

'I will need a little more time before I can answer your question.'

Isobel longed to ask what he meant by that remark, but she let it pass.

'It wasn't very flattering for me, you know. A woman likes to be remembered – even if it's only for making a public spectacle of herself.'

Once again, she got the impression that he chose his words with care, and that he was feeling his way.

'You could never be that, but you will always set yourself apart from others, probably higher than others. It is your nature.'

'I had no idea I was such an interesting subject for observation.'

'As I said, you set yourself apart from others, but probably will suffer more because of it.'

She laughed then.

'You have summed me up perfectly. I seem to always be in trouble of some kind, especially with my family.'

As if to confirm her remark, her eyes wandered again to where Violet sat with Saunders.

After first glaring at Isobel, Violet began to laugh at something Saunders said but even from that distance her behaviour seemed to Isobel to be forced and unnatural. The whole thing was a play designed to cause maximum pain to her sister.

A servant appeared, offering madeira in exquisite long-stemmed crystal glasses etched as usual with the Almeida crest.

Phillipe passed her a delicate flute and for one moment their fingers touched and fumbled as they struggled to stop the glass from spilling. For him it was another unnerving flash of heat that brought on a vague unhappiness along with the thrill. He was flooded with an urgency to tell her of his love for her, to take a risk and ask her to marry him at once, but when he looked at her, she seemed so flagrantly unaware of the passion she had inspired in him that he felt a bit of a fool and drew back, hiding once more under a controlled mask.

Even so, something would have to be done about securing her love as soon as possible, as he could not now endure a future without her.

But Isobel was not as unaffected by his touch as he thought. She too struggled with conflicting feelings. They had been too long together, too long talking intimately, and it had drawn her closer to him in a way that was distinctly uncomfortable.

Their nearness to one another hadn't gone unnoticed. Aunt Bea was again making warning signals at her from across the room that plainly told of her disapproval. She would be difficult later and Isobel prepared herself for the lecture that was sure to come. It was impossible not to be aware of Carolina's stricken look as well and Isobel began to feel sorry for her. It would be an easy thing to excuse herself and move away from him, but something unknown and powerful held her there. Besides, there was no one else in the room she wished to talk to. It was plain he too was aware of being watched and Isobel saw him glance towards Carolina, frown darkly, bite his lip then turn back to face her.

He hurried to find something to say, anything to keep her with him.

'And the cubs, are they well? What will you do with them?'

'I intend to raise them till they are old enough to take care of themselves. That is, that was my plan before—'

Isobel looked away to hide the feelings that threatened to spill over.

He was very moved by her emotion and felt deeply for her pain. It had been so long since he had cared for anyone or anything, the sensation took him by surprise and he forgot his need to hide his admiration for her.

'You are a very remarkable girl.'

She laughed at that.

'Well, that's a change. I'm used to being told I'm a very annoying girl.'

Then Saunders walked past with Violet on his arm, their heads close together as they whispered secrets to each other that only lovers would care to hear.

Her mood darkened at once, and she looked up at Almeida. Defeat mingled with anger showed in her eyes.

'It seems I must sell – and soon, and the cubs will have an uncertain future without me.'

Now that grim reality was before her, she had difficulty keeping the tears out of her eyes.

'What will you pay for Silver Mist?'

He could not reply at first. Her brimming tears struck him to the heart. Then it occurred to him that he had the power to keep her at Silver Mist if he chose. If he refused to buy, then it was very likely she could not leave, at least not yet. It also occurred to him then that this was precisely what he had been doing all along.

He could have finalized the sale in an instant at their first meeting, but again he'd been dishonest with himself and had delayed the inevitable for as long as he could, finding excuse after excuse because he wanted to know more about the bewitching girl before him.

But now, now he knew for certain that he loved her, he would have to further delay the sale of Silver Mist despite his uncle desiring the place with an almost unhealthy obsession for years.

He cared nothing for what the little sister wanted and very much less for Saunders.

All he wanted was a chance to persuade the girl sitting

next to him to love him as he – he was sure of it now – loved her.

'Mr. Almeida? You are dreaming again…'

She smiled as she recognized their shared tendency to fall into daydreams. The thought occurred to her too that he was showing signs of being attracted to her. Other men had displayed that same dreaminess of expression when around her, but still with him she was unsure. He was a different creature to other men, and she reluctantly admitted to herself Phillipe Almeida had affected her emotionally and cracked just a fraction the thick crust she kept over her heart.

There was no time for Phillipe to reflect much on the beauty of her smile or how he could win her heart, as at that moment there was a great deal of commotion at the doorway of the ballroom as a gentleman walked into the room, glanced around at the assembled guests, then fixed his eyes immediately upon Phillipe, who seemed thrown into an immediate uneasiness by his presence.

Isobel looked at the figure walking slowly and with great dignity towards them.

He was a man of around seventy years old but appeared to be very strong still, with a powerfully broad chest and a ruddy, florid complexion. Everything about him exuded pride and undisputed power, along with the easy confidence of an old battle-worn lion, though his scars were well hidden under an expensive swallow-tail black suit.

Draped diagonally across his chest he wore a red and white striped ribbon with an elaborate blue and gold medal that seemed to officially justify his self-importance.

His thick white hair was worn combed back from his forehead in waves; a sharply pointed beard and a well-trimmed moustache gave added structure to his thin, refined face and high cheekbones.

His eyes though were narrowed and suspicious as they caught sight of his nephew and Isobel.

Everywhere the Indian servants bowed low before him as he seemed to expect, and they seemed frightened and watchful even though the old man was smiling. But there was something cruel and cynical about his smile, especially when he approached his nephew and stood before him.

'Phillipe.'

'Uncle, you are very late. I almost didn't expect you tonight…'

'I don't know why. I said I would return, and I wouldn't miss this night for anything.'

Isobel noticed Phillipe Almeida was becoming increasingly agitated.

'I would very much appreciate a few moments alone with you, Uncle. It's important and it can't wait.'

'There is no need, and it can wait.'

Then, turning to Isobel, he bowed in a peculiarly old-fashioned way. 'And to whom do I owe the pleasure?'

'This young lady is Miss Blanchard. She is our new neighbour at Silver Mist. Miss Blanchard, this is my uncle, Count Tiago Almeida.'

Isobel returned a cautious smile, but she felt herself go cold under the man's hard glare.

He looked at her closely for some time without saying a word, then he turned to his nephew and examined his face with a deep and searching scrutiny.

'I see…'

The count smiled, though again it was unpleasant and seemed loaded with a threat of some kind.

He gave a stiff bow in Isobel's direction, said he was charmed by her presence, then turned his back abruptly and made his way through the assembled guests to where Carolina was sitting with her mother. Isobel watched as they kissed each other in a familiar way, then the count took Carolina's hand and led her down the steps to the middle of the room.

Holding Carolina's hand in his own, he raised it in the air and the other in the direction of his nephew while commanding him to join them.

The count's voice boomed across the room.

'Come, my boy, the moment we have all waited for so long is upon us at last.'

There was a hushed silence as Phillipe seemed to stand frozen and aghast, till the old man laughed and broke the tension.

'The young man is obviously shy, so I will perform this most pleasant duty myself. I have gathered you all here this evening to announce the engagement of my nephew, Phillipe Santiago Almeida to our lovely Carolina Maria D'Souza, as was my nephew's stated desire, so I'm sure he will not begrudge me this moment.'

For a long moment Phillipe stood, unable to move, then he turned to look at Isobel with such naked despair, she was shocked. The count's voice boomed across the room.

'This is a most important moment. We have intermarried for generations and with this marriage...' He halted to give added meaning to his words, 'we can resume an almost unbroken tradition...'

Phillipe roused himself then, first glancing at Carolina who stood expectant but ashamed, with the beginnings of tears in her eyes, and at the silent crowd who were showing signs of a faint discomfort at his lack of action. He smiled at Isobel with what she thought was unusual tenderness in a man who appeared at times to be so cold, straightened his back and left her.

Isobel watched then as he took Carolina's hand in his own while everyone in the room erupted into clapping and cheering. Carolina clung to her handsome fiancé with an air of adoration and absolute ownership and Phillipe smiled at the girl and lifted her hand to kiss it in a very tender way.

Then, to save Carolina from further unwanted speculation, he gave a little speech that made Isobel believe she must have misread him after all.

'My uncle knows me and my desires very well, and I hope my dearest Carolina will forgive me for allowing him to speak for me even though I would have preferred to claim that honour for myself … in private,' he added, with a bitter curl of his lip as he glared at his uncle. 'However, the result is, I hope, to everyone's satisfaction.'

The look of devotion on the girl's face was plain for everyone to see, and if there was any doubt about the circumstances leading up to her very public engagement, she showed no signs of it.

Phillipe smiled throughout it all and redoubled his efforts to appear a happy man, even embracing Carolina and kissing her with some passion on the lips, much to the joy of the crowd. Isobel watched him from across the room, and when he lifted his eyes to hers for a stolen fleeting moment, written there she could see only despair and utter hopelessness.

Chapter Twenty-Eight

I sobel woke early the next morning, well before the other occupants of the house were stirring. She had not slept well in the ancient bed even though there was a level of luxury to the sheets and silken quilt she had never experienced before, and for a long time she had lain awake, thinking of the events of the night and especially of Phillipe Almeida.

With the sure instinct of a woman, she felt he had shown more than a little attraction towards her, but whatever she may think he was a lost man now. A little squeak of envy made itself felt in a most unnerving way. It was a new sensation as she had always received the attentions of men with a kind of amused pity, thinking herself immune to their masculine powers. But then, none of the men she had met before had the inescapable air of mystery he projected. It clouded her usually rational brain like a fog and made her want to move closer to him, both physically and emotionally, to entice out his secrets and tell him her own even though she would never have that chance now. That budding tenderness she felt for him must forever lie dormant now he was undeniably engaged to another woman.

Outside the window, a heavy mountain mist had almost enveloped the gardens, muffling all sound and making the house seem more than ever trapped in the stifling white cocoon of a lost world, but as she watched, the shapes of trees slowly emerged with the lifting fog and even showed a cheerful glimpse of the groves of red rhododendrons on the lawn, enticing her to dress quickly and take advantage of the pleasure of being alone to explore the gardens below.

The flagstone halls were empty and there was no one to ask the way out of the sleeping house, but she was imbued with a secret joy in perhaps doing something perilous and forbidden that no one else was likely to be doing at that hour.

It was something she had been fond of doing as a child – creeping out of bed before the household was awake and wandering in the garden in her nightgown and bare feet to splash in puddles, or walking out of the front gate then running back in again, or just lying on the damp ground and looking at the sky simply because she had been told not to.

Then later, at breakfast, she would take a furtive delight in the innocently unaware faces of her parents who, seeing her grinning face, would wonder for a moment what she was up to before going back to their toast and newspapers.

After trying several doors, she found one that opened onto the outside world and to a sudden fresh onslaught of cool, scented air that lifted her mood at once. A stony path she had seen from her window followed the massive banks of blue hydrangeas growing against the house to a path almost as wide as a road, leading away from the formal gardens to the fields, bordered on both sides by an avenue of darkest green cypress trees, thin and tall and half-hidden in the mist. Isobel walked briskly, following the road for what must have been a quarter of a mile, admiring on both sides the long, ordered rows of coffee plants growing under tall silver ash trees while dreaming of the pleasure she might have experienced herself in seeing her own crops under such neatly cultivated order if only she had the chance. But sell she must, and the sale must be finalized as soon as possible to prevent Saunders from interfering, as that possibility was unendurable.

Soon she began to think of turning back, as without warning the fog had returned thicker than before on the wave of a chilly breeze from the towering mountains nearby.

There was no sound except the harsh wailing of unseen crows surrounding her in the mist, filling her with a sense of dread, and she had begun to wish she had not left the safe confines of the house.

As visibility became more difficult, there were some horrible moments of feeling so disorientated she couldn't tell whether she was walking towards the house or away from it, but she clung to the line of trees in the hope they would eventually lead her to safety.

Despite having a beauty of their own, the cypress would always spell graveyards to her, especially as her last sighting of that species of tree was on the day she buried her father.

The trees were traditionally guardians of the dead and in this case too, to her surprise, the avenue of cypress ended by surrounding an ancient graveyard enclosed by a high stone wall and covered in yellowing lichen and green velvet moss.

For some time, she stood outside a pair of slowly rusting iron gates embellished, as everything was in this grand estate, with the Almeida family crest. She thought about entering, even though the swirling mist made it a forbidding place. Behind the gates were several elaborate crypts and a wide scattering of more humble headstones, some of them half fallen over and crumbling into dust. Growing in and out of the tombs was a sticky-looking morning glory that despite its lurid colour failed to give that forlorn place a more hopeful aspect.

Something moved in the nearby undergrowth and a sensation much like having ice-cold water poured down her back rooted Isobel to the spot.

She decided she would try to return to the house at once, and seek comfort in the firm reality of humanity, but when she looked behind her at the path, it had been almost completely swallowed by the creeping mist and the walk back seemed an even more daunting prospect than the comparative safety of the graveyard, so she began to wander amongst the tombstones while she waited for the fog to lift.

It was unnerving to see so many graves of women and girls with her own name amongst the Annas, Marias and Carlotas; but then she remembered the Portuguese queen Isabel, after whom those sleeping there were named and who had inspired so many young men to travel to new worlds in search of wealth and prestige. She was amused to see the name D'Souza repeatedly in the graveyard, cementing what she had already learned in the book by her bed. There was even a Carolina D'Souza, born Lisboa 1746, died 1794. A ripe old age compared to most of the others.

The larger crypts embellished with Romanesque pillars and topped with tall iron crosses were reserved for the superior Almeidas, many of whom bore the title of count.

One name stood apart from the others by the newness of the inscription and the wilting bouquet of flowers placed in a joyously painted Italian vase at the foot of the tomb. The wording was simple:

Silvia Lucia Maria Almeida
My Beloved
Born Palermo Sicily 1885
Died Casa Margarida 1905

Isobel realized then that it was Phillipe Almeida's wife who lay there in that lonely place. To her surprise she saw that the girl was a Sicilian, which explained Marco's brilliant, almost aquamarine eyes, so often found in that country. She heard the sound of faint sobbing on the wind that mingled with the cries of the crows that had begun to hop close to her feet in what seemed to be a threatening way.

Isobel laughed aloud to reassure herself, realizing she was playing a game that every now and again got out of control, by letting her imagination run wild and unfettered till she sometimes scared herself. She thought again of the letter she had found and those bitter words – *I hate him* – but couldn't imagine that the girl who lay under that simple headstone with that passionate epitaph – *My Beloved* – had lived her life in fear. Those words were the undying pledge of a love that would sustain, even after death.

But the image in her brain was so striking that Isobel trembled as the fine hairs on her arms stood up. It was almost as if the girl lying under that hard stone was calling out to her, pleading with her, but though the sight of the grave was unbearably poignant, her practical side rose to the surface and she was inspired more than ever, while it was within her power, to be as kind as she could be to the dead girl's child.

Then, without warning, she heard the sound of a twig snapping behind her and almost fainted with fright. Expecting any moment to be attacked by some beast, she steadied herself by clinging to the iron railing of the crypt and braced herself to confront whatever it was before her.

Then a familiar voice broke the silence.

'Miss Blanchard? Whatever are you doing here?'

He stood before her, nearly as drained of colour as she, casually dressed at that time of day in wool trousers and a thick jersey that matched his dark hair and eyes almost exactly. He held a large bunch of blue hydrangeas in one hand while the other he kept hidden, as it trembled slightly behind his back.

'But then again, I should not be surprised, knowing you as I do.'

'Have I done a very wrong thing in coming here?'

'No. I'm very happy you're here.'

His words unsettled her a little and she covered her nerves by being flippant.

'I'm glad you're here also. I was beginning to wonder how I might find my way back to the house.'

'I will take you back, if you will wait a moment.' Then he added, 'You have seen my wife's grave?'

He took the dying flowers out of the vase with great reverence, replaced them with the bouquet of hydrangeas, and filled the vase with a can full of water that was standing nearby. Then he kissed his own fingers and touched the stone under which the girl lay.

Isobel was moved by his actions but began to feel like she might be intruding.

'Would you like to be alone for a while to, you know, talk to her?'

He smiled at that.

'If you wish, but don't go far. I don't want you out of my sight.'

The words were spoken almost tenderly. Then, as if he had revealed too much of his feelings, he added, 'I haven't lost a guest at Casa Margarida yet, and I don't want to start now.'

Isobel waited by the tomb of Alphonso Almeida, *Morte 1597*, and wondered if it was the so-called Alphonso the Just, as she tried to decipher the Portuguese words written beneath, while at the same time occasionally looking up to watch Phillipe as he knelt in front of his wife's grave. At one time she thought she saw him brush his hand over his eyes, but it was so fleeting she couldn't be sure. Then, after a few moments, he slowly straightened, crossed himself and came to stand before her. Even though he smiled, she could detect signs of a deep sadness lingering in his eyes still. To her surprise, she felt the need to comfort him but could find no words powerful enough.

'I'm sorry. Her death must have been a great tragedy for you all.'

'It was. She was an angel really. Everyone says that about their loved ones, but in her case, it happens to be true.'

'I can believe it, having met your son.'

He said nothing at that, seemingly lost in thoughts of his own. Then, hesitatingly, he said, 'She was alone when she died and for that I can never forgive myself.'

'Not completely alone, surely?'

'No, a doctor was there, and my uncle, but I was away, and she had begged me not to leave her. I had no choice, and the baby came early. By the time I returned she had been buried two days. I kept looking for her in the house – I couldn't believe it – and in her place was a child who for a long time I could not love…'

He had an odd, angry expression on his face; he had slipped back in time and was reliving those moments once more. He spoke as if he were alone.

'And now I betray her memory by—' He halted and held his fist to his forehead as though in pain.

For Isobel, here was an answer for his sometimes-cold attitude towards Marco and his reluctance to re-marry. It was guilt that made him hesitant to commit himself to Carolina. Guilt and a passionate love no other woman could ever compete with. Pity overcame her and she hurried to reassure him.

'I can only imagine your suffering, but her death wasn't your fault. You must believe that.'

'Not directly, but in every other way it was. It is my curse, and I must live with it for the rest of my life.'

'Perhaps with a new life, some of the pain will be lessened.'

She couldn't say 'a new wife', but it was what she meant, even though she knew in her heart that Carolina D'Souza could never hope to fill the gap in the life he had lost.

He was looking at her again in a way that was disturbing, while various emotions swept over his face. Hope struggled with despair and suffering.

Then he brushed his thick dark hair off his forehead and frowned.

'Miss Blanchard, I…'

He looked for a while as though he might say something of importance, as he seemed to be struggling to find the words, but instead, after a few moments, he just smiled a little sadly and asked if she was hungry.

'I am famished.'

He took her arm and placed it firmly in his own, but he was unprepared for the thrill of pure lust he experienced at the mere touch of her warm skin. While he struggled with containing his desire, he fixed his eyes on her white hand as it rested on his arm, then he slowly raised his blazing, almost opaque eyes to hers while she stood both flushed and frozen, wondering if perhaps Phillipe Almeida wasn't a little mad.

'Mr. Almeida? You are a worse daydreamer even than I.'

He roused himself then and laughed, and said being hungry always made him lightheaded, but he thought how amused she would be if she should ever discover how close he had come to declaring his love for her, how he longed to tell her how he only felt alive when he was with her. But there was no choice; he must marry Carolina and be embalmed with her along with the rest of the Almeida and D'Souza clans. There was no other answer.

As they walked back to the house, the fog lifted and revealed that the fields had begun to fill with rows of labourers. A few of them looked up from their work and smiled at Isobel in a puzzled way, while others turned away at the sight of Almeida, showing by their actions that they were not pleased to see him.

'Is there something wrong? Everyone is usually so friendly...'

'There is a question in discussion now and it has not been

resolved to their satisfaction. I am working with my uncle to find an answer.'

He clearly didn't want to continue talking and he lapsed back into silence.

After a few moments, Isobel took the opportunity to mention the inevitable sale of Silver Mist.

'Will you speak to your uncle today about reaching a price we can both agree to? You know I am under great pressure to sell now, due to my sister's engagement.'

'I will speak to him if you wish it.'

'I don't wish it but it must be.'

He said nothing in reply, but her arm felt stiff and uncomfortable in his as she felt his body harden and saw his face become a cold mask. Even so, she found the courage to speak.

'Will you allow me a small favour?'

'If I can…'

'May I take your son with me back to Silver Mist, just for a week?'

'I'm not sure. His lessons…'

'I will speak nothing but French and English to him, if it makes you feel any better.'

'It's not so easy as that.'

'Please. It would make me very happy, and him too, I suspect.'

He turned to face her, a patch of high colour on his cheeks.

'Are you saying my son isn't happy?'

'Well, not unhappy exactly… I want him to see the cubs, and you will be busy with your fiancée. I'm sure you will have many plans.'

His face changed as he remembered. He had forgotten

about Carolina and for a few deliriously happy moments he had been pretending that Isobel was his fiancée.

'My fiancée. Of course.'

Again, she wondered at his manner. It was certainly not the behaviour of a man in love.

He began to walk faster and she had to hurry to keep up. She was innocent, but every word she uttered was like a nail being hammered into his flesh.

'Yes, take Marco,' he finally said. He almost added, 'Then at least one of us will be happy.'

Chapter Twenty-Nine

The afternoon brought another celebration of the formal engagement in the form of a lunch party under the huge magnolias on the lawn in front of the house. Even though Isobel longed to nurse her wounds alone at Silver Mist, it became impossible to leave now. It would cause offence, and Aunt Bea's fine English manners would have none of it. Isobel too was held by a curious desire to see how Phillipe Almeida behaved with the newly engaged Carolina in the cold light of day. She had not forgotten the strange conflicting expression in his eyes the night before.

The guests and the betrothed couple were arranged around a long table covered with stiff white damask linen and set with silver cutlery that had been in the family for centuries.

There should have been an air of happy celebration but, curiously, the sumptuous lunch was subdued, mainly due to the imposing presence of the old count who sat at the head of the table next to his cousin, the countess, his leonine head erect, his hard, sharp eyes keeping a close eye on the events while managing to put a damper over everyone's spirits.

The countess too seemed to be struggling with a range of emotions and it was clear to Isobel she was only just tolerating her daughter's engagement and kept up an air of pained haughty disapproval.

On her right sat Phillipe who Isobel noticed was drinking heavily for the middle of the day, but only showed signs of his overindulgence with the occasional bitter laugh. Most of the time he maintained the image of tepid joy, except when he seemed to come back to reality with a start and remember where he was and what he was there for.

It was only when Isobel wasn't looking that he stole furtive looks in her direction, and a perceptive eye could see the regret and pain written on his face. Then he seemed to shake himself and straighten his back as though he had an unpleasant task in front of him.

Aunt Bea watched over the table with her usual close scrutiny, but Isobel couldn't help but notice she seemed thoughtful and distracted in some way, especially when her gaze fell upon Violet who seemed to be enjoying with an uncritical eye the pomp and splendour laid out for her pleasure. Saunders had given her a huge sapphire ring he'd had made especially by a master craftsman in Panjim. He said the ring had arrived at Cardamon Hills the day before, making it plain he was sure Violet would accept him when he asked her – and that fact irritated Isobel to a new level. He could at least have the decency to be a little insecure about Violet's answer.

Every now and then Violet held the sapphire up to the light

to admire the flashing prism of colours on her still childlike hand. It was only when her eyes met Isobel's almost tragic expression that she flinched, while a fleeting shadow of doubt clouded her happiness.

But she pouted prettily and turned away, making a great show of being hurt.

Harry Saunders broke into the general well-bred murmuring with a loud shout across the table.

'Well, Almeida, have you come to an arrangement about Silver Mist yet with Miss Isobel there? You must admit, old boy, you are being tiresomely slow about it. As I was saying to my fiancée' – here he smiled and put his mark of ownership on Violet by squeezing her around the waist – 'it might be best to leave the whole thing in my hands. Get to the crux of the matter, so to speak.'

The old count turned his head to the right and left as though seeking an answer there.

'What is this? You are saying Silver Mist is for sale?'

Saunders was becoming increasingly belligerent.

'Well yes, that is, it was. Now listen to me, Almeida—'

The count ignored him and, turning to his nephew, he said in a voice that showed his irritation, 'Why haven't I been told of this?'

Phillipe's words were clipped as he fought to control his anger. 'This is not the time or place to talk business, Uncle. We have been forgetting this is supposed to be a celebration of my engagement to our dear Carolina.' Then, lowering his voice, he murmured, 'We will discuss the matter further later. Now—'

Isobel could just hear his uncle's angry response.

'I think you are forgetting who is in charge here.'

Saunders had drunk a little too much of the count's good

wine and was spoiling for a fight. His voice rang out across the table again.

'Then when is a good time? Seems to me you've been putting things off for too long, trying to put it over the ladies here.' He waved his hand at Isobel who was fighting to control her temper for the sake of good manners.

'And so,' Saunders left a pause to allow his following words to have the most impact, 'you've had your chance. I've decided to buy the place. It will be in the family after all, and later, if I decide to sell,' he said, as he inclined his head towards the count, who was making no attempt now to hide his fury, 'you will be the first to know.'

Then he raised his glass and smiled around the table. 'There, it's settled!'

The old count glared at Saunders and then at his nephew. He was about to rise from the table, but Phillipe put out a hand to stop him.

'Please, Uncle.'

The count sat down with a slow but menacing movement and then emptied his glass of wine with a cold smile, but it was plain to everyone his mood had changed for the worse.

Isobel had to crush a desire to scream out her fury but instead she confined herself to a few cold words.

'This matter has not been settled at all, at least not by you. Violet and I alone will decide on the sale of Silver Mist.'

'But Isobel, you must admit it's a wonderful plan, and Harry has such a great deal of experience in farming. He will put someone in to run the place for us.'

'Thank you, Violet, but I think Mr. Almeida is right. This is no place to discuss business.'

Saunders blundered on, fired by Violet's enthusiasm.

'Don't you worry, Miss Isobel, I'll give you a thousand pounds more than Almeida here offered you in the first place, but after all, you will be living with us at Cardamon Hills, and what will you need money for? That is till some lucky man takes you off our hands, and I hear you already have at least one admirer waiting in the side-lines.'

Isobel struggled to hide her fury. 'Please, Mr. Saunders, you go too far.'

Phillipe had by now risen to his feet, almost overwhelmed with the thought that Isobel had a suitor. But then, of course a girl like her would be attractive to other men. He was a fool not to have thought of it before, and he could scarcely keep the disappointment out of his voice.

'I think that's enough, Saunders. We are embarrassing our guests. We will continue this discussion later.'

'What the devil do you mean, Almeida? I'm making a legitimate offer here. You've had your chance, so why are you so damned— Excuse me, ladies…'

Then Aunt Bea hit her wine glass loudly with her knife, stopping Saunders in his tracks and calling everyone else to attention, including the count and countess who were mortified by her daring. Their reaction concerned her very little; she had been watching the events all along with a grim smile.

'Forgive me, Mr. Almeida, but as this question has arisen at this, I agree, most unfortunate time – and for that, Senorita D'Souza and my dear Count, I humbly apologize – I will put a stop to any speculation once and for all. Silver Mist is not for sale.'

Here, like Saunders, she paused to allow her words to make maximum impact.

'Violet has often expressed her desire to sell as soon as possible, though Isobel wishes to maintain control of her half of the estate, making it impossible to sell outside of the family. Therefore, I have agreed to buy Violet's share.'

Her lie was delivered so smoothly there was no question of any doubt of her statement.

'Well! I call that damned cunning.' Saunders was bitterly aggrieved. An estate worth at least six thousand pounds that he was about to get for three thousand, with a lovely wife to boot, had slipped through his fingers. He knew the count wanted it and he had planned to sell it in the following year for ten thousand or perhaps more if he could get it. He kept the fury out of his voice when he spoke to Violet. 'Did you know about this my dear? Surely you would have told me?'

'Of course not darling. Isobel? Is this true?' Violet felt as much for her fiancé as he did himself.

'Well, yes,' she lied, trying desperately to hide her own surprise, 'I was going to tell you after lunch. I think after all it is the perfect solution. I knew you would be pleased.'

There was just a hint of triumph in Aunt Bea's voice when she spoke.

'So, in answer to your question, Count, no, Silver Mist is not for sale. Now, I'm afraid my nieces and I must leave you to your celebrations. It's been delightful but we must be back at our home before dark.' Her extra emphasis on the word *our* caused Isobel to experience a great swell of emotion. Her fears were laid to rest at last.

Aunt Bea rose from the table with great majesty then inclined her head ever so slightly at the count who was almost purple with suppressed rage. Isobel realized then with a little start that her aunt had become what could be described as a handsome and dignified woman.

'Isobel, if you would accompany me to my room?'

Isobel was full of admiration, for her dear aunt – and she had no argument with that term now – had saved an uncomfortable situation and had also rescued her from a future reliant on a man she hated.

'What a cool liar you are Aunt Bea. I'm just sorry I didn't think of it myself. You are serious about buying Silver Mist?'

'Most certainly.'

'Well now that's settled, would you consider eventually selling me your half? At a loan of course. I'm sure I could pay you back within a few years. You see, I would like to be independent...'

'Of me you mean.'

'Well, yes.'

'I'm not such a fool that I could imagine you would be happy with having to consult me over every decision regarding Silver Mist, so to save inevitable arguments I agree, but I want you to pay me back, every penny of it.'

'I will. I want to make Silver Mist a success. I didn't realize quite how much I loved it till I was about to lose it.'

'I confess I'm fond of the place too, but I have other plans, so Silver Mist is yours, as long as you pay me back, and I don't mind admitting that I was wrong about Saunders, and you were right. I don't want that bore being in control of your life as well as Violet's.'

At that, Isobel kissed her aunt's cheek with real meaning.

'Thank you. Thank you.'

'No need to make a fuss. You know how I loathe all public

manifestations of feeling. I have bought us some time, that's all, and now it's up to us both to do something about saving Violet from a fate she will most certainly live to regret.'

Chapter Thirty

Not everyone who drove away from Casa Margarida was in a pleasant frame of mind. Harry Saunders was still stung by being outsmarted by Aunt Bea, Violet was confused as to whether she should be pleased or not to have her long-awaited dowry and Isobel was relieved to be leaving a house where she'd scarcely had a comfortable moment. She was unnerved still by the words in that desperate letter, and Phillipe Almeida's engagement to a woman he was clearly not in love with.

Almeida's genuine emotion at the graveside of his wife had almost changed her opinion of him but she also suspected him of having a basic lack of character, and she could never admire a weak man – or perhaps even worse, a man made brutal by uncontrolled jealousy, or motivated by marrying a woman's fortune. She had seen the consequences of marrying a flawed man and how love had at first blinded her own mother to her husband's faults.

Before now, love and Phillipe Almeida was something that

had never crossed her mind, especially as he would soon be married to another woman, and yet there was something between them now that had not been there before, something indefinable and powerful.

The happiest of all was Marco, who had endured a few uncomfortable minutes when it had looked as though his holiday with the lovely Miss Blanchards might not happen due to the interference of the countess, who believed he should stay at home and study. To his great surprise, his father had been equally insistent he should go, and even gave his son a hug and a kiss when he left – an unusual event in the life of the lonely child. Now he was safely through the iron gates of his home and sitting between Isobel and Violet who, both being equally smitten with his charm, were tickling him to make him laugh.

The tickling was pleasant enough but there was to be a great surprise, and his six-year-old brain could think of and talk of nothing else till they arrived at Silver Mist just as twilight was beginning to descend.

Despite Violet encouraging him to stay, Saunders was anxious to get back to his own estate, having been gone for nearly three days.

Parting with Saunders was tinged with more than a touch of relief from everyone at Silver Mist except Violet, who lingered on the terrace, finding it difficult to let him go. She was trying to recapture some of the first dazzling and euphoric sensations of being in love that had somehow begun to fade with the descending twilight.

She told herself she was tired, and that Isobel's obvious dislike of her fiancé was beginning to have some effect. Almost in an act of desperation, as they were about to part, she reached out for his hand and asked with a touch of anxiety in her voice whether he still loved her.

He answered her question by pulling her to him and kissing her on the lips with an ardour that bordered on brutality, causing her to gaze up at him, entrapped, all fears extinguished and with a renewed and breathless adoration. For a little seed of what she vaguely recognized as sexual passion had been ignited in her very conventional soul and now she longed for more.

He left reluctantly, with promises to return as soon as possible. As Violet watched him disappear down the drive, she sat in one of the planter chairs on the terrace to think about her future with an untainted pleasure; inside the house was her sister, who had the uncanny gift of quashing her happiness with one quick shrewd glance in her direction.

Violet sat for a few minutes, suspending her hatred of the place she had fought so bitterly against, and allowing herself for the first time to really appreciate her surroundings. It was pleasant to breathe in the heady fragrance of the strange flowers surrounding the terrace, though to her mind they could never compete with the delicate scent of roses and lavender of her home country, but it was pleasant enough and she was still tingling with the memory of her Harry's burning lips on her own. For once she was content, and if it weren't for Isobel's penetrating eyes, she could almost be happy.

Then a sound coming from somewhere in the front of the property made her start and she leapt to her feet, her hand on her heart, ready to run through the open front door, but it proved to be only the gentle canter of a horse and rider approaching the house.

She cried out in alarm, her voice trembling. The man came closer and the light from the house fell on his face.

'Mr. Cameron! What are you doing here?'

'Violet! I mean, Miss Blanchard...'

'How wonderful it is to see you.'

It was plain she meant it and his face broke out into a broad smile.

'I've come to say goodbye. There have been some changes back home that require my presence.'

'Oh. You're leaving India? Nothing serious, I hope?'

Charlie thought for a moment. His news was too momentous to talk about lightly, and he was too tired to do it justice. He decided it could wait.

'I don't want to talk about me. I'm so glad to see you! What a pretty place. Are you happy here?'

'Well, yes and no...'

'Your sister wrote to me and told me you had broken off your engagement. I hope it has not been too painful for you?'

A flush of shame first swept over her features, then relief that Isobel had lied. Charlie at least would never know how she had been jilted.

'All that is over now.'

He searched her face for signs she might be hiding her true feelings.

'You are quite well then?'

'Yes, yes. It was all for the best really.'

There was an uncomfortable silence while they both struggled with what was unsaid.

'I passed some men on the road coming here ... a man by the name of Saunders said he knew you all. He pointed me in the right direction.'

'Saunders?' For the past few minutes Violet had forgotten he existed. 'Oh! Did he say anything … about me? I mean, us?'

'No, only that he would see me again as he planned to return here soon.'

'Oh, yes, he visits us often.'

Charlie smiled in a knowing way.

'I'm sure he does.'

Violet felt it was up to her now to enlighten Charlie, but she thought it might appear insensitive to talk about her new fiancé when the other had only just a minute ago been dismissed into history.

'We must not keep the others waiting any longer. They'll be so glad to see you.'

The scene awaiting Charlie as he stepped into the drawing room was a charming one.

Isobel sat on the floor in front of the fire with a baby leopard in her lap and another rolling on the floor in front of her. At her feet sat a little boy with huge blue eyes so enthralled with the cubs he could hardly speak and barely noticed the untouched slice of cake he held in his hand. Monty was making strange little playful leaps and barks at the cubs then retreating, his tail stiff with excitement.

Aunt Bea had seated herself in her favourite chair with Billy half asleep by her side. Mary was bringing in a tray of tea and scones from the kitchen. Then as she looked up and saw Charlie, she almost dropped them.

'Mr. Cameron! This is a pleasure!'

Isobel was the first to rush forward, still with the cub in her arms, to kiss him on the cheek with real delight, drawing him towards the fire as she did so.

'Where have you come from? What a wonderful surprise!'

'Well, you did ask me to come as soon as I could. I had no idea it would be so soon ... but what have you got here?'

He was entranced by the cubs, picking them up one by one to fondle them and declaring them to be beautiful examples of their species. He ruffled the hair of little Marco who gazed up at him with obvious adoration as he listened to the explanations of why the child was there.

'You all seem to have very quickly become part of the life here. It suits you especially Isobel.'

'Thank you, Charlie. I may call you Charlie?'

She smiled at him, tilting her head on one side as was her habit, her grey eyes holding him with her gaze.

'Of course, we are old friends.'

His voice almost purred his reply, and Violet looked up with a start. She was certain her sister was flirting with him. It was a new sensation to experience and even though she knew it was unjust there was more than a tinge of jealousy in her heart.

He was even more handsome than Isobel remembered; there was a new extra confidence in his manner that hadn't been there before, and she especially liked his warm brown eyes and his Scots burr that gave her a little thrill of pleasure when he spoke. Unconsciously, as she looked at his fine figure, she tidied her hair and drew a chair up close to him to hand him a teacup.

Violet kept her eyes firmly cast down; her cheeks flushed scarlet. There was an unspoken tension in the air that no one seemed willing to break.

Isobel asked him how long he could stay and urged him to treat the house as his own. Then she began to talk about her plans for Silver Mist and her intention to cultivate a crop of coffee hopefully by the coming October. Then, being reminded of the circumstances that had brought about her need to take the inheritance more seriously, her face collapsed into a frown.

'Has Violet told you her news?'

From the other side of the room there was a distinct intake of breath.

'Isobel, it can wait till tomorrow.'

'Why?' she said. 'It's joyful news, after all.' A faint tinge of sarcasm slipped through with a smile. 'Violet is engaged … again and will be married soon – as early as next month.'

Charlie Cameron was at first pale, then as he regained his usual ruddy colour there was a distinct curl of his handsome lip.

'The gentleman I met on the way here, I suppose.'

'Yes, Harry Saunders. He owns a big estate near here in Karnataka.'

'A fine man, I'm sure.'

'Yes, he is. It all happened so fast.' Violet tried to be firm, but her voice wavered a little against the silence of the others.

'Well, I offer my congratulations.' With what looked like a great deal of effort, he stood up and went towards her, kissing her on the cheek, though he could not look into her eyes. 'I hope you will be very happy.'

They spent the rest of the evening choosing names for the cubs, and it was Marco who decided on Priti for the female, as he thought she was so pretty, and Sami for the male named after Samson as he was so strong, but it was only after the boy was tucked up in Isobel's room with Monty for company that

Charlie relayed his news with a bitterness of tone that surprised them all.

He had intended to keep the news to himself for a few days at least, but something in him wanted to hurt as well as delight. He was not so completely blind to Violet's faults that he wasn't aware of her love of the finer things in life, and his resentment towards her gave the announcement a special extra relish.

Against the greatest of odds, and against any expectations, his cousin, Lord Cameron, a young man who was childless, had been killed suddenly in a hunting accident in Scotland and Charlie was now the present Lord Cameron, and owner of ten thousand acres of land, various minor properties, and the family estate outside of Edinburgh.

The news of him acceding to the title of Lord Cameron was received with varying responses from the family.

Isobel simply laughed and said he was most deserving, but her behaviour towards him didn't alter; she treated him the same as she had always done and for that he respected her.

Aunt Bea made the effort to get to her feet and curtsy in a most deferential way even though he had protested loudly. Then her eyes went towards Violet, and she sighed, making no secret of her disappointment, but almost instantly she fixed her gaze on her other niece and gave an imperceptible nod in her direction as though giving Isobel the licence to make Charlie her own. Isobel acknowledged the look with a frown, then duly ignored it.

Violet was almost silenced with shock by the news, and Isobel could see she was besieged by a range of emotions. But out of sheer pride, her pretty face was almost devoid of expression as she stared down at her hands and struggled with the thoughts that were torturing her. She had rejected Charlie because of what she thought was her love of John Fitzherbert, but who was he to her now? Isobel had been right after all. He had always been a flimsy excuse for a man; compared to Charlie Cameron he was merely a silly boy.

Now, judging by the way Charlie looked at Isobel, and she at him, there was every possibility he would transfer his former affection to her sister, and she wondered how she would be able to bear it.

Now it felt as though the sun had gone down and she was left in the cold. She felt him withdraw from her emotionally, leaving her with a pained emptiness she hurried to fill with thoughts of Harry Saunders; the feel of his arms around her as he held her tight, and the way he had kissed her when he had left her that evening.

Chapter Thirty-One

C harlie watched Isobel as she sat before the table in the dining room, her head bent over the old estate books. Feeling his eyes upon her, she looked up and smiled and persuaded him with that smile to stay a little longer, despite the need for him to return to Scotland as soon as possible. He wondered at the power she seemed to have over him – almost the same power Violet had exerted over him in the past, but now he turned his face away from Violet. He was disappointed in her. He saw her now as still very sweet and lovely but weak, and with her engagement to a man who was, according to Isobel, not worthy of her, his estimation of her had sunk, never to be redeemed.

It helped that Charlie rarely spent a moment alone with her, as Isobel monopolized his time with her future plans for the estate.

Almost as soon as breakfast was over, Isobel, sometimes dressed in young Quimp's jodhpurs and hat, set off with Mr. Singh and Charlie for the fields, in order to calculate how many workers they would need to bring in the crop in the coming October.

Often Aashi accompanied them as, with her intimate knowledge of plants, she was useful in pointing out what was edible on the estate and what was not. It was due to her that a valuable hoard of wild vanilla plants almost ready for picking was discovered almost hidden in a thicket of coconut palms. But that crop was for the future, as even after harvesting, the vanilla would take nearly six months to cure and give up their sticky fragrant syrup.

Charlie at first laughed at Isobel's jodhpurs but soon saw the sense in them; he came to admire her long striding steps and neat figure as she walked through the fields, stopping every now and then to pull off a dead leaf or admire a bloom. There seemed to be absolutely no vanity at all in her manner and he had never before met a woman like her. She pulled her hair back off her face when it was hot and gathered it in a hasty knot which might have made other women look plain but only managed to make her appear more beautiful.

Her elegance dazzled him, and he found himself mesmerized by her movements, watching her slim hands as they played around her face or smoothed her hair. He admired her narrow waist pulled in with the mannish belt, and the shape of her body, so firm and youthful.

He began to think it would be very easy to fall in love with her.

Then there were the long evenings, when after bathing she would change into a dress and amuse him with her wit or ask him questions about his family, encouraging him to open up and talk about his life before coming to India.

Because of belonging to the poorest branch of the Cameron

family and being the only child of a widow, his childhood had been a lonely and almost loveless one.

Now he basked in the warm, homely atmosphere created at Silver Mist and he knew it was largely because of Isobel and her forceful personality.

His eyes followed her lithe, swift figure as she moved around the house seeing to the servants and making sure his favourite dishes were on the table. She often hummed a tune while filling the vases with flowers, before spreading the afternoon tea on a fresh white cloth under the tamarind tree on what passed as the front lawn, where the family would meet to talk and laugh, but always her eye was upon him, seeing to his comfort and making it almost impossible to part with her even though he knew he soon must.

At times he broached the subject of leaving but his words were met with a pleading look and a hasty, 'No, not yet please. Just a few days more...' and he would comply without too much argument, telling himself that Scotland could wait as there was nothing there but responsibility and formality and inevitable loneliness.

It was easier to warm himself in the sun and the rays of love and esteem from the entire household and to wonder at the loveliness of Isobel, and if it would be possible to ever live without her.

The most pleasant hours were spent with Marco and the leopard cubs in rambles around the garden where they would tumble about together, the child in a delirium of pure delight, often ending with Isobel and the boy lying together on the grass, the cubs' plump little bodies rolling about while nibbling at Isobel and Marco's ears with both in fits of laughter.

Charlie would smoke a cigarette as he watched, longing to join them in their tangle of play but knowing Aunt Bea would find it unseemly. As it was, she often called out an order in an attempt to recall Isobel to more ladylike behaviour.

'Isobel, behave yourself! You're making the boy too excited. He'll never sleep. For goodness' sake girl, your skirt! Pull it down at once!' But always there was a hint of kind indulgence and a general amusement at the happiness of the child who had become a favourite with everyone.

But it was always Isobel that Marco was drawn to the most and the more time they spent together the more he felt secure enough to reveal his childish secrets to her.

His declarations usually came out of nowhere, as was the case one morning when he abruptly stopped in his play then stood silently before her, his huge blue eyes full of anxious appeal.

Usually, it was a small announcement like his great love of chocolate or how Monty liked to have his tummy tickled, but this time his little face was more serious.

She had learned to recognize his moods and gently prompted him to speak.

'Is there something you want to tell me?'

'Yes, there is.'

'Well, don't be afraid.'

He smiled very sweetly and moved a step closer to play with the fabric of her dress, though all the while keeping his eyes lowered.

'I like secrets. I have a lot of secrets. And I like to do things without anyone knowing. Sometimes I hide under Papa's desk when he writes his letters.'

Isobel laughed as a sudden thought occurred to her. Of course! Who else could it be?

'Was it you who sent me the butterfly? Did you put that pretty butterfly in the envelope?'

He considered for a while, then his face broke out into a delighted smile.

'Yes, I wanted to give you a present.'

'But why? You didn't even know me.'

'Because when I asked Papa who he was writing to he said to a lady who lived in a faraway, very cold country that hardly ever saw sunshine. So, when he wasn't looking I put it there. I thought it might cheer you up.'

'It did more than that. Your present brought me here. I really believe I wouldn't have come otherwise.'

'Then I'm glad you did. I was praying for someone like you.'

'But why?'

'To be my mama, of course.'

She was so touched that she leaned down and kissed his sweet face. He smelled like a warm mixture of jam and garden soil.

'Miss Carolina will be your mama, and she will love you as much as I do.'

He looked at her then with such naked delight, tears came into her eyes.

'Do you really love me?'

'Everyone at Silver Mist loves you – Monty and the cubs and Billy too.'

He hid his face in her dress, too overcome to speak. She understood the depth of his emotion and left him there as she smoothed his hair, till a few seconds later Monty broke the poignant moment by rushing up with a ball in his mouth. He stood before them both looking particularly silly, then rudely demanded to be taken notice of, as a result of which Marco seemed to forget everything else except the joy of tearing wildly around the garden with Monty in hot pursuit.

Like most children, Marco lived in the moment and preferred not to think about the inevitability of leaving Silver Mist, but it came upon them all in a most unexpected way just when Isobel and Marco were at their rowdiest and when the cubs had taken hold of Isobel's long skirt and refused to let it go, pulling her to the ground and chewing on her petticoat, pieces of which were scattered about the grass.

Charlie was laughing, and even Violet, who was so often silent and withdrawn, was amused in a quiet way.

Charlie saw the grand carriage first as it stopped in front of the terrace, but Isobel by now was lying face down, her hair loose, with Marco sitting on her back. Both her boots had been kicked off and lay scattered across the grass.

He called out in his soft Scotch burr, 'It appears we have visitors – and very grand they are too.'

Coming across the lawn, he saw a young woman he thought attractive in a way that was not at first apparent, but he thought she had an unusual face and a sweet smile and something very rare: an absolute devotion to the man by her side. She had her arm slipped into his and was smiling up at him with a pure and transparent love that was impossible to hide, but Charlie was sure too, with the instinct of one man towards another, that her partner didn't share her feelings.

As he walked towards the group under the tree, the stranger seemed to have forgotten about the girl by his side and kept his eyes firmly fixed on Isobel, who at that moment was trying to remove the laughing Marco from her back. Again, with the insight of a fellow man, Charlie could read interest there and a tender amusement. If there was love there too it was not yet quite clear, but Charlie felt compelled to make a public claim on Isobel by moving quickly and taking both her hands to help her to her feet.

For a long moment they stood close together, Charlie still holding her hands while looking into Isobel's eyes as though he was engrossed by her, as indeed he was. Then, as though coming out of a trance, they both turned together to greet the visitors, with Charlie at first reluctant to let go of Isobel's hand.

Isobel regained her composure first.

'Mr. Almeida, you are two hours early and I will never forgive you for it. Marco, have you nothing to say to your papa?' The child hung back, clearly disappointed to realize he must return to his home; a lonely home without animals.

'*Bonjour*, Papa. You see I have been studying French with Miss Issie while I've been away.'

'I see you have.' He smiled.

'You have no kiss for your papa?' Isobel coaxed.

The child stepped forward and kissed his father, who ruffled his hair in return.

'You have no kiss for me?'

Carolina leaned forward and Marco gave her a hasty dry kiss on her cheek before ignoring the proffered face of the countess. He went back to hide behind Isobel's skirts.

'He has been spoilt,' the countess said before turning to her daughter with her peculiar nasal whine. 'You must be firmer with the boy. He is obviously out of control.'

Isobel gave Marco a gentle squeeze behind her skirt.

'You have come at a wonderful time for us. We have a

guest. This is our dear friend, Lord Charles Cameron. Senor Phillipe Almeida, Countess D'Souza, and Miss D'Souza. Miss D'Souza has recently become engaged to Mr. Almeida.'

Charlie let out an almost audible sigh of relief and felt secure enough now to take Isobel's arm and slip it through his own.

The old countess was impressed with the title and inclined her head with a cold smile; her daughter also condescended to smile and curtsy and even wished him good afternoon. At first Phillipe said nothing, but his eyes flashed back and forth between Charlie and Isobel as he attempted to assess their relationship.

'You are here for a long visit?'

'As long as they will have me. The thought of returning to Scotland now is a dreary one.'

Then he looked at Isobel with such meaning in his smile that Phillipe was sure the young man was in love with her and would certainly take her away from him.

The thought made him resentful, and almost surly. He wanted to leave at once but there were civilities to observe. He must endure an hour or two of polite conversation in which he had no interest, while his heart was breaking.

Time passed slowly for the party from Casa Margarida, and it was a struggle also for Isobel to avoid the long silences and keep the wheels of conversation turning in the face of Phillipe's sullen manner, then, after exhausting all talk of

Marco's week at Silver Mist, the conversation turned to the cubs.

Phillipe thought they were charming but was concerned about their future.

'You must be careful, Miss Blanchard, they do not become too attached to you.' Here he couldn't help a wry smile; he had become attached to her himself after only a few meetings, and the thought of parting with her forever was already impossible for him.

He was thinking of himself when he spoke again. 'There will come a time when they must survive without you.'

Everyone noticed the break in his voice, but he covered it up quickly with a small cough.

He suggested then that it would be a wise idea to take them walking in the jungle every day, before they were fully weaned, to begin training them to kill other animals in order to stay alive themselves.

Isobel listened to his advice and was grateful, seeing the sense of it. She turned to Charlie and asked him if he would accompany her on the walks.

'It will be the same as walking in the park in South Kensington, except we will have to train our pets to attack other animals rather than restrain them!'

He laughed and said he would be delighted, and Phillipe, longing to be alone on such walks with her himself, lapsed into a moody silence.

Charlie, after failing to engage Phillipe with any topic at all, gave up at last to settle back to smoke a cigarette and observe the party before him. He was almost certain now Almeida was in love with Isobel, though he was sure Isobel did not reciprocate his feelings. He could tell by the intensity in the man's eyes whenever he looked in her direction and he wondered why Almeida had become engaged to the strange young girl by his side who clung to him even though he looked at any moment like he might throw her off and storm out of the room.

Marco was beyond speech and could only wistfully pat Monty, who had crept up to lie on the couch next to him. It was only with the promise that he could visit again in a few weeks that he could be convinced to leave Silver Mist at all.

Phillipe had retreated into a thorny shell and could hardly be persuaded to come out of it. His was a black presence at the table and except for an occasional word of thanks when passed a cup or plate of food, which he scowled at, he kept his lips firmly closed.

There was a moment when his interest was sparked at the sight of Constanza who, when bringing the coffee, bobbed him a quick curtsy.

'It is Constanza, is it not? I didn't know you worked here.'

'Yes, sir.'

'I am pleased you have found such a pleasant place to work…'

'I am very happy here, sir.'

She seemed uneasy in Almeida's company and hurried out of the room.

Isobel was intrigued. 'You know Constanza?'

'She didn't tell you? She worked for my family when I was a child. She was very kind to me, and then later when I came back from Italy with my wife…' He couldn't help releasing a sigh. 'My wife was very fond of her. It is years ago now.' This recollection seemed to cast him into a deeper gloom and for the rest of the time he was unreachable.

After they had left, Isobel asked Constanza why she had left Casa Margarida.

'After that lovely girl died in such a terrible way, I could not bear that house. It is an evil place, Madam.'

'Whatever do you mean, Constanza?'

'The old man … I hate him!'

At first, she couldn't be persuaded to say any more and seemed afraid to do so, but then the words came tumbling out in a torrent.

'I was working for the Almeidas when I was a young girl and Mr. Phillipe was just a little boy. His mother, the Countess Francesca, was very beautiful but also kind to everyone in the house and I loved her. Mr. Phillipe's father was alive then and I have never seen a man more in love with his wife.'

Then Constanza bit her lip and frowned, as though reminded of something unpleasant.

'Life was good at Casa Margarida and would have always been, I think, if it weren't for Mr. Phillipe's uncle who came from Lisbon to help with the running of the estate. I remember like yesterday as he was then, all smiles and flattery…'

'So this is the present Count Tiago, who owns the estate now?'

'Yes, and to my mind it is unfair. Casa Margarida should belong to Mr. Phillipe, but the will left everything to his uncle.'

'So Phillipe Almeida's father died?'

'Yes, when Mr. Phillipe was a little boy, and everything changed. Mr. Phillipe's mother was nothing now.'

'But surely that can't be right. There was no challenge to the will?'

'I think there was, but the lawyer in Panjim said it was all legal.'

'And what did Mr. Phillipe's father die of?'

'It was not certain. Some thought the cholera – we call it the *haiza*

– but it was never clear. He must have been out of his mind to make such a will. I know she wanted to leave but he watched her all the time.'

'And was he cruel to the boy as well? Mr. Phillipe, I mean.'

'Yes, Madam. He would have to stay in his room often without food if his uncle thought he misbehaved, though he never did, not really. He was a very quiet little boy, and I think very unhappy. I think that is what drove the countess away at last. One morning she was gone. She ran away while the count was in Madras on business and took Master Phillipe with her.'

Isobel was sure now that the letter she found was from Phillipe's mother and her fears were not for her husband's treatment of her, but for her brother-in-law's.

'At first he took his pistols and left at once for Bombay but he was too late, as she had caught a ship back to Europe. He was away from Casa Margarida for a few months while he went to Italy to look for her, and it was the best time for us all there. At that time some of the bonded workers also ran away—'

Isobel interrupted at this point.

'Bonded workers?'

'Yes, Madam. They have taken the debts of their parents and must work till it is agreed the debt has been paid, but it is never paid because they earn no money.'

'They must be the men I've seen in the fields at Casa Margarida. Their eyes are full of hate.'

'Yes, Madam. They are very angry but the old count refuses still.'

'But surely it's illegal. The government here must be aware of what the count is doing.'

'The government is very corrupt, Madam, and he has many friends in it.'

Isobel thought of the guests at the engagement party. They had seemed disreputable to her at the time, and now she was sure of it.

'But Mr. Phillipe, surely, he does not believe in keeping things this way?

'I do not know, Madam. I think he has tried many times. The house servants say they hear him arguing with his uncle many times. But nothing changes…' She stopped then, before she said too much.

'And did the countess ever return with her son?'

'No, she did not. I do not know what happened to her, but Mr. Phillipe came back with his own wife twenty years later. He had been brought up in Italy. He met his wife there and it was then that I became a maid to her.'

'You liked her?'

'Everyone loved her, including Master Phillipe. He worshipped her, I think. It was the happiest time for us all.'

Here she halted and her eyes took on a faraway look.

'But the old count didn't like Madame Silvia because she was Italian, like his sister-in-law who had run away from him. He was always laughing at her, calling her a peasant when her back was turned, because she was not from a noble family. But the young people were so happy together – that is, until Marco was born and she died.'

Tears filled Constanza's eyes. 'It is not something I like to remember…'

'You were there when she died?'

'Yes, the baby came early but the old count wouldn't let me near her, even though I could hear her calling out for me.'

Then Constanza began to cry in earnest, great deep sobs that threatened to overwhelm her.

'That is why I hate him. Madame Silvia had no one with her to comfort her when she died. No one except the doctor who came from Panjim with a nurse. They left the same day and I never saw them again, so I could not ask what happened. Master Phillipe was away. I remember he didn't want to leave as Madame Silvia was only a few weeks away from giving birth and he argued with his uncle. I heard the old man saying that his nephew was a parasite on him and should do something to help make some money rather than just spending it. There was more but I couldn't hear it, something about Master Phillipe's mother. It was very ugly.

'Then the count threw me out of the house and I'm sure it was because I reminded him of Madame Silvia. He was guilty of something bad, I know it. I could see it in his eyes.'

Aunt Bea came into the kitchen then with the menu for the evening meal and all conversation ceased, but Isobel was left with a picture of Phillipe and his terrible silent pain that refused to go away for the rest of the evening and tormented her even as she slept.

Chapter Thirty-Two

S aunders arrived the following week as brash as ever but
was taken aback at the revelation that not only had Lord
Charles Cameron taken up residence at Silver Mist, but also
that his favourite chair by the fire had been taken over by the
newcomer. At least there was never any doubt in his mind that
Charles Cameron's principle object was Isobel, as he showed
no interest at all in Violet; he seemed either to avoid her or be
totally unconscious of her presence.

However, if Saunders appeared to be less of a man in
Violet's eyes compared to the very attractive Lord Cameron,
she showed no sign of it, in fact, quite the reverse.

She seemed to admire him more than ever, often being
publicly affectionate and adoring to the point that anyone else
in their presence was made uncomfortable. Especially Charlie,
who would turn away with an expression very like scorn. But
the contemptuous curl of his lip only seemed to spur Violet on
to more obvious shows of devotion, almost as though she was
doing it on purpose.

Aunt Bea had arranged to have the money for Violet's share in Silver Mist to be sent from her bank in London to the Panjim branch. A new deed would have to be drawn up, and it had been arranged that a trip to visit a lawyer in Panjim would take place to finally settle matters. Isobel wanted to go to town too, to visit some of the warehouses to discuss the possibility of selling her crop and make a few much-needed purchases for the household.

Violet had agreed verbally to the new arrangement, but it would be some time still till the deed could be signed. Saunders had accepted his loss but not without a certain amount of bitterness, saying he couldn't understand why Isobel wanted to keep Silver Mist when it was plain she wouldn't stay in India for long in any case.

'After all,' he said, as he played with a long strand of Violet's hair, 'she'll soon be Lady Cameron.'

Violet's complexion, usually so full of bloom, paled to an alarming white.

'That's not decided. There's been no mention of it.'

'Well, my darling, you must be blind not to see how things are between them.'

'They're friends. That's all. He helps her with the estate. That's why they spend so much time together.'

'Friends! I've seen the way he looks at her. It's a done thing, mark my words.'

They walked on in silence, then Violet, afraid to look at him as her eyes were stinging with tears, asked if he would take her away to Cardamon Hills for a few days.

'I can't stay here. I'm suffocating. I must get away. Take me away, Harry, please take me away.'

They left that same afternoon with Mary to act as chaperone, and everyone in the house, for various reasons, breathed a sigh of relief to have them gone. Soon after, it was decided that Aunt Bea and Isobel would go to Panjim earlier than anticipated, and Charlie would accompany them, as he now had pressing business there in regard to his own inheritance.

———————

The next morning, they set off, leaving the cubs with Mr. Singh and Aashi. They were so robust and thriving now, and in fact had become so cheeky and confident, that they had moved into Monty's basket by the fire and left very little room for him. Every night Monty delicately squeezed himself amongst them before settling down with a long, drawn-out sigh and an expression of such pained discomfort it was difficult not to laugh. At no time though did he ever show signs of really resenting them as it was impossible not to succumb to their endearing way of licking him all over whenever they got the chance. Even the constant favouritism for the little creatures did little to dent Monty's usually prickly temper; he rose to the occasion and accepted their juvenile antics as befitting an older, more responsible animal, causing even Isobel to look upon him with more respect.

It was a great wrench to leave the cubs behind, and Isobel had a foretaste of what it would feel like when they did eventually leave Silver Mist for their habitat in the jungle. They had begun to eat meat, and the sight of them sharing a bone and tearing at it with all the savage instinct natural to them reminded her of their need to learn to hunt for themselves. It was a daunting prospect, as learning to hunt meant live animals would need to be sacrificed and die in a horrible way for that lesson to succeed. But she had taken on a responsibility, and she would not shirk it now, no matter how unpleasant it might prove to be, in order that her precious children – because that was how she thought of them – would learn to survive on their own.

Again, Aunt Bea proved her generosity by choosing to make a splash with the break in Panjim as even though it was very cheap to live on a day-to-day basis, Isobel had no money to spare for any reckless spending. Her finances were boosted though by the sale of a much-loved family portrait depicting her favourite ancestor, the reportedly wicked Hortense Blanchard who she clearly resembled in more ways than one. Isobel was reluctant to sell, but in the end she wrote to George Latimer asking him to dispose of it if he could. To everyone's surprise it fetched three hundred pounds, enough to pay the wages of the workers for her first harvest.

The portrait was a painful loss, but Isobel accepted it with at least outward composure. Above all, Silver Mist must survive, and if it meant parting with one of the last remnants of her heritage, then so be it.

Aunt Bea had decided on a charming hotel placed most romantically on the Mandovi River and within walking distance of all the warehouses and shops along its banks. It had been built by the Portuguese in the seventeenth century and painted a brilliant turquoise blue with white shutters on the windows, and it was set in a lush garden with predominantly European trees and plants.

The town was pretty and prosperous and the shops

fascinating, and a holiday atmosphere prevailed despite the seriousness of Isobel's mission there, for along with business necessities she had been asked to bring back some of the best white silk available for Violet to be married in. Isobel had no heart for the task, but the silk warehouses were intriguing, usually semi-dark spaces mostly cooled by overhead fans now that electricity had been introduced, and a pleasant spot to while away an hour or two to escape the heat outside. The fabrics emitted a curious, dusty odour mingled with the scent of patchouli or jasmine so that when unravelled the fragrance flew in the air, assaulting the buyer's senses, making each purchase an intoxicating experience.

In the vast rooms the steady hum of voices in all languages and the smells of tea and coffee intermingled with the heady fragrance of curries coming from the street. It was an atmosphere Aunt Bea especially enjoyed, and she would bargain with an enthusiasm that didn't seem worth the effort for only a few rupees less, despite the embarrassed frowns of Isobel who always quietly paid what was asked and often a little bit more.

For Violet's wedding gown, Aunt Bea chose the most magnificent, buttery silk, so stiff it could stand alone when crunched, and yards of the finest gauze for a veil. There were signs of sadness, though, when she passed over the money and asked if it would be delivered to their hotel. The buying of the silk seemed to seal Violet's fate without hope, and both women left the store weighed down by their own thoughts.

Other days were spent visiting the managers and owners of the large warehouses in order to find a potential buyer for the coffee berries, tamarind and vanilla pods. There was a great deal of amused suspicion when a lovely young lady dressed in her Paris fashions and accompanied by her indomitable aunt requested to meet with them; they were usually only admitted to the sacred offices of commerce out of curiosity alone.

The managers were mostly older men, used to seeing women as only suitable for a range of uses, none of which were flattering. Isobel soon realized they were probably being humoured only out of the necessity of being polite, and of course to see such abnormal examples of womanhood up close.

Even Aunt Bea's steely appraisal and Isobel's clipped, no-nonsense requests were no match for these most hardened of businessmen who made an amused show of taking the women seriously and talked about the new Brazil market and how prices for Indian coffee had been driven down and how the labourers made unreasonable demands for higher wages; in the end they would cautiously agree to accept the future Silver Mist crop if it was so fortunate as to reach its fruition.

But their agreements were superficial, and nothing was on paper as in reality they had no intention of buying the Silver Mist crop at all, except at a price so low to be almost not worth Isobel's time, and usually when the women left these meetings there were the audible sounds of laughter when the doors were closed upon them.

The last warehouse they visited was the most imposing and intriguing of all. The name painted on the board outside was *D'Souza*, and Isobel wondered if there was any connection to Almeida's fiancée Carolina.

They were greeted with great courtesy before being shown into a room decorated with severe mahogany furniture and the only sound the ticking of an ugly gilt clock on the wall. At first there could be heard a hushed murmuring coming from an adjacent room, then the door swung open and standing there before them was a Portuguese gentleman, who was the manager of the warehouse, and Count Almeida himself.

Almost instantly his half-smile faded, but he kept up a show of old-fashioned gentility as he came forward to kiss Isobel's hand.

'Miss Blanchard and Miss McGregor, what are you doing here?'

'Count Almeida, I had no idea you were connected with this house.' Isobel almost added, 'Otherwise I wouldn't have come.' She had no doubt the old man considered her an unwanted presence in his life, though for what reason Isobel wasn't sure, especially as his nephew was safely engaged to another woman.

He turned to the other man with a patronizing smile. 'If you do not mind, I will take care of these ladies myself.'

'As you wish, Count.'

'Will you have some refreshments sent to us? Perhaps some tea for these English roses. I'm sure they must be thirsty.'

'Of course, Count.'

The man bowed in a most deferential way before closing the door behind him.

'I am here to have a look at the accounts.' He added unnecessarily, 'It is part of our dear Carolina's wedding dowry. She inherited it from her uncle, Jose D'Souza, but of course a woman can have no use for it. It is right that I should have it.'

Isobel had nothing to say, but her mind was running riot with his words. It is right *I* should have it… There was no mention of Phillipe Almeida being the beneficiary of such a valuable property. The warehouse and the business must be worth a fortune, and Isobel wondered what the rest of the dowry would involve.

Aunt Bea was undaunted by the cool reception.

'My niece and I are here on business. It is about our coffee crop and of course our need to find a buyer—'

'And you imagined you could find a buyer here?'

Almeida cut her off at once with a cold smile.

'Not imagined, hoped,' Isobel said.

'We deal mostly with rice here, as is usual in Goa. We take only a little coffee.'

'I only have a little coffee.'

'My dear lady, you can't be serious.'

Isobel was at her coolest.

'Why ever not?'

'Surely it's obvious.'

'No,' said Aunt Bea, equally coldly. 'No, it's not obvious at all.'

The old count marched slowly back and forth across the room as stiff as an army major.

'It is a waste of both our time, surely you can see that. Your crops will fail.'

'How can you be so sure?'

'Because, my dear ladies, you will never find the workers to pick it.'

'What do you mean? There must be plenty of people wanting to work.'

'Everyone in the vicinity of Casa Margarida works for me.'

'Not everyone, surely.'

'Yes, everyone, and it is accepted that they will never work for anyone else, and everyone knows this.'

'Perhaps once the people discover they might actually get paid for their work, they will consent to work for us.'

The old count drew himself up to look down his nose at Isobel.

'If you are trying to make a point about the bonded workers, they have no desire to be free from their debt to my family. They know when they are well off. With me they have their clothing, shelter and food. What more could they want?'

'Surely it's obvious…' Isobel echoed the count's words. 'A small matter to you perhaps, but you are aware that slavery is illegal now?'

'Only recently it is illegal – a foolish move on behalf of the government as we are now a poor country when once we were rich, but I repeat, it is not slavery. I look after my people, and they respect me for it.'

'I think perhaps you are under a delusion.'

'And I think you are speaking of things you know nothing about.'

The tea arrived, breaking the mood of hostility for a moment. But the young servant was nervous and fumbled a little with the pouring of it, consequently making the mistake of filling it too full and the tea only just escaped spilling over. He glanced up terrified as he caught the look in the count's eyes, then he fumbled once more but managed to right himself and place the cup before the count with a sigh of profound relief. But his ordeal was not over. After taking a sip the old man threw the cup down in disgust.

'You fool! This is cold!'

There was a moment of intense silent discomfort driving Aunt Bea to speak up.

'No need to make a fuss. I prefer my tea cool, especially in this climate.'

'That is not the point!' he screamed, his face now a violent scarlet and Isobel couldn't help but notice a thin trail of spittle running unheeded from the corner of his mouth.

He turned to the boy then. 'You have two minutes to make another. Now get out!'

The boy stood frozen for a moment at first, unable to take in the order. Then the count pointed to the large clock on the wall. 'Two minutes!'

Not waiting to collect the tea things but with a final despairing look at the clock, the boy stumbled out of the room. An uneasy silence followed as the sound of the inevitable march of time took over every other noise in the room. The black hand moving on began to take on a tremendous importance till Isobel, rooted to the spot by the grotesque scene unfolding before her, began to feel a faint wave of nausea, more for the fate of the servant than for her own situation. Then as the minute hand passed the deadline the old man let out a strange victorious cackle and turned to face her, his eyes wide and staring. 'See! See! He can't do it!' and she realized then she was in the presence of a mad man.

Finally, after a full five minutes, the boy arrived bearing a fresh pot of tea. He stood trembling in the doorway, afraid to enter and showing the signs of tears in his eyes.

This was too much for Aunt Bea who decided to take charge of the matter. She rose and went to the boy and took the tea out of his hands. Then she gave him a generous handful of coins and dismissed him while the count watched the scene before him in a kind of stupor.

For a moment it seemed there would be another outburst of

fury, then he suddenly bent forward, clutching at his head with both hands before his face lapsed into a kind of lop-sided smile. It seemed he had forgotten the whole incident and in a few confused seconds he returned to his almost normal manner.

'Now, my dear ladies, if we have concluded our business, I have other matters to attend to.'

It took Isobel some moments to speak, she was so overwhelmed by the incident that had played out before her.

'We were talking about our need to find workers for Silver Mist…'

His smile buckled at once as he shook himself back to the present.

He became quite intimate as he leant towards her, even putting a hand on her shoulder.

'Listen, listen my dear. There is something you can do to avoid all this unnecessary worry. Running an estate is not for a pretty young lady like yourself. I will take Silver Mist off your hands and save you the trouble of facing ruin. It will be better if you accept my offer now, for in a year's time it will be worth less than half of what it is now.'

'And you will try to make sure it is.'

'If you want to turn this into a battle, I can assure you, you will not win against me.'

It was best to say no more. There was too much anger on both sides. Isobel and Aunt Bea walked out with the utmost dignity, but when Isobel glanced back and saw the count's queer, cold smile, she felt a shiver of pure fear, for in that split second the signs of madness had returned once more to his eyes.

Chapter Thirty-Three

After her meeting with Count Almeida, Isobel struggled with being drawn into a whirlpool of depression at the enormity of the task before her. He was a more dangerous foe than she had first thought as well as being clearly mad, but as was her way she put these uncomfortable thoughts behind her. She was determined she would enjoy this stolen evening to the full and face her problems head on the next day with a fresh purpose.

Her spirits began to lift the moment she stepped out of her hotel room onto the wide balcony looking over the Mandovi River. Little boats with golden sails capturing the last glow from the setting sun floated past, leaving a gentle silvery trail in their wake that caused barely a ripple on the wide expanse of water.

Groups of naked children leapt from the shore into the more placid pools along the bank with wild unrestrained shouts of joy while little babies splashed about in the shallows alongside their mothers who sang sweet lilting songs as they washed their bright saris in the swirling yellow water.

There was the heady smell of salty air on the breeze and with it the muddy stench of the inlets combining with the fragrance from the lush tropical garden beneath her window. In particular, there was a plant large enough to be almost a tree, thickly hung with huge white trumpet-shaped flowers that fascinated Isobel with their strange beauty, but it was at the onset of dusk when the full mysterious power of the plant made itself known.

The perfume from the datura only came into being at night and filled her room with a scent so powerful it acted almost as a drug on the senses. The little maid who had unpacked the luggage noticed Isobel's interest and warned her about it.

'It is a dangerous flower, Madam. It is very poisonous and sometimes some of the Indian ladies use it for a love potion to get a husband – or to get rid of one...'

There she stopped, realizing she may have said too much.

'But it is safe as long as you don't eat it,' she added, then laughed, as of course that was very unlikely.

It was a luxury too to have a bathroom to herself and as much hot water as she wanted. On the first evening before joining the others for dinner, she soaked in a long, deep bath and took the time to really think about the past few weeks.

Uppermost in her mind was of course Charlie Cameron. She would have to be a fool not to notice how attentive he was and the expression in his eyes whenever he looked at her. She slid down further into the scented water and closed her eyes. He was indeed a most attractive man and she had to seriously consider now what she would say when he asked her to marry him, as she was certain he would.

Letting her mind run wild, she allowed her imagination to wander far enough to let children into the picture, something she had never considered before. Little Marco had changed her opinion of children and she could see now how enchanting they could be.

She thought a girl might be nice, with Charlie's thick russet hair and hazel eyes, and a boy, with a thatch of blond hair and grey eyes like her own.

Thinking of children made her think of her body and of course her virgin state, and what she would have to do to get children at all.

Her body was firm, slim and healthy, and she took pleasure in running her hands over her fine skin and watching the islands of her white breasts and pink nipples as the warm water flowed over them.

All her life she had been told by various nannies and her own mother not to touch any area below the navel and had once had her hand smacked sharply by a ruler for daring to point out the difference between herself and a male cousin who had once visited her home. Even so, lately she had found herself preoccupied with so-called wicked thoughts mainly because of a hidden cache of erotic Indian drawings she had found, like the cigarettes and gin, secreted away in one of young Quimp's chests of drawers. At first glance she was so shocked she dropped them as though her fingers had been scorched, so they fanned out across her bedroom floor taunting her with a shameless show of passionate abandon. It was as she was bending down to take a closer look her door flew open revealing her Aunt Bea who had chosen that moment for one of her untimely raids. Isobel hurried to explain herself, but the lady scarcely raised an eyebrow at such scandalous images, only commenting that she thought it all looked rather athletic and uncomfortable and couldn't imagine any decent English person indulging themselves in such behaviour. Then without another word she swept out of the room taking the contraband with her.

But Isobel but had seen enough to excite her interest and from then on could hardly keep those tantalizing glimpses of what was clearly a pleasurable experience out of her mind.

There was something too about the urgent incessant hum of life in India that encouraged an obsession with regeneration and love in all its forms. The very air was steeped in it.

Lately, she had noticed Charlie watching her intently and she wondered if he was thinking about kissing her. So far, he hadn't tried, but there were times, especially when they were alone, walking through the coffee plants, and there was no one there to see, when it seemed that at any moment he would take her in his arms and declare his love for her. There was an intensity in the nearness of him when they were alone together, and he must have felt it too as suddenly, he would make a light joke or change the subject and move away from her. It was all most disconcerting.

But she had been mistress of her own destiny for such a short time and had enjoyed it so much she would not throw it away lightly even for what most women would consider an offer impossible to refuse. Then again it would be so easy to give in and be taken care of. It might be pleasant for a change after having taken care of everyone else for so long. Then the uncomfortable thoughts she had put aside began to resurface once more and a tremor of fear snaked through her body. Count Tiago could take Silver Mist from her by slow calculated steps designed to ruin her and leaving her a victim of his mercy. A great surge of the injustice of it all almost overwhelmed her. It was an impossible notion to swallow. She wanted desperately to win this battle; to gloat over him as she held the sword of victory over his head.

She sank further down into the warm scented water and with that the image of Count Tiago began to dissolve and the image of Charlie took his place.

Marriage to Charlie meant Scotland, and a life constricted by the duties necessary to the running of a grand estate. She would have to behave herself and become something she might not be able to live up to.

But then, Violet was sure to be living in England as well, and the thought of being separated from her forever was not to be endured.

Now, whenever she thought of Violet it was with a great deal of regret and she longed to be able to recapture the old friendship between them. But she had paid dearly for trying to steer the course of her sister's destiny, and now she was beginning to accept the fact that Violet might be right after all in wanting to choose a life for herself. Isobel, too, must forge her own path whether it be the wife of Charles Cameron or an uncertain future of inevitable struggle at Silver Mist.

It was a joy for a change to take pleasure in dressing for the night ahead, and as the evening was warm so she chose her coolest gown – a light-grey silk chiffon that fell in graceful folds down to her ankles. It was perhaps a little too fine for the occasion, but she wore it for Charlie, as in a perverse way she wanted him to admire her, and see her at her best, even though she was unsure about him.

Her bare arms were adorned with only a thin silver bangle and her hair was held with the same fleur-de-lis clasp she had worn on the night of the party at Casa Margarida. Thinking of Casa Margarida prompted her to think of Phillipe Almeida. It had been at least three weeks since he had come to pick up Marco and he had been particularly moody and unresponsive, and shown a side of his nature she felt was not very attractive. He had been almost rude to Charlie Cameron and even curt with her for no reason at all she could think of. Though a piece of her still found him intriguing, attractive even, always there was the persistent thought that if Phillipe Almeida had any courage at all he would stand up for himself and make his uncle release the bonded workers from what was clearly a feudal practice. In fact, the whole estate of Casa Margarida felt to her as though it had escaped the onset of time and remained trapped in an era that should have long ago been left behind with its mistakes.

Under normal circumstances, she would have nothing more to do with the house and its occupants, but there was Marco to consider, and she was prepared to overlook the shortcomings of the father in order to see the child again. It would be cruel to have made him a part of her life then exclude him. She decided she would write to Almeida that very night and ask for Marco to come and stay the following week, but first she would settle down and have a cigarette before meeting Charlie in the dining room.

She had only just settled herself comfortably in a chair on the balcony with her feet up and had begun to savour the aromatic pleasure of her forbidden vice when there was a sharp knock on the door.

It was Aunt Bea, who as usual barged in without waiting for an answer. Isobel had only just enough time to hide the remains of the cigarette in a pot plant.

'Come in,' said Isobel pointedly, as her aunt sat herself down in a chair next to her and turned to face her niece with an expression that did not bode well.

'I wouldn't bother putting it out. I know you smoke.' She added, with a smile, 'You should see your face!'

It was unusual for Isobel to be caught out, and it showed in her expression of pure shock that turned instantly to a sulk.

'Well, if you know so much why didn't you say anything?'

'I know enough about you to know you would carry on behind my back anyway.'

Isobel decided to ignore her and tried to change the subject.

'You look nice,' she said, and it was true. Her aunt was looking particularly elegant in a gown she'd had made up from the dark-blue silk she had bought on her visit to Cardamon Hills. Her silver hair was piled high on her head in a becoming style, and she wore a pair of tear-drop rubies in her ears.

Aunt Bea smiled as she smoothed back her hair.

'You girls have taught me a few things…' She grew serious for a moment. 'Especially how wrong I was to cling to the past. I was stubborn and very bitter, and I wanted to hurt my father for opposing me. By the time he died it was too late and I was left with nothing. Life is for living; I see that now.'

For the first time, Isobel realized how very lonely her aunt must have been for so many years with only servants and a parrot for company.

'Well, it has been nice having you around … mostly,' Isobel said with a scowl. 'I think perhaps you may have even taught me a thing or two as well.'

'Really? My dear child, you are not the type of person who ever learns from other people's mistakes or listens to advice. You will go your own way no matter what.'

'But judging by your expression, you're going to give me some advice now.'

'I'm asking you, for goodness' sake to accept Charlie Cameron when he asks you. You would be a fool not to.'

'What makes you think I will refuse him?'

'I see you are conceited enough not to dispute whether he will ask you or not, but I'm confused. One minute it seems as though you're in love with him and the next minute you treat him the same as you treat Monty. But I'm not convinced you'll take him, and I'm asking you again not to be a fool.'

Isobel picked up her fan from the dressing table and held out her hand to help her aunt up from the chair.

'I might surprise you,' she said, with a sly smile.

'That's highly unlikely,' said her aunt. 'Nothing you do ever does!'

Chapter Thirty-Four

Charlie was waiting for them at their table in the dining room and his heart skipped a beat when he saw Isobel coming into the room with Aunt Bea. She seemed to float towards him in her cloud of grey chiffon. Perhaps it was the gown, but it seemed to him that it was more than that; she imbued everything she did with a sense of beauty and drama.

His heart raced at the thought of the evening ahead. He wanted to kiss her very much and tonight it seemed possible since they were away from—

He almost said Violet, but it was true. Violet's presence did have an inhibiting effect on him. Those eyes ... always following him with an expression he couldn't make out.

Isobel had paused for a moment in her passage across the floor to admire a vase of orchids placed on a table in the centre of the room and the maître d' had hurried forward to present her with one. Her gratitude was so evident and her manner so charming toward the man for his little gift that Charlie found himself falling deeper under her spell. He must have her. He must tell her tonight how he felt about her. He must ask her to marry him.

But then, as he watched, a man walked towards her and took her hand to kiss it in a very European way.

At first Charlie didn't recognize him, but when the man turned, he saw those intense, dark eyes and a face almost contorted by some hidden emotion and he wondered at the strange coincidence of meeting Phillipe Almeida in their hotel.

He saw Isobel's face then, as she raised it to meet his. There was surprise but also something else.

Fascination?

It was as though she was trapped by his gaze. It wasn't love – he could see that. There was even a faint touch of dislike that she couldn't hide; her opinion of him was no secret, and because of this Charlie was incredibly relieved, but there was something between them that was so potent he could feel it from across the room.

Even to another man, Phillipe Almeida had a presence that was undeniable. His movements were almost languid, but there was an undercurrent of latent power in his body that seemed almost threatening. Charlie was reminded of a Flamenco dance he had once seen performed in Seville between a man and a woman that had kept him hypnotized by its blatant sensuality. The man circling the woman, his eyes locked on hers as he moved closer and closer, the dance disguising his real intention to move in and overwhelm her, while the girl was seemingly helpless to resist, but all the while leading him to her with every seductive move of her body, urging him on to an even deeper and more flamboyant display of passion.

Charlie watched as Isobel recovered her self-control,

then her silk shawl slipped, and Almeida caught it before it fell to the floor. With a gesture that seemed to capture her briefly in his arms, he placed it back on her shoulders, his lips lingering for a long moment very close to Isobel's neck.

Even that simple act caused Charlie to bristle a little, as he had begun to think of Isobel as his own; Almeida was an interloper.

The two men faced each other as gentlemen. There could never be even a hint of their true feelings on show, but each in their own way was aware of the subtle battle being played out under the guise of good manners.

The first move gave Charlie the advantage as he quickly shifted the conversation around to Carolina D'Souza and Almeida's upcoming marriage.

At first Phillipe looked surprised, as though he'd been suddenly reminded of something he had forgotten about. Then he frowned as he drank his glass of red wine almost in one throw.

'I have just been to the port. Carolina has had to return to Lisbon. The countess has been taken ill with a stomach complaint and refuses to stay a moment longer, and of course her daughter must accompany her.'

'Oh. Nothing too serious, I hope. I'm very sorry for your fiancée – and for you. It seems too cruel to part those so deeply in love.'

Phillipe shifted impatiently in his seat, picking up on Isobel's sarcasm at once.

'The wedding has been delayed, but only by a few weeks. I must join Carolina then. She has a desire to be married in the European spring.'

'Oh, how lovely. Yes, I suppose there will be daffodils in London now. Sometimes I think I'll never see them again.'

Charlie smiled and took her hand.

'You may be back there sooner than you think.'

They were the words of a lover, and they didn't go unnoticed by either Phillipe or Isobel.

Phillipe lapsed into a moody silence once more and began to think about leaving the lovers alone when Isobel broke into his thoughts.

'We met your uncle today. We thought we were going to be dealing with the house of D'Souza, but it seems the warehouse will soon belong to your family.'

'I suppose it will. I hadn't given it much thought.'

'Your uncle offered to buy Silver Mist from me.'

'I thought he might.'

'I told him it wasn't for sale.'

'Well then, he must accept that, though I don't suppose he will.'

Almeida lapsed back into his shell once more. He was feeling truly as though he was in the way. He had interrupted what he could tell from Lord Cameron's eyes was an intimate dinner between two people who were in love, chaperoned by the once eccentric-looking aunt who was now a rather elegant lady. He could tell by that lady's manner too that she wished him gone, as he was sure she was encouraging a match between the young couple.

With his lovely Isobel, for that was how he secretly viewed her. It was not so clear, but then, she was always an enigma to him. She was always charming and polite, as her upbringing dictated, but he sensed an undercurrent of resentment coming from her that became more obvious as the night went on.

He knew he should excuse himself at once and dine alone but he couldn't find it within himself to do so. He wanted to be near her, to hear her talk, and watch her face as her emotions changed. Even a simple movement like turning her head to listen to her aunt kept him entranced, but he had to stop himself from appearing to be too obvious and he returned to his wine feeling blacker than ever.

Sometimes little wafts of her scent came towards him, provoking sensations in his body that were far from civilized, and again he was amazed at how her presence stirred in him feelings he'd thought long dead. She was his first experience of an English girl, and he was impressed by her apparent self-confidence as his only knowledge of women apart from his beloved Silvia, had been Italian girls, and they played a game he understood.

A game where he flattered and admired, and in return they rewarded him with smiles and love – or something very like it. No one, not even his beloved Silvia, had spun this kind of silken net around him, a net from which he hoped never to be released.

But then the weight of his guilt descended upon his mood as he thought of Silvia's lonely death, making him appear to the outside world surly and distracted.

The conversation throughout the meal was kept strictly to safe topics, but all the while he felt the restraint slowly begin to unravel. It was unusual to see a young lady drinking almost two full glasses of wine and she was beginning to get a little tipsy – and with that a bit argumentative, particularly towards him.

He found it difficult, though, to be offended as she looked

so very lovely with her flushed cheeks and luminous eyes, even though it was because they were enhanced by too much wine.

She began with a hiccup.

'I have been told by Constanza that you still have bonded labour at Casa Margarida. Why don't you set them free? It's a disgrace.'

With that she let out another hiccup.

'Excuse me.' Then she continued, 'Surely the estate can afford to pay them a decent wage? Why don't you sell some of those hideous old relics you keep gathering dust at Casa Margarida if you're so hard up?'

'Isobel! That is quite enough! You can't talk to other people like you do to us at home. We only put up with you as we have no choice. Please excuse her, Mr. Almeida,'

Almeida said nothing, only giving away a twisted half-smile.

His silence had begun to infuriate her, and she started to rage a little, forgetting everything she'd been taught about social behaviour.

'The whole place is like a tomb, to keep alive the memory of a lot of very unsavoury people. If they were my relations, I'd be doing my best to forget them.'

He raised his eyebrows at that but remained silent.

'Isobel, really, I think you have had enough.' Aunt Bea leant over and tried to remove Isobel's wine glass from under her nose, but she wasn't quick enough and Isobel held on firmly and passed it to the waiter who refilled it at once.

Aunt Bea made a gesture that implied she had given up on her niece and rose from the table.

'I think it might be a good idea if you accompanied me back to my room.'

'Why? I'm having a good time for once, and I want to talk to Mr. Almeida about something. Don't worry about me, Aunt. I can take care of myself, thank you very much.'

Both men rose with Aunt Bea, and Charlie offered his arm to her to escort her to her room.

Isobel looked up, a little contrite.

'Don't leave on my account, Aunt. I promise I'll be on my best behaviour.'

'We both know that's highly unlikely. Now, I expect you in my room in ten minutes. Goodnight, Mr. Almeida. Don't take any notice of her. We never do when she's in one of her moods.'

Charlie bent to whisper in Isobel's ear, wanting to make it plain to his rival that he was allowed such intimacies.

'I'll be back for you in a moment,' he said, almost adding, 'darling', but he stopped himself just in time.

'Yes, thank you, Charles. I'll be here waiting for you. I want to ask Mr. Almeida about where I can hire some people … who aren't slaves,' she added rather loudly, so the people at the next table turned to look at her.

Phillipe frowned. She was getting too close to a subject he didn't like to think about, but she was so lovely with the fire in her eyes and her insistence on standing up for what she believed was right.

He watched her as she took another sip of her wine with a pained outrage.

'How dare Aunt Bea imply I've drunk too much? Really, that woman drives me half demented.'

A long strand of her hair had fallen and curled around her bare shoulder, and he could hardly tear his eyes away. When she moved, the curl moved too; now it skimmed the curve of her breast above her gown.

He roused himself to interrupt her then.

'One day I'll tell you why this practice continues, but for the moment I can't.'

'If you mean it's because of your uncle, why don't you stand up to him? It is no example to set for your son.'

'There are some things that must remain private.'

'Nothing excuses it. Nothing.'

'You must forgive me if I change the subject. There must be a thousand more interesting topics to speak of.'

'Not to me. Your uncle informed me today that I have no chance of ever hiring labourers as no one will work for me. He owns everyone, just as, apparently, he owns you!' She looked up to see Charlie approaching the table and couldn't resist making her resentment felt.

'Oh, Lord Cameron is coming back. Don't you think, Mr. Almeida, he is a most wonderful man? I admire him so much, mostly because of his strength of character.'

Phillipe was blunt when he stood abruptly to leave her.

'As you admire him so much, I'll leave you alone with him. Thank you for allowing me to intrude on your evening.'

He walked away then without looking back, only giving Charlie a curt nod as he left the room.

'Almeida doesn't look too happy. What did you say to him?'

'Nothing at all. He's impossible – clearly as bad as his uncle. How could a man like that have such a lovely child?'

Then came the hiccup again and Charlie laughed.

'I have strict instructions to return you to Aunt Bea now … and for once I agree with her.'

'No, I want to go into the garden, with you.'

'Nothing would give me greater pleasure, but I have my orders.'

'Oh alright. Everyone seems to be conspiring to have me locked up and the night is just beginning.'

'There is tomorrow night, and perhaps I can persuade Aunt Bea to let us dine alone.'

Isobel scowled at that.

'It's none of her business. We can dine alone if you wish it.'

By now they had reached the hall and he left her in front of Aunt Bea's door. His face was so close to her own that it took a great deal of effort on her part not to take advantage of being alone to kiss him. Her desire to do so showed clearly on her face as she looked at him with a seductive smile.

Above everything, though, Charlie was a gentleman, and he merely took her hand and kissed it, murmuring almost to himself, 'Isobel, my God, you are the very devil. You can drive a man mad!'

Charlie then, looking as though it cost him a great deal to do so, let her go and knocked loudly on Aunt Bea's door.

'There you are, miss. Come inside at once. Thank you, Charlie. Goodnight…'

The door closed on them both and for a minute Charlie listened while Aunt Bea took Isobel to task for her behaviour. He laughed as he heard Isobel's muffled response that didn't sound the least bit contrite. Then, with great reluctance, he walked back downstairs for a final drink on the terrace. He was burning with desire and had to quash it somehow and a walk outside in the garden seemed the best option. He had made up his mind to ask Isobel to marry him the following night, and judging by the look she had given him, a look that left him with his knees shaking and his head in the clouds, she would accept him.

Chapter Thirty-Five

On the way down the stairs, he passed Phillipe Almeida who was on his way up.

He smiled pleasantly and Charlie was prompted to ask if he would care to join him for a drink, but Phillipe declined, saying he must be up early to attend to some business in the morning.

They parted as friends, at least on the surface, and Phillipe made his way down the hall to his room, but as he did so, the door to another room further down the hall opened and Isobel came out with a rush.

She was clearly very angry and wasn't really noticing where she was going and almost bumped into him.

'Oh, Mr. Almeida! I'm sorry.'

It was semi-dark, being lit only by a soft lamp on a table at the far end of the corridor.

He said nothing at all in reply, but for a long moment he kept his anguished eyes on hers, unable to tear himself away.

'My aunt says I must apologize to you at once, so I do, and I hope you will forgive me for my bad behaviour.'

He was unaware of what she was saying. He was still deeply hurt by her words at the dinner table and had been nursing his suffering ever since. It was plain she loved Charles Cameron and his heart was breaking. A tight knot of pain in his chest was making it impossible to speak. She could only stare at him bewildered. Then she laughed to lighten the mood.

'Well then, I must go to bed at once under strict orders from my aunt.'

Still he said nothing, but she was somehow trapped by his silence and his dark, moody face as he gazed at her. She asked herself then why his air of mystery was so much more appealing than the open, sunny face of Charlie Cameron.

With a great deal of effort, she began to move away from him.

'Goodnight then.'

But then as though in a trance, he reached for her hand, entwining his fingers in hers, at first with their fingertips touching lightly, then their palms pressed together in a gesture so intimate, she was as shocked as if he had suddenly kissed her. His voice came out husky and hesitant, as though he was finding it difficult to speak.

'I must talk to you, but not here.' His hand slid down to her wrist and pulled her ever so slightly towards him.

Now was the time to take away her hand, feel insulted, and walk off in a huff, but she didn't feel insulted at all, and she knew she would not walk away. Even as a child she had never been able to say no to a dare, no matter how risky, and in this moment, she almost ran towards the danger, no matter what the outcome.

'There is a terrace in my room. We can talk there. I want to explain something to you.'

He opened the door, still with his fingers closed firmly over her wrist as he led her inside, his eyes fixed on hers. She followed him like a sleepwalker, her heart thumping wildly. This wasn't just a playful escapade like the one she had enjoyed so recently with Charlie, this was something different and shadowy and most definitely forbidden, but she wanted to be there in the dark with him, even if it meant she would be ruined forever in the eyes of society if they were to be discovered.

This was dangerous territory enough, but this man with his dark presence had the power to engulf her and crush the thought of any other man from her brain if she let him. It was baffling and frustrating because she was sure she didn't love him, and at times was even contemptuous of him and of the way he lived his life, but just the feel of his strong, warm fingers on her wrist had her shaking all over with the anticipation of something earth-shattering.

The room was dark except for the light from the houses on the opposite bank of the river and the soft glow of lanterns on the little sail boats as they floated by. He dropped her wrist at last to light a lamp while she stood patiently by, watching him, her arms hanging limply by her sides. He fumbled for a while with the match, and she could see his hands were shaking and his face, momentarily lit by the flare of light, was paler than usual. There was now every opportunity to make her excuses and escape him, but she longed for the next chapter in this strange night, whatever the result.

Every moment of their encounter began to take on an enormous significance – the sound of his footsteps as he walked close behind her, the feel of his hand on her waist as he steered her past the outline of a piece of furniture, the casual brush of his suit coat against her body that caused her heart to leap, his own indefinable scent, masculine but deeply pleasant... The air was heavy now with tension as she stood alert, the hairs on the back of her neck beginning to prickle with expectation.

Her thoughts flew to her mother and how outraged she would be to discover her daughter alone with a man in his room, but she wanted with all her heart to go down this dangerous path for no other reason than to see where it led her. She convinced herself she was in control as always, and could stop at any time, and then she would make him pay for his daring.

She wanted to humble Phillipe Almeida and then to humiliate him, if possible, for being a fraud and a hypocrite.

'What is it? If my aunt should ever suspect...'

In the half-light of the room, the contours of his face were cast into greater relief. He looked tired, even haggard.

'I suppose I want you to think less badly of me than you do.'

Sensing triumph, she was cool and a little scathing.

'What should it matter what I think of you? We barely know each other.'

He took a step closer, his voice dropping almost to a whisper, his eyes glowing with a fierce, sweet aching. 'That's not true, we know each other very well.'

He came closer to take her hand once more.

'Why are you lying to me?'

This was not what she had planned, and she began to feel out of her depth.

'I think I had better go.'

She turned to leave, but he took a quick step forward and she felt his presence loom over her as he put his hand to her waist.

'Don't go…'

She swung around to face him, and whatever he read there gave him hope.

The next second he had her in his grip, almost lifting her off her feet as he pressed his body against hers, then she felt his fingers through her hair as he held her head back to meet his lips. He sighed as he crushed her with his mouth, covering hers till she was breathless; his arms were tight around her waist, pulling her body to his. His image of her as spring personified was realized at the touch of her warm lips. She was summer rain on a withered plant.

While he was kissing her, she was still cool enough to be stunned by what she had set free in him. It was the first time she had experienced the truly unleashed passion of a healthy young man and she couldn't help but feel there was something rather wonderful about it. He seemed now to be almost devouring her, raining hot kisses on her throat and even on a place so temptingly close to her breast. The thrill of his touch was almost overwhelming now, and she forgot to be analytical about the experience and began to kiss him back with as much wild ardour as his own. She thought about a phrase often quoted ominously by her mother, 'The foolish girl had lost her head and look where it led her.'

Well, her daughter was at the point of losing hers, and

Isobel descended, unrepentant, into abandon with a wild, clandestine joy.

This was the secret that had been hidden from her. This was the feeling considered too dangerous to be spoken of out loud. Here was the line a respectable girl could not cross.

He was murmuring something in Italian... *'Mia cara ... Mia bellezza.'* Then, as he began to realize what he had done, he stopped to look at her.

'I'm sorry. Forgive me. How could I behave like this? Like an animal...' His eyes blazed in the darkened room. 'But ... you do feel it, too? What it is between us?'

'Yes, yes, I do. I always have. I don't understand...'

'No woman has ever affected me as you do. No one, but...'

Then he let her go, his arms free and his hands wide apart, standing before her in a kind of agony.

'I have no right.'

In the silence that followed, Isobel became aware of the overwhelming perfume from the datura filling the room and couldn't help but wonder if the plant did indeed have a magical quality that caused unwary humans to lose their heads and give themselves up to illicit love.

'Please forgive me. I did not intend to... You must go at once, before I—'

He turned away, his head in his hands. For a long moment there was silence, then he heard her soft footsteps behind him and felt her arms around his waist. Her words were muffled from where she had buried her face against his back.

'I don't want to go. I want to be with you.'

He turned to face her then, his own face brightened by hope, and kissed her again and again.

'You could love me then?'

'Is this love? What we are doing now?'

'And the handsome Lord Cameron? You are not in love with him?' It was as though he was trying to will her to answer as he demanded.

Then just for a moment her head cleared.

'I don't know. I thought it was a settled thing. Just this evening I decided to marry him, but now…'

'I couldn't bear the idea of you loving him. I was beginning to 'ate 'im…'

The colour had rushed into his face, but she smiled tenderly at his almost boyish passion and his sudden very Italian loss of the letter 'h'.

'It's impossible to hate Charlie. I thought I loved him, but how much? And is it enough? Oh, don't ask me! I don't know… Everything was so clear before.'

He took her arms from around his waist and stood back from her, hurt beyond words.

'Then why do you allow me to make love to you? If you love him as you say' – he spread his arms wide again – 'this could not happen.'

'I didn't say I loved him, and you have no right to lecture me when you are going to be married to someone you obviously don't love. If you did then you wouldn't be saying these things to me.'

'You're right, I don't love Carolina.'

Then he groaned as he fell back in the armchair on the terrace with his head in his hands.

'But I must marry her. I must…'

'What do you mean?'

It was a ghastly moment, for she realized then with an absolute certainty that he had no intention of breaking off his engagement to Carolina. The wild kisses that had passed between them and were surely the first step to their engagement clearly meant nothing after all. She realized then that she was not as liberated as she liked to think. She had expected him to say he would break off his engagement to Carolina at once and transfer his love to her. A deep shame began to creep over her when she realized he had no intention of doing so.

'Why? Why must you marry her? Because your uncle wants you to and you must always do as he says?'

'You don't understand. There are reasons.'

Her anger took over now, being so outraged by how easily she had exposed her heart to him.

'You thought perhaps I might become your mistress, is that it? That's all I'm good for, but Carolina—'

'That's not what I wanted, but I would be lying if I said I didn't want you. There is something about you that must make every man desire you, but for me it is more than that. It is more than love. Please Isobel, try not to hate me.'

'I do hate you and I hate myself for ever being stupid enough to—' There she broke off as she thought of how she could hurt him with the maximum pain.

'You've made up my mind for me now. I can never love a weak man, and you're weak! At least Charles behaves like a man. Now I feel ashamed for what I've done, ashamed for exposing myself to you in this way. I'm a fool and I got what I deserved.'

'It was all my fault. You weren't to blame, and I didn't mean this to happen.'

'What did you imagine then? What did you bring me here for?'

'Because of the strong feelings I have for you. I wanted to know if you felt the same. It would have been a comfort to me and something to remember when…' He hesitated. 'When I am away from you, probably forever. It was very wrong, but I was crazy…'

'Yes, it was! You disgust me and I disgust myself! When I think of how I betrayed Charlie … a man I love. Yes, love! For something so meaningless!'

'You'll marry him then?'

'Of course I will! As soon as I can.'

'Then you would be mad to do so.'

'How dare you! You let me make a fool of myself. You enjoyed it. I know you did. Don't ever speak to me again!'

She ran to the door with him fast behind her. He grabbed her and pushed her against the wall, holding her tight, willing her to soften under his pleading eyes. 'Isobella…'

At first, she thought he would say that he would give up his engagement, anything to lessen her pain, but he said nothing, only releasing his hold on her before turning away with his head in his hands while she delivered what she hoped would be her final words.

'I'm glad this happened, because now I see Charlie's worth in a clearer light. He is the better man! In every respect!'

Then, not even bothering to see if anyone might be watching, she fled down the hall into her own room where she collapsed onto the bed and cried with bitter shame.

It was only with the dawn that she finally fell asleep, but her first thought on waking was of Phillipe, and what she had done. Her next thought was how would she ever face him again, especially in the cold light of morning. But there was a tinge of hope, too, nestled amongst her pain, that at any moment he might knock on her door and proclaim his love for her and beg her forgiveness. Would he change his mind and ask her to marry him, and scandalize his uncle and Carolina? But it was too late now. It was impossible that she could ever marry him now, even if he asked her. His indecision was enough to dampen her illicit passion for him.

Charlie was the right man for her really; he would always be loving and kind and she was sure she would be able to support him in his future role. But how could she marry him now? He deserved better. It was almost as if she had given herself to Almeida even though they hadn't actually...

But she had encouraged him when she should have left before things became so...

What had she done? As usual, everything was her fault.

Then she blushed, hot and deep, and with that she curled her body into a ball and groaned aloud. She lay there for some time, reliving the night before with a mixture of tingling pleasure at the memory of those staining kisses and horror at her feelings of humiliation. She had allowed herself to be carried away by her own passion and left herself open to Phillipe Almeida's contempt.

The only consolation was that whatever she had done, it would forever remain a secret to everyone but herself.

The warm, scented water from the bath made her feel better, but as she was sponging her arm she noticed a faint blue bruise from where he had held her the night before and another on her breast where he had pressed his lips. At the time she hadn't felt anything except a wild joy at being swept away by a thrilling loss of control, and she had given herself up to it recklessly. Her future seemed more confused than ever. She had indeed stepped over an invisible line that separated her from other girls. She knew things, forbidden things, and she could never go back.

But all these thoughts flew from her mind when a loud knock on her door jolted her out of her trance. She was sure it was he, and she drew her dressing gown around her body, ran her fingers through her tangled hair, and prepared to answer the door, almost frightened by what awaited her.

Before she had time to be disappointed, Aunt Bea burst through the door, her face pale with fright.

She had received a letter from Mary saying they had just returned from Cardamon Hills the day before, and Violet had appeared to be just the same as always, but when she woke that morning she was feeling very ill. Mary asked that Isobel return at once and bring a doctor; she was afraid that it was serious as Violet could not be roused from her stupor and there was a fever that showed no signs of abating.

No one spoke and there was hardly any sound on the journey back to Silver Mist except for Isobel's heart-breaking sobs. Guilt was overwhelming her from every direction.

Again, everything was her fault. If she had not tricked Violet into coming to India she would now not be ill, perhaps dying. Her encounter with Phillipe Almeida was nothing now.

Violet's illness made everything that had once seemed so important irrelevant.

Charlie did his best to comfort her, but he too was frozen into a silent pain that could not be relieved till they arrived at Silver Mist and he could see for himself if Violet was in serious danger. The depth of his pain came as a surprise. He had truly believed he had no feelings left for her, having transferred his heart to Isobel completely. But now, the thought of Violet dying left him with an emptiness that was impossible to deny.

Chapter Thirty-Six

I t was worse than they had feared.

Violet lay helpless in a semi-coma, her lovely eyes sunken in an already emaciated face and her body drenched in a cold sweat. A terrible restlessness had come over her and she twisted and jerked her body in her damp nightgown while she cried out for water, as her thirst had become unendurable. So far, any water she had managed to drink was instantly thrown up, then she would fall back exhausted, calling out again for something to quench her terrible thirst.

Isobel stood at the foot of the bed, her hands clenched till the knuckles showed white and her eyes bleak with fear. She began to regret she had never been religious and all the times she had avoided church when she could get away with it. Now she prayed with an almost demented fervour and promised all kinds of good deeds in return for Violet's life. There was no hiding now from the truth: she had caused this catastrophe and the blame lay squarely at her feet.

Nothing could comfort her, not Charlie's strong arm

around her shoulders, nor Aunt Bea's sensible advice to try not to panic till she needed to.

The doctor had tried to be positive but had also said there was nothing much he could do except make sure she didn't become too dehydrated. Cholera was not always fatal and there were various degrees of severity; he thought her chances were reasonably good but noted on the third day of attending to her that Violet didn't seem to have much of a will to live.

'She is not trying. She has given up. You must remind her of all she has to live for so she will fight harder.'

Soon, the doctor announced that he could not stay any longer and departed, leaving medicines that seemed useless and the promise to return soon.

The home that had once been so happy now lapsed into a dreary routine of boiling water and changing damp sheets and washing hands and bodies with carbolic soap and taking turns to sit with the patient.

Charlie wandered the grounds pale and haunted, for the first time in his life feeling helpless to change the situation. Once he ventured to sit with Violet but the sight of him brought on such agitation and an outburst of weak tears that he had to leave the room. Meanwhile, he was feeling the pressure to return to Scotland and take up his duties, but he knew he could never leave Silver Mist till he knew Violet was safe.

He had thought to return with Isobel as his bride but now there was none of the former intimacy between them. She seemed not to notice him at all but went about the day like a ghost, unreachable and distant, her movements stiff and awkward. He often heard her at night, pacing up and down her room, sometimes breaking out into helpless tears, then in the mornings she would appear, white and drawn, to eat almost nothing and to stare down at her hands with an expression that was pitiful to watch. He longed to comfort her but when he attempted to put his arms around her, she looked at him with wide staring eyes that showed her horror at his touch.

Once she said with tears in her eyes, 'Charlie, I don't deserve your kindness. I'm cursed by my own arrogance. I'm sure of it now.'

Then he would drop his arms and walk away to the wildest part of the garden to release a few pent-up tears of his own.

Not long after Isobel's arrival back at Silver Mist, she received a letter from Phillipe Almeida. He had heard of Violet's illness and was anxious to help in any way he could. He wrote of his very deep concern for everyone in the house but did not renew any signs of his passion for her. He kept his letter formal and almost cold and did not allude to their last meeting until the final line:

'Please try to forgive me, and I wish you all happiness with Lord Cameron.'

Isobel tore the letter into pieces. She was not in the frame of mind to deal with anything other than Violet's illness, but still the letter tormented her and brought back in vivid detail every passionate moment of their encounter.

Harry Saunders arrived with an urgency that made Isobel think that perhaps he was really in love with her sister after all, though when he dropped down to his knees by Violet's bed to remind her of his love for her, he received the same reaction as

Charlie. Violet only opened her glazed eyes for an instant before lapsing into weak tears and an anxiety that brought on palpitations and a renewed fear for her heart.

Consequently, Harry walked aimlessly around the grounds in genuine despair. Even his love of hunting was forgotten, but he found some relief in cursing to himself and lashing out with his riding whip at any plant that hindered his progress. Charlie was a more pitiful sight still as he wandered in a state of helpless agitation through the house and gardens, but he found consolation in picking the most beautiful blooms he could find to make into a fresh bouquet to place by Violet's bed in the hope she would see it and be roused back to life. But it was his expression of hopelessness that terrified Isobel the most, and in her despair, she began to see the bouquets as funeral wreaths and an omen of impending doom.

Even the animals took on the general sense of despair. Monty padded up and down the halls and rooms with his tail hanging limp as well as a tragically woebegone expression on his face. Sometimes he stood at Violet's door and looked longingly at the mostly sleeping figure lying motionless in the bed. Once or twice, he tried to lick her into action, but she only pushed him away with an irritable weak touch of her hand before he wandered sadly away to sit with Aunt Bea, who never sewed or knitted now but often sat for long periods of time staring into space. Their vigorous walks around the house and verandas were suspended and he had nothing to do but nip irritably at the baby leopards when they became too rowdy. They were becoming big enough now to wander around the house and get in everyone's way, but even so, as they were the only creatures that were in any way able to comfort Isobel, they were tolerated as innocent children might be.

Isobel took them on her lap to fondle them with an open affection she denied everyone else or held them to her tear-stained face and kissed their silky fur and took them to sleep on her bed at night. They had, however, begun to awaken to their instincts and often spent the night roaming around the room and pawing at the door. During the day, she walked through the gardens like a sleepwalker with the two of them bounding around her heels, as attached to her as if she were their mother. They were clever enough to answer to their names now, and thinking of how their names had come about brought on thoughts of Marco and how she had let him down. She pictured him in that cold house, probably longing to see the cubs again, then she thought of his father and her anguish would return stronger than ever.

With Violet's illness, Billy seemed to more and more to detach himself from the other residents of the house, almost as though he was deliberately placing himself out of the way so he wouldn't appear to be a burden on anyone. He spent most of his day outside now, looking silently at the world around him and watching the other birds as they flew past or landed in the grass to eat grubs. Every now and then he fluttered clumsily up into a nearby tree and sat there cleaning his feathers and apparently thinking deeply about bird matters. It was only at sunset that he waddled up to the veranda door to join the others for supper.

But even these bleak days held a glimmer of hope, for despite everything, Violet was hanging on; this, Isobel knew, was because of Aashi, and her great skill as a nurse.

Aashi would wander off to the forest and come back with a

handful of various plants and leaves and retire to the kitchen to boil up her secret concoctions. At first, Isobel was alarmed and rejected the potions as being unsafe, but it was when Aashi said she had cured both her parents of the *haiza* as she called it, that Isobel was convinced.

There was a meeting where the contents of the elixirs were examined. Apart from the crushed bark and roots from a tree growing in the forest, they were based largely on the water from fresh coconuts with the addition of lime juice and salt. Other times it was boiled water steeped in cloves or coconut water again with ground nutmeg. There was a herbal tea with mint, ginger and basil combined with black pepper. And there was boiled rice crushed to the consistency of a broth and laced with wild honey and nutmeg.

There was the occasional dissenting voice, but in the end, it was Charlie who convinced the others it was worth a try. 'I've seen people cured of disease in the north with similar mixtures. Give the girl a chance.' He added sadly, making Isobel go as pale as death, 'We have nothing to lose…'

Saunders too agreed, saying he had lived in India long enough to know there were things the natives could do with their herbs that were beyond rational thought. He turned away with a tear in the corner of his usually cold eyes, and Isobel was forced to think a little more highly of him.

The secret in the cure turned out to be in the dosage. Small teaspoonfuls of the mixtures were administered every fifteen minutes throughout the day and night, and to the joy of everyone, she managed to keep them down. The sweet rice gruel was eaten almost voraciously and on the fourth day of the cure, there was a definite improvement in her appearance. Her eyes, once so sunken in her emaciated face, had taken on a more normal expression with the bright hazel colour and light beginning to return.

One wonderful morning she could raise her head to look about her before eating a huge bowl of the rice and bush-honey mixture, then she faltered around the room for a few moments, supported by Aunt Bea, who couldn't hide the tears of joy.

Isobel was by now in an ecstasy of happiness and managed to sit down for the first time in weeks and eat a huge breakfast of toast and eggs and Scotch marmalade – the last survivor of Aunt Bea's trunk. She had been reprieved, and life was worth living once more.

However, with the return of Violet's health there was also the return of the nagging thoughts that haunted her night and day. There was no more news from Phillipe, so she assumed he had accepted the fact she would marry Charlie as she had sworn she would, and he would continue with his plans to go to Portugal to marry Carolina.

The illness had changed Violet, making her for the moment at least more grateful for the simple things in life, and she wondered in her newly receptive state why she had never really noticed the natural world before. For the first time with any consciousness, she admired the silhouettes of the trees against the darkening sky and the brilliant hues of the passionate sunsets that filled her room every evening with a kaleidoscope of changing light.

The sight of a blooming flower now took on enormous importance to her, and she buried her face with a kind of rapture in the frangipanis and jasmine placed by her bed every day by Charlie. The scents and sounds from the garden outside her window cast a sly spell over her as she lay at first too weak to move, but it was as though the power of nature itself, by its incessant force, was compelling her to rouse herself and take her place back with the living.

The little geckoes that ran almost constantly across the walls which had once filled her with terrified revulsion, now became a source of delight, and she watched their antics for hours with the bemused affection of a mother towards her wayward children. Monty was welcomed back onto the bed, though for some time it seemed he couldn't summon the courage to take up the invitation but hung back as if afraid to upset what seemed to be a situation almost too good to be true.

At first, he padded slowly over the quilt towards her, taking one cautious step at a time, then in a sudden flurry of wild abandonment when the realization came over him that life had indeed returned to normal, he threw himself on her, rolling about like a mad thing, licking her face in between snapping at his own tail.

Even Billy honoured her with his dignified presence for an hour or two and condescended to be hand fed his favourite biscuit, but the cubs were too rough with her to be allowed to stay and it was then that Monty imposed his seniority and banished them from the room.

Violet was kind to everyone, especially to Aashi, who she knew absolutely was responsible for saving her life. She was humbled by the girl's selflessness which threw her own selfishness into a stronger light, and for a brief period at least, she resolved to be more like her. Even Isobel was looked upon with a kind of indulged fondness as she moved around the room, almost too afraid to speak for fear of causing a relapse.

But it was to Harry that she showed an especial tenderness. She was grateful for his constant attendance and seemed to love him more than ever. It was more than mere gratitude for his devotion; she had accepted her future as the wife of Harry Saunders without any doubt now, because of the scene she had witnessed when lying half-awake in her bed in the early days of her recovery.

Isobel had been taking her turn nursing and was sitting reading quietly in the corner of the room when Charlie came in and sat down next to her and began to talk in his soft Scots burr.

'She has passed the danger point. Even the doctor has said so. She will live, it's certain now.'

'Yes, yes, thank God.'

'Well…'

Violet heard a sudden shifting in the chair followed by a deep sigh.

'Charlie, I know what you are going to say.'

He in turn took a deep breath, then paused, as though it cost him a lot to speak.

'I can't stay any longer, but I couldn't leave while there was any doubt, and there are other things we must decide.'

For half a minute there wasn't a sound, but Isobel stood then and walked towards the open window. Violet could see her clearly by the light of the lamp on the table, almost wringing her hands in despair, but her face when she turned to him was lit by a silvery glow, turning her into a goddess.

'Just one more week, please Charlie. I don't know what we will do without you.'

Then she began to cry, soft choking tears.

'If Violet had died, I would have, too. She's all I have, and it would have been easier to die than to live with this horrible guilt. Oh, Charlie.'

He went to her then and took her in his arms and Violet heard him say, 'Not all. You have me, and always will.'

From where she lay, Violet experienced a deep stab of pain, with her throat full of an aching grief. She had never valued Charlie even when he had offered his fine, strong heart to her, and now she must live with it.

After a moment, Isobel's voice came muffled from where her face lay against Charlie's chest.

'We will wake her. She needs to sleep.'

Then Violet watched as they walked from the room, silhouetted against the light, their heads close together and with his arm enfolding her waist.

Chapter Thirty-Seven

There was an uncomfortable period of time when the entire household watched each other for symptoms of the disease having infected anyone else, but after three weeks had elapsed, everyone began to relax and think of other things.

For Isobel, her first thought now was for Marco. He had sent a letter written in a childish scrawl accompanied by a charming drawing of himself with the animals at Silver Mist. It was a powerful hint, but she was forced to write back and say that because of the illness he would have to wait a little longer. Considering the scene she had had with his father, there was no certainty he would even be allowed to visit, but somehow she thought Phillipe was more generous than that, and would put aside his own feelings and not step in the way of his son's happiness.

But now even the thought of Phillipe brought on a pang of such complicated feelings she would slip into a dark, restless mood that took her mind away from the daily matters that were pressing upon her. She seemed to drift through the increasingly warm days with a grim frown puckering her forehead.

The coffee berries were beginning to turn the palest pink. In another few weeks they would be red and would have to be picked and labourers would have to be found.

Isobel turned to Constanza, who knew all the families in the area, and on her next trip to the market she made it known that there was work at Silver Mist and that her mistress would pay cash for their labour. She returned with sobering news.

'They want to help you, Madam, but Count Almeida has told them that if they work for you, he will never employ them again. They have their families to think of, Madam. It is better to have food than to starve. There is nothing I can do.'

It was what Isobel had expected, as she was under no illusion as to the depth of Count Almeida's spite, but she was determined still to beat him at whatever cost, even if she picked every last coffee bean herself.

With Violet's sure recovery, Charlie was restless now and eager to leave and take up his inheritance, but only if Isobel accompanied him as his wife, for he was sure now that life without her would be impossible.

It had seemed almost disrespectful to talk about marriage while Violet was so ill, but now that she was so much better and seemed more than ever committed to Harry Saunders, each moment pressed upon him to ask Isobel to marry him at once, before returning to Scotland. After living so long in the sweet cushioning adoration of all at Silver Mist, it would be a great wrench to leave the only place on earth where he had ever felt true domestic happiness. He was aware that he was the envy of many, having a great estate to return to. To him alone his future seemed bleak, and the only way he felt he could survive was to take the very heart of the home he loved with him.

There was no putting it off any longer, and he approached her one evening when he found her alone on the terrace with Sami on her lap and Priti sitting quietly panting at her feet as they all watched the sun go down together.

Charlie noticed the gathering wildness in the cubs' natures as the evening awakened something in them; their magnificent eyes flashed about, alert to every moving thing. He knew they would soon be unable to be restrained and he feared for Isobel's peace of mind when they would have to leave her for their wild destiny.

He had mixed a brandy and soda, more for himself than for her, as all of a sudden he was unsure whether she would accept him. He had decided that he would include a yearly stay at Silver Mist as a lure, along with someone to run the estate for them. The cubs, he knew, were his biggest obstacle, knowing she loved them with a passion, but he also knew that if she accepted him, she would transfer that passion to himself, entirely and wholeheartedly.

Somehow Isobel knew instinctively that the time had come for his declaration, and she smiled up at him with an expression that was encouraging. There was sadness though and defeat showing in her eyes along with expectation, for she had only just at that moment decided to surrender to all the forces that conspired against her.

He sat down next to her and took her hand.

'My dear Isobel, you must have guessed by now…'

She smiled and let him keep her hand. He was just raising it to his lips when galloping horses could be heard coming up the drive. They stood together to meet what was coming towards them, anxious now, as there was a desperation to the sound that was fast approaching them.

It was difficult to see at first, but as the horsemen drew closer to the house the light from the lanterns revealed Phillipe Almeida as he emerged out of the blackness of the night, his proud, handsome face bleached white and stark with terror.

At the first sight of Isobel and Charlie, he registered that he had interrupted an intimate moment and along with his desperate alarm he felt a chilling, deep bitterness as well. Next to all that he had suffered, there was more to come – perhaps worse than before – and he felt himself to be a doomed man, a man with a harsh fate.

'Marco!' he said, his eyes opaque with dread and his voice trembling. 'Have you seen Marco?'

Charlie went to him and placed a comforting hand on his shoulder.

'What is it, man? The boy's not here.'

Phillipe's hand went to his forehead, and he groaned aloud.

'He left a note saying that he was going to see the cubs. No one has seen him for hours… My God!'

Terror had stricken Isobel so she could hardly speak, but she mumbled out a few desperate words.

'But he's so little. Surely, he wouldn't…'

'Senhora Clara said he was in the garden at four, but when she went to find him, he was gone. I wasted a lot of time looking for him around the house, then I found the note in his toy box only an hour or two ago. He had hidden it there – he likes a treasure hunt. We sometimes play a game—'

His voice cracked, and he was unable to speak further, but his expression was ghastly and tormented and Isobel was overcome with pity. For a long moment, she struggled with having to stop herself from going to comfort him and holding him close to her as she had done once before. But it was a fleeting thought and the present horror came rushing back with a renewed panic.

Charlie handed him his brandy.

'Drink this. I'll get my gun. We'll spread out. We'll find him.'

'But surely someone would have seen him along the road, and perhaps taken him home till tomorrow when it's light? One of the local people...?' Isobel was clutching at straws now.

'He would probably hide. He likes to hide when adults are around. He would talk of nothing but the cubs, and the dog. I should have brought him here to visit you but—'

He looked at Isobel, his eyes penetrating through to her soul, but she looked down, unable to face him.

By now, Saunders and Mr. Singh had come out of the house to join the other men. Lanterns were lit and everyone rode away towards the road where they thought Marco must still be, calling out his name as they disappeared into the silence of the night.

This was a time when Isobel wished she could ride a horse and do something practical, but she was forced to wait and watch helplessly as they rode away, leaving her to her terror and her ever-increasing feelings of guilt as she became aware that this was perhaps her fault as well. Every whim of his had been indulged, all the while lavishing him with affection, and to a child starved of love as Marco was, it was an irresistible attraction.

Her tears fell fast now, and she prayed fervently to all the gods she could gather to spare the little boy. A little boy, she realized, to whom she had felt inexplicably bound from the very beginning. The butterfly he had put in the letter was a symbol of it, luring her towards him for a then unknown purpose, but it was a powerful feeling, amplified by her promise to the poor dead Silvia who had cried out to her from the grave.

All the women in the household had gathered in the kitchen to wait and weep and hope, but Aashi was restless and asked if she could take a lantern to look for the child.

'I know the jungle, Madam. Let me help. I cannot bear to think of the little boy alone.'

At first Isobel refused, saying it was too dangerous, but then with a kind of frantic desperation she relented.

'I'll go with you. Anything's better than sitting around here doing nothing.'

There was an outcry from the others, especially Aunt Bea, who put up her hand to stop her niece.

'I won't allow it, Isobel, so get that idea out of your head at once!'

'Issie, no!' Violet had thrown herself around her sister's neck and clung there while Mary pleaded with tears in her eyes.

'Miss Isobel, listen to what your aunt says.'

'I must do something; you know I must. Don't you see? It's my fault again. I seem to have a gift for bringing misery to all I love.'

Then she gently extracted herself from Violet's arms and went to the little room next to the pantry where the firearms were kept.

She had never shot anything in her life, but she knew how to shoot a rifle as Saunders had taught her, along with Mary and Aunt Bea. All the women saw the sense in being able to handle a gun, even though none of them had any intention of using it unless it was absolutely necessary. Isobel had proven herself to be a good shot, though not quite as good as Aunt Bea who rarely missed.

It was Aunt Bea's expertise that drove her now to insist on her rights. 'If you go, I go, and I'm a better shot if there is trouble.'

There was such fierce determination in the woman's eyes that there was no stopping her, so they set out, leaving Violet with Mary and the servants, who lit every lantern they could find to light up the house and grounds.

Aashi suggested they take a path that led down to the stream that divided Silver Mist from the coffee fields belonging to Casa Margarida.

At first it seemed impossible that the child might have taken that route, but then Isobel remembered showing Marco where her house lay nestled in the little valley between Casa Margarida and the estate of Santa Maria, belonging to Count Almeida.

After lifting him in her arms, she had pointed to the thatching on Silver Mist's roof saying how it was much quicker to get to her home 'as the crow flies', and explained the term to him. She remembered too with a blinding clarity how his little face had lit up with delight.

'Then if I run down the hill through the coffee plants and across the stream, I could visit you?'

'Well, I suppose so, but it's a very long way for a little boy and it would be better to wait for your papa to bring you.'

He had looked at her then with his huge blue eyes, almost offended.

'I am a big boy, and I am not afraid.'

At the time she had thought nothing of it, but she was almost sure now that was exactly what he had done. He had run down through the coffee plantation to where the jungle formed a barrier to Silver Mist and must have attempted to cross those few hundred feet of almost certain death.

The night was full of eyes and sounds; monkeys screeched at the light of the lanterns and the trees above swayed with sudden ominous movements that struck terror into everyone's hearts, knowing there may well be leopards on the hunt. Only Aashi seemed calm and moved silently and swiftly through the undergrowth like a wraith, sometimes pausing to listen, before motioning the others to follow along behind.

'We must stay tightly together so we will appear bigger.'

So they moved slowly forward, stumbling over each other, oblivious to scratches and bruises as every moment became more hopeless and despairing.

It felt dangerous to speak at all, but they persisted in calling out the little boy's name despite causing a nerve-wracking cacophony of sound to break out in response. The monkeys especially, woken from their sleep, took great offence and chattered abuse from the height of the shadowy trees. Sometimes a fierce, red-eyed male would rush down in a threatening way but would be driven back at once by a few sharp words from Aashi.

They had been out now for almost three hours, and the moon had risen very high in the night sky, lighting up the forest floor and the trees around them. Huge spider webs draped across their path sometimes caught their faces and hair, causing involuntary screams and frantic beating at their skirts in case they had picked up an unwanted traveller.

They moved on, desperate now, calling out louder and with more urgency. When all hope was lost, they heard in response a faint sound, more a sob than a cry, mingled with the trickling of a running stream.

Not daring to believe they may have found Marco at last, the women looked at each other with a mixture of hope and doubt. Then the noise came again. This time, though, it was plain it was only the bell-like tinkle of water flowing over rocks.

Then there was nothing, and Isobel began to believe they had imagined the sound after all. Hope was driving them to hallucinate.

'It must have been monkeys, damn them! Damn them!' Isobel began to cry now, horrible hopeless sobs of despair, blaming herself over and over for encouraging the little boy to seek her out. She moved into a new deeper realm of suffering. Suffering she felt should only be for very wicked people. Now she understood what it was like to lose one's senses, and a voice in her head tormented her mercilessly.

It's your fault, it's your fault. Every superstitious notion she ever had overtook her. Her luck had run out at last. God had forgiven her and given Violet back to her, but was the death of an innocent child a cross she would have to bear for the rest of her life?

It was too much, and she fell to her knees, insensible to the appeals of Aunt Bea and Aashi. She wanted to beat herself with her fists, to tear at her hair, to punish herself.

Then she screamed out Marco's name, more in despair than with any real chance her prayers would be answered.

Aunt Bea recalled her to her senses with a shake.

'Isobel! For God's sake, pull yourself together!'

'It's no good. My life is over. I can never be happy again.'

Then they heard a hesitant little voice, not far away, coming out of the night.

'It's Marco, I am here.'

The three women looked at each other, not quite believing yet, but running towards the sound, Isobel crying out as she ran, with the others stumbling behind, not caring now if in their delight, their noise disturbed the hounds of hell.

There he was, a small, pale crouching figure on the other side of a fast-running stream, his strange, old-fashioned clothes torn and his face dirty. He had been crying, but his eyes lit up with a mixture of relief and anxiety when he saw his rescuers.

'I wanted to see Monty and the cubs. You won't tell Papa, will you?' he said, as Isobel rushed towards him across the stream, only feet away now from gathering him in her arms.

Chapter Thirty-Eight

I t was painfully moving to witness the first moments of the reunion of father and child. For once Phillipe dropped his proud, arrogant manner and held the boy to him for a long time, unable to do anything other than kiss the child's thick thatch of dark hair and fight back tears.

'Never ever do anything like that again. Can you imagine how dreadful it was for me?'

'No, Papa, I promise.'

Then he spoke as though he was the only person in the room. 'Your mama would never forgive me.'

Marco was in heaven, having achieved his goal of being surrounded by the warm, plump bodies of the cubs and Monty at last. He was exhausted too, and before long he fell into a deep sleep and was carried to bed by his father. Phillipe was reluctant to stay but he saw the sense of it, especially when an almost impenetrable mountain mist descended without warning over the house – everyone acutely aware of what might have been if the mist had come down earlier when Marco was alone in that pitiless wilderness.

The atmosphere in the room would have been almost happily domestic if it weren't for Phillipe's ever darkening expression. It seemed the more comfortable and cheerful the inhabitants of Silver Mist became, the further he slipped into a type of black despair and built an almost impenetrable wall around himself that the others mistook for either arrogant pride or stunned relief.

Isobel sometimes watched him when she thought it was safe to do so. In the soft light of the room, the contours of his face became more defined, and the deep shadows around his cheekbones and mouth carved an expression so full of melancholy that she felt a twist of pity for him. Sometimes, a secret inscrutable look came into his eyes, then he would frown as though reminded of something unpleasant and almost physically shake the thought off with a proud jerk of his head as he attempted to bring himself back to the present.

Throughout the evening, Isobel sometimes felt his glistening dark eyes on her but when she looked up he turned away, as though the very sight of her was distasteful to him, and she was left believing he did indeed blame her for Marco's adventure.

The truth though was very different. He could see now why his son so longed to be in the charming atmosphere of Silver Mist – so different to the cold halls of Casa Margarida – enough to defy all the strict rules imposed on him and risk certain punishment just to be within Isobel's sphere.

Everywhere was warmth and humour and occasional squabbling, but most of all there was a sense of family, and his Italian heart cried out for it. He thought of his own home, his meals usually taken alone in the dining room as his uncle was often away, and when they did dine together there were always the cold formalities to observe. The half a dozen servants always at his shoulder made it impossible to talk of anything other than the most banal of subjects. His uncle always dressed to dine, as though he was in the royal presence, his consistently curt manner when dealing with the servants, the loud clatter of cutlery on plates, the long silences, the unspoken resentment, the reproaches, and at times a furious hatred.

He was finding it almost unbearable to watch the woman he loved in the intimate radius of the man he was sure would soon become her husband. Every one of Charlie's actions seemed to confirm this. If he walked behind the sofa where Isobel sat, he would lean his arms on the settee and bend to whisper in her ear, making her smile and look around at him with an expression that plainly showed her fondness for him.

Phillipe noticed that he was not the only observer of the intimacies of the young couple.

He sometimes saw Violet flinch and turn away with a look of such anguish that it made him wonder if he was not the only person in the room disturbed by the sight of such obvious partiality, despite her being engaged to the rather obnoxious Saunders.

Once Charlie placed his hand on Isobel's shoulder as he passed, but his touch seemed so loaded with meaning and the certainty of his right to do so that Phillipe felt a rush of twisted pain in his chest that shocked him. He was not a violent man, but it took all his strength not to leap to his feet and demand such behaviour stop at once, even though he had no right. He was reliving again, as he had a thousand times since he had seen her last, the night when he had held her in his arms. He closed his eyes and felt again the softness of her warm mouth on his, her slim waist, the lovely smooth skin of her neck, her scent...

The soft radiance of the fireside had cast a golden glow over her skin and hair, illuminating her with a halo of light and setting her apart from anyone else in the room. Her husky laugh rang out as she raised her glass of brandy, then she cried with joy as she told of how they had found Marco. But every now and then, through the laughter and the tears, he saw a brief cloud of what he thought was deep despair flickering over her face. Other times he thought he saw defiance, then uncertainty, and even anger directed towards him, along with other sentiments that were unclear.

He felt no one else would notice these fleeting emotions because he alone really knew her, he knew her intimately, and it was his great consolation that he felt deep in his heart no other man would ever get as close to her.

He was spared further torture as one by one the inhabitants of the house said their goodnights and left, till there was only Charlie, Phillipe and Isobel remaining in the room. There were some horribly long moments of tension while the men circled each other, and Charlie made it plain he wanted to be alone with Isobel.

But Phillipe would not be shifted and poured himself another brandy. He had decided it was his right to have some final moments with her as he would be going away for a very long time – perhaps forever – and would take Marco with him.

At last, he roused himself to speak.

'If you will allow me one moment of your time, Miss

Blanchard? In private. There is a business matter I wish to discuss with you.'

Charlie was startled and clearly wanted to object. He was suspicious too as he had seen the emotion in Almeida's eyes when he looked at Isobel, though he was still unsure what it meant. He was aware too of the peculiar electricity that shot between the pair, even in a crowded room. He was relieved there was no tenderness there, as exists among lovers; it was something else, something dark and a little disturbing.

Isobel too seemed agitated and could not meet Almeida's eyes.

'It's very late. Can't it wait till the morning?'

'I intend to leave at first light. I have much to do at Casa Margarida. My uncle will want to see Marco at once of course.'

'Well then, just for a moment or two.'

Charlie prepared to leave but not before making it plain he was not pleased.

'It seems I probably won't see you in the morning, Almeida, but I'm very happy things turned out so well.'

Then he bent to kiss Isobel on the cheek.

'Well then, I'll leave you to it. Goodnight, my darling.'

There, he had said it, and those two words consolidated their relationship, leaving no doubt in Isobel's or Phillipe's mind that they were engaged.

Isobel was taken aback at first, but hid it well with a dazed, flushed smile.

Charlie shook hands with Phillipe and gave him a final look that included a warning. For Isobel it was a strange feeling to watch the two men facing off, squaring their shoulders, apparently highly civilized, but hiding the current of primitive combat that ran just beneath the surface.

Isobel was forced at last to break the silence.

'What is this business you wish to speak to me about?'

He seemed to consider her for a moment, then he stepped forward to take her hand and raise it to his lips while she sat back, uncertain and vulnerable. His warm lips seemed to linger there, causing a hot prickling sensation to run down her back.

'Thank you, a thousand times, for finding Marco. Do you realize what you have saved me from? A lifetime of hell. It is unthinkable. I began to imagine I was being punished for not loving my son enough.'

She was touched but still wary, then pulled away her hand.

'You know what I feel for the child.' Her tone grew cold once more.

He seemed disappointed to lose the tenderness of the moment but roused himself to face her more calmly.

'There is a local man, Carlito Fonte. He is seen as a leader around here, a fine man. Constanza will know him. He might be able to get some men to work for you, but you must not mention my name, otherwise they will be suspicious and do nothing. No man trusts the name of Almeida around here. My uncle is not popular.'

'You could have said all this in front of Charlie. Why we needed to be alone for me to hear this is beyond me.'

'I must honour my uncle. I cannot speak badly of him publicly, despite his shortcomings.'

'Why? A man like you, his own nephew, surely can change things.'

'There are reasons.'

'Tell me.'

'I have no wish to burden you with my problems, but I'm going away to Portugal very soon and none of this will matter.'

'To marry your fiancée, I suppose.'

Her words came out harsh and bitter, and she could have bitten her tongue for exposing herself, though she was very careful not to look at him. Her eyes would certainly have betrayed her.

He did not answer at first, but she watched his hands clench then unclench, showing his agitation.

'I don't want to talk about her. As my fiancée, I owe Carolina the respect she deserves.'

'Of course, you have respect for everyone but not for me… Your respect is reserved solely for your family and those connected with it. I have read a little of your history. *Uma Familia Nobre*,' she scoffed, 'and Casa Margarida is included in this. No outsider could ever violate those cold consecrated walls.'

'I had no idea you had given my family so much thought.'

'I haven't, except where they intrude upon my rights. I consider your estate and everything attached to it as ridiculously feudal.'

'That is your right, I suppose, and as I said, none of this matters anymore.'

'And little Marco, have you thought of him?'

'As I said, I must go to Portugal, and I must leave as soon as I can.'

'Then I may not see him ever again? You blame me, don't you! You think I'm responsible for him running to me? And you want to punish him by taking him away.'

'How could I blame him for doing something—' He

stopped. He almost added, 'for doing something I wanted to do myself.'

She stood very abruptly.

'Well then, there is nothing more we have to say to one another.'

He stood to face her, though she kept her eyes cast down.

'There is no doubt now you will marry Charles Cameron?'

'None, as you have seen for yourself.'

Before he could control himself, an angry colour flooded his face, giving him away.

'He calls you his darling.'

She picked up on his anger and experienced a little thrill of triumph. So, he was not as unaffected as she had thought.

'People in love say those things to each other.'

He took a step closer.

'In love? Then why do your eyes say something else?'

'You're wrong. There's nothing in my eyes but exhaustion. I'm very tired and I want to go to my room.'

'You don't love him. How could you, after—?'

'You've seen what kind of man he is. Why wouldn't I love him?'

He gripped both her arms and pulled her closer towards him, all the while fixing her eyes with his own.

He kissed her then, harder than he had before on that night where he had been so tender, but for a moment she forgot everything and allowed herself to feel his warm mouth on hers. It was so easy to close her eyes and drown in the passion he inspired in her. She wanted to touch him, to run her hands over his body and press her face into his chest and kiss the bare flesh, to tear at his hair – even to hit out at him for daring to overwhelm her. Why did he have that effect on her when no other man had? He robbed her of her self-control. She didn't like it, but even so she left his arms reluctantly.

'You have no right to touch me.'

'I want you to see… I want you to give me time…'

'Can't you see what is before you? Charlie has offered me his heart, his life, and I've never met a better man.'

He flinched at that, and even in the firelight she could see his face go pale.

'Even after what has happened between us?'

'Why should that matter? I chose to throw myself at you, for whatever reasons I can't say. It was the wine, it must have been, but now … you kissed me tonight because you see me as not worthy of respect. You mistake the freedoms I choose to take for myself as liberties you can take with me!'

They stood opposite each other, both in a kind of impotent despair.

'Isobel, there are circumstances that might make you understand me more, make you hate me less…'

'I don't want to hear your excuses. You mean nothing to me! And what does it matter now?'

She tore her arm away from his grip and left, almost fleeing to her bedroom, where once inside she leaned against the back of the door trying to catch her breath.

A moment later she heard him knock softly and whisper, 'Isobel, open the door. Forgive me, forgive me.'

For a moment her resolve almost deserted her as she longed to part in a kind of peace, but her resentment would not allow her to weaken, and she moved away from his imploring words with her hands pressed firmly over her ears.

Chapter Thirty-Nine

B y the time Isobel left her room in the morning, Phillipe was gone, taking Marco with him. Again, her encounter with Phillipe Almeida left her shattered, unsure and tormented, and it showed in her face at breakfast.

Saunders commented on her frail appearance in a tone of voice that seemed to her to be unpleasant and even disrespectful, and she wished him gone. He had been at Silver Mist long enough and Violet was well now, even though at times she showed signs of a lingering depression, and with the instinct of a sister Isobel felt she knew why.

The wedding was almost upon them – to be endured in only three weeks' time – but Violet showed no signs of backing out and Saunders remained at Silver Mist.

The real reason for his continuing to stay became clear that morning.

'The black leopard has been spotted near here. One of the men saw it down on the path near the stream where you found Marco. The animal is dangerous and it's because of those blasted cubs. He can smell them, I'm sure of it. I told you keeping them alive would bring trouble.'

'You want to kill it because you want the trophy for your collection. At least be honest about it,' Isobel said bitterly.

'That's true, but it's only a matter of time till it begins to prowl around here. In fact, I'm sure I heard it last night. Anyway, I'm going out this evening. Will you come with me, Charlie old man?'

'I would rather not. Hunting is not really something I enjoy.'

'I'm not asking you to shoot it. I'll need a good shot to cover my back, that's all. Come on, be a sport,' Saunders persisted, and Charlie reluctantly agreed. His mind was on other things as he knew he must speak to Isobel as soon as possible. He had made it clear how he felt about her, and she would be expecting a marriage proposal, especially after he had referred to her as 'my darling'.

His chance came soon after breakfast when he followed her into the summer room where she often pored over the old estate books.

'Isobel.'

She looked up and smiled very gently. 'I know what you're going to say, Charlie, and the answer is, my most dear friend, I cannot marry you.'

'But why?'

'Because you don't love me.'

'Of course I love you. We've been so close. We do everything together.'

'As close as a brother and sister, a most loving brother and sister. It's Violet you truly love, and always will.'

For a long time he didn't answer, only running his fingers through his russet hair as he brooded over her words.

'Once upon a time yes, I did love her – you knew that. But now...'

'You are the sort of man, my dear Charlie, who falls in love deeply and forever. I've seen you when you look at Violet. Even now, when you're so bitter about her, even though you have no right to be.'

'I was hurt that she could so easily forget me, when all the time I was in Assam I thought of nothing but her.'

'The love is still there. She's been so unhappy.'

'Perhaps you're right, but I can never forgive her for engaging herself to Saunders when she knew how I felt about her.'

'Well, to be fair, you hadn't asked her to marry you and she was scared, so scared she did something out of character and she accepted Saunders when he asked her. It was my fault really, for bringing her here and leaving her to feel frightened and alone. All I cared about was myself; I can see that now. Poor Violet isn't cut out for a life here anymore than she's cut out for a life with Saunders. She did it to spite me, and I probably deserved it, but she got in too deep to get out of it. You must help her, Charlie.'

Charlie struggled with his thoughts for some time without speaking, then he went to Isobel, took her hand and kissed it.

'Dearest Isobel, I don't think there could ever be a more noble girl than you.'

'You know very little about me if you think nobility is one of my virtues, but I do want you to be happy, and you'll never be truly happy with me.'

'I'm not so sure about that, but I do know you well enough

to know you've made up your mind. And you're right about Violet. Once I did feel we were meant to be together, but now it's too late and I must go back to Scotland empty-handed.'

'She loves you still, I'm sure of it.'

'Then why does she lavish so much attention on that man? There, it's out in the open. I can't like him.'

'Then you must do something, and soon. Please Charlie.'

'But what about you, my dear girl?'

'Don't worry about me. I can take care of myself. Besides, I know it now, my destiny is here, in this place. Perhaps not forever, but for now this is where I must remain.'

'Is it because of Almeida?'

She turned her head and looked out of the window, not wanting him to see her face, for it was sure to give her away.

'Almeida? What makes you say that?'

'I've seen the way he looks at you. It can't be love because he'll soon marry someone else, but there is something there, I know, and I'm sorry to say it might not be entirely honourable.'

He blushed then, as he couldn't say he thought it might be an illicit sort of love. He remembered the night in Panjim, and how he had watched Almeida around Isobel. He was familiar with the actions of men when they wanted a woman. That undeniable, animal-like prowling, the restlessness, being unable to tear his eyes away from the desired one, and the night before he saw it again when Almeida had made it plain he wanted to be alone with her.

A sudden fear for her made him speak more openly than he wanted to.

'Be careful, Isobel. He's the sort of man who might hurt you if he's given the chance.'

It was on the tip of her tongue to say he already had, but she laughed off his warning.

'Hurt me? Never! How could he when I don't even like him? Anyway, he's going to Portugal with Marco, and he may never return to India again.'

Her face clouded when she thought of the night before, of Phillipe's urgent voice imploring her to open her door. If she had, who knows what might have happened?

'Now, if you really want me to be truly happy, save me from a future as the sister-in-law of that damned Saunders!'

Charlie walked away from Isobel with mixed feelings. He needed to think. He needed time.

But there was no time, as that evening, before they could set out in search of the leopard, the leopard came to Silver Mist. It appeared out of the shadows of the jungle at nightfall when Isobel was sitting on the veranda with the cubs.

The babies seemed to sense his presence. They became agitated and began to whimper as they picked up his scent on the air. Isobel was terrified for them as she had heard stories of the males sometimes killing cubs, though somehow, she couldn't quite believe it. It seemed a dishonourable act for such a magnificent creature.

And he was a magnificent beast, bigger than the average leopard with a glistening pure ebony coat that shone silver in the setting sun. There was not a bit of him that was not perfect as he slowly loped around the perimeter of the mowed lawn, keeping in the shadows so at times it was difficult to tell if he was there or not. She knew she should raise the alarm, but something prevented her. If she called out then Saunders would come with his gun and kill the creature without mercy, so she collected the cubs together and slowly attempted to backtrack into the house and close the door. But at exactly that moment, Monty sauntered out to sniff the evening air and to relieve himself at his usual tree in the centre of the lawn.

Monty was only halfway across the grass, busy sniffing at something on the ground, when the leopard appeared like a phantom. It stopped and stared as though deciding what sort of a creature it was before him and whether it was edible or not.

Isobel called out and the dog half turned to look at her. He had never been any good at obeying orders and he gave Isobel a look that implied he wasn't going to start now.

But then he turned and saw the leopard and stood stock still, his little body shivering all over and unable to move.

The leopard began to creep forward just as she had seen the neighbour's cat back home in England do when stalking a bird.

Without thinking, Isobel tried the same tactics she used to employ when trying to distract the cat and rushed forwards screaming and waving her hands wildly about. The leopard stopped moving and stared at this odd creature in a long blue dress. Feeling a little ridiculous she called out, 'Shoo! Shoo!' Amazingly, the creature began to move backwards, all the time keeping his eyes on her. She had read that you should never look into an attacking animal's eyes, so she looked away, even though it was intensely nerve-wracking having to keep her eyes averted. But it seemed to be doing the trick as the leopard was almost back into the safety of the undergrowth when both Saunders and Charlie appeared on the veranda. Taking the situation in at a glance, in a second they were back in the house to get their guns. Saunders was quicker in his desire for a kill and rushed forward, at the same time raising his gun and shouting to Isobel to get back. The animal at first looked confused, then began to crouch and snarl with fear. Saunders stopped to aim but he wasn't quick enough and the leopard sprang through the air, catching him by the arm with his teeth. For an instant the creature raised his head to find the throat and at that moment Charlie rushed forward, raised his gun and fired. At first the leopard appeared not to have felt the bullet, only flinching a little, and his savage attack continued while Saunders tried to beat him off with his arms. Charlie raised his gun once more and fired. This time the animal leapt in the air before falling with a soft thud on Saunders's bleeding body. By now, the rest of the household had appeared, and Violet rushed to where Saunders lay unconscious on the ground. But her reaction was a strange one; everyone including Charlie expected a greater show of passion at the sight of her fiancé lying unmoving and covered in blood. She was white but surprisingly calm. She only muttered, 'Is he dead?' in a voice shaking with feeling.

Saunders was pale and insensible, but his eyes flickered open a few times and he spoke a few incomprehensible words. Mr. Singh set off at once to get a doctor while the injured victim was carried into the house and placed on a bed. Aashi cleaned his wounds with her usual gentle calm and after checking his body all over, she turned to the others standing around the bed. 'I think he will live!'

Violet whispered her relief. 'Thank God,' then had to be helped out of the room as she could barely stand.

After the doctor arrived everyone felt easier. Even though Saunders had lost some blood and as long as infection didn't set in, he would recover – though he would be left with some scars on his neck and arms as a reminder of his experience.

Violet was attentive to his every need; however, it was plain her attitude towards him had changed. At times she was almost cool and watched him as he slept from her chair by his bed with a peculiar half-smile, and later, when he was well enough to sit up and talk, she listened to his account of the leopard attack with something very like cynicism playing around her lips. It was plain he had not learned from the incident and was even blaming Charlie for shooting the beast before he'd had a chance to kill it himself.

There was an argument too about the leopard's body. The pelt and head were largely intact, making it a fine trophy for Saunders's wall, but Isobel had made certain the creature was buried deep in the soft ground under a favourite tamarind tree, giving it the respect in death it would have been denied had Saunders had his way.

When he found out he had been robbed, he accused Isobel of being spiteful.

'What difference does it make when the thing is dead if I have the pelt or not? Is it too late to dig it up?'

Not so long ago, Violet had been excited at the thought of having a hat and muff made out of a leopard's pelt but now the idea seemed to sicken her. The baby leopards had stolen her heart and changed her attitude forever.

She said nothing, only giving Saunders a look that hinted at a quiet loathing.

It was not the look of an adoring fiancée and Isobel picked up on it, hoping the hero had come crashing down from his pedestal at last. Later, when they were alone in the drawing room, Isobel cautiously raised the subject.

'You must be very relieved he's getting better. The wedding can go ahead as planned.'

Violet was sewing the hem of a silk nightgown meant for her trousseau, though her actions were listless and almost haphazard. Several times she made mistakes and had to unpick the false stitches. She put aside the garment with a quite reflection, as though she had finally made a decision that had been weighing heavily on her mind.

'I am relieved, but not because of the wedding. I'm relieved because now I don't have to marry him.'

'Whatever do you mean?'

Violet picked up the nightgown, glared at it, then threw it down.

'Because if he had been badly injured, I would have had to marry him and look after him. I realize now that I don't love him. I never really did.'

Isobel began to prowl around the room, touching things in an absent way, too full of relieved joy to stand still. Violet still spoke as though she was coming out of a dream.

'When he was lying there covered in blood, I should have been devastated, but I wasn't. I cared, of course, as I would for any man who was in danger of dying, but I'm ashamed to say I felt almost as though he deserved it. All that killing was bound to catch up with him eventually.'

Isobel laughed a little dryly.

'My dear child, you sound just like me.'

Violet smiled, but she looked tired and depressed.

'I know now that I cannot marry him. The other day when he touched me, I felt my flesh crawl.' She shivered, as though physically shaking him off. 'I knew then it was impossible, and as usual, Isobel, you were right, and I was wrong, and now there's nothing left for me.'

Then she began to crumble.

'I'll go back to London and live with Aunt Bea, and you'll marry Charlie and go with him…'

Her voice faltered then, as she couldn't go on.

'I'm not going to marry Charlie.'

Violet looked up, alert now, her eyes swimming with tears.

'Whatever do you mean? Everyone expects it, including Charlie.'

'No, he doesn't. He's always known I don't love him. Well, I do, but not enough to marry him.'

'Did he ask you?'

Isobel thought for a moment then decided to lie, knowing that Violet would never forgive her for being asked first. Her vanity would not allow it.

'No, he hasn't asked me, but even if he had I would have refused him.'

'That's ridiculous. You would be mad not to. Anyone can see he's perfect.'

Isobel laughed.

'Violet, you really are a most ridiculous girl. Why don't you tell him you love him?'

'So I can be laughed at and rejected? Anyway, it's up to the man to say it first.'

'Why? Why can't you say it? He's made it plain for a long time that he loves you, and I'm sure he still does even though I'm not sure you deserve it. He was willing to make a fool of himself over you. We all saw it, but he didn't care. Where is your courage, Violet?'

'Do you think he still loves me? Really?'

Her face lit up at first then collapsed back into shadow.

'A man doesn't change that quickly. I was certain he loved you. He spends almost every moment with you.'

'We're friends, that's all. It's always been you.'

'He'll think I only love him now because of his title.'

'Well, don't you?'

'No, of course not.' Violet thought for a while. A faint smile fluttered over her face as she realized she might well become Lady Cameron and be the chatelaine of a grand estate if all went well. Isobel saw the smile and rightly interpreted it as having a great deal to do with Violet's desire to have Charlie, but she kept it to herself. Violet was caught in the dream now, of castles, and gowns and servants.

'The title is wonderful of course, but…' she spoke now with more conviction, 'I honestly think I loved him just as much before. But it was all because of… Oh, I can hardly remember his name now. Because of that silly John. Oh, Issie, I'll die if I can't have him.'

Her tone was exactly as if she were talking about a hat she'd seen in a shop window, and Isobel struggled to hide her irritation. Violet usually got exactly what she wanted and the difference between a man and a hat mattered very little.

'Well for God's sake go and tell him. He's going to leave for Scotland in a few days, and a man like that won't stay single for long. Go to him, Violet! It's your only chance.'

'Are you sure Issie? You're not just doing this for me?'

'There's a lot I would do for you, Violet, but giving up a man I love is not one of them. Now hurry!'

Violet threw her arms around her sister and sobbed.

'I've hated us not getting on. I've been so unhappy, and I do love it here, at Silver Mist, despite what I've always said.'

The two sisters hugged each other for the first time in months and even Isobel, who cried rarely, wept a few hot tears of relief now that the dreaded Saunders would not be her brother-in-law.

Chapter Forty

It took a long time for Violet to screw up the courage to go to Charlie, but she was sensible enough too not to go as a pink-eyed supplicant begging for a favour. She put on her prettiest dress, put cold compresses on her swollen eyes, combed her hair into its most flattering style and borrowed some of her Aunt Bea's rouge to put the colour back into her cheeks. But first she had to rid herself of Harry Saunders. He was up now and walking about his bedroom, even though the wound on his arm had not quite healed, and he was already talking about returning to Cardamon Hills as he was beginning to miss the luxury his own estate provided and was frankly becoming a little irritated by Violet, who he thought was not showing enough loving attention. He noticed that she had been almost surly lately and had changed the subject whenever he talked about their impending marriage. Then, at times he'd thought she looked tired and depressed, and he liked her to be always cheerful and bright. He often thought of her as being a pretty little chirruping bird, much like a budgerigar or canary that whistled and sang on cue, and who was there to entertain and cheer. Except now she was letting him down, and every now and then resembled in expression the glum and lacklustre parrot Billy; even her language at times, especially when addressing him, showed a similarity to the scathing remarks of Aunt Bea, heaven forbid.

His heart softened however when he saw her enter his room, looking for the first time for weeks truly lovely, as if she'd had a long, refreshing sleep.

'My darling, how pretty you look,' he said as she entered his room.

He put out his arms, but she stepped back with a look on her face he had never seen before.

'Harry, now that you're almost better, I'm going to come straight to the point. I can't marry you.' She pulled the sapphire ring off her finger, looked at it with a pang of regret, and placed it in his hand.

'My dear girl, are you quite well?'

His answer irritated her.

'I'm perfectly well – better than I've been for ages. I want to release myself from our engagement. I know now that I don't love you enough. I'm sorry, Harry, but I don't think you would be happy with me any more than I would be happy with you.'

She smiled rather sadly as she put out her hand. 'Forgive me. I hope we can remain friends.'

His was not the response she expected. Instead of surprise or even disappointment, his face flushed a violent red.

'Don't you think it's up to me to decide if the engagement is off or not? I feel I have been most generous in overlooking certain disadvantages. I was willing to take you, despite...'

'Despite what?'

'I was willing to take on that sister of yours, even though her behaviour borders on madness at times, and she's vulgar—'

'What do you mean?'

'I saw her, that night when the boy went missing. She was alone with that Almeida fellow in the drawing room, and she was kissing him. She's playing a double game with Cameron, and I've got a good mind to tell him.'

'You were spying on her?'

'I was passing the room and I saw them, and she was behaving like a loose woman.'

For a long moment Violet simply stared at him, her lips trembling, while all her pity evaporated.

'Get out!'

'What do you mean?'

'You dare to insult Isobel! You know nothing about her, how fine she is and how she has looked after me when I've been too foolish to look after myself. Get out now and don't ever speak to me again.'

'I will, and you can tell your sister it's time she faced up to the fact that she'll never make a go of this place.'

He followed her to the door, taking out his anger on her with one final remark.

'Don't think I'll take you back when you come to your senses either!'

But Violet didn't really hear him; she was transfixed by the idea of Isobel kissing Phillipe Almeida and thought about how Isobel behaved when around Almeida. She realized there was a certain feverishness in Isobel's behaviour and a distinct change in her personality when in his company. She thought of the last time she had seen Phillipe Almeida and how he had watched Isobel with an intensity he had clearly made an effort to hide. Did it mean he was in love with her? Was Isobel in love with him?

In the end, she dismissed the whole thing as being of lesser importance when she thought about Charlie and what she must do. She steeled herself for a scene she prayed would end in her favour.

She found Charlie in the summer room, where he stood leaning against the wide-open French doors, breathing in the beauty of the view of the mountains.

He swung around when she walked into the room then quickly turned away, overcome with discomfort at being alone with her.

'I've grown to love it here. It's going to be lonely without you all. You're the only real family I've ever had.'

'We'll miss you terribly,' she said, then in a whisper, 'much more than you can ever know.' After a moment or two she took a step closer. 'Charlie…'

'How's Saunders then? He was looking much better.'

'He's going back to his estate. Mr. Singh is taking him now.'

'I should say goodbye.'

'He didn't wish to speak to anyone. He was quite angry.'

'You're not going with him?'

'No. He's angry because I've told him I don't love him, and I don't want to marry him.'

He considered her solemnly without a trace of a smile, but he was aware at the same time of a cautious rising elation.

'I'm surprised. You certainly gave a good impression of being very much in love with him.'

He stood quite still, frowning, with his hands in his pockets.

Violet went to him, trembling a little. A thin strain of the notorious Blanchard courage struggled to the surface.

'Charlie, how could I love him after knowing a man like you? In every way he is inferior to you. I compare every action of his to yours, and each time he comes up a very poor second.'

Despite her apparent seriousness, he couldn't help but laugh.

'Are you courting me?'

'Yes, I am. I don't want you to ever leave me. I can't bear it!'

Her courage failed her then and a few tears appeared in her lovely amber eyes.

'I know I'm not as wonderful as Isobel. You know how foolish I can be – Harry is proof of that – but I'll love you forever with all my heart, if you will have it?' She turned away then, her cheeks a flaming red, too ashamed to face him. 'I'm sorry. Forgive me. I shouldn't have … but I felt it was worth it to try, even if you do laugh at me.'

She was very careful not to look at him, but she held her breath waiting for his answer. There were no other sounds in the room except for Monty, who had followed her in and was now nibbling rudely and noisily at his hind leg in search of a flea.

She felt Charlie's arms around her first as he drew her to him, then she closed her eyes and leaned against his warm chest as she listened to the most longed-for words.

'My darling girl, nothing has ever changed. I love you as much now as I did before – more perhaps. You'll have to marry me at once. I don't want to go back to Scotland without you.'

When she looked up at him and smiled, her dimples appeared most charmingly, fulfilling her mother's prophecy that she would one day make a brilliant marriage. She could almost hear her mother applauding from the grave.

'Yes, yes, Charlie. Do you mean it? I will, oh, Charlie, I'm so happy. I couldn't bear the idea of living without you. I couldn't bear it, truly. Oh, my goodness! Scotland! Isobel! What will she do? What will she say?'

Then her face crumpled as she plummeted back to reality.

'I was sure it was Isobel you wanted. You spent every moment together. Did you ask her and she refused? Please tell me the truth. I don't want to be second-best. I couldn't live with that.'

While she waited for his answer, in the following painful silence she was made aware again of Monty's even louder rude snuffling, but this time she turned on him.

'Get outside you wretched animal! Can't you see we're trying to have a conversation here!'

Monty looked up at her with his most reproachful beaten-dog expression. Violet never yelled at him, so for once he took her seriously and left the room, making a great show of his injured manner. The little scene with Monty allowed Charlie just enough time to sound convincing.

'No, I didn't ask her. I'm very fond of her of course, and for a time there, because I thought you loved Saunders...'

'She said you didn't ask her, but I wasn't sure...'

Charlie only smiled and said nothing more. Together, he and Isobel would continue to protect Violet from any of the more unpalatable truths in life. It was their mutual fate.

This time Violet was convinced.

'Oh, is this really happening? You do love me really?'

There was no hesitation. He had no second thoughts. When

he felt Violet's soft, yielding body in his arms and kissed that lovely mouth, he knew it was his destiny.

But coming to him when she did was a deciding moment. She had shown an inner determination to risk humiliation, and he knew what it must have cost her. He could never marry a girl without courage, and she had shown him a taste of what strengths lay beneath that lovely, oh so conventional exterior.

Chapter Forty-One

Aunt Bea was overjoyed with the news. Her lovely niece would soon be Lady Cameron and mistress of a grand estate, though she was momentarily struck dumb by the news, having been so sure it was Isobel who Charlie had had in mind for a bride. She gave Saunders hardly a second thought, except to rejoice over his departure, and when she was quite sure Isobel wasn't unhappy with the announcement and in fact seemed genuinely pleased for the young couple, she felt free to write to her friends in London to spread the good news. Violet was thrilled, for she was relishing her revenge and the effect it would have on London society. She would be Lady Cameron, and everyone, especially John, his family, and all who had laughed at her, could go to the devil.

The wedding was planned for the following week – enough time for Miss Blunt and her husband, Reverend Leigh, to come to Silver Mist and conduct the ceremony. Miss Blunt had written to say they would be delighted to attend as she was

366

expecting a child and would be grateful for a change in the fresh mountain air.

Aunt Bea was at first horrified. 'I would have thought Blunt would have more sense! A mother at her age! Whatever has she been up to?' No one had the courage to enlighten her and let it pass, but Aunt Bea was secretly pleased at the thought of seeing her old companion once more.

The presence of fresh faces would be very much appreciated, especially as Violet would go away with Charlie on the day of the ceremony when they would leave for Bombay and catch the first ship back to England, then go on to Scotland where Charlie would take up his duties at last.

It was both a happy and a sad time as the sisters were stricken with misery at the idea of having to part for what could be many years.

For the first few days, Isobel walked about as though in a daze; she had been responsible for Violet for so long that the thought of parting with her left her with a dull pain in the pit of her stomach and a peculiar restlessness she was finding difficult to crush.

All the passionate love Violet had first felt for John, and then for Harry Saunders, had been transferred to Charlie, and she submitted wholeheartedly to that love, giving up any desires of her own to blend seamlessly into his world. Isobel thought it was a dangerous path to take and wondered if a man like Charlie might eventually become bored with such unquestioning devotion.

Violet bloomed and sparkled under the protection of Charlie and clung to him like one of the orchids growing on the trees in the sacred forest. Isobel couldn't help being vaguely irritated by the behaviour of her sister, mainly because she could never envisage being so happy and fulfilled herself.

It was impossible for her to imagine placing the delicate responsibility of her own happiness entirely in the fickle arms of a man to do with as he saw fit. She knew instinctively the love of a man was only a part of what might bring her joy. A large part yes, but there were other aspects of life that were of enormous importance to her; Silver Mist for one and the people in it, the leopards, and the all-encompassing power of the world she was surrounded by.

But she could also look to the future now with a light heart, having fulfilled her promise to her mother to take care of Violet. She had done that, by carefully manoeuvring her into marriage with a man worthy of her, despite having to endure all the pain and criticism on that journey.

All the energy she had lavished on Violet was now looking for another outlet, and that outlet was Silver Mist and the harvesting of the coffee crop.

For something miraculous had happened – a letter had arrived from a French trader she had first met at Casa Margarida on the night of Phillipe Almeida's engagement. Having heard that Silver Mist was in possession of an old forest crop of Arabica beans, he decided to offer her seventy shillings a hundredweight on the condition that she could have the crop down to him by the end of November. He also mentioned that he had heard of her difficulties with Count Almeida and felt it was his duty to support anyone who was prepared to go against him. In fact, he admitted his dislike of Count Almeida was the prime motivation for his offer. Isobel didn't care what the man's incentive was and she was thrilled at finding a buyer at last. Then a cold reality began to set in. It all meant nothing if she couldn't find workers, so as soon as the wedding was out of the way, she would see the man Phillipe Almeida had mentioned, this Carlito Fonte, in the hope he was brave enough to go against the old count and work for her. It was a slim hope though, and the thought of what might happen if she wasn't successful haunted her, even though she hid her fears behind her apparent joy at Violet's impending marriage.

Even so, for Isobel, Violet's marriage was to take place at a huge cost. Much against her own wishes, Mary was to return to Scotland with Violet. Her mother had been ill for some time and it was of the greatest necessity she should return as soon as possible.

Mary would be a great loss for Isobel, perhaps even a greater loss than her sister. Mary was her champion, even at times her guide, and her only connection with the past. The idea of losing her was almost unbearable, and with Violet leaving, Isobel thought her Aunt Bea would be sure to follow, but when she broached the subject with her, she received a surprising answer.

'I have no intention of going back to England just yet, not only because leaving you here unchaperoned would be foolhardy, but because I have plans of my own that have not quite yet come to my satisfaction.'

'If you mean getting your money back on this place, let me assure you almost every penny I earn will be paid against your loan.'

'It's not the loan. I'm not worried about that. I know that now you have Silver Mist in your hot little hand you won't be giving it up in a hurry. Owning the place outright will make you strive harder to keep it, but there are other concerns in life apart from mere money, even for an old lady such as I.'

Isobel was curious and tried to read the answer in her aunt's shrewd eyes but didn't press her any further. She did though experience a huge sense of relief knowing her aunt wasn't ready to abandon her just yet, for despite their occasional day-to-day differences she had begun to rely on her more than she cared to admit openly.

Chapter Forty-Two

The papers giving over Violet's share of the estate to Isobel entirely had been signed at last; Violet had her long-awaited dowry and Isobel had a debt of three thousand pounds and an uncertain future. But all this slipped into the background with the arrival of Miss Blunt – now Mrs. Leigh. She had blossomed in her marriage state, despite looking a little pale in the first months of her pregnancy. Her husband was attentive and kind and seemed devoted to her. It was touching to see how much in love they appeared to be.

It was decided there would be no other guests invited to Violet's wedding, especially as there would be the inevitable uncomfortable questions to answer regarding Saunders's replacement by an entirely different bridegroom, so it was a small party who assembled on the lawn under the tamarind trees to unite Charlie and Violet.

Violet was enchanting, of course, with her long, fair hair brushed so it fell in loose curls to her waist, with a tiara of orchids across her forehead. The glorious buttery silk gown that had originally been made for her wedding to Saunders turned her into a creature from a fairy tale, a fitting consort for the handsome Charles Cameron by her side.

There was not even a faint twinge of conscience when Violet slipped into her dress on the morning of her wedding, as she could honestly say she had hardly given Saunders a single thought since the day he left Silver Mist. On one occasion, she found a scarf belonging to him left behind in the bedroom he had once occupied, prompting a vague memory of how tenderly she had wrapped it around his neck on their evening walks just as an excuse to touch him, but now she took it and threw it on the fire as a final ritual cleansing act.

The wedding ceremony was over in minutes and Isobel couldn't help but reflect on how what now seemed so simple had in fact taken many months of careful planning on her part to achieve.

When the young couple kissed at the end of the ceremony, it was a sweetly chaste moment, but most inconveniently it triggered a memory of the last time Isobel had seen Phillipe Almeida.

His kisses were not chaste. They were passionate and pleading and they had parted in anger, and now he was on his way to Lisbon to marry Carolina D'Souza.

Her hand went unconsciously to her lips as she relived the feel of his mouth on her own. She realized she wanted him very badly, if only to make peace with him.

But she knew it wasn't possible for them to be anything other than lovers, and she told herself that in time her desire for him would evaporate, and Phillipe Almeida would become nothing more than a faded memory. But even as she searched for the consoling words, she knew she was fooling herself. His presence was everywhere, nearly as strong as if he were with her in the flesh, causing a painful loneliness to almost overwhelm her.

The wedding breakfast was eaten in near silence, as everyone was aware of the inevitability of their parting and how their lives would change forever. There was a moment of panic when Isobel almost begged them all to stay a few days longer, so she could wind up her affairs and go with them, as her future seemed suddenly bleak and inevitably lonely. But when she looked at the cubs, a thin strand of courage crushed those thoughts and allowed her to say goodbye to her sister without clinging to her with too obvious a need.

Violet was not so calm. 'When will I see you again? Oh Issie, what will I do without you? Aunt Bea, Monty and the cubs, even Billy? Oh, I'll miss him too. Please come to Scotland soon. Come soon, otherwise I won't be able to bear it.'

She was led away weeping in Charlie's arms along with Mary's soothing words of comfort to support her, even though Mary was in as much need of comfort herself.

The sound of the wheels of the carriage turning down the drive added a final melancholy note to the hearts of everyone watching as they wondered if they would see the young couple and the dearly loved Mary, ever again.

That same afternoon, because she couldn't bear to be in the house that seemed so empty now, Isobel went with Mr. Singh and Constanza to see Carlito Fonte, who lived in a small house in the village only a mile away from Silver Mist. Their arrival caused a minor sensation, and everyone came out of their houses to surround the group and stare with utter fascination at Isobel, who had dressed with less Parisian style than usual. She had made a point of wearing her plainest dress and an unadorned straw hat. Even so, she appeared an incongruous figure in such a landscape as she picked her way in her fine leather boots through the groups of wide-eyed children, mangy dogs and straying squawking chickens, to a muddy path that led to Fonte's simple hut.

From the outside, his house appeared to be made of a dingy yellow mud but once inside Isobel could see how clean and neat he had made it; the walls were whitewashed and the floor was covered with bright woven rugs. His narrow bed lay against the wall where, embedded into the mud bricks, was a neat shelf on which lay a pile of books in English and Portuguese, showing that he had a curious mind.

He was thin almost to emaciation though it was unclear if it was due to a lack of food or because of a kind of burning inner intensity that made it impossible for him to put on weight.

He wore a light cotton shirt that had seen better days and a pair of almost ragged black trousers, but his head was fine and intelligent, even though his mouth was thin and indescribably bitter.

Isobel soon found out the reason for such bitterness.

Both his parents had been enslaved labourers and had died when he was a small boy. He had had the good fortune – or otherwise – to have been taken to a monastery where he had been taught how to read and write, making him unfit for a future as a simple labourer.

He had lived for some time in the service of the monastery but now, at the age of twenty-eight, as if by some latent homing instinct, he had returned to the village where he had been born and where he worked intermittently picking the coffee crops of the rich estate owners. This was his position when Isobel approached him with her offer of wages for the bonded labourers.

'You are mistaken, Senhorida, if you think the count will lie down and take it if you try to lure his workers away – especially since you are a woman. You must expect he will use his friendship with the governor to enforce the law.'

'It's illegal to use slave labour. It's up to us to remind them of that fact.'

'These men operate above the law, and they know no one will oppose them.'

'If no one opposes them, then they will continue to exploit the people here.'

'That is true, but as I said, no one will take the risk. I have nothing to lose so I will work for you, but I can't do it on my own. You will need fifty men for at least six weeks. But they will be too afraid to leave Casa Margarida because they think their families will starve.'

'But surely nothing will change if no one stands up to him. Please, not only for my sake. Talk to the men and try to convince them they must fight. They will win. I'm sure of it, but they must stay firm.'

'You don't know the evil of this man. If you knew what he is capable of… but I will try not only for your sake but for the people here.'

Carlito left Isobel with very little hope and for the first time she began to admit to herself she may have to accept defeat. It was only when she returned home, and she felt again the mysterious power of Silver Mist, that her confidence returned a little. But without Violet and the support of Charlie and Mary there was now a bleakness in her heart that tested her courage like never before.

Chapter Forty-Three

Three weeks after the wedding, Isobel still had no workers and had begun to despair, and at the height of her gloom a letter arrived from Violet, written from on board ship and infused with all the exuberant joy of a new wife.

> ... Everyone here treats me with a great deal of respect. Oh Issie, it's so wonderful to be Lady Cameron. Charlie says we will stay in Edinburgh through the winter months; it's only in summer that we will move to the estate further north. He wants to stop at the bank there to give me the family jewels. Can you imagine, Issie? He says there is a lovely set of diamonds that once belonged to his aunt, and he longs to see them on me. Diamonds, Issie! Wouldn't Mama be pleased? I do so wish she was alive to see me as Lady Cameron...

She went on to say that her husband was perfect in every way and she loved him more than ever:

Charlie sends his love and wants to know if you've managed to find men to pick the crop yet?

Isobel frowned at that as she had almost begun to accept that she might have to sell Silver Mist to Count Tiago after all and return to England a failure, and she had to crush a feeling very like jealousy before she returned to Violet's letter.

… And you will never guess who is on the ship with us. Phillipe Almeida is here with little Marco where they are on their way to Lisbon for his marriage to Carolina.

He seemed very shocked to see me married to Charlie. In fact, he didn't say a word and went quite pale, but managed to congratulate us after a time – I suppose it was because he expected me to marry that beast, Harry Saunders. Phillipe Almeida is an odd man. Sometimes he seems quite happy then other times his mood is so black I fear for him.

Marco of course asked about you and was so disappointed you weren't with us. He is a very dear child, and of course he wanted to know everything about the cubs and Monty…

Isobel's first reaction at the news was exasperation with her sister. How could she fail to notice what was more important between her promised diamonds and the news of Phillipe Almeida's presence on the ship?

… Almeida asked a lot of questions about you. Was there anything between you and him Issie? I didn't tell you before but that horrible Saunders claimed to have seen you kissing him the night Marco went missing. Of course, I know now that's all nonsense and he was just trying to cause trouble for you. No decent man would ever kiss a

girl then not ask her to marry him at once ... but none of this
matters now for his marriage to Carolina is assured...

She finished the letter with a final plea for Isobel to join
them as soon as possible in Scotland:

Why do you stay there? I do miss you Issie, most terribly...

Isobel was thrown now into a violent restlessness. She
paced back and forth in her room, holding the crumpled pages
of Violet's letter in her fingers.

Now Phillipe knew that she had not married Charlie after
all but still he had no intention of returning to her. If he really
loved her as he claimed, he would be before her now, begging
her to marry him, but there in Violet's letter was proof she had
never been anything other than a dalliance. This truth shook
her to the core and hot tears spilled out of her eyes and down
her cheeks. She was a vain conceited fool after all, and he had
made a mockery of her.

Chapter Forty-Four

So far, despite his truly impassioned fight for the bonded labourers to leave Casa Margarida and work for Isobel, Carlito had been unsuccessful but there had been some incidences of trouble at Casa Margarida too that began to eat away at the already crumbling foundations of the regime.

One of the workers had been beaten for a small misdemeanour and Carlito had made such a public stance against the injustice that the old count had sent for the police to come and arrest him. There had been no choice now but for him to go into hiding.

Carlito appeared at Silver Mist the next morning, having spent the night hiding in a peasant's hut in the nearby village. He was thinner and more ragged than ever, but newly fired with an outrage and determination to change the working conditions for the bonded labourers once and for all.

Isobel began to think there was something rather beautiful and noble about him, but she feared too for the saint-like figure, as he was uncompromising to a degree that left him exposed to constant danger.

Constanza considered him a hero and Aashi also held him in deep respect. They fed him as though he were a prince, placing the bowl of food in front of him, then retreating after giving him a blessing. He ate little and usually outside on the veranda, not being able to tolerate the formality of the dining table in the house.

Soon, the rest of the household joined him there and so began a curious relationship that ripened into trust after only a few days. Fonte recognized a kindred spirit in Isobel, despite her very different background, and together they plotted the overthrow of the dictatorship at Casa Margarida and the future of a more equitable system.

Rumours soon flew that the old count had begun to display more open signs of cruelty towards the bonded workers, and within a few days of Carlito Fonte's arrival, some forty or so men, driven by fear and despair, appeared like phantoms on Isobel's doorstep to begin work. Somehow by his actions, Carlito had inspired them to find the courage to fling off centuries of cruel traditions to make a stand, despite what it must inevitably cost them. But they spoke too of the old count's increasingly bad temper and how he had become more violent than ever. He had changed, they said, especially since Phillipe and Marco had left him alone in that great house.

The sheds were taken over and made into sleeping quarters and a place to cook their meals. Then the following morning they took their baskets and set about picking the first of the ripe berries till, by nightfall, a substantial pile of baskets was mounting up in the store house.

More men appeared, having learned about the wages being

paid to their fellow workers, but soon a policeman appeared at Silver Mist with the warning that the workers should return to Casa Margarida at once. But the men held out, fortified by the hope that Count Almeida would be forced to pay wages if he wanted his workers back.

A month later, the Silver Mist crop had been brought in and every coffee berry, except for the final gleaning, had been sent down to Panjim. All of the vanilla beans had been picked and had begun curing in the sheds, and already promised, with the beginnings of their fragrant stickiness, to be almost as valuable as the coffee. In a few months, when the curing was complete, they too would be taken down to the French trader to sell. The prices for the best quality vanilla had skyrocketed, and Isobel expected to make nearly five hundred pounds after wages and costs had been paid. But that was future money and could not be expected to be in her hand for six months at least. The money from the sale of the portrait had been used up and she had been reluctantly forced to borrow from Aunt Bea against the future profit from the coffee crop to pay wages, but she calculated with the sale of the vanilla there would be just enough money left to carry her over till the next harvest. Isobel thought of young Quimp now and how the fortune he was so desperate to make had been close at hand, if only he had kept his head. Not a large fortune, it was true, but adequate and promising, and it brought with it a great wave of pride every time she walked through her charming house and well-tended fields.

But it was not a time to relax as a greater problem had

begun to make itself felt. The leopard cubs had grown to such a size now that they could only take turns sleeping in Monty's basket.

They still crawled onto Isobel's lap and lay curled up like big babies, their heads resting against her breast, their warm, silky heads purring loudly. At such times it was easy to be lulled into a false sense that they were kittens still, but their natural savagery had begun to assert itself, especially at night as they roamed the house stretching their long sinewy bodies up to the windows while peering out into the beckoning darkness and to the jungle sounds that called them.

All of the household was looking towards Isobel now, especially in the kitchen where a raw chicken or a piece of meat would often be swept off the table and fought over in the corner of the room, leaving a grisly mess to be cleaned up afterwards.

Aunt Bea brought the problem to a head when the cubs tore her best silk gown to shreds and left it scattered around her room. Somehow, too, Sami had discovered the nest of false curls hiding in its box and ran through the house with the piece of hair in his teeth with Priti following, desperately trying to tear it out of his grasp. The result of the slaughter was strewn around the house and for days stray curls were found under couches or peeking out from under rugs, bringing fresh embarrassment to Aunt Bea.

'You must do something, Isobel! You must be practical, even if it means they leave Silver Mist.'

'But where will they go? I can't bear it. Perhaps that horrible Saunders was right, and it was unkind to raise them like this.'

Every day Isobel anguished over their fate and each day she pleaded their case.

'They are babies still, just a little longer please.' But at night, when they slept on her bed, she found they were beginning to disturb her sleep. There was hardly any room for her now, but she found their warm bodies so comforting and couldn't bear to banish them from the room.

It was Mr. Singh who took charge at last.

He began by taking them out every day to teach them how to climb trees – a skill vital to their survival in the future – and on one of these expeditions Priti killed a monkey that had sprung down to taunt but was too slow to retreat. At first Priti behaved like she was in shock, almost as though the monkey had wandered into her paws by mistake. Then instinct kicked in and she bit into the throat, clumsily at first but then with more precision.

Isobel heard the creature's screams from the house and put her hands over her ears, not being able to endure the sounds of agony. The cubs came back with the signs of blood around their mouths and a new fierce look in their eyes that was not sweet anymore. She watched them later as they cleaned their paws, their eyes half closed in a secret pleasure, obviously luxuriating in the kill and behaving with an almost smug animal pride.

It was then that she knew she had lost her babies.

Now when they played with her, there was just a faint sense of impending danger, and when she looked into their yellow eyes she saw that momentarily at least the wild animal had taken over from the domesticated.

But there were many months yet before they could be self-sufficient, and Isobel stood firm. If she was mistress of Silver

Mist, the cubs would stay, but she compromised by making a comfortable bed for them in one of the sheds. For some time, they called to her and scratched at the door with the most pitiful cries, and even though she longed to let them out, she walked away with tears in her eyes and with a very reproachful Monty following at her heels.

That night there was more room on the couch and in the basket, but no one was comfortable. The room seemed terribly empty without them, and at one stage Isobel leapt to her feet determined to release the prisoners at once and bring them back to the warmth of the fire. But one stern look from Aunt Bea settled the matter and she sat down to spend a miserable night thinking she might have done a very cruel thing in saving them from the practical savagery of Harry Saunders.

But Monty at least had the instinct to know that because they had tasted a kill, they might now view him more as a meal than a friend and he crept back into his basket next to the fire with a loud, philosophical sigh. In the times when the cubs did come back into the house during the day, a sort of unspoken truce seemed to exist between the animals: there would be no rough play or unauthorized biting. Inside the house, Monty was master, and they always bowed to this unwritten law.

Chapter Forty-Five

U sually, all the attention of the household centred on or around the cubs, but Aunt Bea had noticed a change in the behaviour of her beloved Billy.

He had become more and more withdrawn from the household, spending most of his time in his favourite tree in the garden. From a bird that had previously been a clever mimic, he had now become almost silent, forsaking human words in exchange for more parrot-like trilling that he had clearly picked up from birds of his own breed as they flew past.

At every sighting of his fellow species, he seemed to become more excited. Once he made the effort to join them in flight, but after a great deal of loud squawking from the other birds, Billy had retreated and from then on never attempted to join the flock again.

Each day he became more daring, flying from one tree to another and sometimes resting in the tallest of them. At first he was a clumsy flyer and gave the impression he might suddenly lose control and fall with an undignified splat onto the earth below but soon he became more graceful and soared over the house on his daily expeditions.

Often Aunt Bea would stand out in the garden and call out to him, 'Are you alright, old man? Time you came in now!'

Then he would waddle into the house and nibble on a biscuit or a piece of fruit and seem to be back to his former self until morning came and he would make his way back to the garden once more.

Aunt Bea watched anxiously as the flights got longer and longer until he was seen no more around the house during the day.

'He is returning to the life he was always meant to have,' she said. But her voice held a sob as if she knew one day the inevitable would happen.

She proved to be right, but not in the way she had anticipated, as one morning Isobel came into the house to break the sad news that she had found Billy in the garden under his favourite tree, lying on his side as though asleep.

The ensuing grief was terrible to see, especially in a woman who had always prided herself on her strength of character, but Billy was her last link to her beloved Archie and the bird's death brought a fresh reminder of what she had lost many years before.

'He must have been very old, Auntie, and think how happy he was to be here in the land of his birth. And he had become such a wonderful flyer,' Isobel added. 'Better he should have these last months of liberty than live to old age as he did before in that house in Mayfair.'

Isobel's words were a small consolation, but after Billy was buried in the Sacred Grove, as befitted the noble nature of the little creature, her aunt's spirits revived a little.

A few days after Billy's burial Aunt Bea came into the breakfast room holding an open letter in her hand. Her face gave her away at once. Something momentous had happened.

'I have some news, my dear. I hope you will be pleased... Colonel Ashworth has asked me to be his wife!'

Isobel opened her eyes wide; a piece of toast poised halfway to her mouth.

'Colonel Ashworth! But you hardly know him.'

'I know him very well thank you, miss. I have been writing to him every day for the past few months. We understand each other better than most people. I know his politics agree with my own and he dislikes red meat as I do. What more do I need to know?'

The toast was dry in Isobel's throat now; she could barely swallow it.

'Does that mean you will accept him?'

'That depends on you, my dear. I can't leave you here alone and unprotected. He, of course, has asked you to consider his home as yours also. He has included a photograph of his house in Simla.

The photograph showed a charming house very much in the English style – a large two-storey building with a pretty garden. Isobel looked closer. Surely, they weren't hollyhocks and roses against the picket fence? It could have been anywhere in England if it weren't for the background of jagged snow-capped hills and the colonel's staff lined up in front of the house with great formality in their turbans and puttees.

'But what about your lovely home in Mayfair? And your independence? Are you quite sure, Aunt? This is a very big step.'

'I will keep the house and a housekeeper to make sure it stays in good condition. Sometimes Edward and I may go back to London for brief visits, and you may find some use for it if you ever tire of living here. And as for my independence, I will still have it. My money will be my own.'

'But I can't believe you can marry this man on such a short acquaintance. I can't accept it.' Isobel kept her face down to hide her tears. She had grown fond of her aunt, despite all their differences, but she was beginning to feel the loneliness of her own situation too. Miss Blunt had gone first, then Violet and now ... she was the only one who was not loved. Even her adored baby leopards spent less and less time with her.

Aunt Bea seemed to sense that there was more to Isobel's reaction than she liked to say.

'He's very like Archie. I like to think he would have lived to become such a man as Edward is now. This is my chance, my dear, to recapture what might have been with the love of my life. It's not a great passion but it's comfortable and kind and I do believe he will love me for the rest of my days, as I will him.'

'I don't want to lose you, but if it's what you want...'

'He's written to say he'll come when the last of the harvest is in. Then I hope you'll accompany me to Simla. You will like him I'm sure, but my dear girl, don't be like me and waste your youth. Fall in love, my dear, as soon as you can. You've proved your independence and how capable you are. You can have both: a man who'll love you for your strength as well as your beauty, without you having to make too many compromises.'

'I've never met a man who doesn't want to dominate me. I want an equal marriage and I'm not sure such a thing exists.'

'It does exist. I'll make sure of it,' she said emphatically. 'But you do realize, don't you, that you can't stay here alone after I'm married? Mr. Singh and the staff aren't enough company for a girl like you.'

'I don't see why. My days are full and I go to bed at night tired. There is nothing I wish for really.'

'That won't last. Edward writes there are many single men in Simla, many of them very eligible. You would be the belle of the district.'

'I can never leave here now, whatever happens. The cubs and this house…'

Isobel could say no more, but in her heart she was really afraid for the first time.

She walked out onto the terrace to admire the view of the mountains as she often did at sunset. This magical place had done its work. Everyone around her had fallen in love and married – or planned to – everyone except herself and Mary. It was clear now that Phillipe had no intention of returning to her, despite knowing she had not married Charlie. He would be married by now and living in Lisbon, and there was never any hope she would see him again. She was overcome with a peculiar listlessness and could not envisage ever falling in love with any man again. She was too deeply hurt. For in her heart, she believed Phillipe had loved her and that if circumstances had been different they might have been happy together. But it was not to be, and her mother's words haunted her once more. *A bitter and lonely old maid...*

Chapter Forty-Six

There was nothing more to do now other than to wait for the end of the harvest and the arrival of Colonel Ashworth when Isobel would indeed go with her aunt to Simla – at least for a few months.

Silver Mist and the cubs would be left in the competent hands of Mr. Singh, Constanza and Aashi until she returned, and then she would make a definite decision about her future.

Carlito would remain to take care of the workers and Isobel made arrangements for them to be kept on at Silver Mist and paid until they found further work back at Casa Margarida, as it was hoped the count would finally bend to their demands for a fair wage. With all this extra expense it was becoming increasingly clear that Isobel's profits would be severely reduced, yet there was no choice but to finish what she had started, regardless of the consequences to her.

But the ominous silence from Casa Margarida didn't last.

A few days later, the count himself arrived with an armed police constable from Panjim with a notice signed by his friend the governor to have the workmen returned to Casa Margarida at once.

The men were gleaning in the coffee plantation with Mr. Singh, and for once Isobel was left unprotected to face the count alone.

For a moment Isobel felt sorry for this clearly isolated figure with his pushed-out barrel chest and thin, bandy legs trying to appear bigger and taller than he was. Away from the trappings of his grand house and fawning servants, there was none of the dignity his title and age conferred.

He refused her offer to come into the house and take some refreshment, just stood at the foot of the steps with his legs apart and arms crossed over his chest like a dictator from a pantomime.

'I believe you have something of mine?'

'I don't think so. They're free men and they can do as they like, and they have chosen to work for me. But if you pay them and treat them fairly they will return to you. I can do no more than that.' Her voice trembled a little as she spoke. She had never once in her life had an incidence with the law, that is, if she didn't count the numerous times the local policeman back home had helped her drunken father up the steps to the front door.

'This is a world you know nothing about. We have privileges at Casa Margarida that are above ordinary men. It has been so for three hundred years and will continue for three hundred more. But I am not here to discuss these matters with you, a mere girl!'

'The world has changed. It has moved on while you cling to this ...' she struggled to find the word, '... this feudal absurdity!'

'Silver Mist is on Portuguese land. It is right that the Portuguese own it.'

'It seems to me that my estate is on Indian land, and it is my responsibility to treat the inhabitants of this country with a little respect in return – and that includes paying them for their labour!'

He only smiled at that and called the policeman to him.

'Round up my workers at once. If they don't come then shoot at them – not to kill them, you understand, just to frighten them.'

The policeman was obviously shocked at this suggestion.

'I cannot. If they won't come, I will get more men, but I cannot shoot at them.'

His answer brought on more rage from the count. This time a wave of scarlet suffused the old man's face, causing him to stumble a little.

'Go away! Get my men at once!'

The policeman thought it best to go, but he left slowly, giving Isobel a warning look before he disappeared around the side of the house.

Then the old man said an extraordinary thing.

'You have tried to take everything from me.'

'What do you mean?'

'Marco, he almost died because of you. If you hadn't encouraged him, he would not have run away from me.'

'I didn't mean for that to happen. I would have died myself if anything had happened to him. I love the child as if he were my own.'

Though they had been intended to calm him, her words seemed instead to ignite a fury in him.

'He will never be yours! What do you know of that child?

What do you know of love? Do you know what I had to do to have him live at all!'

'What do you mean?'

He faltered, his frail hands held out in appeal, then he stared straight ahead, as if remembering a moment in time, something so horrific his face had turned the colour of ash.

'Then Phillipe, when you knew he was betrothed to Carolina, a right and proper wife for him ... a family of royal blood ... I saw the way he looked at you. Well, he would never have married you. He owes me money. A lot of money. And he must pay it back. He is married now to Carolina, as he should be.'

Isobel began to feel sick. Phillipe was married. But there was no time to think of that. Beads of perspiration had broken out on Count Almeida's forehead, and he was walking in strange, irregular circles, muttering to himself. There was the same peculiar lopsided smile she had seen before when he had been bullying the servant over the cold tea. There was the same clutching at his head as though in pain and the same incoherent babbling

A reluctant pity briefly overcame her hate.

'Come into the house. It's very hot at this time of the day. Please, I will make you something to drink.'

She put out her hand as he began to stumble towards her, then with a horrible, sly smile he reached into his pocket and brought out a small silver revolver. Isobel's first thought was that it was so small it seemed incapable of doing any real harm. His hand was trembling as he held the pistol out in front of him. He appeared to be trying to think, to wrestle with an idea that had just occurred to him, all the while mumbling something. A name, an Italian name, 'Francesca, Francesca...'

It was plain now that he really was mad, and in her panic, Isobel screamed out for her aunt to come; it was an irrational plea, but she needed her solid, matter-of-fact presence to bring some reality back to the insanity around her.

But instead, her scream brought Carlito, who had rushed from the side of the house and stood before them defenceless.

The old man seemed to focus for a moment, then with a flash of clarity called out.

'You! You, again!'

And with that, he fired his gun, Carlito stumbled, then he collapsed onto the ground clutching at his side. The old man let out a strange triumphant cry, then he wandered a few feet away, muttering and cursing, lost again in his dark world. Isobel rushed to Carlito and was relieved to see he was still alive, then raising him to a sitting position she held her hand over the wound and watched in a horrified daze as the blood poured in little rivulets through her fingers. Then she realized she was trembling, and could only stare about in shock, in desperation begging to a god she didn't believe in to save this man she held in her arms. For she believed it was her fault Carlito was hurt, and perhaps dying. Life had suddenly become too real, and for the first time she cursed herself for having come to Silver Mist at all.

By the time Aunt Bea came to her and helped her to her feet, Isobel's dress was covered with Carlito's blood. At first it was thought Isobel as well as Carlito had been injured and her anguished screams brought Mr. Singh who came running with his knife drawn, followed by the policeman and a group of workers. When the policeman saw the count wandering in crazed circles still with the gun in his hand, he went to him and calmly took the pistol away. He could only whisper in a kind of awe, 'What have you done, Count? You have shot a man. Perhaps killed him, and even you won't be able to escape justice this time.'

There was no reaction, only the same dazed half-smile Isobel had witnessed before, except this time the old man seemed to have slipped into another time. Then without warning he collapsed into a heap on the ground. The spirit in him had fled, and all his bravado and pride were reduced now to a pathetic bundle lying in the dust.

Aunt Bea by now had roused herself into action.

'We should lock him up in the shed, but I can't bring myself to do it. You had better bring him into the house.'

Isobel managed to collect enough strength to speak.

'We must have a doctor. Mr. Singh, if you would be so kind as to go at once to the village. We must save Carlito.' Then her voice cracked, as the tears she was struggling to contain broke through. 'We must save him; I won't be able to live with myself if we don't.'

Then Aunt Bea added with a bitter smile, 'You had better ask a priest to come as well. Judging by the look of the old man, it might be that he escapes justice after all.'

Chapter Forty-Seven

Carlito did not die. He was not seriously hurt and recovered quickly under the devoted attention of everyone at Silver Mist, especially Aashi, who through nursing him, had grown to love him. The love of a woman was something Carlito had always rejected as a distraction, but as the weeks passed, even his self-denying nature weakened under the power of such devotion, and soon he was returning Aashi's love while he grew stronger every day.

In the room next to Carlito lay the old Count Almeida, rumoured to be dying, and Constanza often gave a hasty glance at the closed door then crossed herself as though in the presence of evil, before moving on.

The inhabitants of Casa Margarida would not believe such a curse could be so easily extinguished and still dreaded the day when the old count would return and cast his wrath over the people there, but if they could see the once terrifying figure now, they would have had no fear, for he lay almost immobile in a heavy stupor, trapped in his nearly paralyzed body.

The doctor had come and pronounced that he had suffered a stroke and would in time most likely have another. Meanwhile, there was nothing anyone could do except nurse him, so Isobel had to accept that this most unpleasant man would be with her most likely till he died, as it was thought too dangerous to move him.

Strangely, his was a benign presence, and caused little trouble to the household. He did indeed seem to have slipped back to another time, and every now and then would relive the past with crooked smiles and groans and incomprehensible babblings. Sometimes his sharp black eyes showed an abrupt renewal of life that brought him back to the present time – usually when Isobel walked into the room to take her place watching over him.

He appeared to have forgotten his old animosity towards her and sometimes tried to smile and reach out his trembling hand to her. Once he called her Francesca, while slow, weak tears trickled down his cheeks. Then he turned his face away and sighed most pitifully.

His reaction to the sight of Constanza though was so violent that she had to be banned from entering the room for fear of bringing on another stroke, as he thrashed about in the bed and Isobel was sure he mentioned the name of Silvia, Phillipe's wife.

Later in the kitchen, Constanza was matter of fact.

'His demons have returned to haunt him. When he sees me, he sees Madam Silvia too. I know something happened that night that he can't forgive himself for.' She added bitterly, 'We have been taught that even the most depraved of sinners will have a place in heaven, but I'm not sure he deserves it.'

Isobel was troubled by the old man's struggles with his conscience and found she could not turn away.

'Perhaps it would relieve him to confess. As a Catholic, isn't it true he must confess before he dies?'

But Constanza was not so forgiving.

'Perhaps that is why God has struck him dumb. He denies this man his salvation.'

The old count continued in much the same way, but one night, as Isobel was sitting with him, he all at once became more alert. He seemed to be gesturing to her to come closer so he could say something, and Isobel leaned forward to put her ear against his mouth. His words came out acrid and foul, like his breath.

'I ... I ... had ... to ... do ... it.'

'What did you do? Tell me.'

'*O medico…*'

'The doctor?'

He moved his head then ever so slightly, but enough to show he was satisfied with her question.

After a struggle he sighed out a name: 'Silvia.'

'What happened with Silvia? Tell me. It will relieve your mind.'

'The child. *O medico* said I must choose…'

With a sudden return of strength, his hand took a tight grip on hers.

'He said I must choose the woman, but I chose Marco.'

With those words he relaxed his grip and fell into a kind of tortured slumber, while Isobel could only stare at him aghast.

He was a murderer after all.

Isobel's pity fled. He had sacrificed Silvia so Phillipe's child could live. It was an unimaginable death for the poor girl.

Isobel sat slumped in a chair by the bed. Why did she have to hear this? It was a secret she must forever hold close and bear alone, for if Phillipe ever heard it his heart would break further. If Marco should ever know, he would suffer unimaginable guilt.

But later that night the old man seemed to rally and for an hour or two became almost lucid. Isobel began to think he may well cheat death after all. He begged her to come close once more, but now knowing what she did, she took his grasping hand with a revulsion she found difficult to overcome. This time, the laboured words he struggled so hard to say were something that could bring a bitter comfort to Phillipe.

He confessed that he had burned his brother's original will that had left everything to his widow and son, then forged another, leaving everything to himself for the duration of his life.

'I hated him. He had everything and I had nothing. Then Francesca, my love, my only love, ran away from me...'

With that, he groaned and wailed till the tears poured down his face. Isobel stood back from him, her hands over her ears and her eyes shut tight. She didn't want to hear any more.

The next morning, on the advice of the doctor, the priest was summoned, and later in the day the old man made his final confession. When the priest returned from the deathbed, Isobel scanned his face for some sign of further horrors, but the man was inscrutable and would forever hold the count's secrets to his chest in the same way as she must.

———————

Later that evening, Count Almeida died, and the next morning Isobel had his body taken back to his ancestral home. There was no one there to grieve for him, so she and Aunt Bea, the priest and a lawyer from Panjim took it upon themselves to arrange his funeral and burial in the graveyard of his ancestors.

As was traditional, the count was laid out in the library, his coffin surrounded by many tall candles in ornate silver candelabras that remained flickering throughout the long night. Armloads of vivid blue hydrangeas were gathered in vases placed around the body, but there were no mourners gathered there to weep for him. His was a wasted life, cursed by a bitter jealousy and a lust for revenge that had stunted his soul.

Hardly anyone slept well that night, knowing there was one who slept the eternal sleep in that cold room below and would never awake again.

Chapter Forty-Eight

I sobel dressed in the same black dress and veiled hat she had worn for her own father's funeral only a year before. As she straightened her veil before the pock-marked mirror and stared into her own clear grey eyes it was astonishing to be reminded of the changes to her life since then. Looking back to what she was then, it seemed she had been a mere child. Now she felt herself a woman, and she experienced a twinge of regret to part with the girl she once was. She had witnessed violence, and an evil she could never have thought possible, and she couldn't imagine ever being light-hearted again.

The funeral cortège moved down from the house with the few officials and household staff walking slowly behind the coffin, completely covered now with the dark blue hydrangeas. It seemed inappropriate somehow to grace his casket with any flower that might be sweet smelling, and Isobel couldn't help but think that if there ever were any such thing as a black flower it would be a suitable embellishment for such a dark soul.

As they neared the graveyard, a thick mist came down in a damp grey wave from the mountains, adding an appropriate atmosphere to the general gloom, but Isobel was reminded of the time when she had walked that way before, with Phillipe's arm supporting her own. Now she walked alone, and despite there being a more hopeful future for Phillipe, she could not rejoice in it. It was too soon, and her wounds were not yet healed.

They came at last to the grand tomb of the counts of the Almeida family. From inside, a dusty, acrid odour flew at them from the rows of stone sarcophagi arranged on the cold shelves with the burnished gold names of the occupants carved upon them glistening in the half-light of the tomb. The body of the old count was laid alongside his ancestors, and with unusual haste the heavy metal door of the tomb was closed upon him.

Later, now in bright sunlight, the little group trailed back through the graveyard. The others went ahead while Isobel paused before Silvia's grave. After all the stress of the past weeks, she longed to be alone, if only for a few minutes.

'You go ahead, Aunt Bea. I'll be along in a moment.'

Isobel kissed her aunt gently on the cheek. Affection was more common between them now, as the two women had reached a higher, more loving understanding.

Isobel emptied out the dead flowers from the pretty Italian vase and replaced them with a bouquet of sweet-smelling frangipani and jasmine she had brought with her.

As she straightened up to brush the dirt from her dress, she felt a brisk movement by her side then a small, warm hand slip into her own.

'Miss Isobel?'

'Marco! Is it really you?' For a moment she was almost overwhelmed with joy, but it was soon followed by sorrow. He was Carolina's child now.

She gave him a warm hug and kiss and smoothed the black hair away from his forehead. As usual, there was a faint smear of jam or chocolate in the corner of his mouth.

He smiled, but his sad eyes were fixed on the grave in front of them.

'That is where my mama sleeps. She is in heaven with the angels.'

'Yes, I know.'

'When can I see Monty and the cubs?'

The child had brought her back to the present time and was looking eagerly into her eyes.

'As soon as your papa says so.'

Isobel heard his footstep then and she steeled herself to face him.

He was in mourning, but there was a new lightness in his expression that had not been there before, and she wondered if it was because of Carolina.

Her voice came out husky and strained. 'You received my telegram then?'

'No, I did not.'

'Then why are you here?'

'I was already on my way back from Lisbon. I only heard the news of my uncle's death when I reached Panjim. The newspapers were full of it.'

'Carolina is with you?'

'She is in Lisboa with her cousin. The man her mother has always wanted Carolina to marry, and as soon as I was sure I was free I caught the next ship home. To you.'

It took some time for the truth of what he said to begin to sink in. She was so used to sorrow it didn't seem possible there could be joy in her life again.

He took her hand then, and she knew it was not a dream.

'But she was so in love with you.'

'I don't think so, not really. It was a little case of rebellion, but not strong enough to sustain. I think too that she always suspected…'

'Suspected what?'

He smiled at her and changed the subject.

'You can imagine my shock when I saw Cameron on board the ship – not with you as I expected but with your sister. It took me some time to recover, especially after all you had said. I believed you. I believed you would marry him. I thought there was no hope. They both send their love, by the way.'

'Were they happy?'

'Very happy, and I was very jealous of their happiness.'

He turned to Marco then.

'You stay here for a moment and talk to Mama. I want to speak to Miss Isobel.'

The little boy nodded silently and smiled, then he took one of the frangipani flowers out of the vase and placed it on the cold marble beneath his mother's name.

They walked together to the tomb of the Almeidas. Phillipe was expressionless.

'I can't pretend to be sorry he's dead. He brought so much suffering to so many people, and to you…' He closed his eyes and rubbed his forehead with his fingers as if reliving some unimaginable thought. 'If something had happened to you…'

Tears sprang to her eyes then. The memory was too fresh. 'He was mad.'

'Mad, yes. He must have been. But his greed and jealousy drove his madness.'

'Yes, I know. Your inheritance … he stole it from you.' She couldn't say – and never would – that the man had stolen Phillipe's wife, too.

'My whole life I resented my father because of that will. I always believed he thought me not worthy of inheriting Casa Margarida. And as for my mother, the laws in Portugal and Goa are very cruel to women. No one questioned it for her sake.'

'You didn't suspect?'

'Deep down I always did. I think that is why I stayed here. I couldn't tear myself away. I wanted to get to the truth, but his secret was too well hidden.'

'But your engagement to Carolina?'

'I owed him a great deal of money. My mother has been very much dependent on what I can give her, you see, and Carolina is very rich. He thought that through me he could get his hands on most of it, and at the time the marriage seemed an answer to my problems.'

He paused then. 'This story is too long to tell here. Later, when we are alone…'

All of his emotion showed in his voice then, and a little shiver ran down her back making her knees go weak.

They were standing very close now; close enough for her to read the expression in his eyes.

'There is so much I want to say to you. So much…'

There was no need for him to say he loved her, but she experienced a rush of feeling that made her dizzy with an exhilaration she had never felt before – at least, never because of a man. There was a definite danger in surrendering so completely, but she had always thrown herself headlong into whatever it was that consumed her interest.

She thought then of Violet on her wedding day and the joy she was so clearly feeling, and how she had felt herself incapable of ever experiencing such emotions. How wrong she was, but there was no regret at giving herself up to those dangerous feelings, for in her heart she knew her love for Phillipe was stronger and deeper than anything Violet could ever understand. For a moment she felt a little sorry for Charlie Cameron, despite all his wealth and grandeur.

Her own path had been the more difficult one to negotiate, but in the end the rewards were greater.

'I love you very much,' she said, even though it was a hard and fast rule that a girl must never say it first.

He smiled. 'You must tell me so every hour until I get tired of hearing it. But I doubt I ever will.'

'It's your turn now,' she said.

'I adore, worship and revere you. "I love you" isn't enough.'

'It will do for a start.'

Phillipe looked to where Marco was dutifully waiting by his mother's grave, then, seeing the boy was occupied, he kissed her on the lips. Because of the presence of the child and because of where they were, it was intended to be brief, but they clung to each other, desperate for each other's touch after being so long apart.

'We must go back to the house,' he whispered. 'A child shouldn't be long in such a place.'

They walked together then, with his arm still around her waist, and with Marco skipping happily ahead like a little colt. Every now and then he looked around and smiled at the two people he loved most walking together. He crossed the fingers of both hands and squeezed his eyes shut while he made a wish. He had performed this act many times before, but surely this time it would come true at last.

When they arrived at Casa Margarida, Isobel couldn't help but allow her imagination to run wild. Surely the house was more beautiful than she had ever thought it before. The stones seemed to glow with a golden light now; the flowers growing in the garden around the house were surely more vivid and more fragrant. The scarlet rhododendrons waved lightly in the warm morning breeze and butterflies floated lazily in and out of the blooms. On such a day it seemed to Isobel an earthly paradise.

There was the subdued laughter of the servants coming from inside the house and the sounds of the table being laid in the dining room, but now the doors hung wide open to let in the sweet scents from the outside world.

It was plain to everyone there had been a shift in the relations between Isobel and Phillipe Almeida. Isobel's already abundant beauty had flared into something almost unearthly. An inner radiance glorified her and watching her from afar, her aunt felt a lump in her throat that threatened to turn into tears at such a sight. It seemed her passionate, strong-willed and wayward niece had at last found a man who was worthy of her.

It was too soon to be openly joyous, and at times the

funeral guests were subdued and solemn as the ghost of the old count had not yet been vanquished. His presence lingered in the air still, but his power was fading in the face of the strength of the lovers. Marco felt it even more than the adults and couldn't help but wriggle in his chair with a secret happiness. Ahead of him were endless hours of play with the cubs and Monty, and he couldn't stop himself from laughing out loud.

That ringing laugh seemed to signal the end of all the pain of the past.

Hate would not be allowed to flourish in such a place. Now was the time for love and peace and happiness.

Chapter Forty-Nine

Their love for each other was too powerful to be soon parted so Phillipe insisted Isobel stay with him for a few days before returning to Silver Mist. Over those days, drop by drop he revealed something of his past and why he had been so much in the grip of his uncle's desires. Isobel listened and watched his handsome face as the various moods played over his features. Sometimes she put out her hand to touch his hair and comb it back from his forehead with her fingers as she did with his son, then he would kiss her soft palm with his warm lips before returning to his story. She never tired of the sight of his black lashes against the half-moon of his eyes as he bent over her hand, and always a little thrill of pleasure shot through her body as she relived the night before.

He spoke of his early happiness when his father was alive and how Casa Margarida had been a very different place. It was only when his father became ill that a cloud descended over his childhood. His father became weaker, so he decided to send for his younger brother, Tiago, to manage the estate till he was strong enough to resume the running of it. But he never recovered his former strength, even though the doctors said his sickness need not be fatal, and he came to rely on his brother more and more.

Isobel's mind automatically flew to the possibility that Phillipe's father had perhaps been helped towards his death, but if Phillipe had any suspicion, he kept it to himself, perhaps finding the idea too unpleasant to voice out loud.

'Bit by bit my uncle became indispensable, and as his power increased, the strength of my father declined. Soon, Uncle Tiago took my father's place at the head of the table.

'I remember as a child how I was never allowed to speak unless spoken to, where before I would chatter away unrestricted. My mother too became increasingly silent and our mealtimes became a torture. Then Mama started taking her meals in her room and had me join her there. She seemed afraid of my uncle, but never actually said why.

'Then my father died, and all hell broke loose. At the height of my mother's grief, she discovered she had been left penniless and totally reliant on a man she hated.'

His voice had become hard, while his handsome mouth began to tremble with an impotent anger, but it was the constant presence of Isobel that soothed away these moments and restored him to a kind of peace.

It was a wonderful period for them both, a time when they could spend every moment together. They luxuriated in their freedom and in the knowledge that all obstacles in the way of their happiness had been removed. Even the servants were moved by the sight of the lovers and would smile to themselves as they served at table or came into the room unannounced to see them kiss or clasped in an embrace.

Isobel's feminine touch was making itself felt in the most natural of ways – her bright cashmere shawl flung casually over the back of a chair, or a hair clasp or ribbon left on the mahogany table where she had taken it off.

It gave him great pleasure to see her move about his home and replace the ancient horrors with her fresh, charming presence. He would pick up the discarded ribbon and bring it to his lips to breathe in a little of the scent of her hair or smooth the shawl with a smile of real pleasure. Marco's childish possessions were more in evidence now. His train set was left on the floor in the sitting room, his favourite stuffed toy – a little brown monkey wearing a blue waistcoat and red fez – lay on the couch next to a story book Isobel had been reading to him.

Phillipe played with the sash on her dress as he talked, sometimes haltingly, then in a rush as though he wanted to expel the evil in his story.

'Uncle Tiago became obsessed with my mother. She was very beautiful, and even as a child I could see how he wanted her. I remember her face when he came near her, sometimes to stand behind her chair. Once I remember him putting his hands on her shoulders and his fingers moving up her throat. Her face went as white as this.' He picked up the white fabric of Isobel's gown and stared at it as he remembered. 'But she had to bear it as even the food she was eating belonged to him.'

'He spoke your mother's name often before he died.'

'It was his tragedy, but I cannot forgive him. He caught up with us in Italy two years later where we had been living with my grandmother, but she had died, and my mother had no money at all and was living on the charity of her relations. I was only ten years old so I could do nothing to help, but I always felt the shame of being a burden and feeling helpless.'

Isobel kissed him most tenderly then and had to suppress a stinging tear of pity for the child he once was.

'He said he would support both my mother and me in my education if I came back to Casa Margarida when I was twenty-one. But there was something else I didn't know about. He made my mother sign a contract that if she ever married again, I would not inherit anything. If he could not have her then no one else would. She accepted this for my sake, and because she wanted me to have what had once been my father's.'

He stopped for a moment, his eyes suddenly blank with despair, and Isobel saw then what it had cost him in pride to remain at Casa Margarida with a man he despised.

'He was generous, and we could live with some dignity at last, so I kept my promise to return to Casa Margarida when I was of age, but I came back with Silvia, and he was furious. I think in his distorted brain he saw me as his son and hoped to restore some sort of lost dynasty through me. Then, after Silvia died, he made me feel like I owed him. It was years before I could even contemplate re-marrying but when Carolina appeared he made me feel my debt. He threatened to stop sending money to my mother if I didn't marry Carolina and I was too heartbroken and guilty to care. It was only when I met you that I was somehow brought back to life. I really believe I was frozen till then. Is it possible?' he murmured, as he buried his face in the soft curve of her throat and kissed her above her breast.

'Yes, now I know it is. I am melting, I am melting in the rays of your glorious sun. One day I will ask my mother to tell you the story herself. I have written asking her to come to our wedding.'

'Wedding?' she murmured. 'I suppose there had better be one, and soon.'

Isobel thought of those nights and the first time she had gone to his room.

She had found him pacing the floor, obviously as restless as herself.

'I couldn't sleep. My bed is full of ghosts – mostly your ancestors. I thought perhaps a brandy might help.'

He laughed almost nervously as he stood at the doorway of his room. At first, he was hesitant. He had not made love to a woman since Silvia and his all-encompassing sense of guilt ensured that part of his life had died with her. But his beloved Isobel had awoken so much in him already; he could see beauty and joy in life again, he could laugh again, so perhaps he could love again.

'You know that if you come into my room, I cannot let you go. Not this time.'

'I don't want to be apart from you even for a minute, and the nights seem very long without you.'

She began to think she had made a terrible mistake as he did not reply at first, only smiled and fixed her with his glistening dark eyes.

But he was only teasing her.

'You know, there is an old Portuguese saying that says if a man looks into a woman's eyes and she returns his gaze then she wants him to become her lover.'

'There seems to be a lot of room for mistakes in that.'

He laughed.

'Will I ever get used to your charming English humour?'

'I hope not. I want always to be a surprise to you.'

'You don't want to wait till we are married?'

'We are married now in my eyes, but if you won't have me then I'll leave.'

He put out a hand a grabbed her wrist and pulled her to him as he had done once before in the hotel in Panjim.

'No! I'll have you, but it must be forever. You cannot escape me now.'

It all happened naturally, as he hoped it would.

Everything after that moment was a blurred and dizzying thrill. She wondered at the primitive beauty of their young, strong bodies entwined in each other's arms, and how nothing in the world mattered except those private hours devoted to each other's pleasure.

His body was very hard and lithe and sometimes he hung over her, fixing her with his gaze while she lay prone and unable to move, almost anaesthetized by an overpowering ecstasy till he ravished her in a kind of frenzy. Other times he lingered over her body, taking his pleasure lazily and unhurriedly, his eyes as dreamy as an opium eater but all the while transporting her with him to a higher bliss and encouraging her to give more of herself.

But she drowned willingly in his softly murmured words of love and the feel of his thick shoulders and arms under her hands as she moved beneath him, till finally, the stealthy exquisite flutter permeated her body, before a long, sweet spasm that left her shaking and panting and her body shining with sweat.

The morning after she had first made love, Isobel had wondered at the miraculous event that had turned her from a girl into a woman. As Phillipe slept, she had crept out of bed to look at herself in the mirror thinking that surely after such a night there would be visible signs of her transformation, but to anyone other than herself there was nothing significant to betray her. Instead of looking tired as she should have done, she looked, if anything, rejuvenated, as well as appearing to be, even to her own eyes, more beautiful than before.

Her hair, usually so neat and well behaved, was tangled and caught in the brush as she ran it through. In addition to a noticeable glow to her skin, her mouth appeared fuller and rosier, but that was inevitable after those long, bruising kisses that left her with her head spinning and her legs shaking. It was the expression in her eyes though that gave her away to anyone perceptive enough to notice; she was a girl no longer, and magically had become a woman, bringing with it all the complications and responsibilities accompanying that state.

Isobel recalled overhearing a conversation between her mother and a friend. They had been talking about their husbands and discussing a topic of which Isobel had been innocent at the time. Her mother's rather peevish voice had complained, 'Gerald makes too many demands on me. I would be almost pleased if he takes a mistress.'

Well, Isobel had discovered that far from finding the act of lovemaking a chore, she had enjoyed it immensely and couldn't wait to do it again.

Phillipe had woken then and lifted a lazy arm to feel the empty spot beside him in the bed. Looking up through sleepy eyes he called out to her. She noticed when they were making love that he seemed to become more Italian in both mannerisms and his speech. He forgot more than ever to pronounce the 'h' when he spoke, but she found it particularly endearing.

'You said you would never leave me. Come 'ere to the bed at once.'

She would not have thought it possible, but when they made love again only moments later, it was as he had promised: even better than before.

It was while they were lying in each other's arms that they talked with the comfortable ease of lovers about when he first fell in love with her.

'It was the night of my engagement to Carolina. I believed you had hypnotized me at the time and turned me into a cad. I could see nothing in the room but you. You must wear that lovely dress on our wedding day. No, it was before that. From the very beginning I was under your spell. I can see you now, skipping up the steps of the hotel in Cairo and that proud look you gave me. My heart and my life were yours from the first moment of seeing you, and I suffered a thousand times while I could not have you. You must never let me suffer again.'

It was decided for so many reasons that their home for the present must be at Casa Margarida, but there was now the problem of what to do with Silver Mist. After the final gleaning of the crop, there was hardly enough money left to say that the estate was a success, but it had held its own and promised greater profits if worked all the harder the following year.

But Isobel had decided on a different plan of action.

In a final act of generosity, Aunt Bea made over her share to her niece, so now Isobel was the sole owner of the estate, but with the signing of that paper and her heart's desire in her grasp at last, Isobel felt with a sudden flash of realization that Silver Mist did not belong to her at all. What she had now was the means of giving it back to the people and animals who really owned it, and with a great deal of internal turmoil she made her decision.

Aashi was foremost in her mind. She must be rewarded for saving the lives of both Marco and Violet, and mere money did not seem enough, and now she and Carlito had decided to marry, Isobel intended to deed the estate over to them both.

Silver Mist would be worked no more, and the crops would be allowed to return to how mother nature intended. It was a small compensation to the local people for the burning of the sacred forest on which Casa Margarida had been built three hundred years before. The coffee plants would be dug up or absorbed back into the jungle, the vanilla plants would remain to flower at will and the massive tamarinds would be allowed to embrace each other's branches as they grew bigger still. But most of all, the leopard cubs must always have a place to live as it became clear over time they may never become fully acclimatized to the jungle. They must be nurtured and guided and tended in ill-health, if needed.

Phillipe too struggled with his newfound ownership of Casa Margarida. It had not been a happy place for him after his father died, and the ghost of the old Count Tiago and the crimes of the past were not easily banished, but he felt compelled to stay on for the present. His father was buried there, and his beloved Silvia, and he could not yet abandon her to the loneliness of a country not of her birth and allow her resting place to grow wild with weeds. He was rooted there too by a deep obligation to the people of the estate, who relied on its income, but he felt his time in India was ending, and his future lay in Europe.

Constanza returned to Casa Margarida as housekeeper and was happy there, as she had been in the days when Silvia had been alive and before the old count had brought a curse upon the house.

Mary's decision to return to Scotland with Violet proved to be the right one. When Violet's son was two years old, Mary married a farmer on Lord Cameron's estate and settled in her own home at last, but often thought with a great deal of pleasure of her time in the jungles of India. Aunt Bea did marry her Colonel Ashworth and grew younger still with the love of a devoted and indulgent husband by her side. Monty went to live with her and the colonel's cantankerous bulldog in Simla and spent the remainder of his years as a spoilt lapdog, only occasionally longing for his past as a London dog about town, a seasoned traveller, and a tamer of wild leopards.

Mr. Singh had been missing his home in north India so he would return there now he felt he was no longer needed, though Isobel found his leaving almost as difficult as parting with her Aunt Bea. Fortunately, their separation was not forever, as Mr. Singh's friendship with Aunt Bea proved to be an enduring one, and over the years he made many visits to Simla, where the family would meet and relive their adventures at Silver Mist.

Isobel married Phillipe Almeida in her lovely yellow gown, and was at times blissfully happy, but her spirit was not one to be easily tamed by marriage. She was often wayward, and often argumentative, but their love for each other was deeper and more intense than most, and it endured throughout the years, and became worthy of being called 'a grand passion,' both in their eyes, and by everyone who knew them.

Italy drew Phillipe back more and more, both for the sake of his mother and because he was an Italian at heart. He bought a house there, large enough to accommodate them all, so Marco could become familiar with the culture of his poor dead mother. In this way Silvia became more alive in Marco's heart, and her memory less connected with tragedy.

All this suited Isobel very well and it also became a regular event to spend a month each year with Violet and Charlie in Scotland, even though Violet could not quite forgive Isobel for not taking the title of countess with her marriage.

But Isobel only laughed at Violet's snobbery; neither she nor her husband had a taste for it. They were both more than content to be mere citizens of the world, neither higher nor lower than their neighbours.

In all this Marco was perhaps the happiest of all. He loved his new mother and the little sister who came a year after his father's marriage, and never once regretted the day when, on a childish whim, he had slipped a beautiful butterfly into an envelope directed to an unknown girl, with a fervent wish that was somehow magically fulfilled.

Acknowledgments

A deep and sincere thank you to my editor Charlotte Ledger for her considerate collaboration, unfailing support and gentle understanding, and to Tony Leach for always championing me.

ONE MORE CHAPTER

One More Chapter is an
award-winning global
division of HarperCollins.

Sign up to our newsletter to get our
latest eBook deals and stay up to date
with our weekly Book Club!
<u>Subscribe here.</u>

Meet the team at
<u>www.onemorechapter.com</u>

Follow us!

 @OneMoreChapter_

 @OneMoreChapter

 @onemorechapterhc

Do you write unputdownable fiction?
We love to hear from new voices.
Find out how to submit your novel at
<u>www.onemorechapter.com/submissions</u>